THE SILENT WITNESS

A NOVEL

SIR LIONEL A. LUCKHOO
AND
DR. JOHN R. THOMPSON

OLIVER
NELSON

THOMAS NELSON PUBLISHERS
Nashville • Atlanta • London • Vancouver

Published in Nashville, Tennessee, by Thomas Nelson, Inc., Publishers, and distributed in Canada by Word Communications, Ltd., Richmond, British Columbia.

The Bible version used in this publication is THE NEW KING JAMES VERSION. Copyright © 1979, 1980, 1982, 1990, Thomas Nelson, Inc., Publishers.

The characters in this historical novel are real characters of public domain or are those whose names and character representation are used by written permission. All other characters are fictitious and are not those of any person living or dead.

Although this novel is based on documented historical events, some of the details are not factual.

All legal and trial procedures are those of the authors and do not necessarily follow those of the judiciary system of the United Kingdom or the Central Criminal Courts of London, England, or of those of the court known as Old Bailey.

Library of Congress Cataloging-in-Publication Data

Luckhoo, Lionel Alfred, Sir, 1914–
    The silent witness / Sir Lionel A. Luckhoo and John R. Thompson.
      p. cm.
    ISBN 0-7852-8007-3
      1. Jesus Christ—Fiction. I. Thompson, John R., 1932–
II. Title.
PR6062.U23S57   1995
823'.914—dc20   94–24278
                                            CIP

Printed in the United States of America.

1 2 3 4 5 6 — 00 99 98 97 96 95

This book is dedicated to Lady Jeannie Luckhoo and to my children: Deborah, Sharman, Michael, Marina, and Mark.
L. A. L.

This book is also dedicated to my wife, Susan Thompson, and to our children, Eric and Kristen, as well as to my daughter Tammy and to the memory of my daughter Kimberlin.
J. R. T.

Friends by the hundreds also deserve our dedication as they have sown so much into our lives as we have walked on God's earth in His Grace and Mercy.

Acknowledgments

Our sincere thanks to Lady Jeannie Luckhoo and Susan Thompson for their giving of their advice, encouragement, and time in the writing of this book.

Our thanks also go to the late Demos Shakarian and the Full Gospel Business Men's Fellowship International for following their vision and providing a global ministry to businessmen where we, Sir Lionel Luckhoo and John R. Thompson, were able to meet the Messiah in our hometowns of Georgetown, Guyana, South America, and Kokomo, Indiana, U.S.A., respectively.

Special appreciation goes to the FGBMFI international directors and supporting members of the Texas State Office for their vision to reach out and bring words and testimonies of life to the developing countries of Central and South America.

A special thanks to the late author, Irving Stone, and his words of encouragement for us to write this book and his direction on how we could accomplish it.

Special thanks to our many friends whose prayers made it possible to continue writing this book over a period of nine years.

And our eternal thanks to

THE MESSIAH

Prologue

It was almost midnight as a rain-filled wind out of the northwest was bringing an early spring deluge down from the Florida panhandle. The old Blanchard home on Meadow Wood Drive firmly resisted the cold pelting rain just as it had for the past sixty-one years.

Inside, the fireplace in the great room burned brightly with its yellow-orange flames throwing dancing shadows on the mahogany-paneled walls. Above the fireplace mantel hung an original Carol Matthews oil painting of the warm and sunny beach at Marco Island, a favorite resort that I thought of, especially on cold dark nights. One solitary lamp offered the only other light in the room.

My good wife, Susan, was already asleep in the master bedroom with her head under a mountain of covers, so as not to hear the thunder. Mitty, the faithful foot-warming cat, was at her usual place at the end of the bed. Kristen was in her room doing her eternal homework with her overnight guests, Sheri and Sue. Earlier in the evening, Eric had zoomed off in his sports car to his classes at Palm Harbor Community College.

Sir Lionel Luckhoo, our famous boarder, as we lovingly called him, had just turned seventy-nine years old and was off somewhere in a distant country. He was speaking to some group about his life's experiences, which included earning his title of "The World's Most Successful Criminal Lawyer" in the *Guinness Book of World Records*.

As usual, he would be sharing some of the victories of accomplishing the world's record of 245 successive murder acquittals that he had achieved before English judges and juries where he practiced law as a barrister. However, he probably would be reluctant to relate the fact to his audience that he once was legal counsel to the infamous "Bishop" Jim Jones when Jones was in Luckhoo's home country of Guyana, South America.

If he mentioned the cult leader at all, Luckhoo would tell his listeners that Jones was a "self-proclaimed messiah" who had persuaded some twelve hundred misguided religious disciples to follow him from the United States to his new "promised land" in Guyana. Eventually, they died there in vain for their beliefs.

But mostly, the quiet and modest barrister would be telling his audiences about his newfound relationship with the man called Jesus of Nazareth, whom Sir Lionel believed to be the Hebrew Messiah, the Promised One, the Christ of the Christian Bible. Luckhoo always warned his audiences not to follow religious leaders whose words and actions did not match up with those of the life of this Jesus of his.

The evening newspaper lay open in my lap with the headlines silently screaming an unwanted memory: "COURT DEBATES KENNEDY'S DEATH!" It seemed like only yesterday when that terrible chain of events surrounding the death of America's thirty-fifth president caused a shock wave that traveled around the world in the hearts of humankind.

It seemed like an eternity ago in November of 1963 when I, and millions of others, sat in front of a television set and watched with horror as Kennedy's life ended in Dallas, Texas. As it has happened for many, suddenly and without warning, life came to an abrupt stop for this world leader in the prime of his life.

I turned the paper over and saw a pre-Easter advertisement of J. D. Summer's Cadillac dealership. He annually carried a full-page story about another world leader, Luckhoo's Jesus of Nazareth, whose life came to an abrupt stop in Jerusalem almost two thousand years before Kennedy died. Summer's ad headline stated the premise of a two-thousand-year-old debate: "DID HE RISE FROM THE GRAVE?"—a reference to the death and resurrection of Jesus.

I noted the stark similarities between the two headlines: each heralding the still-debated controversy about the deaths of the two world leaders.

I stared back into the fire and pondered what would happen if Jesus, the Messiah, were brought to a modern trial with "The World's Most Successful Criminal Lawyer" as His defense barrister. Would the outcome of such a court debate still be the same?

If Sir Luckhoo were to be the barrister for the defense, it would be only proper to have a prosecutor who was equally talented at law and equally strong in his beliefs about this world-acclaimed Messiah, Jesus of Nazareth.

My thoughts went immediately to another famous attorney. He had earned my deep respect for his defense of oppressed people. He was a man who had also achieved world recognition as a lawyer: Clarence Seward Darrow. *Yes, I thought, Darrow and Luckhoo would make a great pair of adversaries; both have been world-famous attorneys; both expressed opposing religious views.*

I pondered, *No, such a thing is impossible. Darrow died in 1938, and Luckhoo has already stated he has retired from his practice of law and . . . oh, well.*

I sat watching the fire and began to doze again. A deep sleep suddenly overtook me.

I rarely dream in such a fashion as what I am going to share with you. Perhaps it was real. You will have to be the judge and jury of that. I simply want to share it as I saw it happen in my dream.

The last sounds I can remember consciously hearing were made by the hall clock as it began to strike midnight on its Westminster chimes: "Bong . . . bong . . . bong . . . bong . . . bong . . . bong . . ."

THE SILENT WITNESS

1
LONDON, ENGLAND

Glynn Morris walked down the main hall of Old Bailey toward Number One Court and stopped in front of the great oak doors. He turned the key and heard a "klunk" as the deadbolt receded into the massive lock. He pushed the door open as he had done for the past few years as chief of maintenance in the Central Criminal Courts Building.

Looking up at the skylight, he could see the gray dawn breaking through the cloudy London skies. As he walked in front of the prisoner's dock, a sudden cold chill went up and down his spine. He heard a faint hiss like that of a snake when it is ready to strike, and he smelled a fetid odor like that of burning sulfur. The hair on the back of his head stood up, and his heart began to beat rapidly.

Morris could see nothing out of place in the famous courtroom that had been there for over a hundred years. Yet there was something different. His nervous system was screaming to his brain: *Caution! Caution! Run! Run!*

His lips trembled as he barely said the words out loud, "For God has not given us a spirit of fear, but of power and of love and of a sound mind." The second time he spoke it out strong as he walked quickly to the justice's bench and turned on the lights.

The hiss stopped, but the smell of sulfur and the clammy cold in the room seemed to remain. Morris looked around the courtroom, but he saw no one else. He felt as if he had been in the presence of the devil himself as the room was filled with deathly silence.

The door slowly opened, and Morris held his breath as a black shoe began to move into the room.

"My word, Adams, what are you doing?" Morris demanded of the chief of security.

"What am I doing? Let me ask *you* the very same thing, Mr. Chief of Maintenance! I'm sitting at my desk downstairs, and I see the fire alarm sensor going off in Number One Court. The next thing is that something has set off the air-conditioning sensors, and it's colder than a bloomin' iceberg here in the building. So I come runnin' up the stairs and find the whole court floor stinks. And the most stink is coming out of Number One Court. Now you tell me what's been happenin' in here!"

Jaymes Adams smiled broadly. "I probably scared you to death. Your face looks white as a sheet!"

Morris did not smile as he told Adams what had just happened to him.

"Jaymes, it's something evil . . . something in the spirit realm. I feel as if I just walked by the devil himself."

Adams turned, looking pensive. "I think you're right, Morris. I think you're right. It's been a long time, but we've both met that evil one before, and his calling cards are still the same. Be alert, Morris. Be alert. Our lives may depend upon it!"

Adams turned and walked out of the courtroom, leaving Morris nodding his head. He walked into the hallway and down the marble steps to the ground floor, quickly making his way to the security booth. He unlocked the door and picked up the telephone. He dialed and waited as the phone rang several times. Finally a sleepy voice answered on the other end: "Hello."

Adams spoke hurriedly into the phone: "Jody! Jody! Wake up, honey. Wake up! This is Jaymes."

"What's the matter, Jaymes? What's going on? Are you all right?"

"Jody, listen to me. Call Frances, Kaye, Esther, Naomi, and the other women. We need some prayer and we need it started now!"

Adams went on, hardly stopping to take a breath: "The clerk's Plan of the Day published yesterday says that today's trial in old Number One is the trial of Jesus of Nazareth, and I thought some joker had changed Plan of the Day sheets on me. But I just came from the Number One Court, and I find Morris standin' inside lookin' like death warmed over and white as a sheet . . . like he'd just had an encounter with the devil himself. And not only that, the whole buildin' went cold, plus the place smells like the sulfur pits of Sicily. And then my fire alarm sensors were goin' off like London was on fire again."

Jody's reassuring voice came over the phone: "Honey, it's him again. But it's a different situation from what it was years ago when you met him face-to-face in India. There are two of us now."

Adams smiled as he said, "You're right! I love you. And I'll talk to you later, love."

Adams hung up the phone. Taking out a small book from his shirt pocket, he began to read out loud, "The Lord is my shepherd, I shall not want. . . ."

Big Ben was just sounding seven chimes from the Westminster Tower in unison with the church bells at St. Sepulchre, across the street from Old Bailey. Somehow they seemed loud and ominous in their ringing, like a last warning.

2
THE WORTHY OPPONENTS

The morning air was filled with the mixed aroma of baking bread, brewing tea, automobile fumes, and fish. Usually foggy, London was experiencing a rare day as the sun emerged through a cloud-laden sky.

A black limousine turned the corner onto Newgate Street and proceeded up the street.

Limousines were nothing new to Londoners. Since London was the capital city of the United Kingdom, it was not uncommon to see diplomatic licensed limousines flying the flags of their sovereign nations.

But the diplomatic limousine driving on Newgate Street was different from most. Instead of one flag flying from the vehicle's front bumper, there were two flags.

The flag on the left was a green, yellow, and red flag of Guyana, a new and emerging country of South America that had once been part of the British Empire. On the right was a more elegant flag, complete with gold tasseling around the edge. The flag was white, with the exception of a square of blue in the top left-hand corner. In the middle of the blue square was a blood red cross, a symbol of Christianity.

In the passenger compartment sat a small brown-skinned man in his mid-seventies. He was dressed in the traditional attire of an ambassador. He wore a black morning coat with striped trousers. His vest was black. The black-and-gray-striped cravat at his neck was accented by his white shirt. His shoes and hosiery were black.

In the ambassador's right hand was a pair of dark gray suede gloves, and next to his hand sat a matching top hat. Beside him, on his left, lay a well-worn book with a small red ribbon hanging out of the bottom.

The ambassador was quiet as he rode through the busy street. His eyes were closed, but his lips were silently moving, as if in prayer to his God. Like his flags, the ambassador would be serving in two capacities today. One, as an ambassador representing the white flag, and the other, as a world-famous lawyer from Guyana.

The limousine stopped near the corner of Newgate Street and the street known as Old Bailey. The ambassador looked out his window and recognized the building where he had practiced law on several occasions.

Crawford, the chauffeur, opened the door and stood to attention, looking to his passenger in case his assistance was needed.

The ambassador handed him his book and his top hat, then got out of the vehicle. As soon as he was on the sidewalk, he was handed his top hat, which he put on his head. He kept his gloves in his right hand as he took his black book in his left hand and walked toward the door of the building. He paused for a moment and looked back at his chauffeur. "Thank you, Crawford. I shall ring you up when I need you to come for me. Be sure you and your Julie say your prayers for me. I'll need them especially today."

Crawford nodded. "Yes, sir. We'll do that, Sir Lionel."

Just as the ambassador reached the door, Chief of Security Jaymes Adams opened it. "Top of the morning, Sir Lionel. Welcome back to Old Bailey."

The ambassador took off his top hat. "Good morning, Mr. Adams. It's good to see you again. God bless you!"

He walked down the hall with its richly decorated frescoed walls, his footsteps resounding on the inlaid marble floors. Coming to the private elevator, he pushed the button. The door opened after a few seconds, and he stepped in.

"Good morning, Sir Lionel. It's good to see you back here, sir."

"Thank you, Mrs. Alexander. So kind of you to say that. How is that splendid husband of yours getting along?"

The tall thin elevator operator perked up immediately: "Oh, Richard is doing very well. He always remembers you in prayer!" The aged elevator stopped at the court floor.

"Tell him God loves him and so do I, Mrs. Alexander," Sir Lionel said as he stepped out of the elevator and turned down the hall.

The combined smells of cleaning chemicals and wood polish reached his nostrils as he came to the door marked PRIVATE—BARRISTERS AND SOLICITORS ONLY. Inside, a dark-moustached young man took his hat and his book, and he assisted the ambassador with removing his morning coat.

"Fine morning, Sir Lionel."

"Yes, it is, Mr. Hancox. Are things well with you?" The groomsman was opening a small closet door marked with a gold-leaf inscription: "Sir Lionel A. Luckhoo, KCMG, KT,

BACH, CBE, QC" (Knight Commander of the order of Saint Michael and Saint George, Knight Bachelor, Commander of the British Empire, and Queen's Counsel).

"Yes, sir. God's still number one in my life."

"Splendid, my boy, splendid," Sir Lionel replied.

"Sir Lionel, are you ready for the silks?"

"Yes, if you please. I also covet the prayers of you and your lovely wife, Cheryl, today."

"Absolutely, Sir Lionel. Consider it done," he said as he assisted the ambassador into his court attire, laying the powdered court wig on the table.

"Thank you, Mr. Hancox. God bless you." The ambassador went on quietly dressing in the traditional garb of an English barrister, and he put on the powdered wig.

Outside, a taxi pulled up to the curb. The passenger held out a crumpled bunch of bills to the driver. The driver took several of the bills, and his passenger added him an extra one as a tip.

The man stepped from the taxi, looked up and down the street, and then began to look at the building. His eyes caught the sixteen-foot-high statue *Justice,* standing on the golden dome of Old Bailey.

The man wiped a wisp of gray hair from his eyes as he looked up and said, almost with desperation, "Ah, there you are, Lady Justice. I knew you'd be here." And with a cynical tone he continued, "But I never expected to see you without a blindfold covering your eyes. Perhaps this trial will be one of full justice of law!"

Adams was watching at the door as the American got out of the taxi. He knew from the various articles he had read in history books that he was looking at the world-famous attorney, Clarence Seward Darrow.

The physical descriptions matched, including the craggy features of the man's face, complete with the long and deep lines that went from the corners of his eyes down his face, like deep scars of pain. His ears were rather large, but they were in proportion to the great six-foot-high frame on which they were carried. A small puffy bag was under each deep-set eye, and his brow looked like a great wave had crashed across it, leaving its wavy mark etched on his forehead in grooved lines. A gust of wind blew open the coat of his wrinkled suit, revealing the wide suspenders that had become part of his trademark. His cleft chin stood out like granite, and his nose jutted forth like the prow of a great ship.

Clarence Darrow pulled out a pocket watch from his vest pocket. It was 7:33.

"Good morning, Mr. Darrow, sir. Welcome to Old Bailey," was the greeting that reached a surprised attorney as the door opened.

"Well, thank you, sir. Thank you. What's your name, sir?"

"Adams, sir," the chief of security replied.

Darrow looked like he had suddenly lost his train of thought. He stared into space for a few seconds before regaining his composure: "Uh, yes, Mr. Adam. Seems to me you had a relative way back there by the name of Adam who started all this mess. I hope you're guarding this door better than he guarded that Garden of Eden, if there was one. Might have saved all of us a lot of trouble if he had watched."

Adams looked at him in a quizzical fashion and was going to correct Darrow's pronunciation of his name. Instead he said, "I believe that you need to get to the courtroom,

Mr. Darrow. Just go down this hall to the elevator and Mrs. Alexander will direct you from there."

The tall attorney turned and slowly walked down the great hall toward the elevator. Adams watched him as he went, a man in his eighties, wearing a suit that looked like he had been sleeping in it. Coming to the elevator, he pushed the button, and the door opened.

"Good morning, Mr. Darrow," the operator greeted him brightly.

"Morning, lady. What do you have to be so bright about?" he asked.

"I'm just happy to be alive, sir," she replied.

Darrow's face darkened a bit. "I bet you are. I just bet you are."

They said nothing further as the elevator came to the court floor. The door opened and Mrs. Alexander pointed to the door for barristers and solicitors.

The once-fiery lawyer bent forward and walked with some difficulty caused by the twinges of arthritis. Mrs. Alexander watched him as he opened the door and disappeared inside.

Hancox stepped forward to greet Darrow. "Good morning, Mr. Darrow. Welcome to Old Bailey. I'm here to help you dress for court, sir."

Darrow looked down at the man with a puzzled look. "Dress for what? I'm already dressed, young man."

Without a pause, the groomsman began to assist Darrow in removing his coat, saying, "It is the custom of the English court, sir, that all barristers and solicitors appearing before the Crown should be attired in traditional silks and wigs. The fact that you are an American lawyer is no exception to this rule. My responsibility is to assist you in your attire."

Darrow held out his long lanky arms to receive the silk gown provided by Hancox. "Well, I'll be!" A smile flashed across his face. "It looks like I'm trapped in the trappings of tradition." He laughed as he grabbed his suspenders. "Well, let's get on with it. The trial starts at eight o'clock, and I never was one to be late for a trial."

Darrow turned and looked at himself in a floor-length mirror, first at one side, then the other. He looked at himself under the powdered wig and said, "If anybody would have told me I'd have to wear this getup in order to come back and do this trial, I'd have said, no way!"

Hancox turned from hanging Darrow's coat in a locker and said, "I beg your pardon, sir?"

"Oh, I was just talking to myself, son. Let's get on with this masquerade anyway. . . . I've only got so much time here," he said as he turned and followed the groomsman to the end of the dressing room.

Hancox opened the door, allowed Darrow to step into a large law library, and said, "Mr. Clarence Darrow, this is the barrister for the defense, Sir Lionel Luckhoo. Sir Lionel, this is the attorney for the prosecution, Mr. Clarence Darrow." Then he turned and left the room, closing the door behind him.

There was a long oaken table in front of Darrow. On either side were rows and rows of law books from floor to ceiling. At the end of the table stood his worthy opponent, a man quiet of speech, but with an impressive record of murder acquittals.

Fully erect, Luckhoo stood not quite five feet six inches tall. His features were West Indian, and his accent British. His bushy eyebrows looked like dark arches over twin gorges of deep-set dark eyes. The bridge of his nose was fairly wide between his eyes, sloping down above his strong mouth, giving him a well-proportioned face. Some people thought he was a double of the French emperor Napoleon.

Luckhoo looked up and saw a tall man. Dramatic in his courtroom presentations, Darrow was known throughout the world for his able defense of Eugene V. Debs of Terre Haute, Indiana, for his part in the 1894 Pullman strike in Chicago, and for defending Loeb and Leopold in the famous murder trial in 1924. Perhaps the most notable trial was Darrow's defense of schoolteacher John Thomas Scopes, called the Scopes Monkey Trial, in Dayton, Tennessee, in 1925, where evolution was the central issue.

Luckhoo bowed stiffly but made no move toward Darrow. He looked him in the eye and spoke.

"Mr. Darrow, I consider you a formidable adversary. I have studied your life and your life's work at law. I admire you for your brilliant legal career in which you defended the indefensible and maintained a profound concern for humankind. You have pitied those less fortunate than you, who found themselves in bondage and slavery of some kind, even though slavery was supposed to have been abolished from your country. I see you as bringing a measure of humanity into the American courts of law and to law itself, providing those who needed redress of their bitter grievances. Many of your clients were destitute in body, soul, spirit, and finances."

There were tears of compassion in his eyes as Luckhoo looked across the long table into the eyes of Darrow. His voice was soft.

"Mr. Darrow, throughout the centuries of time there have been countless books written about the value of human life and about creeds for living. There have been great personages who have walked this earth, leaving behind them the fruits of their good deeds, and they all have left an indelible mark on the pages of time." Luckhoo paused, taking a quiet breath.

"History has recorded that you, Mr. Darrow, have lived your life as one of those, possessing a quality of humility as expressed by Origen and Andronicus. You apparently have lived a life, in deed, that is close to that of Jesus of Nazareth, of whom we bring to trial. Yet, sir, you verbally deny that He is who He says He is. It would appear to a commoner of human judgment that you were somewhat incredulous." Luckhoo's voice dropped to just above a whisper.

"Mr. Clarence Darrow, I have great respect for what you have accomplished in your lifetime on this earth. You have made great accomplishments of humanitarian works. When you finally stand before the great white throne on Judgment Day, as you surely will, the Judge of this earth will judge you according to your acceptance or denial of one thing, and one thing only . . . His Son, the Messiah. I have no right to judge you, nor will I do so. I want you to know that I am committed to this trial and to proving that the man we bring to trial here this day, the man called Jesus of Nazareth, is the central figure of not only the Torah and the Christian Bible but of the human race as well. I intend to prove, beyond a shadow of a doubt, that He is the Messiah!"

Luckhoo placed both hands on the table in front of him, and leaning over, he looked up into the face of the tall American lawyer.

"Mr. Darrow, I would have preferred to meet you under different circumstances, but regardless of the occasion, it is an honor to do law with such a distinguished adversary as Mr. Clarence Seward Darrow!"

Luckhoo folded his hands in front of him as he concluded his remarks and stood, with apparent respect, waiting on the expected reply of his worthy opponent.

Darrow blinked his eyes as if he had, for just a moment, been in another world. His countenance changed, and his eyes seemed to blaze with fire while he looked at the small man standing at the other end of the table.

The Yankee lawyer had stood with his hands in his pockets, as was his custom, listening to his opponent, seeking to catch every inflection and the hidden meanings of the statements being spoken to him. He said nothing for a few moments.

Darrow was no fool. He recognized that he had a formidable opponent, one who knew a great deal more about law and about the true meaning of the Bible than those he had debated previously.

For a moment, it was as if time was suspended. Neither man moved until Darrow took his hands out of his pockets and pointed a long bony finger at Luckhoo: "I guess I call you Sir Luckhoo, which is fine." He dropped his arm and opened the front of his court gown with both of his hands and placed them on his red suspenders.

"Sir Luckhoo, I trust you do not see yourself in a metaphoric dream where you believe that you are another David, coming against me as some sort of modern-day Goliath who has rattled the armies of you Christians."

Darrow turned to his right and slowly looked up and down at the volumes of law books, taking his time to gather his words very carefully.

"Now I don't have anything personal against your Bible and this Jesus of yours. I am well aware of the influence that your Bible and this man have had on the people of this earth.

I am cognizant of those who believe in Him and try to live as He lived . . . a peaceable man, a loving man, a genuine man, a holy man, and certainly a determined man."

He turned back from the law books. He took his hands out of his suspenders and placed them on the worn oaken table, deliberately rubbing his hands over the wood of the table, as if in deep thought. Darrow had a way of letting his opponents know that he researched and studied for his trials. His voice was firm.

"Your Jesus was a very good man, Sir Luckhoo, but He sure isn't the Messiah you're looking for. He might have been a prophet like Mohammed or a great philosopher like Socrates or maybe a good preacher like John Wesley. But, Sir Luckhoo, you need to understand that I am going to prove to you and to that jury out there in that courtroom that He was a deceiver, a fraud . . . a good one . . . but still a fraud."

Darrow's voice became mocking in tone as he spoke. "I give you credit, Sir Luckhoo. You've made a big change in your life. You now go around the world telling anybody who will listen your little story. Let's see, how does it go? Oh, yes. 'It is wonderful to be cleansed of my sins by the blood of Jesus, because He died for me at Calvary. He died in a sacrificial and substitutionary death for me two thousand years ago so I could have eternal life in heaven!' What happened, Luckhoo, are you as deceived as your precious Jesus is? You used to be a well-to-do attorney who had a worldwide law practice. Now you're nothing more than an itinerant evangelist!"

Clarence Darrow leaned over and placed his hands on the desk to be eye level with his opponent.

"What about your former client from Jonestown, Guyana, South America . . . you know, Bishop Jim Jones? What about his religion? Didn't he claim to be one of you Christians at one time who eventually took over twelve hundred of his religious disciples to their deaths? When I look at religion across the years and see what it has done to people, I get sick."

Darrow paused, then took another breath. Luckhoo did not interrupt.

"Some folks say that I'm an agnostic, and probably I am. It's hard for me to understand how just one God could have all the religions we have. Nor do I believe you can prove that one God made this universe and everything in it. In eighty-one years of walking around on this earth, I never found very much of that love your Jesus was supposed to represent. And I'm not the only one!"

Darrow paused for a moment, and his countenance changed immediately.

"After our great Abraham Lincoln freed the slaves, a former slave by the name of Frederick Douglass wrote these words about Christians, and I quote: 'Were I to be again reduced to the chains of slavery, next to that enslavement, I should regard being the slave of a religious master the greatest calamity that could befall me. For of all slaveholders with whom I have ever met, religious slaveholders are the worst. I have found them the meanest and basest, the most cruel and cowardly of all others.'"

Lionel Luckhoo stood with tears coming from both eyes. Inside he felt sick and ashamed, for the moment, that he was a part of any organized religion.

Darrow continued in a strong, but quiet voice.

"When I got to be a lawyer, Sir Luckhoo, I had just one year of college in Ann Arbor, Michigan. I wasn't like you. I sat before several lawyers who asked me a lot of law questions. They said I passed their exams and I became a lawyer. You attended Queen's College and Oxford University. You have been knighted twice by the queen of England. You still hold the world's record for the most successive murder acquittals in history. You were the only ambassador to ever have represented two sovereign nations at the same time. You see, sir, I do know something about you, and I consider you a worthy opponent."

Darrow stooped and reached into a well-worn briefcase. He pulled out a tattered book, with papers and cigar wrappers sticking out of both ends of the book.

"Sir Luckhoo, I have studied all the laws listed in this Bible of yours. I also have studied all of the Old Testament prophetic Scriptures that are prophecies of this Messiah that you all claim are fulfilled in the New Testament by this Jesus. I know that the recorded trials given to this man at His death in Jerusalem were all a farce . . . that is, if your Bible is true. You see, I've done my homework. We're ready to see if you've done yours, sir."

Two giants of law stood facing each other. There was silence in the room as the two opponents respectfully looked at each other like two fencing masters poised with sabers raised in salute; the call "On Guard" already given, the question "Ready?" having been asked, and each anticipating the order: "Fence!"

The door to the courtroom opened, and the groomsman Hancox stepped in and quietly shut the door behind him. Standing at attention he said, "My lords, the assistants of the court are in place, the jury is in position, the accused is in the dock. Will you come and take your place in the courtroom as it is time for the trial to begin and for the lord chief justice to take the bench. Gentlemen, please follow me."

Not waiting for an answer, Hancox turned, opened the door, and held it for the men.

Luckhoo bowed to Darrow, and since he was familiar with the courtroom, he proceeded first. Darrow returned the bow stiffly and then followed.

The air seemed full of electricity, just waiting for some spark to ignite it and cause a great explosion. A great duel was about to begin.

3
THE TRIAL BEGINS

The huge clocks just finished tolling eight o'clock as the bailiff stood, took the court scepter, rapped it sharply on the floor three times, and spoke with a loud voice: "Silence. Be upstanding in the court."

At that command, everyone in the courtroom stood, eyes focused on the door to the right of the justice's bench. The door quietly opened and a distinguished-looking man walked out toward the only seat behind the justice's bench.

The lord chief justice was dressed similarly to the other members of the official court, with a full wig. But his red cloak was much more elegant than all the others, and it was trimmed in ermine fur.

He had a neatly trimmed white beard and a moustache. His ocean blue eyes seemed to sparkle at times. His teeth were as white and perfect as rich pearls. His hands were tanned and very strong.

The lord chief justice sat down as the bailiff of the court

spoke the age-old statement of Old Bailey, which seemed to echo around the giant courtroom.

"All persons who have anything to do before my Lords, the King's Justices of Oyer and Terminer and general gaol delivery for the jurisdiction of the Central Criminal Court, held here this day by adjournment, draw near and give your attendance. God save the King and my Lords, the King's Justices."

The bailiff tapped the court scepter on the floor one time and everyone sat down.

The lord chief justice turned to the court secretary and spoke, "Take the book and call the roll."

The secretary stood, picked up a leather-bound book from the end of the clerk's bench, and began to read. As he read each name aloud, the reply came back: "Here am I."

"For the prosecution, Clarence S. Darrow."

"For the defense, Sir Lionel A. Luckhoo."

"Instructor Solicitor of Prosecution, Mary Houston."

"Instructor Solicitor of Defense, Diane DiPietro."

"Honorable Clerk of the Courts, Sir Robb L. Thompson."

"Bailiff, Sir William S. Griggs."

"Court Parliamentarian, Sir George M. Walters."

"Court Recorder, Sir C. S. Brooks."

"Court Linguist, Glenn L. Norwood."

"Evidence Foreman, Edgar N. Longworth."

"Representing the House of Lords, Sir John M. Lloyd."

"Representing the House of Commons, Alvin K. Tasker."

"Usher of the Court, Sir Stephan M. Steinle."

"Marshall to the Court, Sir Edward P. Kuhn."

It seemed like an endless roll call of names until suddenly he called: "The accused, Jesus of Nazareth."

Jesus' voice was strong and pure as He replied: "Here I am!"

Those were the only words He would say during the entire trial.

"The lord chief justice, Secretary Hugh M. Richeson, and the court are present and accounted for. Mr. Parliamentarian, please!"

Parliamentarian Walters stood and turned and faced the lord chief justice.

"My Lord Chief Justice, let it be known all here about that there is a quorum of the court. Let justice have the day!"

The bailiff banged his scepter one more time on the floor and shouted the call: "The court is in session. Let the trial of the accused proceed. The honorable clerk of the courts, please."

From the bench in front of the chief justice stood the clerk of the courts, Sir Robb Thompson. He stood facing the dock and read from the document that he held in his hands.

"Will the accused please rise."

The accused man stood in the dock with His hands at His sides. He looked directly at the clerk as the charge was read against Him.

"Be it known throughout the land that as the clerk of the criminal courts, I am commanded forthwith to cite and admonish the defendant that the Crown does herewith bring charges against You, Jesus of Nazareth, for the complaint of the crime against society of capital fraud. It is alleged that You, the defendant, Jesus of Nazareth, have fraudulently presented Yourself and subsequently been presented fraudulently as the Savior of the world, as the Messiah, and that You claim that You died, and on the third day You were raised again to life from the physical act of death, and that You are now alive. How does the defendant plead to this charge?"

Luckhoo stood up straight as an arrow, looked at the chief justice and, in a loud voice, opened his case.

"My lord, the defendant pleads not guilty!"

The clerk turned to Luckhoo.

"The court records the statement for the defendant as 'not guilty.'" Both men sat down.

The lord chief justice spoke and his words were filled with authority.

"Mr. Clarence Darrow, as the appointed prosecutor of this trial, you may proceed with the prosecution of the defendant."

All eyes turned to Darrow. Houston kicked him gently on his leg and said with a loud whisper. "You're on Darrow. Give it to 'em!"

Darrow stood in front of the bench where he had been sitting. He looked first to the chief justice, then to the jury. He wiped a wisp of hair off his enormous forehead and tried to push it under the uncomfortable wig on his head. He put his hands inside his court gown and brought out his bright red suspenders.

"Your Honor," and he paused expectantly, "uh, Your Lordship Chief Justice and members of the jury, I hope you will be gentle with me as this is the first time that I have practiced law in your country. When I practiced law in America, it was just a tad different, so I hope you will bear with me." Darrow beamed a confident smile to the jury.

"It is necessary in opening this case that I should be able to relate to you the setting in which the accused, Jesus of

Nazareth," Darrow turned his eyes toward the dock and the accused and dropped his voice before he said, *"lived."*

Darrow was a master of communication. He seemed to be able to pick out each member of a jury and talk to that person just as if he were back at his first law practice in Ashtabula, Ohio, and talking to one of his neighbors who happened to be on the jury.

"To set this very important trial on its proper foundation, it is necessary for me to give you some of the history of Israel and this nation's continuous quest for the elusive person they call," this time Darrow's voice was somewhat mocking as he said, "the Messiah!" He paused.

"This folk teaching," Darrow's voice carried a tone of authority, "about their Messiah was from the Hebrew religion. And it came primarily from two books of religious literature, the Torah and the Talmud. The Jewish Torah is their law comprising five books written by a patriarch of theirs—whose name was Moses—and it became the mainstay of the religion of Judaism."

He continued to stand with his hands in his red suspenders while reciting the scholarly dissertation.

"Their Torah became their written law as time went on. It came to have a wider meaning among the Jews, and it embraced the religious literature of Judaism."

He kept his eyes on the jury.

"They also had an important religious group called the Pharisees and their religious teachers called rabbis, who also recognized an early oral Torah, or law. It was comprised of some specific and some additional applications of the general principles of the written Mosaic law. In other words, these religious leaders added verbally a bunch of laws to those that Moses had reputedly received from the Hebrew God."

Darrow's voice seemed to gain momentum.

"In their early history there was a great dispersion of the Jews throughout the world, and all the sources of the written and oral law were drawn upon with traditional interpretations and opinions of generations of rabbis. They compiled a great corpus of religious literature. With that were embodied legends, history, and homilies delivered in their synagogues. The whole of this was completed in the fifth century A.D., and it is called the Talmud. It consists of six major parts and sixty-three volumes. Its influence on Judaism has been great, sustaining the Jewish people through long centuries of difficulties and severe persecution."

He started to walk over to where the jury was seated, but Houston grabbed the tail of his court gown and gently pulled him back.

"Hold it, Darrow," she loudly whispered, "you're in Old Bailey. You have to stay behind the bench!" Several of the barristers and solicitors behind Darrow overheard Houston's comments and snickered.

Darrow showed his years of persuasive courtroom practice as he humbly looked up at the chief justice and said, "Oh . . . uh . . . sorry, Your Lordship. I'm used to getting close to the common people," an obvious reference to the jury. He quickly returned to his former demeanor.

"Their law started with Moses and the Ten Commandments. Evidently that wasn't good enough for a bunch of rock-ribbed religionists who added their own laws, one of which was that a hungry person couldn't pick an ear of corn to eat if it happened to be on one of their so-called Sabbath days."

Darrow fumed, and he began to walk back and forth a few paces behind his bench. He took his hands out of his suspenders and held the sides of his black court gown.

"You see, folks, this Messiah who was looked for by the common folk of the Jews was purported to be a future great leader like their King David had been. This Hebrew Messiah would be that leader who would free their land from all the oppressors. They had oppressors coming out of their ears, including the Assyrians, then the Babylonians, the Persians, and finally the Romans."

Darrow stopped pacing and looked intently across at the jury.

"Ladies and gentlemen of the jury, I believe that the Jews deserved to be a free people. It was no small wonder they were all looking to anybody who had the appearance of being their Messiah person that their religious leaders had told them about."

Darrow's voice softened.

"The hope of the Jewish people was their *Deliverer* or *Savior*, other terms used for the name Messiah. This great Deliverer or Savior was to redeem humankind by restoring the fabulous glories of King David and King Solomon and by bringing the whole world under the benevolent leadership of the God of the Hebrews. It just so happens they would once again become a powerful nation with this kind of philosophy." He gestured to illustrate each point.

"You see, they were tired of living under a series of tyrannical governments. The Jews, throughout history, have long been a subjected people, a conquered people, and a widely scattered people. The religious promise of a Messiah was obviously a great hope to the Jews."

Darrow made a surprise move. He held up a small leather-bound book.

"Your Lordship, at this time, I wish to enter as evidence this New King James Version of the Bible because it contains most of the historical writings that we have today about the life of the accused. That is, if my distinguished opponent has no objection."

Luckhoo looked a bit puzzled as Darrow brought the Christian Bible into his opening statement, but the defense counsel made no move to object to its admission as evidence.

The chief justice looked at Luckhoo, then back to Darrow, and then nodded his head in approval. Darrow held the Bible up, and the evidence foreman came to the bench, took the Bible, and returned to the center table.

"My lord, I mark this as Exhibit A," and he put a large tag on it.

"So be it," was the comment of the chief justice, and Darrow continued.

"Now Exhibit A, that Bible, contains some interesting details, similar to those found in the Torah. It has some history, some poetry, and some nice stories in it, like the one about this young fellow David killing a nine-foot-tall giant with a rock."

Darrow smiled condescendingly at the accused and then turned back to the jury.

"Now, that's a nice story, folks. I don't care how you cut it. That's a nice little story."

Darrow seemed to be like a baseball pitcher up on the mound. Every eye in the courtroom was on him, and with every statement that he pitched, he felt more secure in his prosecution of the case against Jesus of Nazareth. He continued his slow and easy presentation.

"Later on into the scene of history comes the accused, Jesus of Nazareth."

Darrow delicately stepped into an area of very personal religious views intermingled with one of pure history.

"I wish the jury to be aware that the major portion of first person information about the accused comes from one source . . . Exhibit A . . . the Christian Bible. In the latter sections of the Bible are four books, which are commonly referred to as the Gospels. The titles of these four books, or the Gospels, are supposedly the names of the authors of these books and men who were friends of the accused. They are titled Matthew, Mark, Luke, and John."

Darrow was deliberate in his speech.

"A study of these books, which I have done, gives a person a picture of a very definite personality. The books carry the same conviction of reality that this man did indeed exist."

Darrow pointed to Jesus, sitting in the prisoner's dock.

"The prosecution does not doubt that this man did indeed exist."

He paused for a moment, dropped his hand, and looked back at the jury.

"But I wish to bring to your attention that the personality of Gautama Buddha has been very much distorted and obscured by an image of a stiff squatting figure, known as the gilded idol of Buddhism. Therefore, is it not reasonable to believe that the lean and intense personality of this simple man, Jesus of Nazareth, as portrayed in the Gospels, has been equally distorted? His life has been painted by the masters as that of a humble, gentle, and divine person. Idols of this Jesus hanging on a Roman cross of crucifixion are in every Catholic and Orthodox church in the world."

Darrow pointed to Jesus again.

"On the one hand, it seems to be that the accused, a handsome, unmarried, itinerant Jewish teacher, wandered about the dusty, sun-bleached country of Judea for a period of about three years, living on gifts of food and money, much of it from women He influenced."

Turning his head sideways and holding the palms of his hands upward as in a futile gesture, Darrow continued.

"He gathered about Him twelve men who, when approached by this Jesus, reputedly left their occupations, left their families, and immediately followed this itinerant preacher of a new religion. They slept out on mountainsides and had very little to call their own. They were perhaps a ragtag bunch. Yet on the other hand, this son of a carpenter is frequently represented by His followers as immaculately clean, well groomed and sleek, wearing spotless raiment."

Darrow continued carefully weaving his tapestry of the alleged deception of the accused.

"Let me tell you about the amazing recorded birth of the accused, that is, according to the story in Exhibit A, and with what little recorded history we can find, and from what history records of the customs of the Semites of the fourth century A.D."

Darrow held up his own Bible by one corner.

"The story in Exhibit A portrays that precious little scene we have seen on courthouse lawns for years: the shepherds, the Magi, the animals, and the father of the baby standing next to the mother, all looking at the baby in the manger."

Darrow spoke with disdain and folded his arms across

his chest. He used his voice like an expert fencing master, a jab here, a thrust there.

"I wish to paraphrase the story as it appears to have happened, in Nazareth, Israel, in about 4 B.C. The parents of a Jewish girl, approximately thirteen years old, whose name was Mary, and of a Jewish boy, approximately seventeen years old, whose name was Joseph, were in formal discussions concerning the forthcoming marriage of their children, as was their custom. There had been agreement on the marriage, and a binding engagement took place. It also was the custom of these tribespeople that the girl would live with her parents until the actual marriage ceremony, after which the married couple would consummate their marriage with sexual intercourse."

Darrow seemed somewhat pleased with himself that he could remember these things from the Hebrew books that he had studied over the years. He smiled to himself as he followed his notes.

"Now sometime between the engagement and the wedding ceremony, this thirteen-year-old Mary, who claimed that she was a virgin, was reputed to have been alone in the home of her parents one day. It was reported that she was visited by an angel named Gabriel."

Darrow flashed a wide grin at the jury.

"Now, folks, the Jews do not believe angels to be those cute little chubby girl or boy angels with wings, harps, and little bows and arrows. No, sir, they believe them to be giant, fearsome beings, a little bigger than me."

Darrow grinned again and looked down at his desk as if he were trying to be modest.

"Now this large angel told this teenage Jewish girl that she had been chosen by God to give birth to a baby boy who was supposed to be no less than the Son of God! She was told that she was to call His name Jesus. This girl was told that her son was going to be great. He was the One sent by God to take over the throne of David, and He would be the King of Israel, over the house of Jacob, one of the Jewish patriarchs, and be a Savior of His people."

Darrow laid the Bible down, then held his hands out, palms up, toward the jury as if he were trying to hold something in them. His words were incendiary.

"Her baby was supposed to be the centuries-awaited Jewish Messiah." Darrow paused and smiled at the jury.

"Now, folks, what do you think that a gentle little thirteen-year-old virgin girl would say to a great big angel that suddenly appeared before her and told her that she was going to be the mother of the Son of God?" Darrow paused, looking at the jury.

"I'm amazed at what she said. In fact, she asked a very profound question: 'How am I going to have this baby since I am a virgin?'"

Darrow paused and put his hand under his chin as if he were thinking.

"I find it very unusual to believe that this child, who was facing an awesome angelic being direct from the throne of God, would think to ask that kind of a question. But Exhibit A . . . indicates that is what she said."

Darrow's voice got a bit louder.

"This huge angelic being told her that she was going to have an intimate experience with the Holy Spirit of God, and then she . . . would be pregnant . . . with the Son of God . . . even though she . . . would still be a virgin!"

Darrow spaced his words slowly and distinctly to let each word sink into the minds of the jurors.

"I must say, with my limited knowledge of the sciences, that throughout all of recorded scientific history, never has a virgin been pregnant and at the same time remained a virgin. I've never read of that kind of a thing happening, except in some folk and fairy tales. But here," he pointed at his Bible before him, "this very young child, Mary, this reputed Jewish virgin, said that the angel departed from her. And later on, she found out that she was indeed pregnant!"

Darrow pecked his finger up and down on his Bible.

"That is as her version . . . in Exhibit A . . . is recorded!"

In his presentation, Clarence Darrow always tried to be very logical.

"What happened next was that when her seventeen-year-old husband-to-be heard about her pregnancy, according to this Bible story, his first thought was to have her 'put away,' and not marry her."

He scratched his head under his wig.

"Now, folks, before he did this, an amazing thing happened. He had a dream!"

His voice portrayed a false sense of jubilance.

"Dreams are wonderful, aren't they? In this teenage boy's dream God told him it was all right to marry the girl! That may well have been what he told his and her parents because he did marry his pregnant girlfriend. That appears to be very commendable for a seventeen-year-old boy to do who supposedly did not get his thirteen-year-old girlfriend pregnant, don't you think?"

Luckhoo rose to his feet as if to object to this statement, but he decided to sit down and did so. This movement threw Darrow off for a second, but he went on with his opening statement.

"Oh, wait now, folks. There's more to this . . . uh . . .

Bible story! They did get married, and about the time she was supposed to have the baby, they had to go to Bethlehem for a census. Because of the census, called by the Roman government, Bethlehem was overcrowded. The only place these two teenagers found to stay was in a clean stable of an inn."

Darrow smiled.

"Now that night this teenage girl gave birth to a baby boy in that stable, and they named Him Jesus, which was a very common name of that day. Later on, some astrologers from the Orient had been following a new star that appeared to be moving across the sky, and they came to Bethlehem seeking a newborn King. Like a lot of things we don't know for sure, this may have been a part of their superstitious beliefs."

The tall, lanky lawyer shook his head and smiled to himself.

"And again, according to this fine Bible story, this star seemed to stop over the house where Jesus was now about two years old. Here was a slight diversion for the astrologers who were on their way to find this God-child. Remember that they were following some sort of a star they said was moving. Before they got to Bethlehem, they stopped in Jerusalem and talked with the ruler of that area, a despot named Herod. Supposing he was a religious man, they asked where they might find a new King born in Bethlehem. This jealous and crafty old king encouraged them to find the new King and bring back news to him."

Darrow rubbed his hands together, as if portraying an evil person.

"Well, they found the baby Jesus and determined that He must be the child they were looking for. Then they gave

Him presents. They never went back to Herod because they, too, had a dream! Amazing, isn't it? Everybody is dreaming," he said in a burlesque fashion.

"Well, what does an angry, evil king do when he hears of possible competition? Why, he had all the baby boys in that area under two years of age murdered!"

Darrow paused and pointed at the Bible lying on the evidence table.

"Now at least that part of this incredible tale is documented in history!"

He made the statement with a note of frustration in his voice.

"Now before Herod could kill Jesus, the teenage Joseph had another one of those dreams. He took Mary and the baby Jesus and fled to Egypt. Egypt was a land of magic and the occult as well as a land of ancient religions." Darrow again took his hand in his chin.

"Then that Bible is silent about the life of Jesus for about ten years. The next time you read of Him, He is twelve years old and apparently is some sort of genius. He was found in the Jewish temple teaching the learned doctors of law."

Darrow's voice lowered to a loud whisper as he said each word very distinctly.

"Then once again . . . we do not hear one word about the life of this person! This time it is for eighteen long years. Think about that, folks! The first time Jesus and His family supposedly hid out in Egypt, the land of mystery and magic. The second time, Jesus simply disappeared into His father's carpentry shop for eighteen years. Don't you find that very interesting, especially for a Messiah?"

Darrow paused to let the thought sink in.

"Members of the jury, let me share with you some similar evidence of another religion, according to a very reliable source . . . the historian H. G. Wells."

Darrow's voice sounded like that of a college lecturer.

"Gautama Buddha was born in India about 563 years before the accused, Jesus of Nazareth, was born. Records indicate that the Buddha's mother, Maya, was the wife of King Suddhodana Gautama, a ruler from the Kshatriya caste of that great nation. In the writings about the life of the Buddha, the queen had a dream, and in her dream, she saw a white elephant entering into her womb through the right side of her chest. Shortly thereafter, she was found to be pregnant with child, and she bore a son whom they named Siddhartha."

Darrow had a big smile on his face.

"They say that a hermit, named Asita, came from the Himalayan Mountains to the castle to see the newborn child. He predicted that if the child would stay in the palace, he would become a great king of the whole world, but if he embraced a religious life, he would become the savior of the world. Buddhist history records that Siddhartha forsook the pleasures of the palace for a pious life and later became Gautama Buddha, the leader of the worldwide religion of Buddhism." He paused but a second.

"Now which story can you accept? The girl becoming pregnant after the visitation of an angel or the girl becoming pregnant after a dream of an elephant entering her womb?"

Darrow held up his notes as he talked.

"The historian, Wells, also gives us some insight regarding a third and similar religious leader, the founder of Islam, Mohammed. Wells records that Mohammed was born in a city called Mecca, in Arabia, about A.D 570. This recognized historian tells us that Mohammed, in contrast to Buddha, was born in considerable poverty and was an uneducated shepherd boy. But later he had the good fortune to marry a prosperous woman. Wells states that Mohammed was a shy, sort of a poetic man, and he says that Mohammed seemed to lack incentive to do much with his life."

Darrow continued his detailed opening statement.

"At age forty, this Mohammed had a visitation from an angel, who gave him some verses of writings. From this, Mr. Wells gives us evidence that Mohammed became a 'prophet,' saying that there was 'one God,' and that there was a 'future life,' and that there were a 'paradise for the believer' and a 'hell for evil persons.' Mohammed, according to this respected historian, claimed that there were other lesser prophets, and this Jesus, the accused, was one of those prophets."

Darrow's voice was like a painter's brush on a canvas of words, giving a wide strong stroke here and a gentle light touch there.

"Mohammed had a difficult time getting started, as history records it. He, like Jesus, had been an itinerant teacher, and he had a few followers here and there."

Darrow stood behind his bench, feeling as if his feet were nailed to the floor because he could not walk in front of the jurors' box as he was used to doing.

"Interesting group, these religious types. Mohammed led raiding parties, killing his fellow countrymen in the name of religion, and he proclaimed that Allah was God. Mohammed also proclaimed that he was the divine prophet of God in this earthly kingdom."

Clarence Darrow looked at the jury. He saw faces that were somewhat hostile to his agnostic beliefs; people with various other religious beliefs displayed expressions of mild aversion, disbelief, and prejudice over what he had just told them. Although he wanted to influence them, his heart burned that they would be open to hear all of the evidence against and for the accused. He was a lawyer of law, a devout seeker of truth as he knew it.

"I have presented to you a very brief look at some rather strange similarities of three of the so-called great religions of the world. I have given you some background on the Hebrew religion. I have provided this information not to indicate to any of you that you are not knowledgeable about one or any one of them but to remind you that they all have some precepts that are strange and strangely alike. Please permit me to provide a bit more of the parallel history of these religions. I believe it will allow you to place in perspective the capital fraud that has been perpetuated on humankind because of this man called Jesus, declared by His followers to be the Messiah."

Darrow straightened his court gown, then cleared his throat with a dusty-dry cough. There was a suppressed eagerness in his manner that revealed the old warhorse in him, anxious to get into the questioning of the witnesses. He grinned his broad boyish grin and continued to speak.

"Between 600 B.C. and A.D. 600, five of the world's so-called great religions were founded: Buddhism, Christianity, Confucianism, Islam, and Judaism. They are all dependent upon and draw their inspiration from their own sacred scriptures. Buddhism and Confucianism, however, are different in that they are not religions with a personal God as the center of their worship, as Judaism, Islam, and Christianity are. These three God-centered religions do worship a personal unseen God, and their faiths are closely related, with all three of them growing out of a root of Judaism."

Pleased with his notes and his memory, Darrow continued his remarks.

"They all are the religions of the primitive Semite tribes, and they were founded in the great quadrilateral that embraces the Arabian Peninsula of Mesopotamia, Palestine, Lebanon, and Syria. All three of these religions were propagated by so-called prophets of God. Each religion is somewhat bound to its own culture. Buddha, Mohammed, and Jesus all claim to have been supernatural beings, yet they claimed to be human beings as well! They enjoyed the worship of their followers. They ran into severe problems from groups and authorities who opposed their beliefs and the methods by which they propagated their beliefs."

Darrow added a final statement, like a signature being added to a painting.

"And . . . they . . . died!"

Every eye in the courtroom was on Darrow. His reputation had preceded him, and he was not one to disappoint his audience. He simply turned and looked directly at the accused with a blank expression on his face, showing no emotion at all. It was as if time were suspended. No one coughed. No one moved. The only noise was the ticking of the clock.

"There is no doubt that the accused, Jesus of Nazareth, is the central figure of a worldwide religion today. The adherents of the Christian religion are found in every nation on the earth. We have before us Exhibit A, which is their Bible, containing the sixty-six books of the Old and New Testaments."

Darrow gave the jury a condescending smile as he held up his Bible.

"This is a wonderful book, folks. It has inspired thousands for centuries. It contains Scriptures on how to live a good life in the short time we are here on this old earth. It tells some prophecies about something called the Rapture of the church . . . about a second coming of their Messiah person . . . about a heaven and a hell . . . and about the destruction of this earth."

Darrow used pauses effectively. He paused and looked back at the witness section.

"And, oh, yes, in here is the story of an evil supernatural personage named Satan, the devil."

He paused again.

"This religious book tells us stories about the accused, Jesus, mainly in the books of Matthew, Mark, Luke, and John. The authors of those books were followers of Jesus. But how much truth is in their book? The Mormon religion is considered part of the Christian religion, yet the Mormons have a different book." He paused to let the point sink into the minds of the jurors.

"The Jehovah's Witnesses are considered part of the overall Christian religion, yet they have a different book. There are several versions of the Christian Bible, including Exhibit A, the New King James Version. But, on the other hand, there appear to be lots of differences in the Christian religion."

Darrow laid his Bible gently on the table in front of him. He smiled a wily smile.

"In my country, members of one religious group consider themselves evangelical Christians. Every year they gather in convention and verbally degrade people within their own denomination. Yet they say that their Jesus is reputed to have said, 'A new commandment I give to you, that you love one another; as I have loved you, that you also love one another. By this all will know that you are My disciples, if you have love for one another.'"

Darrow's voice rose to a higher pitch, and the tone of authority was carried on the back of every word.

"Folks, even those with no religion know they have to get along together and support one another . . . or else, what value is religion?"

His tone suddenly turned to anger.

"I say that it is because of men like this Jesus, who foist their ideals on the superstitious people of the world. They are told of some great Promised Land, only to find that they have to fight for every inch of it."

He turned and looked at his worthy opponent, sitting to his left. Luckhoo had his eyes closed, as was his custom in a trial.

The thought entered Darrow's mind: *This is going to be an easy trial. The defense counsel is asleep already!* But something seemed to warn him that was not the case. He proceeded cautiously.

"Now, you fine folks of the jury, let me tell you what the accused, Jesus of Nazareth," and he paused again for effect, "is not!"

His words rang out in the huge courtroom like a shot: "The accused, Jesus of Nazareth, certainly is not a true historic character. We are hard put to find any authenticity in written history as a religious leader by qualified historians! This indicates that the man is a FRAUD!"

Some of the jurors covered their mouths to hide their feelings about this statement. The barristers and solicitors leaned over and loudly whispered comments to each other. A dull roar rumbled in the courtroom.

The lord chief justice banged his gavel. "Silence in the

courtroom." Looking directly at Darrow he said, "Proceed, Mr. Darrow."

"Thank you, Your Lordship."

With the response from his statement, Darrow knew that he had hit a nerve with several people in the jury as well as with the gallery of barristers. He proceeded delicately.

"In the early part of the last century, a historical attitude became popular in most fields of true study, including that of religion. Those pioneers attempted to seek, on a historical level only, information considered to be available on the founder of one of the most successful religions known to humanity." Darrow assumed his lecture voice again.

"Most of what we know about the accused comes from a very biased group of sixty-six books, Exhibit A, the Bible."

Darrow picked up a folder containing several sheets of typewritten paper. Unconsciously, he reached up and whisked the wisp of hair that had escaped from under his wig. He read from the paper in his folder.

"We have some insignificant facts about the accused from some writers of history. I would like to enter some of them as exhibits at the proper time, if I may, Your Lordship."

He did not look up from his reading of his file as he continued.

"There was a letter written to Emperor Trajan in A.D. 112 by Pliny the Younger, who was then the governor of Bithynia. The governor stated that he had discovered Christians in his province, and his letter indicated that he had them arrested and that they had confessed they held meetings before dawn to sing hymns to this Christ, as God."

Putting his file down before him, Darrow opened the front of his court gown and grabbed a suspender, one in each hand. He looked squarely at the jury while he spoke.

"Celsus wrote, about A.D. 180, a book against the Christians. But he neither affirms nor denies a historic Jesus. There was even supposed to have been an official document between Pontius Pilate and Emperor Tiberius, which discussed the accused. The historian Justin is the first to allude to this elusive document, and then Tertullian follows him in this belief."

Darrow hunched his shoulders and put his hands into his front pockets.

"However, the pursuers of authentic history have come to an agreement that Justin believed that there was such a document . . . Tertullian assumed the same because of Justin, evidently without verification. Somewhere in the fourth or fifth century," he droned on like a college professor, "on the authority of Tertullian's assumption, it is believed that a faithful believer forged the document."

In an animated fashion he said, "By the way, the name of Claudius had replaced the probable one of Tiberius. It would be unscientific to base any evidence of a historic Jesus on any forgery."

Darrow smiled confidently. "This evidence is from valid historians."

He took his hands out of his pockets and again picked up the folder. He turned the pages, glancing at them for a few seconds, and then directed his gaze toward the jury with a quizzical look.

"Wouldn't you folks expect that if there were a Messiah born to the Jewish nation . . . or at least someone who professed to be a Messiah . . . wouldn't you expect that some Jewish somebody would write that important fact somewhere in their history?"

Looking back at his notes, he proceeded.

"Philo of Alexandria was born about thirty years before the beginning of what we know as the Christian era, and he died about fifty-four years after Jesus died. This man had an interest in the country of Israel. He wrote over fifty works that we have today."

Darrow shook his great head.

"But not one of them alludes to this Jesus or His followers! I find that extremely interesting, don't you?"

Darrow turned the page, stood up straight as if he had just discovered something in the folder, and spoke in artificial excitement.

"Wait . . . I do have something from the Jewish historian Josephus, from his writings the *Jewish Antiquities*. He wrote, 'At that time lived Jesus, a holy man, if man he may be called, for he performed wonderful works, and taught men, and they joyfully received the truth. And he was followed by many Jews and many Greeks. He was the Messiah. And our leaders denounced him. But when Pilate had caused him to be crucified, those who had loved him before did not deny him. For he appeared to them after having risen from the death on the third day. The holy prophets had, moreover, predicted of him these and many other wonders. The race of Christians takes its name from him and still exists at this present time.'"

Darrow rubbed his chin as if in deep thought.

"I thought that true historians were supposed to be unbiased about their writing of history!"

He paused for a moment and placed both hands on the railing in front of his desk.

"It would appear that the Jewish historian got caught up in the story he heard from the Jewish and Greek converts to this new religion, or Josephus had become a convert himself."

Darrow took the folder again and focused his attention on his papers.

"Several investigative historians, including Dr. Charles Guignebert, professor of the history of Christianity in the Sorbonne and author of the book *Jesus*, do not believe what is attributed to Josephus in this case . . . is truth!"

He raised one finger in the air to emphasize his point.

"Dr. Guignebert, speaking specifically about the quote I just read to you from *Jewish Antiquities*, said in his book: 'We have italicized the phrases that no Jew could ever have written, save one, indeed, who was on the verge of conversion to Christianity. Their glaring improbability was attacked as early as the beginning of the eighteenth century by a Swiss philologist called Otto, and nowadays all the critics take them for what they are worth. The question, however, is still open whether we have here an authentic rhetorical outburst of Josephus, amended by a Christian, or, as the writer inclines to believe, a pure Christian forgery.'"

Looking full into the faces of the jurors, Darrow spoke with fervor.

"Members of the jury, how many kinds of frauds has the human race endured throughout history in art, in literature, in precious jewels, and . . . ," Darrow paused and looked directly at Jesus, "in people?"

Darrow continued to hammer away at any case that Luckhoo might try to build for the accused.

"One of the oldest religions, that of the Hebrews, centered on one God, Jehovah. Their patriarchal Bedouin founders, Abraham, Isaac, and Jacob, were reputed to have conversed with their supernatural God. He reputedly led them throughout their history as a nation and supposedly gathered this nation in the country of Egypt. I personally have no quarrel with the Jews, but historians have a very hard time validating stories of the Jews. One historic record of the Egyptians shows the settling of a tribe of Semitics in Goshen in Egypt under Pharaoh Rameses II."

Darrow looked up sharply.

"This seems to corroborate the Hebrew Old Testament account in the first book of this Christian Bible, the book of Genesis."

Darrow picked up his well-worn copy of the Bible, held it by one corner, and flapped it back and forth like a thick fan.

"However, the Egyptians are strangely silent about any person named Moses or like Moses. They also show no account at all of any of the so-called supernatural plagues that were supposed to have been placed on Egypt, like those listed in the book of Genesis."

He paused and shrugged his shoulders.

"There is no Egyptian recording of any miraculous parting of the Red Sea and the subsequent loss of the entire army of Pharaoh by drowning as was stated in the very first book of this Christian Bible. And remember . . . this Christian Bible contains most of the recorded history of the accused."

Darrow smiled a fatherly smile at the jurors.

"Perhaps since their Bible cannot be fully verified by qualified historians . . . perhaps their Bible is just a collection of nice stories, told over and over by older people around campfires throughout time. Perhaps it was the only thing the dispersed people could hang on to for their very survival. I most assuredly would not fault them for that."

He paused for a moment to catch his breath.

"But the fact is, several historians state that the beginning of the Bible cannot be historically verified. The historians of the accused's day say that only a few brief sketches indicate that Jesus even existed. But none, except Exhibit A, can point to His being any kind of a religious leader. And, members of the jury, I hasten to point out that the Bible was written by no one else but the biased believers of these two religions, Judaism and Christianity!"

Darrow reached down and picked up the folder from which he had been reading.

"Your Lordship, I would like to enter into evidence this file of quotations, with appropriate biographical information, from Guignebert, the great historian Wells, and the writings of others recognized as historians of their day."

The foreman of evidence rose and walked over to Darrow, took the file from him, and returned to the center table. He looked up at the lord chief justice.

"My lord, I mark this Exhibit B."

The lord chief justice stated, "It is so received as evidence. So be it."

Darrow placed both of his huge hands flat on the bench in front of him and leaned toward the jury. He knew that the things he had to say in the opening hours of pleading could very well be the most important of the trial. He was not content to plead merely on the basis of hearsay; he wanted his arguments to be based solidly on historical facts and on the law. He believed that religious freedom was important to everyone in that courtroom, even those like himself who did not believe in religion per se.

His opponent, Luckhoo, sat with his eyes closed, shutting out anything that might divert his attention from what

Darrow was saying. Luckhoo never took written notes in his trials. Once, when asked about this, he stated, "I make my trial notes on the backs of my eyelids."

Once again Darrow looked at the jury, this time with a smile across his face, as if he were going to tell them an interesting story.

"Remember the story of the elephant who enters the womb of the wife of a king in India in a dream . . . and she is pregnant with the leader of a world religion."

He paused.

"Remember the story where a male angel visits a young Hebrew virgin in Israel . . . and she is pregnant with the leader of a world religion."

Again he paused for the effect it would have.

"And remember the story of a poor uneducated shepherd boy of Saudia Arabia who had a visitation from an angel, and he became a self-proclaimed prophet of God and the leader of a world religion."

Making his point with his long bony finger, Darrow spoke quietly.

"Remember that all three of these religious leaders are males who have pictured themselves as the savior of the world and have established bona fide religions that are dominant in the world today."

He pecked his fingers on his desk loudly.

"Remember that all three have had very strong women in their lives, which may have influenced them a great deal."

Darrow placed his hands together in a prayerful position.

"Remember, too, that all three have had very unnatural, or if you prefer supernatural, things happen in and to their lives, according to their own writings or those of their devout followers."

He picked up his notes again and read.

"Let me quote once more from Dr. Guignebert, a statement about the accused, which seems to cover all three of these religious leaders: 'Psychologically, Jesus seems to have been of the type, common enough in history, produced by an environment in which religious interests could take tyrannical and exclusive possession of the mind, and, in this particular case, in which obsession with the Messianic hope created a predisposition to an ecstatic state. Under these conditions, the slightest impulse from without was sufficient to produce a sense of vocation.'"

Without looking at the lord chief justice, Darrow continued.

"That quote and the references to it will also be found in Exhibit B, Your Lordship."

Darrow picked up his Bible and held it high as if he were holding some sort of prize for all to see. He looked up at it, brought it down to his eye level, and then threw it with a light toss onto his desk. He looked back to the jury.

"In that book, which is Exhibit A, are the Gospels . . . the books written by Matthew, Mark, Luke, and John . . . all followers of the accused, Jesus. They all tell different and somewhat conflicting stories about the religious and Roman trials held for the accused, the poor carpenter from Nazareth. But according to three out of the four Gospels, the blame for Jesus' arrest is placed directly on the religious Jews of His day."

He smiled again.

"I would consider that an appropriate thought process for persons leaving their Jewish faith to start a new faith, wouldn't you?"

Darrow paused once more.

"Now as a lawyer, I have had some interest in the arrest and legal proceedings in the case of the accused. I have argued with those who have looked at the Gospels as they would points of a case, even in view of the inconsistencies the Gospels present from a legal viewpoint."

He pointed to the witness section.

"For instance, they have argued that the arrest of Jesus by the Jewish authorities was illegal because a capital offense was involved. The fact is, in religious matters the members of the Jewish Sanhedrin were qualified in all cases and they had full authority to issue a warrant for the arrest of Jesus."

He crossed his left arm across his chest and placed his right elbow on his left hand, using it as a resting place. He then placed an index finger at the side of his mouth.

"Claiming to be the Jewish Messiah was certainly a religious matter. To claim such was a religious crime of blasphemy, according to their religious beliefs, and that was punishable by death by stoning, the stake, strangulation, or decapitation. I might mention that crucifixion on a cross was strictly a Roman method, and the accused ended up on the Roman cross instead of being put to death by a Jewish method."

Once more Luckhoo's eyes popped open, and he turned his head toward Darrow. The thought went through his mind that he had not underestimated his opponent's ability to research and argue against his case. Darrow was doing well enough to keep Luckhoo alert.

Luckhoo turned to DiPietro.

"You'll do well to take as many notes as you can. You can learn a lot from Mr. Darrow." She nodded and held up her partially used notebook.

Darrow pointed to the Bible on the desk before him. He picked it up and then put it back down quickly.

"There are many other discrepancies in the common beliefs about Jesus of Nazareth, whom His followers called the Messiah."

Darrow's huge eyebrows knitted together, and his craggy features stood out even more.

"I should like for each of you of the jury to decide for yourself whether or not He is who He says He is. I think that the best way for that to happen is for us to question those who were intimate with the man when He walked upon the earth."

Darrow stood and looked directly at the accused in the dock.

"I have brought you information on Buddha, Moham-med, and Jesus as well as facts about the religions they perpe-trated upon humanity. I wish to clarify why only Jesus is being brought to trial for capital fraud instead of all three of these mortal men."

Like an expert marksman taking aim at his quarry, Dar-row slowly raised his arm with one outstretched finger and pointed it at Jesus. His voice was almost a hiss.

"It is because that man, sitting in the prisoner's dock here at Old Bailey, is the only one who claimed that He rose again from the dead . . . and . . . is alive today."

He dropped his arm and looked directly at the jury.

"The prosecution will prove that not only is He guilty of capital fraud upon the people of the world, but He is guilty of perpetuating an illusion on His followers and converts."

Darrow paused and spoke in a loud whisper.

"One other thing we all should remember . . . we are here to make a decision of guilty or not guilty."

Darrow stood up to his full six feet. When he wasn't standing in his usual slouch, he looked like a giant of a man.

Luckhoo sat watching him, not moving. Jesus sat expressionless in the prisoner's dock, as He had during the entire opening statement by Darrow.

"Members of the jury, if the accused, Jesus of Nazareth, were actually a Messiah, the Savior and the Deliverer of humankind from their mortal sins, who came to this earth almost two thousand years ago, He has failed miserably. For which of you, sitting on the jury, is not beset by some kind of mountain of a problem of one kind or another, and even this moment needs a Messiah, a Savior, or a Deliverer?"

He looked from side to side at the jurors. All eyes were on him, but no one answered his rhetorical question.

"Which one of you can pick up today's newspaper or listen to a radio or television broadcast and find that there is not war or famine somewhere on this planet? Which one of you is ignorant of the history of the failings of humankind, even with the hundreds of thousands of so-called gods in this world?"

Darrow's voice began to rise and the blood vessels were beginning to stand out in his forehead. His fists clenched and opened intermittently.

"Although religion is not on trial here and should not be so, the rock-ribbed religionists of the world should be."

He shook his fist in the air. Darrow picked up a copy of a folded newspaper and held it as if he were reading from it.

"The religionists of Germany sat back and watched Hitler take over and destroy millions of Jews. Even at this moment, some people work to save the whales and yet stand by to allow pregnancies to be terminated. In my day that was murder."

His face was red with anger. Darrow hated injustice, especially to those who could not defend themselves.

"Blacks the world around are still not allowed in some white churches. Murders are still going on in the name of religion. So-called evangelists are taking in millions of dollars a day on television from the fruitful faithful with a promise that if they make a vow and pay that vow to the particular ministry, then will God bless them!"

He slapped the paper across his hand, making a loud noise. A few people jumped at the sound.

"Parents refuse needed medical or psychiatric treatment for their children because it conflicts with the religious doctrine of 'our Father' or 'our bishop' or 'our elder.' The Klan still burns the cross of this Jesus as the symbol of white supremacy."

Darrow had again started pacing behind the bench. His face was the color of volcano smoke. With almost a shout he spoke.

"When are we going to call a stop to this? When is enough going to be enough? Ladies and gentlemen of the jury, I say that the time is NOW! That is why this man is being brought to trial!"

Luckhoo jumped to his feet as if he had been hit with a bolt of lightning.

"My lord, I should like to remind my esteemed counsel that the accused is not being brought to trial here for the sins of the world or even for the sinners of the world. He's already done that in my estimation. The accused is charged with capital fraud, more specifically not being who He says He is. The crimes of those involved with religion, even in His name, should not and cannot be laid at this man's feet and cannot be considered evidence against Him. My esteemed counsel has already stated in his lengthy and wearisome opening oration that religion per se is not the charge here, and if it were, Jesus would be just as innocent as He is of capital fraud."

The lord chief justice nodded his head.

"The objection is sustained. The jury is instructed to disregard the prosecution's references to the crimes of religionists. Proceed, Mr. Darrow."

Darrow was used to these detours in his court presentations and went on without missing a beat. His voice was now very calm.

"According to Jewish beliefs, the Jewish Messiah is to be a human, God-elected redeemer for the Jewish nation and, coincidentally, for all of humankind through the intermediation of Israel. This Messiah is pictured as God's messenger, the human instrument of God's divine will, who will, at an appointed hour, be sent by God to redeem Israel from its long martyrdom of suffering, humiliation, and oppression. The predetermined mission of their Messiah is clearly stated: that of establishing God's kingdom on the earth. At that time, brotherhood, peace, and justice will usher in the eternal Sabbath for Israel and for the rest of humankind as well, provided that humankind accepts the belief in one God and His Torah."

Darrow took a deep breath, then placed his hands together with his fingertips pointing upward. His words were like blows from a sledgehammer hitting against a rock.

"Ladies and gentlemen of the jury, I hasten to remind you of a very important fact in this case. The very devout holders of the original belief in the Messiah, the Jews, do . . . not . . . believe . . . that . . . their . . . Messiah . . . has . . . come!"

Darrow let the words sink into the minds of the jurors for a moment or two. A smile of confidence played over his lips.

"The Jewish hope is in that they are still looking for Him to come!"

Darrow turned and placed the flat side of his huge left hand, palm up, toward the prisoner in the dock.

"Here, brought before us in this prisoner's dock, sits Jesus of Nazareth, born in Bethlehem, of the tribe of Judah, and the nation of Israel. This man emerged from the Jewish welter of overheated fancies, esoteric notions, wild-eyed prophecies, and folk legends that accumulated about their Messiah for three thousand years."

The lanky attorney took hold of his red suspenders and looked at the accused. Jesus looked up directly into the eyes of His prosecutor, and Darrow turned and looked at the jury.

"According to Exhibit A . . . He says that He is the promised Messiah. I believe that the prosecution has already shown that Jesus of Nazareth is *not* a historic Messiah, and I intend to prove through actual witnesses who lived on the earth with this man that beyond a shadow of a doubt, He is simply one of several would-be messiahs. Most of all, you have been provided with historic evidence that Jesus of Nazareth is not who He says He is! Now, it is time that others, who actually saw the man, verify these facts for you."

Darrow's blue eyes had a twinkle in them. This was the time that he seemed to relish the most, that of interrogating witnesses, of interacting with them. His prime interest in religion was to bring it into an open debate and discussion.

"Your Lordship, that concludes the opening statement for the prosecution."

Darrow sat down with a look of satisfaction on his face. His legs ached from standing.

The lord chief justice looked at Darrow, then at Luckhoo.

"The counsel for the defense may proceed with his opening statement. Sir Luckhoo."

Luckhoo stood, placed the tips of his fingers on the desk in front of him, then made a slight bow to the lord chief justice.

"My Lord Chief Justice, the defense wishes to make no opening statement."

The faces of the court officials and those in the spectator section were mirrors of disbelief. Muted conversations broke out all over the courtroom.

Darrow turned his head so quickly his wig almost fell off. Houston dropped her pencil on the floor.

The members of the jury looked at each other in surprise.

DiPietro bit down hard on the pencil that she had been chewing nervously. She looked up sharply at her senior partner in the defense but said nothing.

Only three people in the courtroom seemed to be unruffled by the announcement: Luckhoo, the lord chief justice, and Jesus. Jesus nodded affirmatively; a great expression of satisfaction settled down over His face.

The lord chief justice banged his gavel on the pad.

"The bench acknowledges that the defense does not wish to make an opening statement; is that correct, Sir Luckhoo?"

Luckhoo was quiet and respectful.

"That is correct, my lord."

Luckhoo sat down as quietly as he had gotten up. He contrived to appear as cool and unemotional as ever, but on the inside he was excited, anticipating the testimonies of the coming witnesses.

"So be it duly recorded in this trial."

The lord chief justice banged his gavel one more time on the pad.

The pages of history were ready to be related by those who lived them. Time was going to go backward . . . again!

4
WITNESSES FOR THE PROSECUTION

MORNING, DAY ONE

Mr. Prosecutor, you may call your first witness."

Darrow had just stood for over an hour, giving his opening statement to the jury. His legs felt like timbers that had been bent in a high wind. He had wanted to sit down and listen to Luckhoo's rebuttal of his verbal attack against Jesus, but the unpredictable Luckhoo had just changed directions in the trial.

A suppressed eagerness in Luckhoo's manner made Darrow vaguely uneasy.

"What is he up to, Houston?" Before she could say a word, Darrow stood up slowly, trying to get all his thoughts moving in the same direction.

He looked over at Luckhoo and spoke under his breath, "Well, Sir World-Famous Big-Shot Attorney, two can play that game. I'll give you one to try on for size!"

Darrow smiled to himself, then looked at the lord chief justice.

"Your Lordship, I wish to call as my first witness, Joseph, the carpenter, of the house of David, the father of the accused, Jesus."

This was becoming a bizarre trial. The defense had just refused a golden opportunity for his opening statement, and now the prosecution called for a hostile witness to testify in his case.

The barristers and solicitors again burst into muffled conversations, gesturing to make their points.

The bailiff of the court stood up and spoke in a loud voice: "Joseph, son of Jacob. Call for Joseph, son of Jacob."

From the witness section behind the dock, there rose a man who appeared to be in his late forties. He made his way from the witness seating, crossing in front of the jury, to the witness box.

He stopped momentarily between the jury and the prisoner's dock, where Jesus sat. He turned his head and just for a moment his eyes met those of Jesus. Their expressions held something of great respect and unfathomable love for each other. He then continued to the witness box.

Joseph was wearing the traditional clothing of a Jewish workingman with an inner garment made of cotton, an outer garment of coarsely woven goat's hair, and a girdle, or belt, around his outer garment. He wore crudely made sandals on his feet.

The carpenter's olive skin was deeply tanned, and his hands were calloused from using them in his labors as a craftsman. His eyes were dark in color, and they seemed to be like deep pools of peace. His hair, which hung to his shoulders, was gray with a tinge of black still showing here and there. He had a leather thong tied around his head to keep it from flowing into his eyes.

The bailiff handed him a Bible to place in his left hand.

"Do you understand the language being spoken here today?"

His answer was in a rich, clear voice with an Aramaic accent: "Yes, I do understand your language."

The bailiff said, "Repeat this after me: I solemnly swear to tell the truth, the whole truth, and nothing but the truth, so help me God."

Joseph repeated the pledge and placed his hands on the front of the witness box where he stood. He turned and looked at his son, sitting in the prisoner's dock. He gave Jesus a look of confidence.

The lord chief justice spoke up: "Mr. Darrow, you may proceed with your examination in chief of the witness."

Darrow seemed to identify with this carpenter-workingman. Then he remembered that he was there to prosecute the accused, the son of the witness.

"Mr. Joseph, I am reading from Exhibit A, the book of Matthew, chapter one, verses fifteen and sixteen: 'Eliud begot Eleazar, Eleazar begot Matthan, and Matthan begot Jacob. And Jacob begot Joseph the husband of Mary, of whom was born Jesus who is called Christ.' Are you the Joseph mentioned there?"

"Yes, I am."

"I am reading from Exhibit A, the book of Luke, chapter three, verses twenty-three and twenty-four: 'Now Jesus Himself began His ministry at about thirty years of age, being (as was supposed) the son of Joseph, the son of Heli, the son of Matthat, the son of Levi,' etc., etc. Are you the Joseph mentioned there?"

"Yes, I am."

"Did I mispronounce any of those names?"

"No, sir, you did not."

"In one of the genealogies you are given the father of Jacob and the grandfather of Matthan. In the other, you are given the father of Heli and the grandfather of Matthat. Doesn't this appear to be a contradiction in Exhibit A, the Bible?"

Luckhoo rose to his feet, his eyes aglow with an expectation of doing battle with his worthy opponent.

"I object, my lord. The witness is not an expert on the Bible, having neither read nor studied it and only having heard what has been elucidated here in this courtroom this morning from it. The learned counsel is projecting his opinion upon something that has not been proven or disproven here in this court, that being the validity of the Bible."

Before the lord chief justice could reply, Darrow quickly spoke out.

"Your Lordship, I will rephrase the question! In one Scripture I just read, you are shown as the grandson of Matthan and the son of Jacob. In the other Scripture, you are shown as the grandson of Matthat and the son of Heli. Which one is correct, Mr. Joseph?"

"They are both correct, sir."

"How can that be?"

"The first mention of ancestors of Jesus is shown from my ancestors, showing my name as the son of Jacob. The other ancestors were given in accordance with the usage of our people and our time. They are those of my wife, Mary. Women's ancestors were directed to the males, the husbands; therefore I am the son of Jacob and the son-in-law of Heli."

Darrow thought to himself: *You should have remem-*

*bered that one, Darrow. Watch out. This one may be uned-
ucated, but he's sharp as a tack!*

From Darrow's courtroom appearance, he had not missed a beat and was unruffled by this response. His next question was already on his lips.

"Are you a carpenter by trade?"

"I am."

"Are you married to a woman by the name of Mary?"

"I am."

"Did you and she have children?"

"Yes, sir."

"I quote again from Exhibit A, Mark 6:3, here speaking about your son, Jesus: '"Is this not the carpenter, the Son of Mary, and brother of James, Joses, Judas, and Simon? And are not His sisters here with us?" So they were offended at Him.' Are those mentioned here in this Scripture, namely, James, Joses, Judas, Simon, and the reference to His sisters . . . are those your children that you and your wife, Mary, had through physical intimacy, therefore naturally producing human babies?"

"Yes, sir."

"Now, Mr. Joseph, are you the father of the accused, Jesus of Nazareth?"

"No, sir, and yes, sir."

"Mr. Joseph, would you please explain your totally contradictory answer to the jury."

"Yes, sir, I will. I am not the natural father of Jesus, but I am the husband of His natural mother. And I raised Jesus from His birth as His father."

"Who then is the natural father of Jesus?"

"Jehovah God, the Creator of heaven and earth, is the supernatural Father of Jesus."

"And *how* did your wife get pregnant with Jesus, Mr. Joseph?"

"I cannot tell you, sir. Jehovah God did not provide me with that information on how He did it. All I know is that He did it!"

Darrow's voice immediately rose to an intense pitch. He had learned to deal with facts. Dealing with religious faith made him very uncomfortable.

"And how did you know that God did it? Tell us the details of it . . . in your words!"

"As was the custom of my people, our marriage was contracted by our families. Mary was thirteen and I was almost eighteen. It was some months after the engagement that I found out she was pregnant . . . when she returned from three months at her cousin Elizabeth's home. And after I had a dream, I believed by faith."

"By faith, huh? Mr. Joseph, as a seventeen-year-old Jewish boy, did you have sexual intercourse with Mary after she became engaged to you?"

"No, sir, I did not."

"When was the first time that you did have sexual intercourse with her, Mr. Joseph?"

Luckhoo jumped to his feet again and looked over at his adversary.

"My lord, the esteemed American counsel is attempting to turn this trial of a very holy event of Christendom into a circus. I object to this line of questioning."

The lord chief justice said, "Sir Luckhoo, while we are examining the very basic tenets of the Christian religion, we are also concerned with the natural side of the birth of the accused, since it plays an important part of this trial. Objection overruled."

He looked back to the witness.

"The witness will answer the question, please."

Luckhoo sat down, accepting the decision as simply a part of trial proceedings.

"The first time I had sexual intercourse with my wife, Mary, was about a month after Jesus was born."

"Thank you. Now how did you feel about the girl you had planned to marry when you found out she was pregnant and it wasn't your unborn child . . . before your dream?"

"I was upset. I was hurt. I felt betrayed. I was angry. I felt as if I had been cheated."

"Did you ask her how she became pregnant?"

"Yes, sir."

"And what was her answer?"

"She told me it was Jehovah God. She said that I would have to trust her and that Jehovah God would provide me with the answer."

"'God would provide' you with the answer, is that what she said?"

"Jehovah God, yes, sir."

"And what did you intend to do in this case?"

"Under our Jewish religious customs, it was a great sin to be pregnant and not married. In fact, it was punishable by stoning. For all intents and purposes, I was her husband, and despite this conflict in our relationship, I dearly loved her. I wanted to believe her with every fiber of my being. I didn't want her stoned to death. The only thing I could think of to do for the honor of my family was to put her away privately until she had the baby, and then we'd have to work something out. This was allowed under Jewish tradition."

Darrow's attitude changed toward his witness with the

mention of Jewish tradition. He began to treat his witness in more of an indifferent manner.

"Go on, Mr. Joseph."

"I was very concerned about this, and I thought about it a lot. One night, I cried out to Jehovah God and asked Him for a solution to this great problem."

"Do you consider yourself a devout religious person, Mr. Joseph?"

"I believe in Jehovah God, and I try to live my faith!"

"Go on."

"I went to sleep that night and I had a dream."

"I suppose you have a lot of dreams, Mr. Joseph."

Luckhoo stood to his feet again, his hand raised in the air like a short sword.

"My lord, I object to counsel's badgering of the witness at every turn. Let the man tell his story."

He sat down with his arms crossed. His brown face had turned reddish.

Darrow always liked to intimidate his opponents. He started questioning again before the lord chief justice could intervene.

"Mr. Joseph, do you often dream? Perhaps that will appease my esteemed opponent."

"No, sir."

"Go on with your dream, sir."

"In my dream I saw an angel of the Lord, and he called me by name. He said, 'Joseph, son of David, do not be afraid to take to you Mary your wife, for that which is conceived in her is of the Holy Spirit. And she will bring forth a Son, and you shall call His name Jesus, for He will save His people from their sins.' And then I woke up from my dream."

"And what did you do then, Mr. Joseph?"

"I remembered the words of the prophet Isaiah: 'Therefore the Lord Himself will give you a sign: Behold, the virgin shall conceive and bear a Son, and shall call His name Immanuel.'"

"You said you named Him Jesus, not Immanuel, is that correct?"

"Yes, sir. Immanuel means 'God with us.'"

"What did you do next, Mr. Joseph?"

"At the proper hour I ran to the home of Mary and told her of my dream. Then I told her that I was happy . . . that I was going to go ahead and marry her. We then made arrangements for the wedding ceremony."

"Did you have friends or acquaintances who knew of the pregnancy of Mary?"

"Yes, sir."

"And how did they know?"

"Through gossip. Both good and bad news traveled fast."

"That hasn't changed much, Mr. Joseph . . . that hasn't changed much."

Darrow seemed to mentally slip away from the courtroom for a few seconds. Then he caught himself and quickly recovered his composure.

"Uh, what did your friends think about you marrying a pregnant teenager, Mr. Joseph?"

"Some of them thought that I had lost my mind or that I was the one responsible. Others thought that I was getting a secondhand woman. It really didn't matter what they thought. I believed that it was Jehovah God who had caused her to get pregnant. I never had stopped loving Mary, and I wanted to marry her."

"That was very gallant of you, Mr. Joseph."

"No, sir, I didn't feel like it was gallant. I just felt like it was Jehovah God's will for my life. That's all, sir."

"Now, what kind of questions did you ask your wife about her pregnancy?"

"I didn't ask her any questions about her pregnancy, only about what the angel looked like and who she thought he was."

Darrow thought to himself: *That sounds like a boy! His girlfriend is pregnant before their marriage, and he wants to know what the angel looked like!*

"Was this purported angel supposed to have a name?"

"My people believe that Jehovah God has a messenger angel in heaven named Gabriel. I believe it was he."

"Do your people believe in other such special angels in heaven, Mr. Joseph?"

"Yes, sir. We believe that Jehovah God has a warring angel named Michael and that He once had a worshiping angel named Lucifer."

"Do you believe these angels still exist?"

"Yes, sir."

"Where do you believe these angels are today?"

"I believe that Michael and Gabriel are still in heaven with God and that Lucifer is on the earth somewhere, now known as Satan, the devil."

"Oh? What happened to this worshiping angel named Lucifer, that you say is now the devil, Satan?"

"The sin of pride was found in Lucifer's heart and he and one-third of all the angel host of heaven, those who followed him, were kicked out of heaven. Lucifer, now with his name changed to Satan, and his demon spirits became the archenemies of Jehovah God."

"Would you say, Mr. Joseph, that you and your people are a very superstitious people?"

Luckhoo moved quickly to his feet, surprising many of the barristers and solicitors behind him because of his age.

"I object, my lord. The counsel is leading the witness with an assumption that he would know whether or not all the Jews were superstitious as well as casting aspersions on the Jewish people."

Like a fencing master avoiding a thrust, Darrow tartly replied but did not look at Luckhoo.

"If it pleases the court, I chose the word *superstitious* specifically from the very definition of one of our English ancestors to the colonies in America, a Mr. Webster. He defines *superstition* in this way: '1. An irrational abject attitude of mind toward the supernatural, nature, or God, proceeding from ignorance, unreasoning fear of the unknown or mysterious, a belief in magic or chance, or the like. 2. Any belief, conception, act, or practice resulting from such a state of mind. 3. Such conceptions, practices, etc., collectively.' Does Your Lordship wish that definition to be entered as evidence for my esteemed colleague's benefit?"

The lord chief justice shook his head at Darrow's question.

"Mr. Webster's dictionary does not need to be in admission as evidence. The objection is overruled. Answer the question to the best of your knowledge, Mr. Joseph."

Luckhoo sat down, closing his eyes again. Joseph's voice continued strong as he spoke.

"My people are a very fearful and superstitious people, and they have been for centuries. They seem to live under a spirit of fear."

"You were living in Nazareth at the time. Is that correct, Mr. Joseph?"

"That is correct, sir."

"Did you complete the wedding ceremony as planned?"

"Yes, sir."

"Then I believe it was the custom of your people that your new wife come and live with you and your family. Is that correct?"

"Yes, sir. That is what she did."

"Your baby was born in Bethlehem, however. Please tell us how that happened."

"We Jews were ruled by Caesar Augustus from Rome. There came a decree from Rome that all subjects must return to the city of their fathers and there be counted and taxed. Since my family was of the house of David, I had to take my family, which was my wife and myself, to the city of Bethlehem. She was in the ninth month of her pregnancy and was great with child. I went to the representatives of Rome in Nazareth to see if I could get a waiver for my wife. They would have nothing to do with it. I had no choice, except to take my very pregnant wife with me to Bethlehem. She couldn't walk there. The only other way for her to get there was on a pallet or on an animal of some sort. I had no one to carry a pallet, so the only alternative was to let her ride the only animal I possessed, a gentle donkey that I had owned since I was a boy."

Darrow interrupted: "How long was the trip?"

"It took five days, as there were no sand or rain storms."

"Proceed with your story, Mr. Joseph."

"I had heard stories from various caravans going through Nazareth that there was an inn where we might stay in Bethlehem. Mary and I started out with a caravan. On the evening of the fifth day, darkness overtook us before we could reach the town. Mary was feeling strong labor pains, and a cold wind was coming up. It felt like rain, so I said we'd better go the last three miles before we stopped. She gritted her teeth and agreed. The closer we got to town, the more discouraged I became. I could see campfires burning all around the town, which meant that everything was probably full, and it was too late for me to think of pitching a tent. I could see the pain in Mary's face from the combination of the long hard ride on the donkey and her labor pains. The only thing I could think about was getting her into a private room and getting a midwife, which was required by our tradition."

"So you came into Bethlehem and found the town full of people. What did you do?"

"I asked directions to an inn from a local merchant. He told me where to go but said I might as well not go because it was probably full. I got there and he was right. People were sleeping all over the place, including on the floor of the main room in the inn. I found the innkeeper and told him about my wife. He said he had even rented his own bedroom! I didn't know what to tell Mary. I was just ready to leave when the wife of the innkeeper came up and whispered to him. Then the innkeeper told me that he did have a stable, really a cave, where he kept his animals. He said that we could stay there. He said at least it would be dry and it had just been cleaned that day. I ran back to Mary and led her and the donkey down the incline behind the inn to a cave."

As the gentle carpenter spoke, his face was wrought with the emotion of remembering the events. Darrow opened his Bible and was searching for a reference.

"Go ahead with your story, Mr. Joseph."

"Mary's face was white, and I didn't know whether it was the dust of the road or the effects of her pain. I lit a lamp and went inside. I found some of the innkeeper's animals and a couple of clean stalls. I went back out and brought Mary in on the donkey and laid her on some blankets in the stall. That night she was delivered of her child. We named Him Jesus."

"That was a fairly common name for a boy, wasn't it?"

"Yes, sir."

"Did anything else happen that night?"

"Yes. Later Mary and the baby went to sleep. I had started a fire in the entrance of the cave to keep us warm, and I woke up just as dawn was breaking to tend the fire. It was then that I saw a group of men moving quietly toward the entrance to the cave."

"What did you do?"

"I picked up my staff and motioned for them to come and warm themselves by my fire."

"And who were these men?"

"They said that they were shepherds."

"What did they want?"

"They said that while they had been guarding their sheep in the field just outside Bethlehem during the night, they had seen an angel standing in the sky. And the angel had spoken to them!"

"An angel, huh? Did the angel speak to all of them?"

"All of them standing in the door said they saw and heard the angel. There were about twelve of them."

"And what did this angel say to them, Mr. Joseph?"

"They were an excited bunch to say the least, and the best I could get out of them was that they were tending their sheep, as was their custom. It was around the time of the end of the second watch, and they were waking up their relief watches when the night became like day with a blue-white light from a star. I remember that they said they were very afraid. The next thing they saw was an angel standing in the sky."

"You're telling me, Mr. Joseph, that these ignorant sheep-herders showed up at the cave where you and your wife and baby were staying, and they told you—"

"I object, my lord. It would be in keeping with the rules of evidence to allow the witness to tell the story without the prosecution making judgments about the intelligence level of the shepherds." Luckhoo nodded abruptly at Darrow and sat down.

The lord chief justice spoke matter-of-factly.

"Strike the word *ignorant* from the record. Mr. Darrow, we ask you not to impose your opinion on the witness. Proceed, Mr. Joseph."

"Yes, sir. They said it was very strange because the shepherds were all awake and excited, but the sheep were chewing their cud and were very peaceful."

"So the only knowledge of seeing this angel was that of the sheepherders, is that right?"

"Yes, sir."

"And what did they tell you that the angel did and said next?"

"They said he spoke and said, 'Do not be afraid, for behold, I bring you good tidings of great joy which will be to all people. For there is born to you this day in the city of David a Savior, who is Christ the Lord. And this will be the sign to you: You will find a Babe wrapped in swaddling cloths, lying in a manger.'"

Darrow stared at Joseph in amazement. He read those exact words in print before him in his Bible. It was as if he were in a daze, as if he had gotten hold of something much bigger than even he could imagine. Almost a minute of silence elapsed. Every eye in the courtroom was on a time-frozen Darrow.

Houston yanked on her associate's court gown: "Where are you, Darrow? . . . Where are you?"

Darrow blinked, took a deep breath, and continued, almost methodically, on the prosecution's case.

"Mr. Joseph, do you know that you just quoted, word for word, what is written here in the book of Luke in this Bible?"

Joseph's voice was slightly wavering.

"Sir, I have not so much as heard whether there be a book of Luke or a Bible, except what I heard here today in this room."

Darrow's hand shook on the page, but he maintained his tone of authority in questioning the witness.

"You appear to have an excellent memory, Mr. Joseph. Are you quoting these things word for word as you remember them, or are you just generalizing what was said?"

"Sir, everything I have ever learned had to come by memory, including what I know of the Law and the Prophets. As a young lad I learned to grasp on to every bit of knowledge that I could. I would rehearse it over and over in my mind as I worked in my shop. I am speaking what the men said to me word for word years ago. I have noticed, sir, that you have done the same from your memory, earlier in this trial."

Darrow turned in his Bible to the book of Luke, the second chapter. He ran his finger down the verses and stopped at the thirteenth verse.

"And what kind of event happened next, according to these simple sheepherders, Mr. Joseph?"

Joseph's tone of voice was the same as when he started his testimony.

"They said that there were music and singing all around them like they had never heard before, even in the great temple in Jerusalem. They said a host of voices were praising God and saying, 'Glory to God in the highest, and on earth peace, goodwill toward men!' They said they just stared at the sky, and little by little it returned to what was normal except the bright star was still in the sky. According to the shepherds, it looked brighter and bigger than all the rest."

Joseph gestured, making a large circle with his calloused hands.

"They then said they went to their campfire, and all of them sat around it, talking about what they had just seen and heard. They said they kept asking themselves and each other, Did this really happen, or was it a dream? And all of them, including the young boys, said it was not a dream, and it really happened to them."

Joseph closed his eyes in an attempt to remember the exact words that were spoken on that special night.

"Finally they said, 'Let us now go to Bethlehem and see this thing that has come to pass, which the Lord has made known to us.' The head shepherd told his men that they would cast lots to see who would stay with the sheep and who would go into Bethlehem. He told me that by this time dawn was beginning to break in the east."

"How far from Bethlehem were these sheepherders? Did they tell you, Mr. Joseph?"

"They were about an hour's journey away."

"How did they find you, Mr. Joseph?"

"They told me that they had asked people in Bethlehem about a newborn baby or a pregnant woman, and they were told to come to the inn."

"Mr. Joseph, did anyone mention a bright light or the singing to the shepherds that you know of?"

"No, sir. They said that they asked, though."

"Now let's get this straight, Mr. Joseph. The people in Bethlehem . . . you say that the sheepherders asked them if they had seen this bright light or the angels or had heard the voices or the singing, and none of them had this unique experience. Is that correct, Mr. Joseph?"

"Yes, sir. The ones they asked had not seen anything."

"Did you or your wife hear any singing or angels or voices or see any great light, Mr. Joseph?"

"No, sir."

"By your standard of education, did these shepherds appear to be uneducated, Mr. Joseph?"

"I make a general statement here, sir, for it is not for me to judge. Jewish boys learn much of the ancient truths orally from their mothers and fathers. Each boy is expected to be able to recite the ancient wisdom in the Hebrew language. At the age of five, those who are fortunate enough, as I was, attend daily teachings at the synagogue with much more advanced teachings. Most of the shepherds were very poor and probably not able to attend synagogue teachings from the rabbis or attend the rabbinical schools."

"So from what you are saying, Mr. Joseph, in your opinion, these men were, for the most part, uneducated men. Is that correct?"

Darrow's face was expressionless. He was like a miner patiently digging for gold. He kept at it, looking for one nugget of a word here or there before he would stake his claim for a complete prosecution.

"Compared with others, they had the least, sir."

"Thank you. Proceed with your story, Mr. Joseph."

"I offered the shepherds some food. They sat by the fire and ate some bread and cheese, and then they told me their story, which I just told you. Then I excused myself and went back into the cave and told Mary what they had said. She said that she felt comfortable enough to invite them in, so I did. They came in and stood around just looking at the baby Jesus. He was lying quietly asleep in the manger we were using for His bed."

"Is that all they did . . . look at your child?"

"No, sir. I stood by my wife and by the baby and watched the faces of the men. Every one of them had a look of wonderment on his face. And every one had tears that flowed quietly, like streams of hope, and their tears fell on the stable floor onto the straw." Joseph paused and cleared his throat, wiping tears from his eyes with his sleeve.

"Was there anything unusual that happened?"

"Well, yes. When the baby woke up, opened His eyes, and started to cry, every one of them dropped to his knees and began to quietly praise Jehovah God. After a period of time, the head shepherd stood up. Then the bunch of men stood up and walked out, each saying only one more word . . . 'Shalom!'"

"Did you ever see these men again, Mr. Joseph?"

"No, sir, I never did."

"And what did you and your family do next?"

"I took care of Mary and the baby as best I could. I bought food and did the daily tasks necessary. When Mary felt stronger, we went to the location where the Roman authorities were registering the people. She and I registered ourselves and the baby, then located the synagogue."

"Did you have any other visitors while you were in Bethlehem?"

"Yes, just about two years later."

"You weren't still living in that cave at that time, were you?"

"Oh, no, sir. The innkeeper found that I was a carpenter, and he had already hired me to build a large addition onto his inn. He offered us the use of a small home that he owned on the outskirts of Bethlehem as part of my wages. Mary and I thought that it was wise to stay there until she and the baby were stronger, so we took him up on his offer and moved our meager belongings into that house. He had sufficient tools for me to do the work and paid me well to support my family during that time."

"Now what about the visitors?"

"They first appeared at the inn, and I saw them as I was working. There were three of them. They appeared to be rich foreign Gentiles. They quietly inquired about a newborn king, and they specifically said, 'Where is He who has been born King of the Jews? For we have seen His star in the East and have come to worship Him.' The innkeeper said he didn't know anything about any 'King of the Jews' being born, but he did have an unusual event happen back during the Roman census. He told them about the first human baby that was ever born in his stable, and then he pointed to me. They came over to me, bowed down to me, and introduced themselves as astrologers, scientists, and philosophers from Persia."

"Could you speak their language?"

"No, sir, but they spoke perfect Hebrew, and we conversed in the Hebrew language."

"What happened next, Mr. Joseph?"

"They asked if they could see the baby. I said that I would be happy to take them to the baby and that I would come for them after I completed my work that evening."

"And then what did you do?"

"I thought about it all afternoon until I hit my thumb with my hammer about three times. I decided I had better keep my mind on my work. I left my work at the usual hour and ran to the house. I told Mary about it, and I helped her prepare a simple meal for the expected guests." Joseph smiled as he was remembering the event. He closed his eyes and then laughed.

"I even ran to the brook and took a bath before I went back to the inn to get them. I was shocked when I saw them."

"What do you mean, you were 'shocked' when you saw them?"

"When they arrived in Bethlehem and during the time they were there, they dressed as well-to-do people would dress. But when I went to bring them back to my home, they were dressed like three kings! They had rings and bracelets on. They wore fine shoes and turbans. The men were regal looking! They had several big servants with them, strong men with swords." Joseph was now comfortable in the witness box, and he began to loosen up. He flexed his muscles in both arms as he described the guards of the Gentiles.

"They followed me outside the inn and mounted their camels, and I led them to our house and I invited them all in, including their guards and servants. But one of the Magi spoke to their servants in their own language, and only the Magi followed me into our little house. The rest stayed outside with the camels."

"And what did they do when they saw your baby, Mr. Joseph?"

"'And when they had come into the house, they saw the young Child with Mary His mother, and fell down and worshiped Him.'"

Darrow turned the pages in the Bible lying open before him. He ran his finger down a page and stopped on verse 11. He was in somewhat of a daze as he looked up at this simple carpenter.

The American attorney stared at this Jewish carpenter and tried to comprehend whether it was circumstances or part of a historical plot concerning what he was hearing and seeing repeated word for word in his own Bible.

The frightening thought passed through his mind: *Perhaps it is true after all. Perhaps after all the years of resistance, all the years of denial, all the years of debating the Bible . . . perhaps it is true after all!*

The thought sent a chill up and down his spine. Darrow had always been a seeker of truth, and this turn of events deeply bothered him. He regained his presence and continued his questioning.

"What did they say and do when they, uh, worshiped your child, Mr. Joseph?"

Joseph shrugged his shoulders. "I did not know what they said because they were speaking in their own language. But I saw them fall to their knees before the baby and bow their faces to the ground. They had tears coming down their faces. They did this for more than just a few moments."

"And what did your wife, Mary, do?"

"She was holding the baby so that the Magi could see His face."

"Did they do anything else, Mr. Joseph?"

"They looked very perplexed. They studied the baby's face as if they were trying to memorize what it looked like. They sat quietly for a long period of time, and finally one of them said something in their language. Immediately one of their servants came in with a large basket."

"And what was in the basket?"

"They brought out a box that looked as if it were solid gold. They opened it up and took out several items and laid them at the feet of the babe."

"By chance were these items of gold, frankincense, and myrrh, Mr. Joseph?"

"Why . . . yes, sir, they were."

"What did you think they were for, Mr. Joseph?"

"I had no idea. I had heard stories, from my childhood, about such gifts. I had been told that gifts like this were considered a tribute to sovereign rulers and kings. But I had never seen such wealth, even at the temple in Jerusalem. They gave the gifts to the baby."

"Did Mary or the baby do anything special when these gifts were given, Mr. Joseph?"

"Yes, sir. Mary smiled and expressed our thanks because I was totally speechless."

"And what did the men do then?"

"They rose, bowed to the child and bowed to us, and then left."

"Was it the custom of your people to bow upon greeting one another?"

"Yes, sir."

"Did you ever see these men again, Mr. Joseph?"

"No, sir."

"Did you ever leave Bethlehem prior to this visit, Mr. Joseph?"

"On the morning of the forty-first day we left Bethlehem for Jerusalem for the rites of presentation of the firstborn at the temple and the rite of purification of the mother."

"And how far was Jerusalem?"

"It was five miles to the north."

"What did you do in Jerusalem, Mr. Joseph?"

"I took Mary and the babe to the Gate of Women. I gave her some coins, and she went to the temple area where the women who had recently given birth to infants were coming for purification. I took the babe and bought two turtledoves for a sacrifice and waited for Mary to return. She joined us, and we went to the sacrificial section of the temple."

"Was there anything unusual about that trip?"

Joseph put his finger to his forehead, in thought.

"We were ready to give the babe to the priest when an older man, whom I had seen in the temple even when I was a lad, came up and asked if he might see our child. He had prayed for every child brought to the temple for years. We handed Him to the man and opened up the baby's blanket, and the man uttered a cry."

"What do you mean, he 'uttered a cry'? What kind of a cry, Mr. Joseph?"

"It was as if he were shocked at what he saw but he wasn't scared at what he saw."

"You mean when he saw the face of your baby? Who was the man? What did he say and do?"

"Yes, sir. Simeon was his name. He 'took Him up in his arms and blessed God and said: "Lord, now You are letting Your servant depart in peace, according to Your word; for my eyes have seen Your salvation which You have prepared before the face of all peoples, a light to bring revelation to the Gentiles, and the glory of Your people Israel."' He then blessed all of us in Hebrew, and then he turned to Mary and said, 'Behold, this Child is destined for the fall and rising of many in Israel, and for a sign which will be spoken against (yes, a sword will pierce through your own soul also), that the thoughts of many hearts may be revealed.'"

"This Simeon character prayed for every child who was brought into the temple, is that right, Mr. Joseph?"

"Every newborn child, I believe so, sir."

"Was this Simeon character considered in any way a nuisance or a pest at the temple by the priests?"

Luckhoo jumped to his feet.

"I object to counsel soliciting an opinion on the part of the witness as to what the priesthood at the temple thought of the man called Simeon. The witness is not a priest and therefore could not officially speak for the priests, my lord."

He sat down abruptly. The lord chief justice quietly spoke, "Sustained. You do not need to answer the question, Mr. Joseph."

Darrow countered immediately with an angry tone at the interruption.

"Mr. Joseph, you said that you had seen this man in the temple even when you were a young boy, praying for the babies brought in for the Jewish religious presentation of the firstborn, is that right?"

"Yes, sir."

"Have you ever heard gossip or comments, made by the common people who came to the temple, concerning this man Simeon and his preoccupation with seeing firstborn babies?"

"I heard some things. Yes, sir."

"Tell the jury what you remember people said about him."

"Well, sir, over the years, I overheard several priests say that he was a bother and they wanted him removed from the temple, but no one ever did. One of my relatives said that he thought he was just a nice older man who loved God and blessed the little children being brought for presentation."

"Thank you, Mr. Joseph. Now what happened next?"

"There was a woman, probably over a hundred years old, who had been a widow for around eighty-four years. Her name was Anna, the daughter of Phanuel of the tribe of Asher, and she was considered a prophetess. When she heard Simeon's cry, she came over to where we were and looked at the babe. The moment she saw Him, she gave great praise to the Lord. As she walked away from us, we could hear her telling people to repent, and that the redemption of Israel was present."

"This is another person well up in years, is that right?"

"Yes, sir."

"And this older person named Anna hears Simeon cry out, and she comes over and makes a commotion over the baby like Simeon did and disrupts the presentation ceremony, is that right?"

"She didn't disrupt any ceremony."

"Now, Mr. Joseph, had you ever heard anyone make any statement about this Anna similar to what you have told us about Simeon? Perhaps a priest or a temple official?"

"Yes, sir, I have."

"So now we have two . . . older people . . . and so named by the testimony of you, Mr. Joseph, of what you heard temple officials say . . . and these two religious people caused a commotion in a religious temple over your baby boy. Is that correct?"

"To a certain extent, yes, sir."

"Did you finish the presentation of the firstborn male child, Mr. Joseph?"

"Yes, sir."

"Then what did you do?"

"We went back to Bethlehem because I had not yet finished the work I had agreed to do. When that was finished, we planned to return to Nazareth."

"But you did not return to Nazareth, Mr. Joseph. Why not?"

"That night I had a dream. I saw the same angel in my dream that night that I saw in my previous dream."

"So you had another dream, Mr. Joseph, right?"

"Yes, sir."

"And you acted on that dream, is that correct?"

"Yes, sir."

"And what did the angel tell you this time?"

"I shall never forget, sir. He said, 'Arise, take the young Child and His mother, flee to Egypt, and stay there until I bring you word; for Herod will seek the young Child to destroy Him.' That was exactly what he said, as I remember it."

Darrow knit his bushy eyebrows together, took a deep breath, and pursued the witness.

"Did your wife have the same dream?"

"No, sir."

"Did you tell your wife about this dream?"

"Yes, sir."

"Did she agree with you that you should take your family to Egypt?"

"Yes, sir."

"How old were you both at this time?"

"I was almost twenty, and my wife had just turned sixteen."

Darrow shook his head, smiling a bit. He was having some difficulty comprehending all he was hearing, yet he seemed to feel a deep respect for his witness.

"Your wife is just sixteen, you are nineteen, and you have a dream that you need to escape from your home country and go to the foreign country of Egypt. Now this is a very, very long way for you to travel with your little wife and your infant on your little old donkey, isn't that correct?"

"Yes, sir."

"And, Mr. Joseph," Darrow said confidently, "would you say that this kind of behavior defies all bounds of common sense of your time and people?"

"Yes, sir."

"Going back to the Magi who visited you . . . did any one of them mention that they had stopped in Jerusalem and had talked with King Herod the Great about looking for a newborn king?"

"Yes, sir, they did."

"And did they tell you what King Herod asked them to do?"

"Yes, sir."

"And what was that?"

"They were asked to bring back to him the news of the newborn king. They said that he told them that he wanted to go and worship the newborn king."

"And what was your opinion of Herod the Great?"

"He was a ruthless, sick old man who was greatly feared by the Jews and even some of the Romans. He ordered the drowning of the Jewish high priest Aristobulus, a brother of his wife, Mariamne. He had his own wife, Mariamne, and two of his sons executed. He was a liar and a murderer!"

"Would the word *butcher* be a word that the common people might have appropriately applied to Herod?"

"Yes, sir."

"Did in fact, after you had gone to Egypt, Herod the Great in a great wrath have all the baby boys in Bethlehem, who were two years old and under, killed by the sword? And did he also order the murder of infants throughout that area of Palestine?"

"Yes, sir, he did." Joseph's countenance, for the first time, changed expression. A cloud of anger covered his face and the blood vessels stood out at his temples.

Darrow studied the carpenter's face. He could see the rich heritage of an honest, hardworking human being written in the deep-set lines across Joseph's face. Joseph was a man who hated injustice.

Darrow began to feel somewhat guilty in having to question Joseph as a witness hostile to his case. He felt a lump in his throat until Houston yanked hard on his court gown. "Where are you, Darrow, asleep?"

"Uh . . . Mr. Joseph, did the thought occur to you, after hearing what the Magi said and prior to the dream, that perhaps your baby might not be safe in your homeland as far as this wicked Herod was concerned?"

"That thought did cross my mind, sir."

"So you took your wife and your baby, and you started off to Egypt. Is that correct? Tell us, in your own words,

Mr. Joseph, as a nineteen-year-old husband and father, what were your thoughts about Egypt?"

"My ancestors lived for years in Goshen, in Egypt. Our people were called out of Egypt by Jehovah God to come and claim the Promised Land, the land of Israel. The word, told among my people, was that the Roman Mark Antony, an ally of Herod, had ruled Syria and the East, including Egypt. We had been told that Antony took his own life in Egypt and that the Egyptians had never expressed any love for Herod. I felt it would be a safe place for us. But it didn't make any difference what I thought! I believed that Jehovah God was sending us to Egypt!"

"Wasn't it commonly known by your people that the Egyptians were great practitioners of magic and that they worshiped many gods?"

"Yes, sir."

"And this was the land that your angel told you to flee into for the safety of your family. Is that correct, Mr. Joseph?"

"Yes, sir."

"Tell us what you did after this unusual dream."

"I told my wife about the dream and she agreed that if I saw the same angel I had seen in an earlier dream, she, too, thought it was from Jehovah God. I gathered what gifts had been given to the babe and took a tithe to the synagogue. I inquired about caravans going in and out of the city, and I found that one would be leaving for Alexandria that afternoon. I bartered with the caravan master, and he agreed that we could go in the safety of the caravan. I told him that we would join the caravan one day's journey out of Bethlehem. I finished my work at the inn and we left that night."

"What did you do in Egypt?"

"We found a group of Hebrews living there. Within a

short time, I found work. Most people there spoke the Aramaic language, which I also speak. By using some of the gifts as barter, we were able to sustain ourselves."

"And how long did you stay in Egypt?"

"Just about a year."

"And there, I suppose, Mr. Joseph," Darrow said with scorn, "you had another dream, is that right?"

"Yes, sir. It was just before Passover. The same angel appeared to me in a dream and said that Herod was dead and we could return to our homeland. We made plans and found a caravan that was going into Israel. We left with them just before dawn."

"So you went back to Bethlehem?"

"No, sir. We were just south of Bethlehem, in Hebron, when we met some Jewish merchants who were coming from Jerusalem. They told us that Herod had died just before the Feast of the Passover. They said that his evil son Archelaus was now the king. I felt that it would be wise for us to avoid Bethlehem and Jerusalem since we had a boy child the age of Jesus. Archelaus's father had murdered many children who were the same age as Jesus. Mary agreed so we took an eastern route around Bethlehem, then on to Jericho, through Bethany. We then went north to Nazareth."

"You did end up back in the hometown of both you and your wife . . . that being Nazareth?"

"Yes, sir, we did."

Darrow paused and looked directly at Joseph. A thin smile broke across his face, almost a smirk. He put both hands inside his court gown and brought out his bright red suspenders. His tone was mildly mocking as he continued his questioning of this hostile witness.

"Let me see if I've got your story correct now, Mr. Joseph.

At the age of seventeen, you are engaged to this thirteen-year-old girl . . . and you find out she is pregnant. Your Jewish tradition says that an unmarried pregnant woman is to be punished by being stoned to death, but you gallantly agree to marry her after you have a dream. Now your friends think you are touched in the head, but you and she believe that Mary is pregnant with no less than the Son of your God." He took a breath and paused.

Joseph stared at Darrow.

"Now more changes come into your life and hers. You marry her, and your little world turns upside down because you have to take your pregnant wife to the city of Bethlehem to be registered with the hated Roman government. So off you go on your faithful little donkey. You and your nine-month-pregnant wife arrive in Bethlehem, along with a few thousand other people. And when you get there, as the old saying goes, 'There is no room at the inn.'"

Darrow let his suspenders snap back inside his court gown. He leaned over his desk and placed both hands flat on the table and looked directly at Joseph. His voice was strong and accusing.

"Since there is no room at the inn, you and the missus end up staying in the stable at the inn. That night your little baby Jesus is born. A group of uneducated sheepherders come to the stable and tell you they have heard angels singing in the sky. No one else heard or saw them singing! A short time later you move out of the stable into a house and the three kings of Orient show up to worship your baby and give you some very expensive gifts. Am I right so far, Mr. Joseph?"

Joseph looked at Darrow pointedly. He made no move to acknowledge the prosecutor's tacit scorn.

Darrow continued without Joseph's affirmation.

"Then you have another dream and you leave town with your wife and baby boy and head to the land of magic and illusion . . . the land of Egypt. You all are in Egypt for about a year, and you have still another dream. This one tells you that dirty Herod is dead, and it's safe to go back home. So with a detour here and there, you end up back in Nazareth with a child you claim is the one and only Son of God." Darrow stood up straight and pulled out his suspenders again. He stood quietly and then took one hand and rubbed his chin.

"Mr. Joseph, if you'll pardon the pun, that's one Jonah's whale of a story! Now we come to the everyday part of your tale. You raise this Son of God right there in your own carpenter shop just like He is your own boy and—"

Luckhoo stood and slammed his fist on the desk.

"My lord, the American counsel has vividly demonstrated that he has a track record of courtroom theatrics. I trust that this court will not encourage the same level of debasing decadence in the examination of these witnesses." His eyes flashed with anger.

The lord chief justice spoke with sternness. "The prosecution will not demean the witness."

Darrow changed his tone to a very serious one. He looked at Luckhoo and then back to the witness.

"Mr. Joseph, my track record will verify that I have been a champion of working people all my life, so when I ask you this question, I'm not derogatory . . . but as honest as I can be. My question is this: How did you, a simple, and by your own terms, uneducated carpenter, ever see yourself as the earthly father raising the divine Son of God in a humble carpenter's shop?"

Joseph's countenance changed once again. His chin jutted out like granite. He stood erect in the witness box and clenched his fist, holding it in his other hand. His eyes blazed with determination. His words echoed out of every corner of the courtroom. Every eye in that courtroom was upon him.

"Mr. Darrow, I do not understand some of the words that you just spoke and retold my story, but I do understand the meaning behind your words. While I am uneducated by your standards and even those of my day, I, Mr. Darrow, am not an ignorant man! From my childhood I was taught that there is a God. I have been taught that Jehovah is a great and awesome God! In my life I have seen the works of His hand, and I have seen Him make the foolish wise and the wise foolish. I don't know why I was picked to be the earthly father of the divine child Jesus, nor can I tell you why His mother, Mary, was picked from thousands of Jewish virgin girls."

Joseph paused a moment to catch his breath.

"I can only tell you that given that responsibility, I took what I had, and I raised that male child as my own flesh and blood. I believed that any knowledge of the divinity of Jesus must come from His divine Father and not from an earthly human father. Therefore, sir, I taught the boy the same skills that I had been taught. I taught Him from the Word of God as I had been taught. I taught Him reverence for Jehovah God as I had been taught. I taught Him the same basic values that I taught to each of my children who came from my own loins." Joseph slammed his fist on the edge of the witness box, and the sound resonated throughout the courtroom. People suddenly blinked their eyes. Others sat up straight as if they were being scolded by a parent.

"Most of all, Mr. Darrow, I taught all the children that Jehovah God gave unto my care . . . including Jesus . . . that integrity and honesty were virtues honored by God. Mr. Darrow, I have told you the truth about all you have asked me and I will continue to do so, sir!"

Joseph looked over to his right to the prisoner's dock into the shining eyes of Jesus. A gentle smile broke across His face as He looked at the man who had raised Him as his own.

Once again the famous Clarence S. Darrow seemed to be caught off guard by the comments of his witness. The words seemed so profound coming from this apparently uneducated man. Darrow's mind was racing, not only trying to comprehend what was being said, to remember the Scriptures that Joseph had quoted, but also to present his next question in order of the prosecution. His next words were somewhat sharp.

"Thank you for that testimony of your integrity, Mr. Joseph. Now let's go back for just a moment and determine some very important facts. When Jesus was born, was He born naturally, as you had knowledge of other children being born?"

"Yes, sir. He was born naturally."

"There was nothing extraordinary about the physical birth of Jesus as, say, opposed to how your later children were physically birthed?"

"That is correct, except we had no midwife as we did for our other children."

"And you have told us that you raised Him as you did your other children. And was that similar to the way other Jewish children were raised?"

"Yes, sir."

"What kind of schooling did Jesus receive?"

"At the age of six, Jesus attended the school in the synagogue."

"And what was He taught?"

"He was taught the scrolls of the Law and the history of the Jewish peoples. At the age of ten, He studied the Mishna, or traditional law, and He continued until He was fifteen."

"Was He taught about the Jewish Messiah in those schools, Mr. Joseph?"

"Yes, sir."

"Would that have been taught in both schools to one degree or another?"

"Yes, sir."

"Under the parental care of you and Mary, did either or both of you tell Jesus about the Messiah, and perhaps the meaning of the coming of the Messiah?"

"Yes, sir."

"Now during the time from your return to Nazareth until the time when Jesus was twelve years old, did He evidence any events or unusual signs to show that He might be the Son of God?"

Luckhoo stood quickly to his feet.

"I object, my lord. Counsel has not stated what form of evidence he is referring to that would lead to such a conclusion. He cannot ask the witness to make such a conclusion without laying the foundation."

The lord chief justice looked at Luckhoo.

"I cannot agree with you, Counselor. The prosecution asked the witness merely to conclude whether or not in his view he saw any signs to lead him to a conclusion that Jesus was the Son of God at that stage growing up as a young Jewish boy. Your objection is overruled. Proceed."

Darrow smiled sarcastically.

"Did you ever feel like you were raising a special child, Mr. Joseph?"

"Yes, sir," Joseph paused, "I knew He was not just an ordinary child, like His brothers and sisters. When He was twelve, we and our families went to Jerusalem to the Feast of the Passover. We were returning to Nazareth when we noticed He was not with the other children, as was His custom. We returned to Jerusalem and looked for Him for three days. On the third day we found Him 'in the temple, sitting in the midst of the teachers, both listening to them and asking them questions. And all who heard Him were astonished at His understanding and answers.' Times like that led me to believe He was special. Then there were other times He was just an ordinary boy."

"Did Jesus ever say to you, as His earthly father, that He was the Son of God?"

"I cannot recall that He ever did, but with the dreams and with the visitation from the angel that Mary had and—"

"No, I'm not asking for those details, Mr. Joseph." Darrow paused, looked at Jesus sitting in the dock, and then turned his attention back to Joseph.

"Mr. Joseph, other than the one example of Jesus' religious knowledge shared with the religious scholars, did you ever see Jesus do any miracles in your lifetime?"

"No, sir, I did not."

"Did Jesus ever express His feelings about the sickness and poverty in His world?"

"Yes. He seemed to be very concerned about those things."

"Did you ever see Him lay hands on anyone in your lifetime?"

"No, sir."

"Mr. Joseph, would it be an honor to be the promised Messiah of Israel?"

"Oh, yes, sir."

"Would it be considered a great honor?"

"Yes, sir, very much."

"Was the Messiah to be a deliverer of His people?"

"Yes, sir, not just *a* deliverer but *the* Deliverer."

"Could that Deliverer mean freedom for the nation of Israel from the oppression of the hated Romans?"

"That was a common hope among the people, sir."

"Is it your considered opinion, Mr. Joseph, as a business-man in your country, that the Jewish religious leaders were looking for a spiritual deliverer Messiah or a warring deliverer Messiah?"

"Objection, my lord! The witness has not been presented to this court as an authority on the opinions of the Jewish religious leaders in his country, and he is unqualified to answer that question," Luckhoo said as he rose to his feet and sat down abruptly.

The lord chief justice nodded his head to the defense counsel's objection.

"Sustained."

"Mr. Joseph, I want to go back to your genealogy, to your ancestors. Are you aware that there are four women listed in your genealogy, the one listed in the book of Matthew of Exhibit A?"

"I am aware that there are four women listed in my family genealogy. I am not aware of the book you mentioned, as I told you before."

"Two of the women in your genealogy were not Jewish born. Do you know their names?"

"Yes, sir. They were Rahab a Canaanitess and Ruth a Moabitess."

"That is correct. Now three out of the four women were known, under your Jewish religious code, as adulteresses or harlots. Is that correct?"

Luckhoo's face was a livid red. He turned toward Darrow, and his voice rose nearly to the level of a shout.

"My lord! I would ask the lord chief justice what on earth this line of questioning about the women in the genealogy of the witness has to do with the guilt or innocence of my client?"

Darrow was quick to answer: "Your Lordship, if it please the court, the witness has indicated that both he and his wife, Mary, were especially picked by God for an assignment to raise this alleged Son of God. It is the intent of the prosecution to show that these two individuals were no more special than most of their contemporaries, but in fact, they, too, had a skeleton or two in their closets, so to speak. Those skeletons were their ancestors who were adulteresses or harlots, which was a very serious religious offense in their day."

The lord chief justice looked at the exasperated defense counsel.

"Sir Luckhoo, I must concur with the prosecution. Overruled. Please answer the question, Mr. Joseph."

"Would you repeat the question, sir?"

"Were three out of the four women listed in your genealogy known as adulteresses or harlots?"

"Yes, sir, they were."

"Mr. Joseph, did you raise Jesus with the same amount of care, affection, love, and discipline as you did with your other children?"

"I surely tried to do that, sir."

"Did your wife, Mary, appear to do the same?"

Luckhoo raised his hand at the same time as he jumped to his feet.

"Objection, my lord. The witness obviously cannot answer for his wife, and her testimony has not as yet been entered into evidence." Luckhoo sat down.

Darrow rose to the challenge. He turned to the lord chief justice with a look of disgust on his face.

"Your Lordship, I am not considering this witness as an expert witness in psychology or in child rearing. However, I believe that I am within the rights of rules of evidence to ask this husband's perspective of his wife's affection and care of their child, and his observations of such."

The lord chief justice calmly stated, "Sustained."

"Mr. Joseph, was your wife as objective and fair as you appear to have been in raising Jesus and the other children?"

"Well, no, sir. She tended to favor Jesus more than the other children, but that is natural because He was her first child and—"

"Just answer my question about being objective and fair, yes or no."

"No, sir."

"Did you two have any conflicts over raising Jesus?"

"No, sir."

"Did you ever hear your wife telling Jesus that He was the Son of God, the Messiah, or a divine child, or making any other reference that His conception and early childhood were supernatural?"

"Yes, sir, she told Him the facts as she knew them."

"Did you tell Him some of these kinds of things, also?"

"Yes, sir. I told Him about the shepherds and the Magi and about Herod killing the babies while looking for Him."

"So basically, both you and your wife told the stories to Jesus that there was something very special about the events of His birth and His life as an infant. Isn't that correct?"

"Yes, sir, we did because He was!"

"Did you teach Jesus about the Jewish beliefs concerning the Messiah?"

"Yes, sir, I told you I taught Him as much as I knew."

"And did anyone else ever teach Him about the Jewish Messiah?"

"Yes, sir. I told you that our rabbis of the synagogue taught Him our traditions in the schools."

"Did Jesus attend any schools of higher education other than the synagogue school?"

"No, sir, He did not."

"Mr. Joseph, in your lifetime, were you ever interviewed about Jesus by any person who claimed to be a historian, a court official, a writer, a scribe, or any other such title?"

"No, sir."

"Do you have any knowledge that your wife was interviewed about Jesus by such a person or persons?"

"No, sir."

"Thank you, Mr. Joseph. Now when was the last time you remember being with Jesus?"

"I remember that we had just celebrated His twenty-eighth birthday. I became ill suddenly, and the next thing I remember is that I passed to the realm of the dead."

Darrow felt a cold chill run up and down his spine. His hands suddenly felt clammy, and there was a hard knot in the pit of his stomach. He muttered to himself, "It's a dream. It's a dream . . . wake up!"

He blinked his eyes and felt Joseph looking at him with anticipation.

"Your Lordship, I have no further questions of this witness in examination in chief."

Darrow took out his red bandana handkerchief. He wiped his forehead and sat down. Houston took his hand and squeezed it.

"You're still a good old warhorse, Clarence Darrow! Take a break."

It was twelve o'clock. The Westminster tower bell began its deep chime in the distance, and the bell at St. Sepulchre sounded almost simultaneously. It had been a laborious morning for all in the courtroom, and yet not one person in the courtroom moved from a seat.

They all turned and looked at the lord chief justice.

"The court will recess for lunch and return to session at one o'clock this afternoon. The cross-examination of the witness will begin at that time."

The court bailiff stood, rapping the court scepter on the floor three times. "Be upstanding in the court."

Everyone rose, and the lord chief justice exited through the door on the left of his bench. The bailiff recited his statements, and people began leaving the courtroom.

Jesus turned and went down the stairs to the floor below. Court officials led the jurors to their lunchroom and the witnesses to their lunchroom. The barristers and solicitors went out the doors closest to them in an attempt to get to a restaurant and find something to eat.

Darrow and Houston walked toward the barristers' law library, talking quietly.

Luckhoo turned to DiPietro, "Diane, you go and get something to eat. I'm going to stay here and pray. I need God's wisdom, and He says He will give it to all who ask."

She left, as directed. The courtroom was silent. Luckhoo

could feel the presence of his spiritual enemy in the huge room, but he also knew that there were unseen angels somewhere behind him. He took off his court wig, laid it on the bench in front of him, and quietly began to pray.

5
WITNESSES FOR THE PROSECUTION

AFTERNOON, DAY ONE

Everyone was in place at one o'clock. The jury sat watching the door where the lord chief justice would emerge shortly. People were talking quietly around the courtroom. The bailiff stood watching the justice's door.

The church and tower bells chimed one time. The door opened, and the lord chief justice entered the courtroom. The bailiff recited the traditional words of the court, and everyone sat down.

"Sir Luckhoo, as counsel for the defense, do you wish to cross-examine this witness at this time?" asked the lord chief justice. He looked at Luckhoo, who was already standing behind the bench.

Sir Lionel Alfred Luckhoo again found himself in the position of counsel for the defense. He had defended many persons accused of murder and had obtained acquittals for them. This client was charged with a less serious crime of capital fraud, but the implications in this trial were far greater than all of his previous trials. Luckhoo was participating in the most important trial of his life. He was defending a personage who was loved and hated by people, perhaps more than any other, and he himself was a follower of Jesus!

Despite his advanced age, Luckhoo's voice was strong as he spoke the first words toward his overall defense of the accused, Jesus of Nazareth.

"Yes, my lord."

Luckhoo paused, looked at Joseph, and proceeded.

"Mr. Joseph, there has been a great deal of effort on the part of the esteemed prosecution to demean your heritage and to portray you as a liar! Have you lied in this trial, Mr. Joseph?"

"No, sir, I have not. Jehovah God is my witness!"

"That means that you were not intimate with your betrothed before the accused, Jesus of Nazareth, was born, as you have stated. Is that true?"

"Yes, sir, that is true."

"You did have intercourse with your wife, Mary, after the birth of Jesus, and you did have male children by the names of James, Joses, Judas, and Simon, as well as female children by this union, is that true?"

"Yes, sir, that is true."

"Your explanation of your dreams to the jury . . . was it the truth?"

"Yes, sir. I told you all that I tell the truth."

"Thank you, Mr. Joseph, I believe you. But I want the jury to know that you are telling the truth. Now all the events that you describe in Bethlehem, in Jerusalem, in Egypt, and in Nazareth . . . they are all absolutely correct as you stated them to the jury. Is that also true?"

The color of Joseph's countenance changed from an olive to a deep red. There was frustration in his voice.

"Sir, do you and these people not believe what I say? I tell the truth! I told you all when I came into this box that I would tell the truth! I told the truth and now again I tell you I told the truth! What more do you want me to say about the truth?"

"Again, Mr. Joseph, I believe that you have told the truth. I want to reassure the jury that you are a truthful man . . . a man of integrity. Now I want to ask you some questions that the prosecution did not ask, Mr. Joseph. You knew your wife and lived with her for over twenty-eight years. During that time, did you ever find that your wife had lied to you about anything, including the supernatural conception of Jesus?"

"No, sir, I have no knowledge of any kind that my wife ever lied to me."

"During the time that Jesus was growing up, did He ever tell you that He believed that He was the Son of God or make a statement to that effect?"

"Only on one occasion . . . when He was left behind in Jerusalem. We went back and found Him in the temple in discussion with the religious doctors. I remember His mother was very concerned about Him, and she said, 'Son, why have You done this to us? Look, Your father and I have sought You anxiously.' And Jesus turned and looked at us. I'll never forget . . . He made a statement that hurt me and yet it confirmed my thoughts. He said, 'Why did you seek Me? Did you not know that I must be about My Father's business?'"

A tear rolled off the leathery cheek of Joseph and fell onto his calloused hands, folded before him on the edge of the witness box. He looked from Luckhoo to the prisoner's dock and saw the appreciative smile of Jesus. Another tear escaped from his eyes. He took the sleeve of his cloak and wiped them dry. Luckhoo waited for Joseph to continue.

"I always believed in my heart that Jesus was the Son of God and that His conception was supernatural. For twelve years I walked by faith, with the belief that the child that I was raising was the Son of God. When I first found out that Mary was pregnant, I asked her how this happened. She simply told me that I would have to trust her and 'that God would provide me with the answer.'" Joseph looked up at the skylight. As thoughts of his past flooded his mind, he smiled.

"On that day when we walked into the great temple . . . and when I saw the boy that I was raising . . . standing in the midst of the most learned and religious scholars of Is-rael . . . and I saw that they sat listening to His every word . . . I knew that Jesus was not the son of any earthly father, but the true Son of God! When His mother said that she and His 'father' had sought Him with concern . . . His reply was that 'did you not know that I must be about My Father's business?'"

Joseph slowly looked back at Luckhoo.

"I knew I had no further business in the temple. Three days previously we had sacrificed and worshiped, and we were finished with our temple business. I knew that Jesus could only be talking about His real Father . . . His heavenly Father . . . Jehovah God. At that instant I received my answer from God. That answer allayed all the doubts that had tormented me for almost thirteen years about the pregnancy of my wife and the divine nature of Jesus."

Luckhoo interrupted with a question to clarify a point.

"You said earlier that His comment 'hurt' you. Was He rude or arrogant when He said it?"

"Oh, no, sir. It just reminded me, at that time, that I was only a steward of God's Son and that I had to really let go of Him in my mind so that He could be what His heavenly Father had called Him to be."

"Mr. Joseph, was it general practice of your day for believers in Jehovah God to be called the sons or the children of God?"

"No, sir. Most Israelites referred to Abraham as our father, and we are sons of Abraham."

"I have one more question, Mr. Joseph. Out of all the children that you raised, were any of them, in your considered opinion, perfect or near perfect in comparison with other children?"

Darrow came alive from the bench where he was sitting like he was shot out of a gun.

"I object, Your Lordship. The witness has explained that he is a carpenter with little education. He does not have any knowledge of child psychology or sociology, and he has not indicated that he is qualified to discuss developmental psychology. He is untrained and unqualified to make such an evaluation."

Darrow sat down just as quickly as he had risen.

The lord chief justice quickly commented on the objection. He nodded his head.

"I find that the question is asking for an opinion from the witness based on his experience as a father raising children. I find no objection to that, Mr. Darrow. Please answer the question, Mr. Joseph."

"Yes, sir. Jesus was as near perfect as you could imagine a child to be. As an infant He would cry when He needed to be fed or to have His underclothing changed. He would get a scratch or bruise on Him while He was playing. In the shop it was not uncommon for Him to get splinters in His fingers or to hit His finger while learning the trade of carpentry. He laughed more than the other children. He cried like the other children, although not nearly as much. But He never complained or argued about doing anything He was told. He had a hunger for studying from the scrolls. He always was respectful and obedient. Always!"

"Thank you, Mr. Joseph. My lord, I have no further questions of this witness at this time."

"Mr. Darrow, do you wish to reexamine?"

"No, Your Lordship." Darrow shook his great head.

The lord chief justice looked at Joseph and said, "You may step down and return to your seat, Mr. Joseph."

Joseph left the witness box and walked back to the area set aside for the witnesses, pausing adjacent to the prisoner's dock to look at Jesus. Each man smiled a confident smile at the other.

Darrow was clearly perturbed. While his first witness had provided substantiation that there had been no historic basis for Jesus, Joseph's testimony had been highly emotional and reinforced that he had been telling the truth. There now existed the possibility that Jesus could be a special or divine personage. It was necessary for Darrow to try to rehabilitate the situation, and he resolved to call as his second witness a man he had reserved as a concluding witness.

The lord chief justice spoke.

"Mr. Darrow, you may call your next witness."

Darrow stood, rubbed his chin for a moment as if he were pondering the witness to call next, yet he had already made up his mind during lunch and had discussed it with his instructor solicitor, Houston.

"Your Lordship, let the Jewish high priest, Joseph Caiaphas, be called."

Everyone in the courtroom appeared to be amazed that Darrow would call such a controversial witness at the beginning of the trial. Whispering filled the courtroom.

Luckhoo leaned over and said something quietly to his associate barrister. DiPietro nodded her affirmation.

Bailiff Griggs stood at his seat for the call.

"Joseph Caiaphas, Jewish high priest. Call for Joseph Caiaphas, Jewish high priest."

A rustle was heard behind the prisoner's dock in the witness seating area. A short man arose and moved regally toward the aisle.

He was impeccably dressed and was wearing an elegant turban, the official headdress of the high priest. It was made of fine linen with many folds. On the front of the turban was a gold plate bearing a Hebrew inscription: "Holiness to the Lord."

His neatly trimmed white hair matched his combed beard. His face was a tanned color, and his skin was without spots or blemishes. His dark eyes glared and were in stark contrast to his thin pale lips.

All eyes were turned to him, except those of the accused, Jesus.

Caiaphas marched, as if to some cadence, toward the bailiff, his face expressionless.

He wore an ephod made of gold, blue, purple, and scarlet threads, which were intertwined with fine linen. The back and the breastplate of the ephod were held together at the shoulders by beautiful large onyx stones.

Beneath the ephod he wore a blue robe. It had no sleeves, only slits for his arms. The fringe trimming of the bottom of the robe had embroidery of blue, purple, and scarlet pomegranates. In between each pomegranate hung a tiny gold bell, which rang faintly as he walked.

His breastplate was an elegant piece of embroidery about ten inches square, doubled over to make a pouch. It was adorned with twelve precious stones, each one bearing the name of one of the twelve tribes of Israel. The two upper corners were fastened to the ephod by gold laces, and the bottom of the breastplate was attached to his girdle by gold rings and chains. He wore a lustrous white linen shirt and matching breeches under his other garments. On his feet were slippers of gold mesh.

Caiaphas stepped into the witness box, and the bailiff stood before him and held a Bible. He looked at it suspiciously, then placed his hand on it as the bailiff asked him a question.

"Do you understand the language being spoken here today, sir?"

Caiaphas spoke in icy tones: "Young man, I am an educated man. If the man before me knew the language, I certainly should!"

The bailiff didn't bat an eye. He swore Caiaphas in as a witness, then returned to his seat.

Houston leaned over to Darrow and whispered, "Look at that one, will you! You've got yourself some sort of holy royal lion there! Get him to chew up some of those Christians for you!"

Darrow looked at her and smiled. "I believe you're right," and he added cautiously, "but I'll have to be careful that he doesn't turn and bite me!"

Darrow looked down at his notes and then at his witness. He smiled at Caiaphas.

"High Priest Caiaphas . . . in my country I would call you reverend. Is that appropriate, sir?"

Caiaphas's reply was precise and cold.

"You may call me reverend if you wish, Mr. Darrow."

"Yes, sir. Reverend Caiaphas, if my recollection of history is correct, I would like to verify some things with you, sir."

Darrow was uneasy with his witness. He didn't know whether it was because of his royal-looking attire or because of his pompous attitude.

"Reverend Caiaphas, you were the Jewish high priest in Jerusalem, having been appointed to this post by the Roman curator, Valerius Gratus, and you eventually ended up under the procuratorship of Pontius Pilate, is that right?"

"Yes, that is correct." His words were precise. One got the feeling that Caiaphas was used to asking the questions rather than answering them.

"Your appointment came indirectly, through Gratus, from the Roman emperor himself, Tiberius Caesar, and was reaffirmed under the governorship of Pontius Pilate."

"I was so appointed, sir."

"Would it also be proper to say that as the Jewish high priest, you were the president of the Jewish Sanhedrin?"

"I was."

"At the time that you were the president of the Sanhedrin, was it considered to be the supreme Jewish court of justice?"

"I would believe so, yes."

"Allowing me to use terms from my own country, would

you have been considered the chief justice of the Supreme Court of justice of the Jewish peoples?"

"I know nothing of your country, sir, but the title would also be a correct one."

"Then perhaps I should be calling you Mr. Chief Justice. Is that correct?"

"Mr. Prosecutor, you may call me chief justice or reverend or Mr. President. All are correct titles of my position!"

"Thank you, sir."

"Thank you, Mr. Prosecutor."

Luckhoo stood slowly to his feet, almost in a slow-motion style with both hands stretched upward.

"My lord, I find no reason why this court and the jury should be forced to endure this meeting of this mutual admiration society between the witness and the prosecution." Luckhoo sat down with his hands still in the air and then clasped them across his chest in an act of frustration.

Darrow moved quickly to solidify his point.

"Your Lordship, rather than acquiesce to this outburst by my esteemed counsel, the prosecution is intent on bringing to this court the knowledge of the proper title and authority of this witness who was the first to bring legal charges against the accused in a court of law."

The lord chief justice simply nodded his head in the affirmative.

"Proceed, Mr. Darrow."

"Reverend Caiaphas, please give this jury a very brief history and description of the Jewish Supreme Court, the Sanhedrin."

"Most members of the Sanhedrin trace its beginning to the council of seventy elders named by the patriarch of my people, Moses. It was first mentioned in history in the time of Antiochus the Great, who lived from 223 to 187 B.C. The Sanhedrin existed and continued its legal functions under the Hasmonean princes and the high priests. Under the Roman emperor Pompey, the title of the high priest was governor of the nation. However, in my term in office, the jurisdiction was over the eleven toparchies of Judea proper but did not extend into Galilee. We did exercise authority over the congregations of the Jewish synagogues in other countries as well. I must say, however, that the extent to which the outreaches of Jewish communities were willing to yield obedience to the orders of the Sanhedrin depended on the extent to which they were favorably disposed toward us."

"So your legal authority extended beyond Jerusalem and beyond the boundaries of Judea?"

"Yes, it did, in the context in which I explained."

"Under the Roman authorities, did the Jewish Supreme Court continue to function?"

There was a note of pride in Caiaphas's voice.

"We did. The Roman authorities imposed certain restrictions only with regard to competency."

"Can you give the jury a very brief summary of the working arrangement between the Roman government and the Jewish Sanhedrin?"

"Of course! To the Sanhedrin belonged all judicial matters and all measures of administrative matters that could not be competently dealt with by lower local courts or those that the Roman procurator had not especially reserved for his judgment. The Roman authorities considered the Sanhedrin the final court of appeal for questions connected with the Mosaic law. But I must point out that it was *not* open to anyone to appeal to it against the judgments of the lower courts. Rather, it was requested to intervene in cases in which the lower courts could not agree as to the judgment. Once the Sanhedrin had given a judgment, there was no further appeal. We were the Supreme Court!"

"Who might call the Sanhedrin into session?"

"The group came at my call. The tribune of cohorts stationed at Jerusalem could call, and of course, the procurator could order us to assemble."

"Did you have legal authority to pronounce the sentence of death on any prisoner brought before the Sanhedrin?"

"Yes, we did have that authority, although it was necessary that it be ratified by the procurator."

"Now, Reverend Caiaphas, I direct your attention to the prisoner in the prisoner's dock. Have you ever seen this man before?"

"Yes, I have seen this man before."

"And by what name do you know this man?"

Caiaphas spoke with disdain.

"He is known by me and others as a Galilean called Jesus."

"Did He ever come to trial before you?"

"Yes, He did."

"Using that trial as a point of time reference, when did you first hear of this Jesus?"

"I remember hearing stories of Him from some of my friends about a year prior to His trial."

"Would you share some of the things that you heard and share your response to them."

"I had some friends in the area of Galilee who said that the peasants were saying that this man had the power of healing and casting out demons and had been doing both in that region."

"Wasn't that somewhat of an uncommon thing?"

"Oh, no. Throughout our land there had been magicians and sorcerers doing their tricks of magic. This Jesus just seemed to be another one of them."

Darrow did not want to be interrupted by Luckhoo. He chose his words very carefully.

"Did He ever do anything that was, let's say, more unusual than the so-called tricks of the so-called other magicians and sorcerers?"

"I heard that He had cured a man with leprosy and two blind men. They said He made a mute man talk and cast demonic spirits out of several people. He became brazen and cured a man with a disabled hand . . . right in front of a crowd on the Sabbath, which was against the Jewish laws."

"Did that impress you?"

Caiaphas's eyes narrowed. He raised his hand and pointed at Jesus in the dock, but he did not look at Him. His voice rose with every word to a high pitch.

"Yes, that impressed me. It impressed me with anger. Devout Jews have long been looking for the promised Messiah-King who would deliver the nation of Israel and bring forth the everlasting kingdom of God on the earth. That charlatan is an absolute fraud as a Messiah. He continued to break our laws. He and His disciples picked corn on the Sabbath and ate it, just as one offense. I do not understand why He is back on trial here. We tried Him in Jerusalem and found Him guilty. And the Romans put Him to death by crucifixion."

"Certainly you did not have a man put to death simply because He healed a man on the Sabbath or because He picked some corn to eat on the Sabbath?"

Darrow's voice wavered. He asked a sincere question of

his prize witness, and his own feelings were in conflict against those in organized religion.

Other than pointing at Jesus, Caiaphas had been standing like a soldier at attention during the questioning. This question seemed to strike a tender nerve in him. His face turned red, and he took hold of the front of the witness box with both hands. His voice continued in the high pitch.

"I am the high priest of the Jewish people, and my record for integrity stands, Mr. Prosecutor. Your question shows your lack of knowledge of the jurisdiction of the Sanhedrin. We never went beyond the bounds of our authority. I am a Sadducee who lived by the precepts of the holy Mosaic law. This man Jesus created problems for our nation and for Himself. His every act drew the people away from the authority of the Sanhedrin. His next step undoubtedly would have been to incite the people to riot, as had many false prophets before Him, thus giving the Romans one more chance to bring destruction down on our heads."

"Were the people beginning to follow Jesus?"

"Yes, especially after some sort of miracle that He performed on a man from Bethany named Lazarus. He reputedly was dead three or four days, and this Jesus is supposed to have raised him from the dead."

"Are you saying He actually performed such a miracle?"

"We've heard of these things throughout history of how the evil one, Satan, can do supernatural things by using men. This, no doubt, was one of those events. By the next morning, the gossipers had told the story all over Judea."

"What did you do?"

Caiaphas seemed to be back in control of himself.

"I called an informal meeting of the Sanhedrin at my home and asked their counsel as to what to do with this man. They had all heard of Him and His followers, a band of itinerants. Everyone had the same fear . . . if this man were allowed to continue stirring up the people, they would once again be led to riot against the Romans. Not only would we be an oppressed people, but we would be slaves as our people once had been in Babylon. The Passover holidays were almost upon us, and there would be a horde of people in the streets, including the usual rabble-rousers. Following the discussion, I made a decision. I spoke to my colleagues: 'You know nothing at all, nor do you consider that it is expedient for us that one man should die for the people, and not that the whole nation should perish.'"

"Did Jesus cause you any problems during the Passover holidays?"

Caiaphas sighed and said, "Oh, yes. He did one of His typical theatrics, which drew attention to Himself and encouraged the feebleminded poor people as well. He made a whip, and He tipped over the tables of our money changers in the temple. He opened the cages of sacrificial doves, and they flew all over the place. The ignorant crowd cheered Him on!" Caiaphas was visibly agitated.

"Didn't the temple have a group of security people, called the temple guard, to maintain peace and order?"

Caiaphas threw up his hands in a gesture of futility.

"Oh, yes! I could have done more with a group of old women than with them. The captain of the guard reported the episode to me, and when I asked him why he didn't make an arrest, he told me that he and the men were afraid because of all the people cheering for Jesus. He was afraid an arrest might start a riot. He was probably correct, but I chastised him anyway."

"Reverend Caiaphas, what did you do next?" Darrow's

use of the title seemed to calm the witness down, and he once again stood at attention.

"I called the Sanhedrin into session once more and told both parties, the Pharisees and the Sadducees, what had happened. Instead of being behind me as before, they were greatly divided. His turning the tables over and defying the temple guard put even more fear into some of them. They made ridiculous statements, such as if He could raise the dead, He could cause all of our deaths. And since He had defied the temple guard, He was already out of our control. Others said that He had done nothing that deserved the death penalty according to our law. I dismissed them with the statement that if He caused a riot, He was going to cause our deaths, also. I went to bed very frustrated that night."

"Did you ever confront Jesus yourself?"

"I did."

"Would you tell the members of the jury what happened on that day, Reverend Caiaphas."

"The seditious event of His upsetting the workings of our great temple happened on the first day of the week, just six days before the beginning of our Passover holidays. Our informants told us that Jesus left with His rabble-rousers and went to the home of the man He reputedly raised from the dead, the man called Lazarus. His home was in Bethany."

Caiaphas's face was stern as he remembered the events.

"I felt that I had full authority to arrest Him for His vile actions," he paused, "but with the mood of the populace, I wanted the counsel of our leaders. The next day this arrogant carpenter returned to the temple. He had somehow gathered a bunch of little innocent children to shout, 'Hosanna to the Son of David!' When I heard that greeting, which is reserved for our Messiah-King, I was furious. The gall of the man. I went into the courtyard and confronted Him, which was foolishness on my part."

"What do you mean . . . 'foolishness' on your part?"

"The man made no sense. When I asked Him by what authority He upset the tables of our legitimate money changers and those responsible to provide the unblemished temple sacrifices, He said that He would answer my question if I would first answer His question. Such insolence!"

"Did He ask you a question?"

"Oh, yes . . . you couldn't stop the man in front of all those people."

"What was the question that He asked you?"

"The baptism of John—where was it from? From heaven or from men?"

"Was Jesus referring to John the Baptist, who had been beheaded by Herod?"

"Yes, He was."

"And what was your answer, Reverend Caiaphas?"

"It was a trick question. I knew that some of the crowd were followers of John and the mood of that crowd was to cause problems, or they wouldn't have been following this man. He made me look like a fool. The only answer I could give Him was that I couldn't answer His question, so He simply parroted back that He couldn't answer my question."

"And what did you do then?"

"I left that bunch of scoffers and went to my quarters."

"Did you plan to arrest Jesus for His violations of your religious laws?"

"Yes, we did."

"Reverend Caiaphas, why didn't you do that at that time?"

"I was the chief justice of Israel at that time, and I did

believe in the Mosaic law. I was also under Roman law, and it was my duty to follow that law. It was my plan to seek their advice, assistance, and direction."

"Prior to that, had you sought any other advice in this matter?"

"Yes. I certainly am not some sort of dictator. I had sought the counsel of my father-in-law, Annas, as well as that of some of the elders of the Sanhedrin."

"And what was their recommendation?"

"That we arrest Jesus."

"Reverend Caiaphas, would you tell us something of your father-in-law, Annas, that we might have as reference for his judgments?"

Caiaphas seemed to stand taller and his face shone.

"My esteemed father-in-law was a very respected and influential man. He was appointed high priest by Publius Sulpicius Quirinus, the Roman legate of Syria. My father-in-law's wisdom and influence extended far beyond the borders of our country. Five of his sons became high priests of our nation, which should speak of his influence."

Luckhoo sat motionless with his eyes closed, but his ears picked up every word and recorded them. His colleague, DiPietro, squirmed in her seat and was rapidly taking notes.

Darrow seemed very pleased with the testimony of this star witness, and Houston sat with a smile on her face.

Jesus, the accused, sat inside the prisoner's dock looking down. The jury seemed fascinated by the testimony of this elegantly dressed priest.

"So at this point, you have all the members of the Sanhedrin and your esteemed father-in-law behind you, and your plan is to arrest Jesus. Is that right?"

"Not entirely. At least one of the members was known

to be in sympathy with this Jesus. I really didn't know who else might have been smitten with His new religion."

"And what did you do?"

"I can honestly say that I believe it was the divine providence of Jehovah God that one of the very close disciples of this Jesus came to us with very grave concerns about his teacher."

"What was the man's name?"

"He said his name was Judas Iscariot. He was the man who carried the purse for this group . . . their treasurer."

"What did he say to you?"

"He told me a number of things as I questioned him. He said that when he started with the group, he believed that Jesus was truly the Messiah who was going to deliver our nation from the heel of the Romans. He then said that the teachings became confusing to him because Jesus would talk about His kingdom and then He would talk about loving others, including the Romans."

Caiaphas paused, with a look of satisfaction on his face.

"Jesus' disciple said that our beloved King David would have never talked like that about his enemies. Judas said that when Jesus turned the tables over in our temple, He was like a madman. In his judgment, if Jesus were to continue with His erratic behavior, He could create problems that would send our nation back into slavery, with no chance for any freedom from the Romans. The man made good sense! Judas said that one of Jesus' followers, a fisherman named Peter, had even called Jesus the Messiah. Judas stated that he thought that was very dangerous. And I agreed with the man."

"What did you do then, Reverend Caiaphas?"

"I directed one of the guards to take Judas to the courtyard for a few moments while I called another meeting of the council. I told them that one of the close disciples of Jesus had come with information that His followers believed that Jesus was the Messiah. It was of great concern to us that Judas indicated that Jesus had prophesied His own death on several occasions. If that were the case, it was apparent that some sort of rebellion would again break out and that this Jesus was prepared to die for His cause. There had been other lunatics who had been false messiahs in the past, and we didn't need another one to disrupt what little peace we had with the Romans."

"What happened next?"

"The council agreed that we should use the temple guards to take Jesus into custody . . . only if that could be done at night and very quietly. They agreed that we should then turn Him over to the Romans."

"Now, Chief Justice Caiaphas . . . and I said that to preface my question . . . was what you were doing legal as far as the Sanhedrin was concerned?"

Caiaphas drew himself up to his full height. His hands tightened on the front of the witness box. His voice quivered with anger as he began.

"Sir, I was the high priest. I did not do things that were dishonest in my position. I am a Sadducee and I follow the Mosaic law. I am not on trial here. It is Jesus who is on trial here, just as He was on trial in Jerusalem. He was found guilty there, and He certainly should be found guilty here. I, as the high priest, had the right to call into session, at any time, the priests, elders, and scribes who made up the Great Sanhedrin. And I had the privilege of doing it at the Temple Mount in Lishkat Hagazit, which is the Chamber of Hewn Stone, or at a chamber in my home. The Sanhedrin had the authority to sit in judgment with just twenty-three of the seventy-one members present. The court sat from the morning sacrifice until the evening sacrifice. There were times when the court would hear arguments all night."

Caiaphas's voice calmed.

"Would you describe the court's general procedure for criminal cases to our esteemed jury?" Darrow asked.

"The high court usually began in the midmorning. The accused was brought in, charges were read, and the witnesses were examined. Convictions or acquittals were based on the evidence presented by the witnesses, and our practice was that we accepted little of what the accused had to say. Each witness was first questioned on the seven points of the Mosaic law. After the evening meal, the council would sit in the chamber and argue the merits of the testimony. We would then come to a judgment of the accused for conviction or acquittal. As you can imagine, some of our cases took a few hours. Others took all night to reach a decision."

"Was the Great Sanhedrin authorized, under the Roman rule, to administer capital punishment?"

"We were allowed to administer capital punishment. However, this right was restricted to religious law."

"And was it under the recognized religious law that the council sought to arrest Jesus?"

"Yes, it was."

"And was it under the recognized religious law that the accused, Jesus, was arrested and brought to trial?"

"It was."

"Did you ever give any thought to whether or not this man might be the promised Messiah?"

"I did. But the evidence against the man was overwhelmingly in favor of His being a fraud. We knew of the so-called miracles that He did. On every occasion we attempted to prove or disprove them as being from Jehovah God or from Satan, the devil. He was constantly breaking our laws on the one hand and on the other telling His disciples that He came to fulfill the Law. He told others that the temple would be destroyed, and in three days it would be rebuilt. There was much more. Such babbling was preposterous."

"Who led your soldiers to Jesus?"

"One of His disciples, Judas Iscariot, the son of Simon."

"And when and where did they arrest Jesus?"

"The captain of the temple guard along with the tribune of the Roman guard arrested Jesus at the foot of the Mount of Olives at about two in the morning on the Friday before Passover."

"Who gave you the use of the Roman guard to assist you in this matter?"

"The Roman procurator, Pontius Pilate."

"When your soldiers found Jesus, how was He identified, Reverend Caiaphas?"

"Judas Iscariot was with the soldiers. He told us that the one that he kissed would be Jesus. He walked over and kissed Jesus on the cheek."

"Then your soldiers did arrest Jesus at the place where Judas Iscariot said He would be. Is that correct?"

"Yes, it is."

"Where did the soldiers take Jesus after His arrest?"

"They had been instructed to bring Him to the council chambers in my home, and they did so. They arrived there a little after two o'clock."

"What did you do when they brought Him to you at that early hour of the morning?"

"I immediately questioned the captain of the temple

guard as to the details of the arrest to ensure that we had handled it properly. After all, the man was a Hebrew citizen. We were there to protect His rights, even though He was a troublemaker. The members of the Sanhedrin are for justice, you know."

"What did you do next, Reverend Caiaphas?"

"I wanted to be lawful in all that I did, so I had the guard take Him to a former chief justice of Israel, my highly esteemed father-in-law, Annas."

"Did Chief Justice Annas question Him?"

"I learned from the captain of the guard and from my father-in-law that he did question Him."

"What was the outcome of this questioning of Jesus?"

Luckhoo was on his feet with his hand waving in the air.

"My Lord Chief Justice, I object to this question. This calls for a hearsay answer. The witness was not at the scene of this questioning by his supposedly 'highly esteemed' father-in-law."

The lord chief justice turned toward Luckhoo and nodded his head.

"Objection sustained. The foundation of any questioning by Chief Justice Annas with the defendant has not been established. Continue your questions, Mr. Darrow."

"Thank you, Your Lordship. Chief Justice Caiaphas, why were you in such a rush to arrest Jesus?"

"Our Jewish Passover and our Sabbath would commence at sundown on Friday. During that seven-day period there can be no trials, and no punishments can be meted out. Prisoners are simply held in confinement during that time."

"What was so dangerous about holding Jesus in prison for a week or so, as you saw it?"

"The man was obviously deranged. But at the same time, He was very charismatic, as I have said. We believed literally thousands of people might rise up and free Him from a Roman prison. Not only that, if they were to accomplish that feat, that could be just one more step toward inciting a national riot against Rome. Caesar would have his crack troops at our borders within the week. Our people would again be taken captives and taken to foreign lands. Our walls would be broken down as they were in the days of Ezra and Nehemiah. More than any other imposter from the past, this Jesus had many of what I considered messianic traits. Many of the people were soundly convinced that Jesus was the promised Messiah. He was dangerous."

"Since you had Jesus in custody, what did you do next?"

"I had servants go with messages to all of the members of the Sanhedrin who lived within an hour's journey of Jerusalem. I told them to be at my home as soon as possible. I told them it could be the most important trial that they had ever attended. I had a large room in my apartment that was sufficient to handle the complete council, if necessary. One by one the members arrived, even at that early hour of the morning. I then had a guard bring Jesus into the council."

"Was there a charge against Jesus before the council?"

"Certainly. The charge was blasphemy, which was punishable by death under Jewish law. On several occasions the accused had proclaimed Himself to be the Messiah, the true Son of Jehovah God."

"How did Jesus plead?"

"The man made absolutely no defense for Himself. He was as different in that courtroom as night is from day! When He was on the streets or in the hills, preaching to His precious flock, He was Mr. Charisma. But before His elders, He said nothing."

"Was He resistant in any way, Mr. Chief Justice?"

"Not at all. One time previously He had been reproached by His elders and they were going to stone Him for His blasphemy, but He turned and somehow walked right through the middle of them. But in our council meeting, He was quite passive."

"Chief Justice Caiaphas, did you follow the legal procedures of the Sanhedrin that early morning?"

Caiaphas did not get angry at this question as he had done in the past. He looked directly at Darrow. He held on to both sides of the witness box as he spoke.

"Mr. Darrow, I do not know the exact number of council members we had in that room in that early morning hour. But I do know that the council clerk stated that we had over the required quorum of twenty-three present."

"So you were legal."

"Not only were we legal, Mr. Darrow, but you should know that the Great Sanhedrin was a very religious, very legal, and very political group of influential men. Regardless of this one insignificant trial with this one Jesus, I had to serve with these men for the rest of my tenure as chief justice. I was a Sadducee among many legalistic Pharisees, so I endeavored to satisfy all points of the law . . . sir."

The American lawyer felt the sting of Caiaphas's words and some of the power that he must have wielded in his day. Having to walk on a tightrope between the Jews and the Romans required great ability.

"Were you required to call witnesses?"

"Yes, and we did."

"Did you call for witnesses for the accused?"

"We did, and none came forth."

"Did the witnesses against Jesus present valid testimony?"

"For the most part, yes."

"Would you explain that, Mr. Chief Justice?"

"Several witnesses presented conflicting testimony. But considering the early hour of the morning when we called them, we felt that was reason to accept their testimony. By and large, the witnesses presented convincing evidence against the accused, although that was not necessary for His conviction. Eventually, His own words convicted Him."

"And how did this come about?"

"Although I think the man is deranged, He certainly is no fool. He was well-versed in our law. I presented Him, as a devout Jew, with a question that I felt He must answer. And He did."

"What was that question, Mr. Chief Justice?"

"I said these words: 'I put You under oath by the living God: Tell us if You are the Christ, the Son of God!'"

"What was the answer of Jesus, the accused?"

"His answer was blasphemous. He said, 'It is as you said. Nevertheless, I say to you, hereafter you will see the Son of Man sitting at the right hand of the Power, and coming on the clouds of heaven.' That statement alone was more than sufficient, under Jewish law, to convict a person of blasphemy."

"What did you do then?"

"We have a traditional ritual that we are bound to do when we have heard blasphemy. We tear our outer clothing in such a way that it cannot be repaired without being noticed. Blasphemy is an irreparable religious offense. I tore my outer garment from top to bottom."

"Did the others of the council follow you?"

"Yes."

"What did you say next?"

"When blasphemy is committed, my response is, 'He has spoken blasphemy! What further need do we have of witnesses? Look, now you have heard His blasphemy! What do you think?'"

"And how did the members of the council answer, Mr. Chief Justice?"

"They all answered with the traditional saying: 'He is deserving of death.'"

"The official quorum of the Sanhedrin answered in one voice the same? 'He is deserving of death,' is that correct?"

"Yes, that is correct."

"And is that a pronouncement of death upon that person, Mr. Chief Justice?"

"It is."

As a student of law, Darrow was fascinated by what he was hearing of ancient Jewish religious laws. He had read some of the books, but it was as if he was hearing a book being spoken by a historical participant.

"What happened next, Mr. Chief Justice?"

"I told the temple guard to take Jesus and hold Him until after dawn when we would take Him to Pilate, the Roman procurator."

"What was your reason to send Him to Pilate since you had already judged the accused to be guilty of a crime punishable by death?"

"Our Roman governors had long prohibited us from carrying out many of our laws, including that of delivering the death penalty. We had to have the approval of the procurator."

"And why didn't you take the accused to Pilate at that time?"

"Sir, it was about five o'clock in the morning. I was aware that the accused was a Hebrew citizen and that He had His rights. Therefore, it was important for a trial to take place in the Chamber of Hewn Stone in the temple. That was our next step. Also, I might add, the procurator was a most unhappy person to deal with whenever he was disturbed at such an early hour. I felt that it was important to follow our laws, then awaken the procurator."

"What happened next?"

"We took the blasphemer into the chambers of the Sanhedrin in the temple. The charges were again proclaimed that the accused had blasphemed in the presence of the high priest and other members of the Great Sanhedrin. It was my responsibility as chief justice to remind the court that this offense required the death penalty. I called the roll of the council members present, and each, without exception, stood and stated, 'The accused is guilty. His punishment is death.' The clerk of the court wrote the prisoner's name, the charge of blasphemy, the finding of guilt by quorum vote of the Sanhedrin, and the sentence. This would be taken to the Roman procurator for his confirmation of the sentence."

"Did you then take Jesus to the Roman procurator, Pontius Pilate?"

"We did."

"Where was he, Mr. Chief Justice?"

"He was in the Praetorium, just north of the temple."

"And you went next to the Praetorium, is that correct?"

"I did."

"And did you go into the Praetorium?"

"No, sir. To enter the residence of a Gentile would have caused me to religiously defile myself."

"So what did you do, Mr. Chief Justice?"

"I sent a Gentile messenger into the Praetorium with a message."

"And what was that message, as you remember it?"

"I remember what I stated. I said that if it pleased the honorable procurator of his imperial majesty, Tiberius Caesar, the Jewish Sanhedrin, with the authorization of Roman rule, had found a Hebrew, one Jesus of Nazareth, guilty of blasphemy, which is punishable by death. I further requested that the Honorable Pontius Pilate confirm our sentence and arrange for the execution to be carried out before the beginning of the coming Jewish Sabbath. I also expressed my concern that there was a danger of serious rioting if the matter of this Jesus were not adjudicated promptly."

"Mr. Chief Justice, will you please tell the jury what ensued?"

"Our guards were bringing the criminal up at the same time the procurator stepped onto his balcony. His chair was brought out for the procurator, and he sat on a platform in the courtyard."

"Did you enter the Praetorium area, Reverend Caiaphas?" Darrow stood with his hand on his chin.

"No," Caiaphas explained, "as I said, our laws state that entering that area would defile us, making us unclean. We could not eat the Passover Seder that night."

"So what happened?" Darrow asked impatiently.

"I sent another messenger to Pilate asking if he would be so gracious as to come out to us in the esplanade, where he normally sat in judgment in the afternoons."

"And did he come out?"

Caiaphas frowned. "Reluctantly, yes."

"Tell the jury what happened then with the official Roman procurator, Pontius Pilate."

"Instead of proceeding with the formality of accepting our verdict, the procurator asked us: 'What charge do you bring against this man?' which basically was the opening of a formal Roman trial."

"And what did you do, Mr. Chief Justice?"

A faint smile came across Caiaphas's face: "I simply stated that if Jesus were not a criminal, we would not have brought Him before the procurator for judgment."

"And what was the reply of Governor Pilate?"

"His reply was a typical sneering Roman remark!"

"And what was that?"

"He said that we could take this Jesus out of his court and judge Him ourselves. He knew well that we had already done this." Anger came into Caiaphas's eyes, and he turned and glared toward the section of seats where the witnesses for the trial were sitting.

"Did you reply to his remark?"

"I did. I reminded the procurator that we Hebrews could not carry out the sentence of execution under Roman law without the permission of the Roman government, of which he was supposed to be the local administrator."

A warped smile crossed Caiaphas's lips.

"What was the governor's reply to that?"

"He stubbornly asked us again concerning the charge against Jesus. There was quite a gathering of people in the area where we were, and I believe that Pilate was attempting to show his usual disdain for the Hebrews and to demonstrate his authority. I instructed the members of the Sanhedrin to present the formal bill of indictment, which said that we had found Jesus guilty of inciting the people of Israel, that He forbade them to pay tribute money to Tiberius Caesar, and that He claimed to be Messiah, that is, the King of the Jews."

Caiaphas stood up straight in the witness box and placed his hands together in a gesture of strength and composure.

"What happened next?"

"The governor stood up and walked inside his courtyard. He then motioned for his guards to bring the prisoner before him. I could not hear what they said. Pilate took his time and then walked back out onto the esplanade. Then Jesus was again brought before Pilate. The governor said that he found no guilt in Jesus."

"Can you summarize the rest of the events with Pilate?"

"Yes, sir. We followed the precepts of Roman law and presented our witnesses against the accused. Pilate asked Jesus if He had witnesses on His behalf or if He wanted to say anything on His own behalf. No one spoke up, and the accused had nothing to say in His own defense. Then Pilate remarked that Jesus was a Galilean and therefore should be under the jurisdiction of the tetrarch Herod Antipas. Then he adjourned the tribunal. We had no choice but to take the accused to Antipas, who was in residence at the Hasmonean Palace."

"And tell our jury what happened with Herod Antipas, in summary form, please."

"We took the accused to Herod and formally informed him of the charges. He talked to the accused and then told us to return Jesus to Pilate."

Darrow looked quizzically at the chief priest.

"Did you have any indication as to why he was sending you all back to Pilate?"

Luckhoo stood to his feet quickly and quietly.

"My lord, counsel is soliciting an opinion from the witness concerning what he thought was the reason for the actions of Herod Antipas. Such testimony would be hearsay testimony and I object to that."

The lord chief justice looked at Darrow.

"Sustained. You may proceed, Mr. Darrow."

"Mr. Chief Justice, what happened when you returned to the procurator with the prisoner Jesus?"

"Pilate still expressed his opinion that the accused was innocent and that He only needed to be flogged and shamed. He said that he felt that those who were following Jesus would leave Him when they saw the power of Rome exercised."

"Did you agree with the verdict of the governor?"

"No, I did not."

"Continue with the facts of the story, Mr. Chief Justice."

Darrow was playing to his witness.

"The governor never was a strong man, and he even let his wife influence some of his decisions. The next trick he tried to pull on us was to use amnesty. It was his custom each Passover to release one prisoner of Rome, with the choice of prisoner being given to the populace. He offered them a man who had been found guilty of murder and insurrection, a man called Jesus Barabbas. He also offered them our prisoner, Jesus of Nazareth, which he had no right to do. Immediately the cry went up from the people for Jesus Barabbas to be released. Pilate wavered, then had Jesus flogged, and tried to release Him, even though his word was that he would bow to the wishes of the people. He brought Jesus out after He had been flogged and said that he still found no crime in Him. Our lawyers finally had to inform the honorable prefect that Tiberius Caesar had given the law that the religious customs of the Hebrews would be upheld. This Jesus had claimed that He was the Son of God. That was blasphemy . . . and punishable by death."

"Did the governor then pronounce the sentence of death on the accused?"

"No. He called for a bowl of water and washed his hands of the affair, saying that his hands were clean of the prisoner's blood. Finally, when the crowd of citizens kept shouting for crucifixion, the governor acquiesced and accepted his responsibilities." Caiaphas's voice rumbled with the hatred he held for his ancient enemy.

"He eventually gave the order for Jesus to be executed. And in his true slinking nature, this Roman weakling had the inscription made for the cross to read, 'THIS IS JESUS, THE KING OF THE JEWS.' It was just one more of the insults that Rome laid on the back of God's chosen people."

"Mr. Chief Justice, was the trial of Jesus of Nazareth in front of the official sitting representative of Rome? In other words, was it a legal Roman trial as far as you were concerned?"

"It was. It was an investigation by the prefect granted such authority. The stated charge against the accused was treason against Rome. The secondary charge against the accused was the endorsement of the Great Sanhedrin's conviction of Jesus on a capital religious offense. He was found guilty of both charges by the Roman governor. Because Jesus was not a citizen of Rome, He had no right to any appeal."

"And was Jesus executed and found to be dead?"

"Absolutely. There is no doubt that the man died on a Roman cross of execution on a hill called Golgotha, or Place of the Skull. I and two of my scribes stayed and watched until after His death."

"Why did you do that?"

"We waited in vain for this rabble-rouser to recant His statements so we might absolve Him of His sins and at least assure Him of dying a blessed death. But He did not."

"Doesn't it take quite a while for someone to die on the Roman cross of execution?"

"Yes, for some it took hours and even days. But since it was the eve of our religious festival, we asked that the Romans break the legs of the crucified criminals early."

"What was your reason for this request?"

Caiaphas seemed very matter-of-fact as he explained, "It was a way to hasten death . . . less suffering for all concerned."

"Would you explain what you saw the Romans do to Jesus at the place of execution."

"The prisoners were stripped naked, and a large crossbeam was laid on the ground behind each one of them. The Roman soldiers forced the prisoners to lie face up on the beam. The executioner took their arms and stretched them flat against the beam. He then placed a large nail in the hollow spot where the hand and wrist join. He drove the nail through each hand and into the beam. A piece of cloth was wrapped around the prisoners' loins so their nakedness wouldn't be offensive to the women and children who came to watch. The crossbar with the prisoner nailed to it was hoisted to the top of a large upright that had been placed in the ground previously. The executioner took the feet of the prisoner and nailed them to the upright with the right foot over the left foot."

Caiaphas paused to take a breath.

"The pain in the prisoners' arms, from the hanging, becomes so great that the arm and shoulder muscles become paralyzed down to the chest and they are not able to breathe. Using their legs to raise themselves up for a moment allows them to breathe. This can go on for hours, depending on the strength of the prisoner. To hasten the process the executioner will sometimes break the legs of the prisoners so they cannot raise themselves up to breathe, and they suffocate."

Caiaphas returned to the specifics of Jesus' crucifixion.

"The Roman soldiers broke the legs of the two prisoners who were on each side of the accused, Jesus. They were pronounced dead by the executioner. When the Romans came to Jesus, He was already dead, so they did not break His legs. They did, however, run a spear into His side. He did not move when that was done. I think that was about the ninth hour."

"Were you satisfied that Jesus was dead?"

"We were." Caiaphas smiled slightly but looked straight ahead at Darrow.

"And was this the end of Jesus?"

"Unfortunately it was not."

"Will you please explain your statement to the jury."

"Yes, I will, Mr. Prosecutor!"

"We learned that a confederate of the crucified criminal Jesus of Nazareth went to Pilate and asked for His dead body. The man was a respected member of our Great Sanhedrin ... Joseph of Arimathea. Pilate didn't believe that the prisoners were dead, so he dispatched a Roman soldier to go to Golgotha, the place of the execution, to see if it were so. When the soldier returned with the affirmative answer, Pilate gave his answer to allow Jesus' body to be removed."

Luckhoo rose to his feet: "My lord, I object to this hearsay testimony of the witness. He was not present at this conversation and is presenting a biased opinion."

The lord chief justice looked over at Darrow and nodded. "Sustained."

Darrow was quick to reply.

"How do you know what was said at the home of Governor Pontius Pilate, Mr. Chief Justice?"

Caiaphas's answer was given with a smirk of satisfaction.

"Because we had spies everywhere—including in his bedroom!" came the shocking announcement.

"You dog of a Jew! I told Rome that we should have annihilated every Jew on the face of the earth when the great legions of Rome marched into your detestable nation!"

The words exploded from the witness section behind the prisoner's dock. A man, dressed in the toga of an elite Roman citizen, stood shaking his fist at the high priest, who continued to smile even as he was being degraded.

In an instant, Caiaphas drew himself to his full height and pointed his finger at Pilate and shouted back, "You can't do a thing to me now, you foul demagogue. It's too late! It's too late for you and your stinking empire!"

The gavel's bangs punctuated the words of the lord chief justice.

"Order in this trial! Order in the trial! Order in the trial! I command you in this courtroom to come to order!"

His gavel fell again, sounding like a clap of thunder from the heavens. "You witnesses and you of the legal profession are here by the grace of the court to hear all the testimony given. If there is another outburst in this court of law, I will remove all of you."

The lord chief justice's eyes were as fire as he sat down.

He looked directly into the eyes of the prosecutor and spoke with a calm voice.

"Mr. Darrow, you may proceed with the examination of this witness."

Darrow felt he had lost some hard-earned legal ground when two of his key witnesses engaged in a shouting match. But Darrow's famous courtroom skills were in evidence as he immediately brought the trial back with the focus on the accused.

"Mr. Chief Justice, we were talking about the convicted, sentenced, and executed Jesus of Nazareth and His dead body being requested by one of the unfaithful members of the Great Sanhedrin, that being one Joseph of Arimathea. This information came to you by way of an informant in the household of the Roman governor, Pontius Pilate. Is that correct?"

"It did." Caiaphas's face was still red.

"And did your informant tell you that Pilate gave the Arimathean permission to take the body?"

"He did."

"Did you also have loyal informants following the Arimathean?"

"Yes, sir, we did."

"And what report did they bring to you?"

"They said that the Romans had left the area of the execution. Two men, the Arimathean and one identified as John, a disciple of the deceased, came and took the dead body down from the executioner's cross. Several women were still standing around weeping, including the mother of the deceased, a woman by the name of Mary. One of our informants said it was a pathetic sight, this Mary woman as she sat on a rock, holding the body of her dead son across her lap, sobbing as though a sword had pierced her soul."

"Did you identify any of the other women?"

"Yes. They were followers of Jesus. One was Mary, the wife of Clopas, and the other was a woman who was known as having been mentally disturbed. Her name was Mary Magdalene. I don't remember the names of the others."

"What was done with the body of the dead criminal?"

"It was reported to me that there was some sort of conversation between the men and then they washed the body. What looked to be a servant of one of the men brought some spices and perfume and did the customary task of anointing the body and wrapping it for burial."

"Was this the usual procedure for preparing a body for burial?"

"Basically, yes."

"Then what did your loyal informants tell you that they saw?"

"They reported that the men carried the body to a tomb. We found out later that it had been previously purchased by the Arimathean. They put the body in the tomb. A great round stone in front of the tomb served as the door. It was held in place by a smaller stone. The two men began to rock the great round stone, and one of the women pulled out the small rock from in front of its edge. The greater stone rolled in front of the tomb entrance, closing it with a loud thud."

"How many loyal informants did you have watching what was going on?"

"There were three trustworthy men who were part of the temple guard."

"Please tell us what happened next."

"I had instructed the leader of the informants to come

to me immediately as soon as he knew that the body of this problem maker had been sealed in the tomb."

"And did he do that and report as you have stated?"

"Yes, sir, he did."

"And what did the other two men do?"

"One of them was instructed to stay at the tomb until further notice. The other was told to follow those who had just left the tomb."

"What was the reason for ordering those actions, Mr. Chief Justice?"

"We were aware that this Jesus had a great following of rabble-rousers, and we did not want these feeble followers to incite a riot because of the death of their leader. But that did not happen, and His followers scattered like a flock of sheep without a shepherd."

"Why did you leave the man at the sealed tomb?"

"One of the heresies espoused by Jesus of Nazareth was that He would rise from the dead in three days. No man had ever done that before, and that includes the Nazarene."

"Was a guard put around the tomb of Jesus?"

"Yes. We wanted to put the Roman guard around the tomb. We felt that if they were there and anything happened, it would not appear to the people that the Sanhedrin was reacting in any way to this fake Messiah. We did not wish to give credence to any of His claims, especially that of His rising from the dead."

Darrow had been standing in one spot for quite some time. His bones were beginning to ache, and he shifted from one foot to the other. His assistant, Houston, passed a note to him: "Watch the time! Don't get cut off in the middle of examination by the afternoon teatime recess!"

Darrow agreed. He wanted the testimony of Caiaphas complete by the end of the afternoon.

"Did you send to Pilate and request a Roman guard at the tomb?"

"We did."

"And when did you do this?"

"That very day."

"And did the Roman governor send a detachment to the tomb?"

"No!" Caiaphas spoke in disgust. "He told us that we had our own guards and to guard it ourselves."

"Did you then dispatch the temple guards to the tomb of Jesus?"

"Yes."

"And when did they arrive?"

"In the late afternoon of the day after the crucifixion of the accused."

"What happened next?"

"The captain of the temple guard reported back that they had sealed the tomb with ribbons and attached the seal of the Great Sanhedrin. I then went to bed."

"And what report did you next receive?"

"I was rudely awakened just after dawn of the first day of the week by someone pounding at my door. I shouted an order for one of my servants to see who it was. It was the captain of the guard, and he brought with him one of the guards who had been on watch at the tomb. The guard was almost out of breath, having run all the way from the tomb."

"And what did the captain of the guard tell you?"

"He told me that the temple guard had something to tell me directly."

"And what did the guard say?"

"He said that the morning watch was guarding the tomb and there was a sudden earthquake. He said that the seals on the tomb were broken and the stone rolled to the far side of the tomb. He said that he saw a man sitting on the tombstone and that 'his countenance was like lightning, and his clothing as white as snow.' He said they were so much in fear that the guards fainted. When they came to, they all fled the area and ran to the barracks to make their report."

"Did the guard look into the tomb before he fled the area?"

"No, sir. He said that he was too fearful to do so."

"Did you know if the body had been removed?"

"The captain of the guard dispatched two guards to the tomb site, and they found the tomb empty. They reported this back to the captain as we were questioning the guards who had been at the tomb."

"And what do you believe happened, Mr. Chief Justice?"

Luckhoo jumped to his feet with the pigtails of his wig bouncing up and down. His voice rang throughout the courtroom.

"My lord, we are dealing with the facts in what happened at the tomb where the dead body of the accused, Jesus of Nazareth, was laid. The esteemed Reverend Caiaphas was not at the scene. He did not witness the resurrection of Jesus or anyone removing His body from the tomb. I am willing to allow what Reverend Caiaphas's loyal and paid captain of the guard told him and what the soldiers told him, even though we are dealing with third party conversations, which at best provide concern for legal creditability."

Luckhoo was angry as he spoke.

"But I am definitely not interested in a biased religious

dissertation on what the Reverend Caiaphas believed to have happened at that tomb." Luckhoo sat down.

The lord chief justice nodded his head in approval and looked back at Darrow.

"Sustained. Mr. Darrow, rephrase your question."

Darrow smiled at his witness and put his hands in his suspenders.

"What happened next, Mr. Chief Justice?"

"I told the captain of the guard to take the guards who had been at the tomb and allow them to talk to no one else until I called for them. I then called another emergency meeting of the Sanhedrin to meet at my home."

"Will you summarize the contents of that meeting for our jury, Mr. Chief Justice?"

"I reminded them that this rabble-rouser Jesus still had many friends who were in the city for the Passover holidays . . . that Jewish holidays were always a time when the spirit of nationalism seemed to be at an all-time high. I reminded them again that all we needed was for some of the leaders of this Jesus movement to spark the crowds of people with the exciting statement that their leader, who had said He was the Messiah, had risen from the dead. We would have a fire of a riot on our hands like never before. The elders were in total agreement with me. One angry member recommended that the guards take the full guilt for the botched-up affair. They should say that they had fallen asleep and Jesus' disciples had stolen the body in order to make it appear that He had risen from the dead. We had witnessed how far this lunatic was prepared to go to compel events to answer to the prophecies that He was the Messiah. Even a dead Jesus was a serious matter."

"How did you feel about this, Mr. Chief Justice?"

"Well, the men indeed had failed in guarding the tomb. I could not explain how several of them could have seen this light thing at one time. But the fact was that the body of Jesus was gone without a trace. I ordered the tomb guards to come into the Sanhedrin with the captain of the guard. We told them that they should be severely flogged for failing in their duty of guarding that tomb. We told them that we were not going to flog them but we were going to be gracious at this time of Passover and were going to suspend them from duty with pay. To prevent any possible riots by the followers of Jesus, we said to tell anyone who asked, 'His disciples came at night and stole Him away while we slept.' We told them that if Pilate heard of it, we would protect them, and we were true to our word."

"Did Pilate raise any questions in the matter?"

"He did not. He could care less about our problems."

"Did you hear anything further of Jesus?"

"Oh, yes. His disciples perpetrated stories that He was seen alive again in bodily form."

"Did you investigate any of these reports?"

"We did."

"And what did you find, Mr. Chief Justice?"

"We found that the stories were always reported by His disciples . . . those who believed in Him. We heard of nine or so incidents of His followers supposedly seeing Jesus or someone who looked like Him."

"Did that bother you?"

"Not really."

"Why not?"

"Because we had seen or heard, over a period of centuries, about the works of magicians and illusionists. In the history of Israel, there have been many deceivers, and this man Jesus was just another one of them. His disciples certainly had reason to want people to believe He was alive."

"I have only one more question, Mr. Chief Justice. I certainly appreciate your in-depth testimony. My final question has to do with your conscience. Did you ever consider the possibility that this Jesus was the true Messiah that every devout Jewish believer had been seeking for centuries?"

"I must say, Mr. Prosecutor, that during the time I first knew of this Jesus and went to see Him, I did indeed have hope that He was the promised Messiah. I have dreamed of Him in my sleep, and I have tried to be as fair and as impartial as I can be to examine His claim to messiahship. But I cannot find sufficient evidence that would lead me to believe that Jesus of Nazareth, the man we found guilty of blasphemy and subsequently executed, was the Messiah of Israel. Many things that happened were very coincidental, making Him look like He could be the Messiah, but I do not believe that He was or is the Messiah-King."

"Thank you, Chief Justice Caiaphas. I have no further questions of this witness, Your Lordship." Darrow sat down on the bench behind his desk. He took his red bandana handkerchief from his back pocket and wiped his brow. Houston poured him a glass of water from the Waterford pitcher on the table.

Luckhoo glanced at the slowly ticking clock on the wall but made no move to stand or to speak. Caiaphas stood motionless with his hands still on the edge of the witness box. Jesus looked straight ahead with His eyes on the lord chief justice, who banged his gavel on the walnut block and spoke.

"The witness will be cross-examined by the defense before being excused as a witness. This trial is recessed for tea and will resume at eight o'clock tomorrow morning."

The bailiff of the court rose and spoke in a loud voice to formally end the day's proceedings. People began to move from their seats toward the doors of the courtroom. The jurors were led out the door through which they entered the court just hours ago. The witnesses left by a door at the rear of the courtroom. Jesus, the accused, was led to the back of the witness box and down a flight of stairs to a row of cells.

Darrow put his papers under his arm as he and Houston walked toward the barristers' room without acknowledging their opponents, talking in lively but muted tones.

Luckhoo and DiPietro sat staring at the empty prisoner's dock until DiPietro quietly said, "Sir Lionel, you look like you need to have some tea. It feels cold and clammy in here, and it still smells like the stinking devil."

Luckhoo didn't say a word. He nodded his head at the same time the church bell at St. Sepulchre began to toll four times. It was teatime in London, and it looked like the prosecution had won the day.

6

WITNESSES FOR THE PROSECUTION

MORNING, DAY TWO

London was having a typical morning. The fog quietly entered the city and enveloped everything that stood upright. The mournful foghorns could be heard sounding their warnings up and down the Thames River. Anything that moved seemed to be gliding from place to place as if in a ghostly dream. Even the tower bell at Westminster rang with a chill, announcing that it was eight o'clock.

Inside the courtroom, everyone was assembled. The bailiff banged his scepter one time on the hardwood floor.

"This court is in session. Let the trial of the accused proceed." He paused for a moment. "Be seated." Again he paused in rote. "The honorable clerk of the courts, please."

Sir Robb Thompson stood in his robe and wig, looking very similar to all who were in the well of the court.

"Jesus of Nazareth is accused before the Crown of the crime against society of capital fraud. He has pleaded 'not guilty' to this offense."

He paused and looked at the witness box where the witness stood, anticipating the next action of the court.

"The witness before this court is Joseph Caiaphas, Jewish high priest, who is ready for cross-examination by the defense, Sir Lionel A. Luckhoo, my lord."

The lord chief justice nodded as the clerk took his seat.

"Sir Luckhoo, you may cross-examine the witness."

Luckhoo looked at the accused, and Jesus passed a quiet smile of encouragement to him. Luckhoo grasped one side of his gown, looked directly into the eyes of the lord chief justice, and bowed.

"Thank you, my lord. I shall do that with great delight."

He turned and looked directly into the eyes of Caiaphas. Both men were approximately the same height, except the headdress on the priest made him appear taller. As he began to speak, Luckhoo closed his eyes, as was his custom.

"Reverend Caiaphas, I believe that one of your religious titles was high priest. Is that correct, Reverend Caiaphas?"

Caiaphas bristled: "You could at least respect me enough to look at me when you speak to me!"

The tension could be felt throughout the courtroom.

Darrow leaned over to Houston and whispered, "Looks like little old David has one of those Judah lions that's gonna chew him up!" Houston smiled and poked him in the ribs.

"Reverend Caiaphas, while I do not owe you an explanation of why I choose to examine or cross-examine a witness with my eyes closed, I will afford you the courtesy of a reply. It is a practice that I learned as a young man. It has nothing to do with your personality, your position, or your popularity with the prosecution, which was portrayed so unashamedly yesterday afternoon in this courtroom." Luckhoo opened his eyes, looked directly at Caiaphas, and closed his eyes again.

"Now, Reverend Caiaphas, will you please answer the question for the benefit of our jury?"

Caiaphas's answer was tart: "Yes! I am known by that title."

"The esteemed prosecution also referred to you a great deal by another title, that being the chief justice of the Supreme Court of the Jewish peoples. Is that also correct, Reverend Caiaphas?"

"He did call me that, yes."

"But indeed, Reverend Caiaphas, was there ever such a title officially given to you?"

"No, sir."

"So that title came from Mr. Darrow's vivid imagination, is that correct?"

"He first called me by that title, yes, sir."

"You accepted that title and said that it was correct, did you not?"

"I said that Mr. Darrow could call me chief justice or reverend . . . both were correct titles of my position."

"Wasn't your correct title president of the Sanhedrin instead of chief justice?"

"Yes, sir, it was, and I believe Mr. Darrow referred to me as the president of the Sanhedrin as well, if you can recall."

"Thank you, Reverend Caiaphas, I can recall!" Luckhoo seemed to be impervious to the verbal jabs of the high priest.

"Reverend Caiaphas, isn't it true that in your day, there were two distinct Jewish views of the Great Sanhedrin . . . one being that it was the highest legislative and judicial court of the rabbinic law, directed by two leaders, and the other view being that the Sanhedrin was a political and judicial body headed by the high priest?"

"We were not political—"

Luckhoo interrupted. "I did not ask your opinion, Reverend. I asked if it were true that there were these two views of the Sanhedrin in your day. Yes or no?"

Luckhoo's voice rang throughout the courtroom. Caiaphas looked as if he had lost his self-control at being questioned in such a manner, but he put his hands together and cracked his knuckles. He then smiled patronizingly at his questioner. His voice seemed once again under control.

"Yes, there were two or more views about the Great Sanhedrin in my day!"

"My questions to you, Reverend Caiaphas, will be about the Great Sanhedrin in Jerusalem in your day and not some other place or period in time. Was it not true that the Sanhedrin was made up of Pharisees and Sadducees who were from the aristocracy of your nation?"

"For the most part, yes."

"Compared to others who had served as high priest under Roman rule, the period of eighteen years that you served was considered an unusually long tenure, is that correct?"

Caiaphas took this question as a compliment. "I would say that is true."

"Then, Reverend Caiaphas, is it also true that you served totally at the pleasure of the Roman prefect in power, and at the time of the so-called trials of the accused, that Roman prefect was Pontius Pilate?"

Caiaphas was caught off guard. He stuttered for a moment. A look of frustration came over his face, as years of oppression by the Roman government were brought back to his memory. He exploded with anger. His voice was shrill.

"Yes, I did serve at the pleasure of Pontius Pilate! We Hebrews had to have that weak despot's permission to do just about everything, including living and breathing. We had to run bowing and begging to a man who was so full of fear that he made life miserable for us. But I am not under that dog now! Not now!"

The courtroom was buzzing with muted conversations.

Darrow leaned back in his seat with a look of disgust and whispered to Houston through gritted teeth, "All that work to get some semblance of facts and order out of that priest, and Luckhoo makes him look like a rubber-stamp puppet!"

Houston didn't say a word but just shook her head in sympathy.

Luckhoo paused, looking at the jury.

"I should like to remind the jury at this time that the Holy Bible has been introduced as Exhibit A."

Luckhoo then looked back at his witness.

"Before you came into this courtroom to be a witness, did a court solicitor give you a book called the Holy Bible to read, Reverend Caiaphas?"

"Yes," he answered in a matter-of-fact manner.

"Were you given specific instructions by a court official to read the sections of that Holy Bible denoted as Matthew, Mark, Luke, and John?"

"I was."

"And did you read those four books of the Bible?"

"I did. I read much of the book, including the portion called the New Testament."

"Do you recall if your name and title were mentioned in any or all of those books of the Bible?"

"Yes, I recall!" His answer was abrupt. "I was mentioned

in a book titled Matthew, a book titled Luke, a book titled John, and a book called the Acts of the Apostles."

"And where these books of the Bible mentioned you personally, were they historically accurate, Reverend Caiaphas?"

"It is somewhat astonishing, but they are accurate from a historic point of view. I hasten to say that they are not particularly flattering, but every historian is entitled to his bias," Caiaphas said resolutely.

"Then Exhibit A is historically accurate in reference to the statements that relate to you or to the events in your country and in your time. Is that correct?"

"Yes, they are."

"Is it correct that the chief priest and the elders of the Jewish people who constitute the Sanhedrin are in fact a judge of anyone who is accused of a crime under their jurisdiction?"

"That is correct."

"And under your law, the prosecutors are the citizens who will bring such a case against any person they wish to have charged?"

Caiaphas loved to debate law, and it seemed that he might have a chance to match wits with Luckhoo. He felt an exhilarating tingle go through his body.

"Yes. The witnesses to the offense are not only witnesses; they are the virtual prosecutors who present their case before the chief priests and the elders who, as a body, act as a unified impartial judge."

"Then is it against Hebrew law for you to be a prosecutor or a witness in your own court where you are a judge?"

"It is."

"Reverend Caiaphas, it is written in the book of Matthew, in chapter twenty-six, verses three through five: 'Then the chief priests, the scribes, and the elders of the people assembled at the palace of the high priest, who was called Caiaphas, and plotted to take Jesus by trickery and kill Him. But they said, "Not during the feast, lest there be an uproar among the people."' Do you remember that incident?"

Caiaphas hedged.

"I don't remember that anyone mentioned killing Jesus, as in murder, at that meeting. But He was a very severe religious and political problem to our nation . . . and growing worse by the hour."

"So you were part of that specific group of people mentioned in that chapter and those verses of the book of Matthew?"

"Yes, I was, but—"

Luckhoo interrupted Caiaphas: "The assembly spoken of here in the book of Matthew was held before you had Jesus arrested, and it consisted of members of the Sanhedrin. Is that correct?"

"Yes, it was."

"Then according to your own testimony of moments ago, you and that group of conspirators from the Sanhedrin were witnesses against Jesus, and therefore, according to your own law, that placed you in a position where you would be a prosecutor of Jesus in your own court. And you have testified under oath that this procedure is illegal by Hebrew law! That miscarriage of justice with the Sanhedrin in your home was illegal by your own law. That is correct, isn't it, Mr. Chief Justice Caiaphas?"

Caiaphas sputtered, then regained his composure: "I am not on trial here!"

Luckhoo banged his fist on his table and shouted, "You already answered that question in the affirmative . . . moments ago, Mr. Sanhedrin President!"

Caiaphas retaliated. "I've read a few other books before I came here and I am not required to make any statement that may incriminate me," he said sternly.

Luckhoo looked at the lord chief justice: "My lord, please let the record state that the witness refused to answer the question."

The lord chief justice nodded his head in the affirmative.

"Let the record so state. Proceed, Sir Luckhoo."

"Was it your plan to arrest Jesus?"

"Yes," Caiaphas said cautiously.

"When you were planning to arrest Jesus, did you expect that His disciples would retaliate with force?"

"Yes, we expected His disciples to be as erratic as that madman Jesus was in our temple when He caused havoc, turning tables over and whipping innocent men."

"Did you consider it a possibility that if there were such a physical confrontation, Jesus and some or all of His disciples might be killed in such a fight?"

Caiaphas's tone was patronizing: "My dear esteemed law colleague, you, above all people, who have successfully defended two hundred forty-five persons accused of murder, certainly should know that when there is violence, there is a chance somebody will be killed." Caiaphas's words were almost a jeer.

Darrow punched Houston in the ribs with his elbow and whispered, "By golly, it looks as if that old rock-ribbed religionist has done a little homework and he's as spunky as all get-out." Houston grinned and nodded her head.

Luckhoo ignored Caiaphas's negative insinuation and continued.

"Did Judas Iscariot, one of the disciples of Jesus, come to you and offer to sell you information by which Jesus would be betrayed into your hands?"

"The man came of his own free will, yes."

"To summarize the action that took place between this betrayer and you . . . Judas was paid thirty pieces of silver to inform you where and when you could find Jesus and to specifically point Him out because you did not have such exact up-to-date information, is that correct?"

"Basically, yes."

"And did you not pay Judas Iscariot exactly thirty pieces of silver for his betrayal services in this conspiracy?"

Darrow couldn't stand it any longer. He jumped to his feet with his long arm in the air.

"I object, Your Lordship. The esteemed Sir Luckhoo is trying to suggest that exercising the legal right of the chief justice of the Sanhedrin to arrest a Hebrew for a religious crime was a conspiracy. It obviously was because the chief justice wished to keep violence at a minimum, and not endanger his own nation, that he sought the best time and the best place to arrest Jesus."

Luckhoo spoke quickly, with his eyes closed.

"Thank you for that added bit of testimony for your witness! To assist the learned prosecutor, a conspiracy is the act of conspiring. With illegal trials being directed by the Sanhedrin President Caiaphas, with his paying blood money to Judas to betray the accused Jesus, and with this very group of conspirators getting involved in their own illegal trial, my question is entirely appropriate and admissible."

The lord chief justice nodded his head.

"Overruled. Proceed, Sir Luckhoo."

"My question, Reverend Caiaphas, was: Did you or did you not order exactly thirty pieces of silver to be paid to Judas Iscariot, the son of Simon of Kerioth, for information that would lead you to Jesus of Nazareth, the accused sitting there in that box?"

"I did!" His reply was tart.

"It was Judas who asked for an unspecified amount of money to betray Jesus into your hands, isn't that correct?"

"Yes, Judas asked for money. We did not volunteer to pay him to lead us to Jesus."

"Was it your choice to pay him thirty pieces, or was that at his request?"

"That was my choice, of course!"

"Why did you choose thirty pieces of silver?"

"I don't know why thirty pieces of silver. What difference does it make? I paid it to the man for the man. He led us to Jesus. It was my decision alone to pay him thirty pieces of silver, and I paid him THIRTY PIECES OF SILVER!" he shouted.

"And do you know what he did with the thirty pieces of silver?"

"Yes, I know!" Caiaphas spoke with exasperation.

"What did he do with them?"

"He brought them back to the temple the following morning and threw them on the temple floor."

"And what was said at that time?"

"As nearly as I can remember, Judas said that he was sorry that he had betrayed his Messiah. He said, 'I have sinned by betraying innocent blood.' One of our members simply told him that was his personal responsibility. He then threw the coins down on the temple floor and left dejectedly."

"What did you do with the coins?"

"One of our staff picked up the coins and was going to return them to our temple treasury, but they were defiled because they were the price of blood. Later our members took counsel and decided to purchase a potter's field so that we could bury strangers in it. It earned the name of Aceldama, the Field of Blood and it is called that to this day. We put the money to good use," Caiaphas said with pride.

"Do you know what happened to Judas or where he went?"

"Yes. One of our servants was instructed to follow him in the event that he would try to get a crowd together to release Jesus and thus attempt retribution for his disloyalty. We instructed our servant not to reveal himself to Judas under any circumstances. He came running back to report that Judas went to the side of one of the mountains, where a tree had grown out of the rock, and tied a rope to the tree and then to his neck. He immediately jumped off the side of the tree in an attempt to hang himself. However, the rope broke, and Judas fell headlong several hundred cubits below onto the rocks. His bowels gushed out onto the rocks. Our servant reported back that Judas was dead by suicide."

Caiaphas spoke with little emotion.

"Reverend Caiaphas, it was very compassionate that your loyal servant let a man take his own life without intervention. I believe that speaks very clearly of the quality of the leadership of the Sanhedrin and of your—"

Darrow leaped to his feet shouting, "I object, Your Lordship! Counsel has taken it upon himself to impugn the character of the chief justice of the Great Sanhedrin because of his own religious bias! Reverend Caiaphas is not on trial here. Jesus is! And He has already been convicted before the respected Jewish leader Annas, before the Sanhedrin late at night, before the Sanhedrin early the next morning, before Pilate, then before King Herod Antipas, and then back to the legal authority of that land, the Roman governor, who ordered that the accused be crucified! Regardless of the actions of Reverend Caiaphas and the Sanhedrin, the Roman governor was the one who had the authority to crucify or not to crucify the accused. He made the decision to crucify!" Darrow's face was blood red with anger.

Luckhoo turned calmly toward the bench where the lord chief justice sat listening. He spoke quietly.

"My lord, the case against the accused concerns whether or not He has committed a crime of capital fraud, whether or not His role as a religious leader of His day and of our day would indicate that Jesus of Nazareth is the promised Messiah of the Jewish people and of the world itself. The weight of the evidence against Him is primarily from live witnesses of some of the events in the life of Jesus. The witnesses cannot confirm or deny that Jesus is qualified to be that Jewish Messiah. They only bring authenticity to the happening of historic events. It is only by the fulfillment of every one of the predictions of the promised Jewish Messiah that you have the Jewish Messiah! The defense is now proving that these ancient predictions happened, regardless of the bias of those who witnessed their happening."

Luckhoo pointed to his Bible, lying in front of him on the desk. He repeatedly tapped the book with his finger as he talked.

"The defense is also providing undeniable proof, beyond a shadow of a doubt, that Joseph Caiaphas was and is prejudiced against the Nazarene and that he did everything in his power to destroy Jesus. Reverend Caiaphas was an adjudicator of illegal trials against Jesus. In his personal rejection of Jesus of Nazareth as the Messiah, he unwittingly fulfilled ancient prophecy. While this witness holds an important place in history, while his life is intertwined with that of the accused, Jesus, and while he was the highest religious personage of his place and his time, Joseph Caiaphas still expresses only his biased viewpoint. Although he may display the virtue of sincerity, the defense believes him to be sincerely wrong!"

Luckhoo nodded to the lord chief justice and waited for him to speak.

"Members of the jury, Reverend Caiaphas, Mr. Darrow, and Sir Luckhoo, we are not trying the president of the Sanhedrin for any offense here in this trial. Bias and prejudice are particular tendencies or inclinations within a person that prevent him from being impartial. While Reverend Caiaphas has a right to his bias, prejudice, or interest as to how he performed his duties as president of the Sanhedrin in a nation that was governed by a foreign power, the jury is to consider such bias, prejudice, or interest in the deliberations. The objection is overruled."

The lord chief justice turned and looked at Darrow, then at the jury.

"You are to regard the comments by the prosecution concerning the Roman governor and his authority to crucify and his decision to do so as hearsay evidence. You may proceed in your cross-examination of the witness, Sir Luckhoo."

Luckhoo nodded toward the bench. He closed his eyes and continued his questioning of the high priest.

"Reverend Caiaphas, would you state that the Hebrew

law was very strict, particularly in capital cases that came before the Sanhedrin?"

"Yes." Caiaphas spoke in a monotone.

"Was the charge against Jesus one of blasphemy, which was punishable by death by stoning?"

"That was one way it was punishable, yes."

"Was blasphemy punishable under Hebrew law by crucifixion?"

"No. Crucifixion was a Roman form of punishment, not Hebrew."

"Reverend Caiaphas, I am going to cite some points of Hebrew law. If I am incorrect on any one of them, please stop me. First, if one witness failed to agree with another, the evidence of both was invalid. Second, the accused had the right to give evidence in his own defense. Third, even after a trial and conviction, sentence could not be passed on that same day. Fourth, the members of the Sanhedrin could gather the next day in plenary session when each would again make a declaration of guilt or innocence. Fifth, a capital charge, which could require the death penalty, could not be tried at night. Am I correct so far, Reverend Caiaphas?"

Caiaphas stared at his hands, still clutching the edge of the witness box. "Yes! Correct!"

"Sixth, Hebrew law made it mandatory that the arresting officials inform the accused of the charge for which he was being arrested. Seventh, the custom was to warn the witnesses that if clear testimony failed to come up to the required standard of strict corroboration, not only would the accused be acquitted, but they, the witnesses, would be sentenced to death by stoning. Eighth, the Jewish code states that under no circumstances was a man, known to be at enmity with the accused, permitted to occupy a position among the judges. Ninth, the Hebrew law prohibited the Sanhedrin from meeting on a Friday at night or during celebration of any of the feasts. Tenth, unless a prisoner has first been lawfully arrested, no Hebrew court can legally inquire and acquire any jurisdiction over that prisoner. Eleventh, any judgment, verdict, or sentence imposed by a court devoid of jurisdiction would be a nullity and completely void. Twelfth, the burden of proof was on the witnesses to show and to establish by the testimony and evidence, beyond a reasonable doubt and to a moral certainty, that the accused was guilty of an offense within the jurisdiction of the Sanhedrin. Thirteenth, a judge in the trial had no authority to interfere in the trial, and if he did, the trial was ended."

Luckhoo opened his eyes and looked pointedly at Caiaphas. He slammed his fist on the desk in front of him.

"Are these points of the Hebrew law that you so zealously sought to enforce, Reverend Caiaphas, and are they correct as I quoted them to you?"

The high priest's hands pressed against the side of the witness box so hard that his knuckles turned white from the pressure. His head tilted forward, and his eyes fastened on the worn wooden floor in front of him.

His life seemed to pass quickly before him. He remembered his parents and the pride that they expressed when he entered the priesthood. He remembered the zeal that he once had for Jehovah God and his burning hope of the coming Messiah in the early days of his ministry.

He remembered his fashionable marriage to the daughter of the high priest, Annas. It was then he found himself in a world of politics and religion where his zeal for Jehovah God was in conflict with religious political power.

Caiaphas came back to reality when he heard the voice of Luckhoo directed at him.

"Did you hear me, sir? Are these statements correct according to your Hebrew law? Yes or no?"

There was a catch in Caiaphas's voice: "Yes! Yes!"

Luckhoo continued in stern tones.

"Let me go over those points of Hebrew law according to what is historically and legally written in Exhibit A, the Bible. First, your witnesses did not agree. Second, the accused had the right to give evidence in His own defense. Third, He was arrested, tried, convicted, and crucified all on the same day. Fourth, the Sanhedrin did not meet the next day in a plenary session to confirm the sentence of guilt or innocence. Fifth, the so-called main trial was held at night, which was illegal for a capital charge requiring the death penalty. Sixth, Jesus was not informed of the charge when He was arrested. Seventh, the witnesses were not informed about their false testimony and they were not stoned to death when their testimonies conflicted. Eighth, you, Chief Justice Caiaphas, and every one of those council members there at that miscarriage of justice that night were at enmity with the accused. Ninth, it was not only an illegal Friday Sabbath session, but it was a feast day of the Passover as well when this so unlawful trial was held. Tenth, since Jesus was therefore unlawfully arrested, He was unlawfully tried. Eleventh, since He was unlawfully arrested and unlawfully tried, the judgment of that body of men should have been null and void. Twelfth, there was never any corroborated testimony or evidence that established any guilt of the accused. And thirteenth, you, the president of the Sanhedrin, violated your law by standing in the center of the tribunal, and you applied the most solemn and the strictest constitutional Jewish oath possible to the accused, Jesus of Nazareth."

Sir Luckhoo's eyes looked like two hot coals shining in a fiery face. He was clearly agitated as he faced a man who had perverted the justice system to which he was entrusted and he had used it to condemn the man Luckhoo believed to be the Messiah. He almost shouted at the high priest.

"Mr. Chief Justice, every one of those statements is not only true, but every one of those statements proves that your arrest, trial, conviction, and crucifixion of Jesus Christ of Nazareth constituted an illegal miscarriage of Hebrew justice. Isn't that correct?"

Caiaphas's body shook with sobs. His face was twisted with the pain of revisiting his past. Luckhoo's face was void of mercy. He pointed his finger directly at the high priest. His voice remained at an intense level.

"Joseph Caiaphas, I adjure you by the living God, tell the jury the truth. Were your arrest and your trials of Jesus of Nazareth legal and proper under your Hebrew law? Yea or nay?"

Caiaphas whimpered, "No . . . no . . . no . . . oh, no! But you don't understand. He blasphemed! He said He was the Son of God . . . the Christ!"

Luckhoo shouted, "He is the Son of God . . . the Christ. Jesus of Nazareth IS THE MESSIAH!"

Darrow shot off the bench, almost jumping into the air. His wig slipped to one side of his head. He put it back into place with one hand while pointing with the other at Luckhoo.

"I object, Your Lordship. We are in this court to determine whether or not the accused, Jesus of Nazareth, is or is not the Messiah. It is improper for the defense to insert his personal beliefs into this trial. If he wants to be a witness, let him call himself as a witness! Otherwise, let him keep his religious beliefs to himself!"

The lord chief justice gave affirmation to Darrow. He spoke pointedly to Luckhoo.

"Sir Luckhoo, the messiahship of Jesus has not been proven or disproven at this point of the trial. The jury is instructed to disregard the defense counsel's remarks to the effect that the accused, Jesus of Nazareth, is the Son of God, the Christ, and the Messiah. You may proceed with your cross-examination, Sir Luckhoo."

There was an awkward pause. Luckhoo spoke authoritatively in an effort to again control the situation. Caiaphas had regained his composure.

"Reverend Caiaphas, as a Sadducee, your basic belief is only in the written law of Moses, and you are against any teaching that is not based on the written Word of God, given through Moses. Is that correct?"

"Yes, that is correct."

"And as a Sadducee, your belief is to reject the oral teachings of the rabbis. Is that true?"

"Most of them, yes. Our belief is in the written teachings only."

"As a Sadducee, does your opinion lean toward the rejection of the beliefs of the Pharisees, for the most part?"

"Yes. In many cases, we feel that the Pharisees are in conflict with the tradition of the Mosaic Jews."

"Would one of your views be the rejection of the belief in angels?"

"Yes. Sadducees do not believe in angels."

"What about demons or demonic spirits?"

"The Sadducees do not believe in them either."

"And what do the Sadducees believe about the resurrection of God's chosen people after death? Do you believe in the resurrection after death?"

"Absolutely not!"

"Then your concept of the Messiah is as a priestly King who would deliver Israel from the heel of the oppressor and restore Israel to its former glory. Is that a fair statement?"

"Yes." Caiaphas's answer was flat, with no emotion.

"Then you do not believe that the promised Messiah would die, on a cross, as the substitutionary sacrifice for humankind's sins. Is that correct?"

"I believe only what is written in the law of Moses. Jehovah God spoke to Moses that there would be a priestly kingdom."

"And is that your viewpoint of the Messiah?"

"Yes!" Caiaphas felt as if he were being challenged.

"Then you consider the rest of the Scriptures, the Prophets and the Writings, as mere tradition?"

"That is correct."

"But you are aware of the Prophets and the Writings, written by great Jewish leaders, including King David, is that correct?"

"Yes, and I have studied them."

"In your study of the Prophets and the Writings, did you find there were prophetic Scriptures concerning a promised Hebrew Messiah, written under the inspiration of Jehovah God?"

"The Pharisees and the Essenes believed that there were such!" His reply was crisp.

"Were these religious predictions, these traditions, as you call them, were they written hundreds of years before you were the high priest?"

"Yes, they were."

"I should like to test your memory concerning your Pentateuch, which are the books of Genesis, Exodus, Leviticus, Numbers, and Deuteronomy in the Old Testament of Exhibit A, the Bible. Prophetically, these books make a number of statements concerning a Messiah. I ask that you affirm or deny the authenticity of the Scriptures that I will read to you, as best you can remember, Reverend Caiaphas."

Caiaphas interrupted Luckhoo with a curt reply. He looked at the jury and smiled confidently. He then turned and looked back at Luckhoo.

"You are not the only one with the ability to recall, sir. I believe I will be able to tell you in what books they are found, even in your Exhibit A . . . your Bible!"

Luckhoo bowed slightly. "My compliments, Reverend Caiaphas, for this display of your astute ability. Is it written that the promised Messiah would be a male, the seed of a woman?"

"Yes. In the third book of Genesis." Caiaphas offered a bravado smile to Luckhoo. "Verse fifteen!"

"Of the seed of Abraham, Isaac, and Jacob?"

"Yes. In two books. One is Genesis and the other, Numbers . . . sir!" Caiaphas was very self-assured.

"That He would be from the tribe of Judah?"

Caiaphas thought for a second, then answered. "Yes. Moses' book of Genesis. Chapter forty-nine, verse ten."

Luckhoo stood for a moment and looked at the man before him. Though Caiaphas appeared to be in opposition to Luckhoo's beliefs as was Darrow, Luckhoo respected the knowledge of Caiaphas, just as he did that of Darrow. Caiaphas understood this, and he appeared to be using it to his advantage.

"Was it written that He would be heir to the throne of David?"

"Yes. Written in the book of the prophet Isaiah."

"That He would be born in Bethlehem?"

"Yes. Written in the book of Micah, a prophet."

"Reverend Caiaphas, was it written that He would be born of a virgin?"

Caiaphas was proud of his ability to remember the location of these prophetic Scriptures, especially since he had spent only a few hours studying Exhibit A, the Bible, before taking the witness stand. This reminded him of the time when he was in rabbinical school as a young boy, at the top of his class.

His shoulders began to rise, and he stuck his chest out a bit. A slight gleam came into his eyes.

"It was written by the prophet Isaiah."

"That innocent children would be destroyed around the time of His birth?"

"Yes, I remember that. It was foretold by the prophet Jeremiah." He put his hand on his beard and appeared to be thinking, trying to recall something from the past. He was quiet for a moment and then began to speak. He appeared to be in his own world for a moment or so.

"That happened in the Bethlehem area when I was a young student. Strange, isn't it? Prophecy happening in your own time. Very strange."

He came back to the courtroom only when he heard Luckhoo ask him the next question.

"Reverend Caiaphas . . . was it written that the young Messiah would be taken to Egypt, then called back to Israel?"

"Yes. From the book of Hosea." His voice was vague, but he was fully alert.

"Was it prophesied that the Messiah would be preceded by a forerunner?"

"Yes, it was. That was written by the prophets Isaiah and Malachi."

"That He would be declared by Jehovah to be His Son?"

"Prophesied in our great King David's psalms."

"Was it written that He would minister to His people in the area of Galilee?"

Caiaphas paused for a moment, thought, then spoke with assurance.

"That, too, was written by the prophet Isaiah."

Luckhoo noted that Caiaphas gave specific references only when he was quoting the books of Moses. He began to raise his voice.

"Rejected by His own people?"

"You need not shout, sir. I can hear you . . . plainly. The answer is yes. That was written by the prophet Isaiah."

"Prophesied that He would have a triumphal entry into the city of Jerusalem?"

Caiaphas's countenance changed as if it had suddenly turned from day to night. He leaned forward with his chin out. He suddenly realized the direction that Luckhoo had taken him. He felt used and he was angry about it.

"If you consider your Jesus riding into Jerusalem on that little donkey and with those few pitiful children paid to shout their Hosannas as—"

Luckhoo interrupted him. His finger was pointing at Caiaphas like an arrow.

"I didn't ask your opinion! I asked if that was one of the prophecies of the holy writings. Yes or no?"

Caiaphas's answer was seasoned with bitterness.

"Yes. The prophet Zechariah proclaimed this of the true Messiah, the King." He blurted out his answer.

"That He would be betrayed by a friend."

"David wrote of this in his psalms." Caiaphas's voice wavered, and he shifted uneasily from one foot to the other. His answers were cautious.

"And wasn't it prophesied by Isaiah that He would be silent to His accusers . . . He would be spat upon . . . His body would be beaten . . . and He would be crucified with transgressors of the law?"

"Yes, that is true," Caiaphas answered haltingly.

"That He would be accused by false witnesses?"

Caiaphas began to shout, "They weren't false . . . they weren't false. They were confused . . . just confused!"

"Isn't it true that the prophet Zechariah predicted that He would be betrayed for exactly thirty pieces of silver, Reverend Chief Priest Joseph Caiaphas?" Luckhoo's voice was intense as he once again pointed an accusing finger at the witness. Caiaphas hated for people to point at him in such a fashion. He felt a deep sense of guilt.

"Yes, it says that . . . but that was just coincidence, you hear!"

Luckhoo spoke even more loudly, tightening the jaws of a verbal vise on his witness.

"And didn't your own King David write that He would be sneered at and mocked . . . that they would cast lots for His very clothing . . . that He would cry out these very words . . . 'Eli, Eli, lama sabachthani' . . . 'My God, My God, why have You forsaken Me?'"

Caiaphas's voice seemed to tremble more with each answer that he gave. He grasped the sides of the witness box as if he wanted to shake it with all of his fury, but only his body quivered.

"Yes, King David wrote it. Yes, he did!"

Luckhoo shook his fist at Caiaphas.

"When Jesus of Nazareth hung on that Roman cross of execution . . . when He was in a state of suffering that could cause any man to cry out anything that might come to a mind filled with pain . . . didn't your informants tell you that the exact words of Jesus were 'Eli, Eli, lama sabachthani . . . My God, My God, why have You forsaken Me?'"

Caiaphas responded with a groan: "My God, my God! Yes, they were!"

Darrow saw that the creditability of his star witness was being impugned, and he jumped to his feet.

"Your Lordship, I object! I object! The defense counsel is badgering this witness!"

The lord chief justice kept his eyes on the witness.

"Overruled."

Luckhoo lowered his voice, but he continued to put pressure on his witness.

"Reverend Caiaphas, did not the holy Scriptures also prophesy through the prophet Zechariah that His body would be pierced . . . and prophesy in the Psalms that none of His bones would be broken . . . and predict in Isaiah that He would be buried with the rich at His death?" Do you remember these writings?"

"Oh, I don't know." He cried out, as if in pain, "Oh, yes . . . yes!" His voice rose with each word. Caiaphas was clearly losing control of his emotions with each question. His brain was frantically searching his memory of the holy Scriptures for the right answers, and at the same time, the haunting similarities between the prophecies and what he now remembered of the life of Jesus of Nazareth brought fear into his life. Sweat was pouring out from under his elaborate headdress.

The defense counsel had not let up with his relentless questioning of the high priest. Luckhoo's voice was booming.

"And didn't King David prophetically write that this Messiah, who would die on this earth, would rise again from the dead and ascend on high to sit at the right hand of Jehovah God? Isn't that what the holy Scriptures say, Reverend High Priest Joseph Caiaphas? Isn't that what they prophesied? Isn't that what you heard from the people concerning this Jesus of Nazareth? Joseph Caiaphas, I adjure you by the living God . . . are not these things . . . TRUTH?"

Caiaphas was trembling. His grip on the side of the witness box was the only thing that seemed to keep him from falling into a heap. His once arrogant voice now quivered from fear. He turned his eyes toward the prisoner, Jesus.

"Yes . . . yes . . . oh, forgive me . . . yes!" Between sobs he blurted out, "Maybe I was . . . wrong. Maybe . . . I was too zealous . . . for my country. Maybe I . . . acted too quickly. Maybe I should have . . . listened to the . . . members of the Sanhedrin . . . who . . . believed You were . . . the true Messiah. Maybe . . . I wouldn't have . . . had those terrible nightmares . . . the rest . . . of my life!"

Caiaphas was a pathetic-looking sight, a man looking back to a time in his life when he had made a historic decision, and now he was in total doubt as to his wisdom in the course of action he had taken.

Every eye in the courtroom was on Caiaphas. No one moved. No one said a word. Only the sound of his sobbing was heard—and that of the ticking of the clock.

Luckhoo spoke in a quiet voice, his arms at his sides, his eyes fixed on the spent witness.

"Joseph Caiaphas, you have testified in this court of law that it was you, and you alone, who determined that the sum of money paid to Judas Iscariot, the betrayer of Jesus of Nazareth, was exactly thirty pieces of silver. That blood money was returned to you at the temple, thrown down on the floor, and in your own testimony, you stated that you bought the potter's field for thirty pieces of silver."

Luckhoo looked down at his Bible on his desk and turned the pages. Then he picked up the Bible and began to read.

"I am reading from Exhibit A, the Bible, Reverend Caiaphas. I am reading from the book of the prophet Zechariah, chapter eleven, verses twelve and thirteen . . . written over four hundred and eighty years before you and Jesus of Nazareth were born: 'Then I said to them, "If it is agreeable to you, give me my wages; and if not, refrain." So they weighed out for my wages thirty pieces of silver. And the LORD said to me, "Throw it to the potter"—that princely price they set on me. So I took the thirty pieces of silver and threw them into the house of the LORD for the potter.'"

Caiaphas stared at Luckhoo, hardly believing what he was hearing. He vividly remembered it was his decision to pay Judas the thirty pieces of silver. He said nothing, but he stood as if he could not move.

"I have one more question of you, Chief Priest Joseph Caiaphas. With the prophecies you have verified with your own mouth from the holy Scriptures, written by Moses, by the prophets, and by King David, hundreds of years before you became the chief priest of Israel . . . and with what you know of the life of the man called Jesus of Nazareth," Luckhoo paused, "is it now your learned opinion that Jesus of

Nazareth could be the prophesied Messiah of the Jewish peoples?"

In that moment Caiaphas struggled with his long life as a Hebrew priest, the years of oppression by the hated Romans, the apostasy that had crept into his reign as chief priest of Israel, and his hasty actions of his past.

His face was contorted with the pain of the words he was trying to form. His words came haltingly, laden with the fear of the unknown.

"I don't know! I still don't know! It's all there! But I don't know for sure! I don't have the faith to believe! I don't know! If there was just one more sign! If Jesus would just do one more miracle . . . maybe then I could believe for sure. Maybe then!"

Luckhoo looked at the broken man who was now staring blankly at the floor in front of the witness box. With a note of remorse in his voice, Luckhoo said, "Joseph Caiaphas, by the end of this trial . . . perhaps you . . . will know. But for you . . . it is too late!"

Caiaphas fell to his knees in the witness box. His hands and arms felt like chains that bound him so that he couldn't run and hide. His regal headdress fell to the floor.

Luckhoo looked at the lord chief justice and said quietly, "I have no further examination of this witness, my lord."

"Mr. Darrow, do you wish to reexamine?"

Darrow had disgust written on his face. He said nothing but shook his head back and forth.

The lord chief justice then spoke to the usher of the court.

"Sir Steinle, please usher Reverend Caiaphas back to his seat."

Steinle stood, walked to the witness box, and pried Caiaphas's fingers loose from it. His arms fell to his sides. Steinle stooped and picked him up, standing him on his feet. The usher picked up Caiaphas's headdress, took him by one arm, and walked the chief priest back to his seat in the witness section.

The man who walked into the witness box as the arrogant and self-assured Chief Priest Joseph Caiaphas now sat in the witness section as a defeated, haggard-looking man.

Luckhoo was having an internal battle; he had compassion for the man who once earnestly desired to seek the things of God in his life. Somewhere, that desire had changed to seeking the power that such knowledge can bring. Luckhoo hated that as much as anyone.

Darrow sat in his seat, stunned. One of his prime witnesses had just broken down in an emotional scene and almost publicly professed that the accused was the Messiah of the Jewish people!

He turned angrily to Houston and whispered, "That sniveling wimp! He's nearly blown apart everything we've established with his pious display of religious repentance!"

No one seemed to have heard the tolling of the bells at St. Sepulchre and Westminster during the intense testimony of the Jewish high priest. It was almost noon.

The jury and the spectators seemed to be wrung out by the confrontation between Caiaphas and Luckhoo.

The lord chief justice looked at the clock and banged his gavel, recessing the court for the morning.

For Luckhoo, the morning had been a bitter victory.

7
WITNESSES FOR THE PROSECUTION

AFTERNOON, DAY TWO

Time seemed in a rush to be counted. People were streaming into the courtroom as the two famous tower bells chimed one o'clock simultaneously.

The lord chief justice opened his door and entered the courtroom. The bailiff stood with his scepter and banged it on the floor with the usual pomp and circumstance. All in the courtroom sat down, anticipating an exciting afternoon session.

Darrow took a deep breath, straightened his wig, and looked at his notes. Then he whispered to Houston, "Well, this old Ohio boy ain't done yet." He stood up to his full height and looked at the lord chief justice.

The lord chief justice spoke to Darrow.

"The prosecution may call the next witness."

Darrow looked slowly around the courtroom from the lord chief justice, to the jury, to the accused, then back to the jury. Fastening his eyes on the jury, he spoke in a loud voice.

"I call as the next witness for the prosecution Pontius Pilate, the Roman governor of Judea."

Again the courtroom sounded like bees in a beehive as the bailiff stood at his post and called the witness.

"Pontius Pilate, governor of Judea. Call for Pontius Pilate, governor of Judea."

A handsome man of medium build with gray hair moved deliberately from the witness section. He was wearing an expensive tunic, the mark of his equestrian, or upper middle class, rank, which was next only to the senatorial rank of Rome.

A narrow bordering strip of purple ran the length of his garment. Over the tunic Pilate wore the traditional toga, which he tastefully draped across his shoulder and down around his waist. Gold bracelets were around his tanned arms, and the gold chain encircling his neck held a medallion that bore the image of Tiberius Caesar.

Pilate held his hands closely to his sides as he walked like a soldier toward the witness box, showing the pride of his ancestry. He was from the family of Pontii.

His dark eyes shone as he turned into the witness box and stood at attention. The bailiff handed him a Bible on which to place his left hand, and he reluctantly obliged. On his right hand was a ring bearing the seal of the Roman Empire.

"Do you understand the language being spoken here today?" asked the bailiff.

Pilate's answer was assertive. He threw his head back slightly, with a flair.

"Sir, I am a Roman, educated with the finest tutors available in the world!"

"Thank you, sir. Please repeat this after me: I solemnly

swear to tell the truth, the whole truth, and nothing but the truth, so help me God."

Pilate repeated the statement with a heavy Italian accent as he looked first at the lord chief justice, then at the two barristers, then at the accused in the dock. Seeing Jesus, he quickly placed both hands at his sides. His attention then focused on the prosecutor, Darrow.

The lord chief justice spoke in his usual calm voice.

"Mr. Darrow, you may proceed with the examination of this witness."

"Thank you, Your Lordship. Governor Pilate, you were the governor of Judea from A.D. 26 to A.D. 36, so appointed by Tiberius Caesar himself, is that correct, sir?"

"That is correct."

"You have heard the testimony of the Jewish high priest, Joseph Caiaphas, given here in this courtroom. Is that right?"

"Yes, I heard his testimony."

"And specifically, have you heard his testimony as to events that involved Reverend Caiaphas and yourself?"

"Yes, I have. His remarks were considerably more respectful to me and to Rome when the little Jewish priest said them back in Jerusalem!"

Darrow knew that he was handling a delicate situation with the rivalry between Caiaphas and Pilate. He wanted no infighting, but he wanted desperately to confirm some of the testimony of his chief witness, Caiaphas. Rather than try to cover up the remark, Darrow offered measured questions and continued in a matter-of-fact way.

"Without reference to his personal observations and comments, Governor, did Reverend Caiaphas tell the events in their general order of occurrence, and did he give the jury generally correct information concerning the events that took place between Mr. Caiaphas and yourself?"

"Disclaiming his petty references to his bravado before me, the order of events and the general content of conversations were generally correct."

"Are you familiar with the Jewish religious concept of a Messiah, Governor?"

"From my ten years as the Roman governor of Judea, I am aware that the Jews have several concepts of their fabled Messiah."

Darrow smiled slightly.

"Governor Pilate, is the name John the Baptizer familiar to you?"

"It is."

"Will you tell us what you know of this man?"

"Word was brought directly to me from my spies . . ."

Pilate paused and looked directly at Caiaphas in the witness section and spoke with a smirk on his face.

". . . that I had planted in the Sanhedrin . . ," he turned back to look directly at Darrow, "concerning an unusual Jewish man causing a stir in the badlands east of Jerusalem toward the Jordan. The people were calling him the Prophet, the Christ, and Elijah, the name of one of their departed prophets. The man claimed that he was none of these, but he said he was 'the voice of one crying in the wilderness.' The Baptist, as some of us called him, was telling anyone who would believe him that a new kingdom was coming and that people should repent from something called sin, whatever that is."

Pilate seemed to be taunting the Jewish high priest and his religion. For years he had wanted to punish Caiaphas for the frustration he had caused, but Rome had kept a tight rein on the procurator. He quickly looked back at Darrow.

"The Baptist appeared to be in his early thirties. He was clothed in camel's hair, and he wore a leather belt around his waist. They said that he lived on locusts and wild honey. And, oh, yes . . . we discovered that he was a blood cousin of the accused, Jesus."

"Were you concerned about this man?"

"Somewhat. People, by the droves, were going out to see him. But you should remember, the entertainment around Jerusalem was not at all like that in Rome. The people would walk for miles to see some strange person with any kind of a different message. We saw that a lot of people were patronizing this new kingdom and repentance thing that the Baptist was preaching."

"Was he a religious problem for you?"

"Not at all. But one of the responsibilities vested in me by Caesar was to keep the peace. Therefore, part of my job was to be interested in crowds. This man drew crowds. He even had the Jewish chief priest and his crowd very concerned about what he was doing. They were out there watching the Baptist practice his religious water ritual, called baptism. We also learned he did baptize his blood cousin Jesus in water at one of his riverside rites."

"He got into trouble with Herod. How did that happen?" Darrow asked.

"Unfortunately for him, he stepped very hard on the toes of Herodias, the scheming wife of Herod Antipas, the tetrarch of Galilee and Perea. The Baptist had the misfortune to lose his head over the matter of loudly pointing out that Herod had married the wife of his own brother. Although the news of the dramatic death of the Baptist was all over Palestine in less than a week, there were no riots or demonstrations on his behalf. Our spies reported that even Jesus did not change what He was doing!"

"Governor, was Jesus' baptism in the river Jordan the first time you had heard of the accused?"

"It was."

"Will you tell us of your knowledge of Jesus from that point, Governor Pilate?"

"We didn't hear much about Him until He began to gather a dozen or so followers. Then He began to preach some of the things that the Baptist had preached, which were not particularly offensive. I'll say this for Him, the man was a charismatic crowd gatherer like His older cousin, the Baptist. The only difference was that this younger cousin got much bigger crowds . . . so we had spies attending and listening to what was going on with Him."

"Was He a rabble-rouser, as Reverend Caiaphas had indicated?"

Pilate chuckled and looked at Caiaphas.

"He presented no threat to Rome or me! But Jesus had the high priest and his inept staff of guards so frightened of Him that He was able to devastate the outer court of the temple all by Himself one day while the weak guards looked on. That kind of activity made me yearn for a real circus, one such as we had back in Rome."

Darrow was working hard to eliminate any rivalry between Pilate and Caiaphas, yet Pilate seemed determined to continue the verbal battle. He hit the problem head-on.

"Governor Pilate, as the highest Roman authority in Jerusalem, you did not get along well with the Jewish high priest, Caiaphas, is that correct?"

"Let's say that the high priest and I did not see eye to eye on many issues."

"But did you respect Caiaphas for his knowledge of Jewish religious law?"

"To some degree. After all, he was a Sadducee."

"Governor, did you respect him for trying to keep his people from rising up against Rome at other times?"

"Some, yes. Again, it was not because of his respect for Rome, but because he wanted to keep his people from being wiped off the face of the earth by the superior force of the Roman legions."

Darrow was assessing the situation while Pilate spoke. He knew that he had to get Pilate off the subject of his disdain for Caiaphas. Darrow made his move.

"Governor Pilate, you are a cultured and educated man, are you not?"

"In the sight of the greatest civilization on the earth, I am of the equestrian rank, next only to the senatorial rank. I believe that speaks for itself, sir."

"I would say so, Governor."

Luckhoo stood at his desk and addressed the lord chief justice with frustration evident in his face.

"My lord, I don't know how long we can handle this pomp and circumstance by my esteemed colleague, Mr. Darrow. He brings in his witnesses and then proceeds to shower us all with accolades of titles and with the glowing attributes of the witnesses. He wishes to make them appear flawless. I trust we are not going to suffer through such dribble."

Darrow turned to his right and looked at the lord chief justice, interrupting Luckhoo without acknowledging his objection.

"Your Lordship, I wish to establish that my witnesses are quality individuals. They lived at a time when standards of excellence were being set in education and culture. Since the defense brought these witnesses and their backgrounds up, I should like to say that both of these historic leaders represented their respective positions with creditability and rightfully reserved their places in history. We must judge them from their perspective and how they viewed history."

"Objection overruled. You may proceed, Mr. Darrow."

"Thank you, Your Lordship."

Darrow breathed easier. He felt as if he had wiped out some of the enmity between Caiaphas and Pilate, again established his witnesses' creditability, and made Luckhoo look like a complainer.

"Governor Pilate, from your observations of Reverend Caiaphas, would you say that it was the desire of the high priest to maintain order among his people?"

"Yes, I have had long conversations with him on this matter."

"And were both of you in agreement on the issue of law and order?"

"We were as close as we could get."

"What do you mean by that?"

"We were the Roman conquerors. They were our Jewish subjects!" He spoke with scorn.

"Did you talk to the Reverend Caiaphas about the man called Jesus of Nazareth?"

"We had several conversations about Him."

"Would you summarize those conversations for us, Governor?"

"Caiaphas came to me for advice and told me that there was a groundswell of emotion among the Jewish people that

Jesus claimed to be one of their messiahs. The Jews were always nationalistic, and their rally point for this was hope in the coming of their Messiah-King. Caiaphas had told me of his problems, the ones that Jesus had caused him. Knowing Caiaphas the way I do, he probably asked for my advice so that I would be biased against Jesus some time in the future. Instead, I chose to take a position of Jus Representationis—the right of representing or being represented by another—for Jesus, for the sake of argument with Caiaphas."

A smirk came across Pilate's face as he turned again to where Caiaphas was sitting. Caiaphas did not respond but continued to stare at the floor.

"After all, arguing with Caiaphas was always entertaining. I rarely trusted what he told me so I always had my loyal spies telling me what Jesus was doing and saying." He adjusted his tunic. "I knew of Jesus' open pacifist preaching, of His so-called healing of people who appeared to be sick, and of His supposed casting out of spirits from people who either had been possessed or were excellent thespians."

A perplexed look came over Pilate's face. He looked as if he were searching for some thought in his past, momentarily forgetting that he was in the courtroom.

"I can't explain a couple of things that He did. My sources verified more than one occasion when Jesus fed thousands of people from just a few loaves of bread and several fish. At another time He was confronted about His paying taxes, and He used some sort of magic or a miracle and provided money for taxes." Pilate mused. "He even supported Caesar on at least one occasion when some of Caiaphas's friends were trying to trap the man with words."

Pilate shook his head as if he had been somewhere in another world. He regained his composure by a faked laugh.

"Did Reverend Caiaphas and you agree about the things you were seeing and hearing concerning Jesus?"

"Well, yes and no. Caiaphas believed that what He was doing was all illusions and tricks of magic. I believed that He could be a god who had come to earth or that He was simply a person endowed with magic. I never felt, as Caiaphas did, that Jesus was a threat to Rome. He felt that Jesus was a threat to Rome and to the Jewish nation as well. Later on, I could see that he had a point."

"What was that point, Governor Pilate?"

"The man was drawing very large crowds. I mentioned the thousands that He fed. Anyone with that kind of power could cause problems to any reigning power if He chose to do so. Caiaphas probably was correct in his assessment that at the time of the Jewish Passover, when there would be an additional quarter of a million or so people in Jerusalem, Jesus could be a dangerous leader. A force like that could certainly wipe out any Roman garrison we had within miles of the city, especially if they possessed weapons of any kind. And there were ripples of talk, among some of the Jews, that Jesus was their Messiah-King."

"I want to take you to the year A.D. 30, and to your arrival in Jerusalem from your headquarters in Caesarea. Why did you go to Jerusalem just prior to the Jewish Passover holiday?"

Pilate continued to be a very polished and professional witness, pausing for a moment before he made any statement. His manner was that of a statesman, although his reputation included that of being a brutal oppressor.

Pilate stood up straight. "I was their ruler! It was my responsibility to be in Jerusalem. Should any insurrection break out with the Jews, I needed to be there to direct my troops."

"What was the first thing you heard concerning the accused upon your arrival, Governor?"

"My faithful spies came to me after we had settled at the Praetorium. They brought me up to date about events in Jerusalem. That included Jesus and His activities. They reported that they had seen a large number of Jews who had hailed Jesus as 'the Son of David' as He rode into the city on a donkey. That disturbed me a bit because the Jews were ever looking for someone to replace their famous dead King David."

"Did you consider this parade threatening?"

"It is hard for me to visualize any king arriving to lead his people riding on a donkey instead of in a chariot." He sneered somewhat as he looked at Jesus for the first time. Jesus looked back with no show of emotion.

"When next did you hear of the accused?"

"One of the cohorts in Jerusalem arrived to tell me that Jesus had caused a commotion in the Jewish temple outer courts. Reverend Caiaphas and the highly esteemed Reverend Annas seemed to have set up shop in that area of the temple, and this Jesus took offense to it. He became somewhat physical and tore a few things up, but none of the great temple guard did anything about it. I saw no reason to arrest the man on a disturbance charge."

"Did the accused do anything else to stir up unrest?"

"Oh, He continued to prick the hides of the puffed-up Pharisees by calling them names. I had to agree with Him on that count." Pilate laughed nervously.

Darrow continued his efforts to bring Pilate and the high

priest to some point of agreement against the accused, Jesus, but Pilate resisted.

"King Herod Antipas also came into Jerusalem at the time of the Passover. Did you have contact with him concerning the accused?"

"No, although I saw that old fox at several dinner parties, we never discussed Jesus."

"When did you next hear from the Jewish high priest?"

"He sent me a communication by messenger to the effect that he again was concerned greatly about this Jesus and that he planned to arrest Him on religious charges, using the temple guard."

"And what did you do?"

"I sent a note in return that he could arrest anyone he chose for religious violations, but that executionary power was not granted to the Sanhedrin by Rome. I told Caiaphas that I knew that Jesus had stepped on his and his father-in-law Annas's toes at the temple, but that was their concern and not mine. I also told him that I would commit a few Roman troops to arresting Jesus since there was a possibility of a disturbance breaking out."

"Governor, when did you next hear from Chief Justice Caiaphas?"

"It was on their Passover Friday when I received another note from Caiaphas."

"And what did that note say?"

"He stated that one of Jesus' disciples had led them to Jesus and His other disciples and that Jesus had been arrested. He also said that the Hebrew would be given a trial by the Sanhedrin. I did not reply because my troop commander had already provided me with that information."

"Your next contact with either Reverend Caiaphas or Jesus was when?"

"That morning, around seven o'clock, I sat in judgment at the tribunal. I had a full docket of cases for the day. I had just judged the cases of two men and sentenced them to death by crucifixion when one of the cohort officers came to me with a report that there was a procession of priests, temple guards, temple officials, and a large crowd of people coming into the esplanade of the Praetorium. I told him to find out what they wanted."

"And what did they want?"

"He reported that the esteemed chief justice and even his esteemed father-in-law, Annas, and members of the Sanhedrin had found Jesus guilty of breaking a law. They wanted confirmation of their verdict so that they could put Him to death. They were coming for my approval."

"And did you hear them, Governor?"

Pilate looked exasperated. "Mr. Prosecutor, Jewish people are intense people. They will wear you down with their persistence. I ordered that they come into the courtyard with their complaint."

"And did they?"

Anger flashed across Pilate's face. "No. They considered that coming into my house was a defilement before their God because I am a Gentile. I was gracious, as usual, and had my chair moved to the area of the esplanade where the wretched Jews waited with their prisoner."

"They had the accused with them?"

"They had someone with them who had been severely beaten. I give them credit, they knew how to work a man over." Pilate smiled sarcastically.

"Did they identify the man as Jesus?"

"They did."

"Did they present you with charges against their prisoner, Jesus?"

"I asked them what charges they brought against their prisoner. In their usual disrespectful fashion, they said that they would not have brought Jesus to me if they didn't have criminal charges against Him."

Pilate feigned a smile.

"They acted like a bunch of children, playing a deadly game, but I was the authority, not they!"

"What did you do, Governor Pilate?"

"I opened the case by formally asking that the charges against the prisoner be presented, according to Roman law."

"What was their next step, Governor?"

"They had their prosecutors present a formal bill of indictment . . . that Jesus was subverting the nation of Israel, forbidding the payment of tribute money to Tiberius Caesar, and claiming to be a Messiah, which is a king."

"And what did you do?"

"I knew the charges were trivial. However, I did have a concern with the man on the claim to being a king. Tiberius Caesar was king and he only. Anyone else was a pretender and subject to death."

"Did you question Jesus?"

"I did."

"Did Jesus talk to you, Governor?"

"He did, but He offered no defense of Himself."

"What happened then, Governor?"

"The Jews gave me lots of reasons why He was guilty, and one of them reminded me that Jesus had begun being a troublemaker in His hometown of Nazareth. I remembered that King Herod Antipas was in the city for the Passover and Nazareth was under his jurisdiction, so I told them to take Him to Herod."

"Did they follow your orders?"

"Yes. They had no other choice."

"Do you know what happened at Herod's?"

"No. I just knew that for Herod to cause the death of another religious person in Jerusalem could have sparked a riot for him. Neither of us wanted that. Herod simply sent them back to me."

"And what did you do when they returned?"

"I told them that neither I nor the tetrarch, Herod Antipas, had found any guilt in the man."

"And what was the reply of the Jews?"

They wanted Jesus crucified. I even offered to release a prisoner to them because of a Passover amnesty tradition. When I did this, they cried for a convicted murderer, Barabbas."

"Did the Sanhedrin give you a charge for which the sentence of death could be granted, Governor?"

"Yes, finally."

"And what was that charge?"

"Blasphemy under Jewish law was punishable by death, and we were under orders from Rome to uphold the religious laws of the Jews."

"And did you give the order to crucify Jesus, Governor Pilate?"

"I did." Pilate spoke his words with authority.

"As the Roman prefect of Judea, did you have the authority to put Jesus to death?"

"I did." His answer was matter-of-fact.

"Was your trial of Jesus legal in every sense, according to the laws of Rome?"

"It was."

"Thank you, Governor Pilate. Your Lordship, I have no further questions of this witness at this time." Darrow took his seat.

The lord chief justice looked over at Luckhoo.

"Sir Luckhoo, the defense may cross-examine the witness at this time."

"Thank you, my lord."

Luckhoo bowed to the governor and began his cross-examination of the witness.

"Governor Pontius Pilate, I believe that your family were called the Pontii, who came from the Samnites, and the Samnites have an earned reputation of being great warriors who almost conquered Rome on several occasions. Correct?"

Pilate seemed impressed that Luckhoo knew of his heritage and background. He smiled cautiously as he answered.

"Yes, we Pontii are of the Samnites of Italy," Pilate answered respectfully. "Yes, sir, that is true."

"If my memory is correct, the Pontii were great equestrians, and they served Rome in both military and civil positions, attaining high career positions in many instances. Is that also correct?"

Pilate stood more at attention in the witness box. He was a worldly wise politician who knew the pitfalls of anything that might appear to be flattery. He was cautious, but he was enjoying the attention to his nobility.

"Yes, my family heritage includes statesmen and military leaders, all of them with honors."

"Would bravery and honor be considered part of your family heritage?"

Pilate thought that the question was odd, but he answered it appropriately.

"My family has been cited for both on many occasions."

"Very interesting, Governor. Now did you hear of Jesus prior to coming to Jerusalem?"

"Through informants, I had heard of His activities."

"Were you aware of the disruption of activities at the temple caused by the accused, Jesus?"

"I was."

"Will you tell us what you heard concerning that event and how you heard of it?"

"A very loyal centurion, Justus, brought me news of it. He and another centurion were walking near the area of the temple when he heard a great commotion. Justus related that they ran to the outer courts and saw the accused, Jesus, with a whip in His hand, flailing away at the merchants who occupied the temple courtyard. He was driving them and their cattle and sheep, which they sold for sacrifices, out of the temple area. They told me that He then went over to where the doves were penned up and opened the cages and loosed them. Next, they said He turned over the tables of the money changers! Their coins went everywhere!" Pilate laughed. "That old skinflint Annas would have died of rage!"

"Did your centurions call for any help to quiet this disturbance?"

"No. The Reverend Caiaphas had his own temple guard! Justus said that they appeared to be afraid of Jesus, and they did nothing. Since His actions were within their own temple grounds, Justus made a proper military decision that it was no concern of the Roman government." Pilate smiled. "And I approved the action!"

"Governor Pilate, you were the provincial judge, in your region, of all crimes against Rome . . . and you also were the jury, were you not?"

"I was."

"What kind of cases came before you?"

"All capital cases, any appeals, all local disputes between the Gentiles and the Jews, and any anti-Roman political activity."

"In Roman law, was there a prosecutor, as we have here under the rule of English law?"

"No. Private individuals, who were plaintiffs, acted as do your prosecutors."

"Were there lawyers available for those who desired defense?"

"Yes, there were."

"Governor, were you notified by the president of the Sanhedrin of their intent to arrest the accused?"

"Yes."

"Did he ask you for military assistance in doing so?"

"Yes."

"And did you give him assistance?"

"Yes, I already stated that I sent a few soldiers."

"What was your reason for doing so?"

"The chief priest indicated that they were going to arrest Him at night with the guard from the temple, which was more than sufficient. They wanted to be as quiet and discreet as possible. My soldiers would be there in case they botched the arrest."

"And did Reverend Caiaphas notify you when the accused had been arrested?"

"Caiaphas sent me another message early the next morning that Jesus had been arrested. My commander had already brought me word."

"What was your next contact with Reverend Caiaphas?"

"He sent a note saying that the Sanhedrin had found Jesus guilty of blasphemy, which was punishable by death under the Hebrew religious law. Caiaphas wanted me to confirm their sentence and order the prisoner to be executed as quickly as possible. He repeated his concerns about rioting during the religious holidays."

"When next did you see Caiaphas or Jesus, Governor?"

"It was early the next morning when I saw them both."

"Governor, did you believe there was a possibility of a riot starting because of Jesus?"

"Those possibilities are always there, and we were always prepared for them."

"Where did you receive Reverend Caiaphas and his party?"

"I had my judgment chair set in its usual place in the courtyard," he said scornfully, "but the little priest could not defile himself by coming into my courtyard. He sent me a request to move my chair into the esplanade. I did it only because my superiors in Rome had ordered me to stay at peace with these pathetic Jews."

"Was there any lawyer for the defense of Jesus?"

"No. There was none."

"Was anyone there to speak on His behalf?"

"No. No one spoke on His behalf."

"As you understood Jewish law, did you believe that Jesus received a fair trial at the Sanhedrin?"

"No. I did not!"

Darrow sprang to his feet.

"Your Lordship, this witness was not at the trials at the

Sanhedrin, and he made his own judgment at the trial at which he was judge. His opinion of the Jewish trials should have no bearing on the accused."

Luckhoo shot a quick reply.

"My lord, this law judge was a contemporary of the time and of Jewish law. His expert opinion on the due procedures of law would have a definite bearing on my client's case. And I asked the question based on his understanding of that law."

The lord chief justice looked at Darrow.

"Overruled. The answer stands. Proceed, Sir Luckhoo."

"Governor Pontius Pilate, as the prefect of Rome, with full authority to sit as judge and jury of any persons within the borders of Judea, including both Romans and Jews, you had the right to order the crucifixion of any person found guilty of a crime, with the exception of a Roman citizen. Is that a correct statement of your authority from Rome?"

Pilate stuck his square chin out.

"Yes, I had that authority!"

"You also had full authority to release them?"

"Yes, I had that authority, also!"

"Governor, why did you ask for water to wash your hands in front of Caiaphas and his crowd?"

The question seemed to rattle Pilate a bit.

"You couldn't tell those stiff-necked Jews anything! I tried to show them my feelings on the matter!"

"Pontius Pilate, were you afraid of the Jews?"

Pilate was taken aback by the question. His face turned white, then red as he found himself verbally off balance. He looked straight at Luckhoo.

"I was not afraid of any Jews!"

"Were you fearful of the power of Rome?"

"No, but I had a very healthy respect for Rome."

"Governor, were you afraid of Jesus?"

Pilate looked at Jesus.

"Afraid of a harmless, gentle pacifist of a man?" he said in mocking tones. "Absolutely not!"

"Were you afraid of the God of the Jews?"

Pilate responded boastfully, holding one side of his toga, his chin in the air.

"Sir, I never saw any God of the Jews. I saw Caiaphas and his pitiful friends creating a lot of smoke in the air with their animal sacrifices, but there was absolutely no power in their religion. I saw Jesus who said that He was the Son of God, and He demonstrated more power than anything I had ever seen the Jews do. But I never saw any Jewish God, nor was I afraid of their God."

Luckhoo sprang like a lion from hiding and went for the jugular.

"Then why did you let Caiaphas and the few Jews who came to you with an innocent man in their midst . . . force you to act against your beliefs? Why, Pilate, did you lose your family honor and your pride and your integrity . . . and condemn an innocent Jesus to die on your hideous cross of crucifixion? You ceremoniously tried to wash your hands, which you knew were going to be blood-stained for taking this man's life. And where is your bravery now that you hide your hands because they haunt you? Isn't that right?"

The spectators in the courtroom, expecting Luckhoo to quietly complete a detailed cross-examination of the interrogation and trial of Jesus, gasped.

Darrow's mouth dropped open and he frowned, deepening the lines in his face. The courtroom once again was buzzing with muted conversations. The lord chief justice banged his gavel.

"I call for order in the courtroom."

Pilate looked as though he had been expecting to be the central figure in a parade, and he suddenly realized that the parade had passed him by. His tone was icy and strong.

"Yes, I ordered the crucifixion of Jesus of Nazareth. Yes, it was carried out at my command! I had the authority! I am not afraid of the Jews . . . do you hear? And I am not afraid of Jesus!"

Pilate strained his voice as he shouted. He raised his hands in frustration and anger against his accuser and turned the palms of his hands toward Luckhoo.

"Do you see any blood on these hands? Do you? There is none because I have washed them and washed them and washed them and washed them. There is no blood on them! Do you hear! No blood! No blood! Do you hear me, Christian? THERE IS NO BLOOD ON MY HANDS!"

Luckhoo said nothing as he watched Pontius Pilate wrap his hands around himself and hide them under his toga. Pilate glared at his verbal adversary, and his breathing was heavy. Luckhoo quietly asked his next question.

"Did you ever personally examine the census records of Caesar Augustus to see if the birth of Jesus, son of Joseph and Mary, his wife, of the house of David, was ever recorded?"

Pilate stood brooding. He finally answered.

"Yes, I checked the census," he sniffed.

"And Governor Pontius Pilate, did you find the names of Joseph and Mary of Nazareth, and of their son, Jesus, written in that census?"

Pilate's answer was curt. "Yes."

Luckhoo looked at the lord chief justice.

"My lord, I have no further examination of this man!" Luckhoo sat down and waited for the expected ripple effect in the courtroom.

Darrow stared at Houston in disbelief. Houston was smart enough to keep her mouth shut. She simply shrugged her shoulders. Darrow slammed some of his papers around on the desk while deciding who to call as his next witness. His anger was apparent to all.

The lord chief justice looked at Darrow and asked, "Do you wish to reexamine?"

Darrow shook his head.

The lord chief justice spoke to the prefect, "Governor Pilate, you are excused as a witness at this time. You may return to your seat."

It seemed as if every eye followed Pontius Pilate from the witness box back to his seat in the witness section. He had entered the witness box as a proud and arrogant man. He returned looking as if he were a prisoner, manacled by his own hands.

The lord chief justice said, "Mr. Darrow, you may call the next witness for the prosecution."

Darrow was quick to answer. His next witness was one of his heroes.

"Your Lordship, I call as the next witness the English naturalist, Charles Robert Darwin."

Heads were buzzing with conversations as Darrow called to the witness stand one of the most controversial men in history. Darwin's theory of evolution had been a shot that had echoed around the world, starting a war between science and religion.

The bailiff stood at his seat.

"Charles Robert Darwin, English naturalist. Call for Charles Robert Darwin, English naturalist."

A gaunt man, of medium height, stood up in the witness section and made his way to the witness box. He wore a black woolen coat with wrinkled trousers that covered worn black shoes turning up at the ends.

Darwin's thin face was accented by the long white beard that hung to the middle of his chest. The top of the seventy-three-year-old man's head was bald. His broad nose looked as if it held up a long white fuzzy caterpillar that extended over his deep-set eyes. Several waves of lines marked his forehead. His very large ears were covered by white hair, and under each eye was a dark chasm across his face, like a deep trough where tears of hurt and remorse had emptied down to the sides of his beard. He entered the witness box and stood holding onto each side in an effort to steady himself.

The bailiff swore him in, although in repeating the swearing-in statement, Darwin mumbled the last word. The bailiff asked him if he would like a stool on which to sit.

"I don't need a stool, thank you," he replied curtly.

The lord chief justice spoke.

"Mr. Darrow, your witness. You may proceed."

Darrow was already on his feet by the time Darwin had reached the witness box. His eyes shone with admiration, and his face was an expression of awe and respect for this highly controversial scientist. He began his respectful questioning of the English evolutionist.

"Mr. Darwin, you were born in Shrewsbury, Shropshire, England, on February 12, 1809, is that correct, sir?"

"That is correct."

His voice was slightly hoarse and cracked as he talked. But there was firm determination in his eyes.

"I should like to recount some of your scholastic background if I may, Mr. Darwin."

Darrow picked up a file folder in front of him and gazed at it with a look of satisfaction.

"You began your formal education at Shrewsbury School under Samuel Butler, and in 1825 you were admitted to the medical school at Edinburgh University. In 1828 you matriculated to Christ's College at Cambridge University and took your degree in 1831. Is that in order, Mr. Darwin?"

Darwin smiled and nodded his head. "Quite right, Mr. Darrow."

"In December of 1831 you were brought aboard the HMS *Beagle* as a naturalist. The purpose of the ship was to accomplish a surveying expedition, which was partially funded by your government, and you were attached to that ship for almost five years. By October of 1836 you had sailed to several islands in the Atlantic, to South America, to the Galapagos Islands, Tahiti, New Zealand, Australia, Tasmania, the Keeling Islands, the Maldives, Mauritius, St. Helena, and Ascension. Is that information correct?"

Darwin smiled and interrupted Darrow. "Yes. You appear to have done your homework well, Mr. Darrow."

"Thank you, Mr. Darwin. From these voyages, you were able to publish a number of geological studies that are reference works to this day. Is that correct?"

"I can account for time only until 1882, Mr. Darrow. I am aware that they were used as references until at least that time, yes."

"I should say that you advanced a theory of reef formation that is still generally held today, sir."

The white-bearded man smiled and nodded his head. Darrow put his hands in his suspenders and continued, using his notes.

"Will you tell us something about what occurred in July of 1837 and about your notebooks of that period?"

Darwin moved his hands forward on the sides of the witness box and began to share about his life. Every eye in the room was on Darwin, and all ears strained to hear his testimony.

"I began my notebooks on transmutation at that time—"

Darrow interrupted with his finger in the air. "I beg your pardon, Mr. Darwin, but would you give a very brief definition of the word *transmutation* for the benefit of our jury."

Darwin smiled again.

"It's been a long time since I did a lecture, sir, but I will attempt to accommodate you. The word *transmutation* simply means 'fluctuation, alternation, or the conversion of one element or isotope into another, either naturally or artificially.' In my work, it was to change from one nature, form, substance, or species into another, or to convert."

Darwin seemed to get his second wind and stood just a little taller as he continued.

"As a naturalist, I was impressed by the character of South American fossils, as well as species in the Galapagos Islands, and in the manner in which closely allied animals replace one another. These facts were part of the origination of my views on the species."

"Sir, you have published a number of scientific books including the very controversial *On the Origin of Species by Means of Natural Selection*. Did these works come from the very detailed notes that you took on your voyages? And would you please tell our esteemed jury what is contained in this book, in summary form, please?"

"To answer your first question, yes. I used this research to write the *Origin*."

Darwin paused, took a breath, then proceeded. "The first four chapters of my book explain the operation of the artificial selection by people and of natural selection in consequence of the struggle for existence. My fifth chapter deals with the laws of variation and causes of modification other than natural selection. The next five chapters consider difficulties in the way of a belief in evolution as well as in the natural selection process. The last chapters deal with the evidence for evolution as provided by geographical distribution, comparative anatomy, paleontology, embryology, and vestigial organs."

"The publication of this one book caused a storm of controversy and led to a conflict between the adherents of orthodox religions and the scientific community concerning God. Would you comment here for the jury?" Darrow was playing to the jury.

"I feel that my life's work has been the demonstration that the evolving of plants and animals, and the adaptations that they demonstrate, provides no substantial evidence of a divine or providential guidance or purpose in design as the Christian Bible purports. Natural selection of fortuitous variations provides a scientifically plausible foundation for evolution and does not necessitate miraculous interposition or any supernatural interference with the laws of nature as we know them."

"Mr. Darwin, would you summarize the work you have done in the area of organic evolution?"

Luckhoo wanted to jump up and object to this testimony

as irrelevant to the trial, but something on the inside told him to wait.

The naturalist shifted from one foot to another.

"Well, Mr. Darrow, that is probably one of the most difficult tasks I have been given in a long time . . . the summarizing part, I mean!" He smiled at Darrow and stroked his beard with one hand. He looked down at the floor as if his notes might be written on the sanded oak boards.

"I was somewhat lucky and was able to win popular acceptance of evolution, not only by scientists, but by the educated public as well. Some of my contemporaries said that I had the most thorough and objective analysis of the data from all fields of biology of how some previous scientific constructs fell into order under the organizing power of my concept."

Darwin continued to stroke his beard as he spoke.

"I and a colleague, A. R. Wallace, put forward a very simple logical possible explanation of the process. It apparently was of much wider applicability and greater plausibility than any concept previously advanced. We theorized the inevitability of evolutionary change on a planet. That is, each species tends to produce more individuals than can find a place, provided that there is sufficient variability, at least part of which is able to be transmitted to the next generation, giving material for a natural selection within the species involved. That was in comparison with the artificial selection practiced by animal and plant breeders in our day. There is a great deal more to my years of scientific study, Mr. Darrow." Darwin smiled.

"Thank you, Mr. Darwin. Now I want to repeat something that you just said to ensure that our jury heard you properly. You stated that you won 'popular acceptance,' not only by your contemporaries in science, but by those who were of the academic community as well. Would that be correct?"

"Yes, but that wasn't the most important thing in what I just said, Mr. Darrow, although it certainly was important in my life and my work."

"Thank you. I want to change subjects, Mr. Darwin. Would you express your religious viewpoint based on your scientific studies and personal beliefs, Mr. Darwin?"

"When I was a young man, I had a belief in deity and even considered, although not seriously, going into the ministry. After I married, I found that my wife's views concerning religion were much stronger than mine. I respected her views, even though I didn't participate in her opinions. When I was in my late forties, I expressed a thought to the effect that if the devil himself were involved in the earth, then the clumsy, wasteful, blundering, low, and horribly cruel works of nature could be explained. That included people going against other people in wars, of which there have been no end. Some years later, as I had just turned sixty, I believed that the universe was not the result of blind chance. But on the other hand, I saw no solid evidence of beneficent design or of design of any kind in the details."

"Did you ever do any studies, of any kind, about the accused, Jesus of Nazareth?"

"Oh, yes, all sorts of clerics at school forced religion down our throats while I was growing up. The colleges were primarily founded by religious denominations, so you had to outwardly adhere to their religious basics to keep them appeased. That is, if you chose to attend and graduate from their institutions of higher learning!"

"Were you once a member of the Church of England?"

Darwin smiled. "Yes, but I hope that doesn't count against me."

"Would you tell us, Mr. Darwin, why you resigned from the Church of England?"

"I gave it up because I found that church doctrines were contrary to the scientific knowledge that I had obtained in my studies and that I had incorporated into my books on the origin of the species, among other things."

"Did the religious community persecute you in any way?"

Darwin's answer was filled with rage: "No, sir, not just in any way. They persecuted me in any way they could invent."

"Mr. Darwin, do you believe in a Supreme Being who caused the earth and all that is upon it to come into being?"

"My scientific knowledge does not allow me to believe in such a concept."

Darrow knew that his questions needed to be precise.

"Based on your scientific work, have you any variation on which to believe in a Messiah or in a supernatural divine God of some sort or in any kind of religion, Mr. Darwin?"

"No, sir. I do not deny that there was a Buddha, a Mohammed, or a Jesus of Nazareth I believe that they were just men who felt some kind of an inner desire to do what they did. They were those of our particular species who rose to leadership roles . . . nothing more."

Darwin paused and extended his hand.

"Mr. Darrow, I am a true agnostic who espouses the doctrine that the existence or the nature of God and the ultimate origin of the universe are not known or knowable, even with the scientific knowledge we have today. Therefore, I simply could not believe in a divine Messiah."

"Thank you so very much, Mr. Darwin."

Darrow made a surprise move. He made a slight bow to Darwin as his hero stood erect in the witness box.

"Your Lordship, I have no further questions, at this time, of this distinguished witness, Mr. Charles Darwin."

The lord chief justice turned to Luckhoo.

"Sir Luckhoo, do you wish to cross-examine this witness?"

The defense counsel stood immediately.

"My lord, I do wish to cross-examine the highly esteemed and highly controversial Mr. Darwin."

Luckhoo looked directly at Darwin.

"Mr. Darwin, I believe that your mother was the daughter of Josiah Wedgwood. Is that correct?"

Darwin was cautious, remembering those who had debated him or questioned his theories in the past.

"That is correct, sir."

"If I am correct, you married your cousin, Emma Wedgwood, in January of 1839."

"Your facts are correct, sir."

"You went to Edinburgh to pursue a medical career and found out that you were not fitted to enter the high post of caring for the human body as a medical doctor, is that a correct fact?"

"Yes, but—"

Luckhoo interrupted.

"You left Edinburgh to attend the religious seminary at Christ's College at Cambridge because you wanted to please your family so you could continue school, is that right?"

"Well, yes, I wanted to please my family—"

"It was never your wish to become a minister of the gospel of Jesus Christ. Is that a true statement?"

"I did not want to be a minister."

"Then is it a fact that you deceived your family into believing that you wished to enter the ministry in order to achieve your purpose of attending college to be a scientist?"

Darrow was livid. He pointed at Luckhoo.

"Are we on some kind of Salem witch hunt here, Your Lordship? Don't this great man's achievements and works have something to say about his character without having to go back to when he was a changeable, youthful student at school?"

Luckhoo interrupted.

"My lord, the defense indeed wishes to show the character of the witness. The admiring prosecution has sought to place the witness in a position of very high scientific esteem when, in fact, he is no more or no less a human being who, in a given set of circumstances, lied to those closest to him. He did this, based on some sort of learned behavior of his past. His goal was purportedly one of being a scientist, a high profession dedicated to searching for truth. Certainly a message that one could deduce from such behavior in his college years was that his end results justified his means as an impressionable youth in college."

"Overruled." The quick reply came from the bench.

Darwin was used to having his character attacked and took it all with little concern.

"Yes, using your terminology, sir, I did deceive my parents in that matter as a young student."

"In your scientific approach to problem solving, did you use such methods as study and observation, argument and discussion, trial and error, and imagination and memory?"

"Yes. Those methods are basic to problem solving as we know it." Darwin's answer was reserved.

"Would you say that scientific study involves creativity in one form or another?"

"Yes, I would think so."

"In your knowledge of such creativity, might one find an analysis of the scientist's own personality and roots therein?"

"There is that probability, yes."

"Could a man's work involve so much of his total makeup that it might reflect qualities of his personality and beliefs, as an example?"

Darwin pondered the question for a moment. "Yes."

"In constructing your theory of evolution, did you ever encounter any conflicts of your religious upbringing, a fear of ridicule and persecution by your opponents, and/or a pattern of hesitation and delay in the completion of your work?"

Darwin sighed and shook his head.

"I experienced all those things and more."

"If I were to use the term *evolution science*, Mr. Darwin, would I be correct in saying that it meant scientific evidence for evolution as well as inferences and theories from such scientific evidence?"

Darwin appeared impressed with Luckhoo's knowledge.

"Yes, your general statement is correct."

"Would your theory of evolution be considered a part of evolution science?"

"It has proven to be, yes."

Luckhoo stood with his eyes closed.

"Let me be more specific in what evolution science might be. Might it include a scientific theory that orderly processes of the universe came from disordered matter and that life emerged from nonlife?"

"Yes, that is a part of my theory."

Luckhoo opened his eyes and picked up a dictionary from the desk in front of him.

"Mr. Darwin, much of what you have produced, as well as that for which you have received fame, comes from your theories. Is that correct?"

"I believe that it is. Yes."

"Mr. Darwin, would you inform the jury if you can agree with how Mr. Webster, in his dictionary, defined the word *theory*. And I quote: 'theory. 1. Contemplation; speculation. 2. The analysis of a set of facts in their ideal relations to one another; as essays in theory. 3. The general or abstract principles of any body of facts; pure, as distinguished from applied, science or art; as the theory of music or of medicine. Cf. Practice. 4. A more or less plausible or scientifically acceptable general principle offered to explain phenomena. 5. Loosely, a hypothesis; a guess. 6. Math. A body of theorems presenting a clear, rounded, and systematic view of a subject; as the theory of equations.—SYN. See HYPOTHESIS!'"

Darwin was hesitant to answer. "I generally agree with his definitions, yes."

Luckhoo threw the dictionary on the desk in front of him, and it landed with a resounding bang. He closed his eyes and continued.

"Does your evolution science indicate that the sufficiency of mutation and natural selection bring about the development of the present complex living kinds from simple earlier kinds?"

"Again, Sir Luckhoo, my answer is yes."

"Would your evolution science also include the concept that anthropoid apes, for example, the gibbon, the chimpanzee, the orangutan, and the gorilla . . . and human beings all came from a common mammal ancestor, Mr. Darwin?"

"That is a conclusion from my studies, yes, sir."

Luckhoo's voice rose a pitch.

"And, Mr. Charles Darwin, does evolution science seek to explain the earth's geology and the evolutionary sequence by uniformitarianism, a theory stating organisms will have the same or similar form as they evolve, and theorize that the earth is several billion years old?"

Darwin stood erect and smiled at Luckhoo.

"Yes."

"Mr. Darwin, I would like to direct your attention to another term, *creation science*, which is in opposition to your evolution science. You have argued with those who believe that a Jewish-Christian God created the earth and the people on it, have you not?"

Darwin was precise.

"Yes, sir. I have debated those people."

"Allow me to summarize their opposite concepts. First, there was a sudden creation of the universe, of energy, and of life from nothingness, a void. Second, there is insufficient scientific evidence of mutation and natural selection that brought about the development of all living kinds from a single organism. Third, there have been changes only within fixed limits of originally created kinds of plants and animals. Fourth, there were separate ancestries for people and apes. Fifth, a Creator, God, created the heaven and the earth, and the earth's geology has been caused by catastrophism, which included a worldwide flood. And sixth, the earth is not billions of years old but thousands of years old. Now, Mr. Darwin, are those statements of creation science considered as in opposition to your theory of evolution?"

Darwin was nodding his head, looking cautiously at Luckhoo.

"They are certainly in opposition to my theory. However, I would hesitate to call their theory a science."

"Mr. Darwin, you have made an impact not only in the scientific community but in the religious community as well. Are you aware of that?"

"I . . . ," Darwin paused, wrinkling his brow, "am aware that my theory created conflict."

"Do you believe that 'it is bigotry for public schools to teach only one theory of origins,' as the esteemed prosecutor once stated?"

Before Darwin could answer, Darrow jumped to his feet, waving his fist in the air, his face full of anger.

"Your Lordship, I object! My statements are not on trial here! Evolution is not on trial here! Mr. Darwin's beliefs are not on trial here . . . but Jesus is! The counsel for the defense is making this courtroom into another trial base for evolution versus creation sciences."

He sat down and looked at the lord chief justice for his reply.

"Sir Luckhoo, do you wish to offer an explanation for this line of questioning?"

Luckhoo's eyes were open as he turned to the bench.

"My lord, Jesus of Nazareth, here on trial in this courtroom, is on record in Exhibit A that He is the Son of God, who is the Creator of heaven and earth. Evolution science denies that there is a Creator, and this witness also states that, in his opinion, God cannot be proven. Yet his theory of evolution is a theory that requires a premise that must deny a Creator God. On the one hand, the witness says there is no Creator God, and on the other hand, the learned scientist says he is an agnostic because you cannot prove there is a God! Then Mr. Darwin states that life emerged from nonlife and then tells us that present complex living kinds come from simple earlier kinds. What a contrast of testimony! I believe that the jury is entitled to know if this scientist believes in his own theory sufficiently to place it into the open minds of young impressionable schoolchildren throughout the world."

"The Crown finds that line of questioning valid."

The lord chief justice spoke firmly.

"Delete the reference to Mr. Darrow's beliefs, then please answer the question, Mr. Darwin."

Darwin answered the question without batting an eye. His reply was quietly stinging to Luckhoo.

"No, I do not! Science and religion do not mix!"

It was only then that Darrow sat down with a look of disgust on his face.

Luckhoo had already made his point. He turned to the witness and went back to his questioning. The courtroom was tense.

"Mr. Darwin, you were a young man on board the HMS *Beagle* from 1831 to 1836, a period of almost five years, is that correct?"

"Yes." He clipped his answer.

"You wrote thousands of pages in your notebooks of your observations during that time, is that correct?"

"Yes."

"Do you consider them scientific observations?"

"I do."

"When and where did you start your first writing in the notebook called 'Transmutation of Species'?"

"I started that in July of 1837, when I was in England."

"I believe that you stated that the theory of evolution became clear to you in September of 1838?"

"Uh, yes, it was then."

"And it was at about the same time that you were reading the works of T. R. Malthus, concerning his principles of population, is that correct?"

"Yes."

"In fact, this is where you stated that you got the theory from which you could work?"

"Yes, I made that statement."

"Mr. Darwin, are you acquainted with the works of such scientists as Sir Francis Bacon, Lord Kelvin, and Sir John Newton?"

"I am acquainted with some of their works, yes."

"Are you acquainted with the so-called Baconian principles of scientific strategy?"

"Yes, I am." Darwin nodded slightly.

Luckhoo spoke slowly and distinctly.

"In summary form, Mr. Darwin, would the so-called Baconian principles, as applied to your theory of evolution, be basically the following? First, to collect evidence for lower human evolution. Second, to then construct your theory of evolution through natural selection. Third, to research the unique difficulties in the application of your theory to the existing human case. Fourth, to then solve any problems presented by such research. And fifth, to have come to a conclusion that your theory of evolution did indeed apply to human beings as far back as you could trace them."

"That might be Bacon's principles applied to my theories, yes."

"Now, Mr. Darwin, did you use his principles as your scientific model?"

"No!"

"Did you use any of Bacon's scientific principles?"

"No, I did not."

"Did you use any scientific steps in any other sequence that would be considered scientifically or logically prudent by scientific standards of your day?"

Darwin moved back as if he had been pushed, but he hung on to the sides of the witness box. His breathing became heavy. His mind was racing, and he knew that there was no safe answer to that question.

"I used proven scientific methods of discovery."

Luckhoo was very quick to reply.

"Mr. Darwin, your notebooks provide us with the answer to that question. If we study your transmutation notebooks and those you wrote on human beings and the mind, we have your scientific strategy, which was not a proven one as that of Sir Francis Bacon. Fundamentally, you already believed in the occurrence of evolution from lower forms, and you already believed that human beings were part of that evolution process. Is that correct, sir?"

The angry Darwin shouted, "Yes, I believed both of those premises!"

Luckhoo shouted back, "And isn't it true, Mr. Darwin, that in describing your work on the formation of coral reefs, you formulated the whole theory of reef formation BEFORE YOU HAD EVER SEEN A CORAL REEF?"

Darwin raised a fist in the air at Luckhoo.

"Yes, you persecutor. But you don't have to see something in order to study it!"

Luckhoo had a swift response.

"That's true, Mr. Charles Darwin. The exception to that rule is when you are the first one to espouse a theory. At least that is the way it is with most scientists, isn't it?"

Darwin refused to answer Luckhoo, who continued the relentless probe of the witness.

"Wasn't it in college where you began to deny your own father's religious faith?"

"Somewhat, yes," Darwin replied grudgingly.

"And didn't your own wife, in writing to you sometime between 1839 and 1840, tell you that you should be aware that the scientific approach of doubting undemonstrated facts and theories should not be extended to matters of religious faith . . . and didn't your Emma also write of the value of prayer? Weren't these some of the things your own darling wife, Emma, wrote to you?"

Hearing the name of his departed wife and remembering some of her words to him, Darwin began to shudder. Words formed on his mouth, but nothing came out as the pain of being away from her encompassed his complete body.

Luckhoo looked at him with compassion. He spoke with kindness in his voice.

"Mr. Darwin, isn't the answer to that question in the affirmative?"

Darwin nodded his head up and down.

"Mr. Darwin, do you now believe there is a God of creation?"

Darwin's eyes were overflowing with tears. Every fiber of his body was hurting because of the mental anguish he was experiencing. With a sob, he took a big breath and seemed to calm down. He wiped his eyes with the sleeve of his coat.

"Sir, I sincerely must say . . . ," his voice was metered,

"that during my lifetime, I felt that I had no reason to believe in a Creator. I had no desire to prove or disprove the existence of a Creator. I do not know if there is a God or not. My honest answer is that I simply do not know, sir."

"And what now is your belief about the evolution of humankind, Mr. Darwin?"

"I once believed that people in the distant future would be far more perfect creatures than they were in my day. But in this short time I have been back in this realm, reading from a few of the most modern history books, and remembering some of the recorded history of humankind of my own time, I find that people are still savages within themselves and to fellow human beings, just as they always have been. If humankind can send guided weapons into the air to rain down mass destruction on the enemies and the innocents, then there is no future for humankind. Humankind has not evolved . . . but has regressed to the old nature."

Darwin paused. He started life with a dream in his heart, a dream of making a difference in the destiny of humankind. He stood in the witness box, knowing that his concept of the dream never came true. He stood motionless, trapped in time.

Luckhoo closed a folder that had been lying open before him on his desk. He turned to his right and looked at the lord chief justice. He spoke very quietly.

"My lord, I have no further questions of this witness."

Luckhoo sat down quietly and bowed his head. No one in the courtroom moved. No one apparently had heard the chimes of Westminster or of St. Sepulchre during the testimony of the witnesses.

Only now, the ringing of the four o'clock hour seemed to bring the courtroom participants back to reality.

The lord chief justice spoke to Darrow.

"Mr. Darrow, do you wish to reexamine?"

"No, Your Lordship," the prosecutor replied.

"Mr. Darwin, you are excused. You may return to your seat."

Darwin let go of the sides of the witness box, turned around, then walked slowly in front of the jury, looking neither to the left nor to the right. He found the row of seats where he had previously been seated and sat down. The lord chief justice spoke.

"This trial is recessed for this day and will resume at eight o'clock on the morrow." He banged his gavel on the pad.

The bailiff of the court stood to his feet and spoke the ancient words, and the spectators filed out of the courtroom.

As Darrow and Houston were leaving the courtroom, Darrow looked back to the witness section. He tried to focus on his first witness to be called the next day. Turning to Houston, he said, "I don't know whether we won or lost this one, Houston. It's a close match at this point. Darwin gave humanity the thrashing it deserves, but he sure didn't help our cause. We'll see what tomorrow brings."

Across the room Luckhoo glanced to the empty prisoner's dock and then to DiPietro.

"Diane, at times like these in a trial, I always wonder if I did my best, if I asked the right questions and made the right statements at the right times—"

DiPietro interrupted.

"Sir Lionel, we all look back at the things we have done in our lives and wonder the same thing. We and these witnesses cannot go back and change anything in our lives. We just have to accept the things that we cannot change and change the things that we can. I think I've heard that many times before. That philosophy also states that we ask God for the wisdom to know the difference."

She removed her solicitor's wig and laid it on the table.

"You know as well as I that changing anything from the past can come only by faith in God. That faith in God offers forgiveness for the things of the past to those who are living. The Creator of all the earth said that there is only one way to that forgiveness. We're here defending the only way and the only truth. Truth will win out and bring light to those who want it in their lives. Those who don't want to hear or accept the truth . . . won't do so. But all get a choice. Everyone gets to choose while living on this earth. Everyone! That is both fair and just."

Luckhoo nodded his head and put out his arm for his assistant to help him to his feet. It had been a long hard day, and the winner was not clearly defined, at least not here in the courtroom. Tomorrow was another day.

8
WITNESSES
FOR THE
PROSECUTION

MORNING, DAY THREE

The bailiff seemed to be in good spirits this morning, and he smiled as he stood looking about the courtroom. There would be no afternoon session. It was common law practice to give the jury time to digest prosecution testimony before hearing defense testimony. The bells at St. Sepulchre and at Westminster were just ending their eight o'clock chimes as he rapped the court scepter on the floor and got the court proceedings under way.

The lord chief justice looked at the prosecutor.

"Mr. Clarence Darrow, do you have further witnesses for the prosecution? If so, will you call such at this time?"

Darrow nodded his head and felt his wig slip a bit. He put his hand up and pushed it back in place.

"Your Lordship, I wish to call at this time Dr. Sigmund Freud, world-renowned psychiatrist."

The bailiff stood and made his call.

"Dr. Sigmund Freud, psychiatrist. Call for Dr. Sigmund Freud, psychiatrist."

There was a slight rustle of clothing as those in the witness section turned to see a man in his early eighties rise from one of the seats.

His hair was white behind his receding hairline, and it was parted on the left side. A neatly trimmed beard and moustache almost covered his thin lips.

His dark eyes, still with a slight gleam in them, looked out under puffy eyelids. His nose was straight with large nostrils, all fitting proportionately on his face.

Freud's gait was steady as he walked. He glanced at each member of the jury as he passed in front of them.

He wore a brown tweed three-piece suit and black shoes. A gold chain draped from the second button on his vest down to a well-worn pocket where a gold pocket watch nestled. In an upper vest pocket the tops of two cigars and a pair of reading glasses protruded. The only bright part of his attire was his starched white shirt with the small string necktie tied in a precise knot.

Freud stood at attention in the witness box, looking at people around the room, as he assessed his surroundings.

He turned to his left and looked directly at the lord chief justice, then to Darrow standing at his bench, then on to Luckhoo. His eyes stopped as he came to the accused, and for a moment he studied all he could see of Jesus sitting in the dock.

"Do you understand the language being spoken here today?"

Freud replied to the bailiff in a thick German accent, "I do."

"Please place your hand on the Bible and repeat this after

me: I solemnly swear to tell the truth, the whole truth, and nothing but the truth, so help me God."

Freud repeated the vow and dropped both his arms to his sides. He waited with anticipation for the first question from Darrow.

"Dr. Freud, you were born in Freiburg, Moravia, in the year 1856 of Jewish parentage. But you spent practically the whole of your working life in Vienna. Is that correct, sir?"

"That is correct." His eyes fastened on Darrow.

"Would I be correct in saying that you were not a person who practiced the Jewish religion during most of your life?"

"True."

"You studied medicine in Vienna and became a medical doctor, is that correct?"

"Yes, that is true." Freud nodded as he spoke.

"Dr. Freud, during your studies as a medical doctor, did you study under such famous doctors as Brücke, Meynert, and Charcot, the French neurologist?"

"I had that honor, sir, yes," Freud replied with a slight smile. He placed both hands on the sides of the witness box.

"You are known throughout the world as the father of psychoanalysis. Is that correct?"

"There are some who have given me that title, yes."

"As a scientist, could you explain some of what is called unconscious human thought to our distinguished jury? I hasten to add, Dr. Freud, could you do that in summary form that we all might understand?"

Freud threw his shoulders back and smiled.

"I will do it as best I can, Mr. Darrow." He paused. "My model for what I called the unconscious was in the area of primitive psychoanalysis. Thoughts, which can occupy the forefront of the consciousness, can recede into the preconscious, or the unconscious, or using a common term, the background, and they can be summoned forth again."

Darrow interrupted.

"Do you mean that, for instance, if people studied for much of their lives about a subject, and that subject was not in the forefront of their lives for a number of years, they might later be able to summon their thoughts again, and those thoughts would be as real as when they were studied originally?"

"Yes, that is possible."

"Thank you, Dr. Freud. Now did you propose, during your lifetime, that the mind could be examined and understood in the light of scientific principles?"

"Yes, I did."

"And were your ideas well received?"

Freud smiled and squinted his eyes.

"No, in fact they caused as much furor, in my day, as Mr. Darwin's theories had created a few years previously, in his day."

"Did your theories eventually become accepted?"

"By and large, yes. There was always some religious Puritan who rejected scientific knowledge as it was presented."

Darrow pulled on his red suspenders.

"Dr. Freud, will you please summarize for us the psychological terms of *paranoid reactions.*"

"Persons who suffer from paranoid reactions are generally characterized by extreme suspicion and delusions. I would say that there are two basic manifestations of paranoid reactions. One is the state distinguished by paranoid delusions and many times accompanied by hallucinations. The second reaction is characterized by logical, systematic delusions."

Darrow let his suspenders fly with a snap.

"Explain the second reaction further, if you will, Dr. Freud."

"Paranoid people rationalize their own thinking and believe that anyone who opposes or differs from them is wrong."

Darrow seemed to have found a key he had been looking for during the trial. He leaned across the desk with both hands flat on the desk.

"Are there other symptoms that people suffering from paranoia might exhibit or not exhibit?"

"If you are talking about psychological symptoms, the people may not exhibit any other abnormal symptoms. In fact, they may appear perfectly normal in all of their activities except in the area of their delusions."

"Dr. Freud, what kinds of paranoia are there?"

"Well, there is the persecutory type, where people have delusions of persecution. There is jealousness, where they are consumed by jealousy. There is erotic paranoia, where persons believe that others are falling in love with them. And there is grandiose paranoia, where persons believe that they are endowed with extraordinary or supernatural gifts and ability."

"Dr. Freud, what are some ways that grandiose paranoia manifests itself in human behavior?"

"These persons believe themselves to be great religious prophets, gods, social reformers, teachers, and/or some sort of benefactors to humankind."

"Dr. Freud, have you ever studied any of the life of the accused, Jesus of Nazareth?"

"Well, I have certainly not done so in a religious sense,

but I have done so in a historic sense, from a clinical perspective."

"Dr. Freud, do you think it is possible that the accused, Jesus of Nazareth, could have suffered from the paranoid reaction of grandiose paranoia?"

"Yes, sir, it is possible."

Luckhoo's face was red as a beet when he stood and looked at Darrow, shouting as he slammed his fist onto the desk in front of him.

"When, in the name of decency, is the counsel for the prosecution going to try this case in good faith on the merits of what the accused has done or has not done? We have been taken through the academic pits of defamation of the character of the accused, and yet not one shred of evidence has been produced by the prosecution that Jesus of Nazareth is not who He says He is."

Luckhoo pointed his finger at Freud.

"Now, this well-known scientific theorist is in the witness box stating that Jesus of Nazareth, the central figure of the human race, is possibly a person with a mental problem. Your Lordship, I object to this line of questioning!"

Darrow was quick to reply, even before Luckhoo was able to sit down.

"Your Lordship, I am sorry that counsel for the defense has such a tender hide for trial law. Counsel has not stated that the accused is or is not someone who is paranoid. Counsel is simply seeking to ascertain whether or not it is possible that the accused could be a paranoid personality type."

The lord chief justice looked at Luckhoo.

"Overruled. Proceed, Mr. Darrow."

Luckhoo sat down hard in his seat. His anger seemed to radiate from him.

"Dr. Freud, with your theory of the unconscious and what you have told us about grandiose paranoia, is it possible for two psychological factors to work together in one person?"

"Yes, it is possible for two factors to work together in one person." Freud was precise.

Not wanting to lose the jury in this chain of questioning, Darrow continued hammering at this central theme of his prosecution.

"Is it possible, Dr. Freud, that a person could be taught all through childhood about his religious conception of the highest calling to humanity, for example, that of being the Messiah . . . to have that thought so placed in the unconscious mind that this thought would become so prominent as to cause him to become a person with a grandiose paranoia and act out such beliefs, even unto death?"

"Yes, that is possible."

"Dr. Freud, I am going to ask you a personal question about your religious beliefs. What is your belief about religion?"

Freud smiled at Darrow. "Mr. Darrow, I am not a believer in religion, and I have stated, in the past, that I feel that religion is a universal, obsessional neurosis."

"Have you ever read the Bible, Exhibit A?"

"Yes, I have studied it from a historic and clinical perspective. I have also studied other religions and the effect that they have had on human behavior."

"From your studies of religion, your studies of psychology, and your studies of the human mind, what is your professional opinion of the accused, Jesus of Nazareth, based on what you know of Him?"

Darrow planned some of his case against Jesus on the expected answer to this question.

"I am not a religious scholar. I can, as you have asked, provide you with a professional opinion. I have studied some of His life, from His clouded birth to His expected death. He apparently lived an exemplary life, according to the Bible, yet I don't see that many of the things about which He preached have ever come to pass. We never enjoyed peace on earth for long, and we have had very little goodwill among human beings, as an example."

Freud paused and pointed to Jesus.

"He established no kingdom on this earth. His ideals certainly contained greatness and still contain sound psychological principles for life. By all laws of probability, His name and His work should have fallen into oblivion by the time His immediate followers had died. Somehow the memory of His existence has been perpetuated in ways that are foreign to what He preached when He was on the earth. Jesus was supposedly against the organized religious hierarchy of His day. Yet throughout the world, there is the evidence of organized religious hierarchy on every street corner in His name.

Freud shook his head and continued.

"I think the man had a destiny of guilt. His lot was as a caregiver, a sufferer, and a guilt bearer. He appeared to want to change the world, but no one human being can change this world. He died a terrible death, like others before Him who thought they were a messiah. I once did a sample case with this Jesus as a patient, such as we would do in a textbook case provided by our tutors. My diagnosis was of a man who became so engrossed in His idea of being a holy Messiah that He became a classic case of grandiose paranoia."

"Dr. Freud, based on your knowledge of Jesus, do you believe He is who He says He is?"

"I do not believe He is the Messiah of the Jewish people, if they have one. I believe the man is a fraud. I believe that anyone who shares the man's delusion shares in perpetuating that fraud."

Clarence Darrow looked at his witness and nodded his gray head. You could hear a pin drop in the courtroom. Darrow looked at Houston and she simply nodded her head.

"Thank you, Dr. Freud. Your Lordship, I have no further questions of this witness at this time."

Darrow sat down.

The lord chief justice turned from Darrow to Luckhoo. His hands were folded together in front of him as he spoke.

"Sir Luckhoo, do you wish to cross-examine this witness?"

Luckhoo nodded his head in the affirmative as he stood to his feet.

"Yes, my lord."

Luckhoo stood looking at Freud for a moment before he asked his first question. It was like he was sizing up this witness for an expected verbal battle.

"Dr. Freud, your last statement concerning Jesus of Nazareth, whom the world knows as the founder of the Christian faith, do you remember what you just stated about Him?"

Freud looked puzzled but replied, "Yes, I remember what I just said!" He appeared to be perturbed that his memory was being challenged.

"Let me quote from that testimony if I may: 'I think the man had a destiny of guilt.' Then you said, 'No one human being can change this world. He died a terrible death, like others before Him who thought they were a messiah. I once did a sample case with this Jesus as a patient, such as we do in a textbook case provided by our tutors. My diagnosis was of a man who became so engrossed in His idea of being a holy Messiah that He became a classic case of grandiose paranoia.' Are those correct quotes, Dr. Freud?"

Freud bowed slightly and smiled.

"I admire your photographic mind, Sir Luckhoo. Your quotes are correct."

"Then you stated that you did not believe He was the Messiah of the Jewish people, and you stated that you believed that He was a fraud. Is that also correct?"

"Yes, it is." Freud hated being redundant.

"Have you studied any about Buddha or Mohammed, among others?"

"Yes, I have."

"And in your studies of Buddha and Mohammed, could your statement . . . 'I believe the man is a fraud. I believe that anyone who shares the man's delusion shares in perpetuating that fraud' . . . be equally applied to Buddha and Mohammed, Dr. Freud?"

Freud's answer was precise.

"Since Jesus, Buddha, and Mohammed were founders of their religions, I am certain that you remember my exact words concerning any religion. I said that I feel that religion is a universal, obsessional neurosis. That would include all religions as far as I am concerned."

"Then your experimental psychological evaluative work using Jesus as a 'patient' would be very biased because you do not believe in religion at all. Isn't that clinically correct, Dr. Freud?"

Freud was unruffled by the question.

"Every scientific or clinical evaluation will have some bias, yes!"

"I also believe that you said that this 'diagnosis' was done when you were a student in college. Is that correct?"

"Yes, but I was a—"

Luckhoo interrupted and his tone of voice became very serious.

"Did you, during your life as a psychiatrist, ever suffer from any neurosis of the kinds you were treating?"

"Yes, almost every—"

Luckhoo cut him off again with his next question.

"Did you ever experience excessive anxieties about death and fears of long journeys while you were in your practice of helping others allay their own fears?"

Freud's facial expression of someone in control changed dramatically. His answer was terse.

"Yes, many psychiatrists go through what I—"

Again, Luckhoo cut him off with a rapid-fire question.

"It is said that you alternated between moods of elation and depression . . . that you suffered from cardiac and gastric troubles with no apparent physiological causes, is that true?"

"I had those problems, yes. Many people—"

"You used the drug cocaine in the treatment of major and minor ailments of your patients. Not only did you prescribe it for ailments, but you encouraged some of your friends and relatives to use it as well, is that true?"

"Well, I was young in my practice then."

Freud could feel the pressure being applied by Luckhoo through his quick questioning. His voice was beginning to show signs of anxiety and panic. He seemed to be losing his composure at the exposure of personal information from his past. His answers came haltingly and uncertainly.

"I did not properly research this drug and did not know of its addicting effect."

"You also gave the world the concept that children can hold sexual feelings and impulses. Is that correct, Dr. Freud?"

"Yes. But that is a—"

Darrow was on his feet pointing at Luckhoo. He shouted at the top of his voice.

"It wasn't but a few moments ago when the counsel for the defense was screaming like a banshee for decency and good faith. Counsel has attempted to impugn the character of every witness presented to this court. I object to this line of questioning by counsel, Your Lordship!"

Darrow stood with his fists doubled on the desk in front of him as he awaited a reply.

The lord chief justice spoke quietly to Luckhoo.

"Please inform the court as to the direction you are taking in the cross-examination of this witness, Sir Luckhoo."

"My lord, our long-suffering jury has once again been presented with a world-renowned personage in the form of Dr. Sigmund Freud. Inasmuch as Dr. Freud's considered opinion has been presented to the jury as coming from another so-called scientific authority, it is counsel's intention to show not only that Dr. Freud is a human being in every sense of the word, but also that he is a person with natural and learned bias, and that his academic and scientific background is woven with such bias."

Luckhoo was very logical in his presentation.

"It is also the intention of this defense counsel to present to the jury evidence that everything that this scientist and any other scientist presents as scientific and true . . . may not be scientific or true! Inasmuch as his professional opinion is biased, it is the defense counsel's responsibility to show the basis for such bias that reflects against my client."

Luckhoo banged his right fist into his left hand.

"Before I was interrupted by the esteemed prosecutor, I was attempting to show that Dr. Freud's theory on childhood sexuality shocked the sensibilities of the people of his own generation, and that many learned psychiatrists and psychologists of succeeding generations do not accept that or other theories of Dr. Sigmund Freud. The jury needs to know the difference between what is scientific evidence presented by a professional and what is biased scientific opinion presented by that professional."

The blood vessels stood out at the temples of Luckhoo's head. His eyes were fully open and staring in anger at Darrow. Tension filled the courtroom.

The quiet, strong voice of the lord chief justice seemed to restore a more peaceful atmosphere in the room.

"During this trial, we have heard the witnesses testifying of both their knowledge and their opinions concerning the accused. The evidence code states that any witness who is not testifying as an expert may give testimony containing forms of inference and opinion. The court finds no fault with the prosecution or the defense in the presentation of either knowledge or opinion that relates to the guilt or innocence of the accused. The objection is overruled."

Darrow was not pleased with the ruling as Luckhoo continued his examination.

"You were born of Jewish parentage in a predominantly Catholic Austria, is that right?"

"Yes."

"Were you persecuted and abused as a young Jewish boy growing up, and subjected to anti-Semitism even while you were going to medical school, much of this abuse coming from so-called Christians?"

"Yes!" Freud replied coldly.

"Were you persecuted by the Nazi government at the beginning of World War II because you were a Jew, and did you have to leave Austria because of your being of Jewish parentage?"

Freud looked at Luckhoo with feelings of both fear and anger, hearing the mention of Hitler's Germany.

"Yes, I was!"

"Did you consider the Germans to be Christians?"

"THEY SAID THAT THEY WERE!" he shouted.

"In your earlier years, did you wonder how these so-called Christians could persecute you and at the same time confess a belief that the world should know them as Christians by their love?"

"I did not believe them! I still do not believe them! They were liars! THEY ARE ALL LIARS!"

Years of persecution seemed to be vented all at once. Freud's eyes blazed with anger. In addition, Luckhoo's closed eyes seemed to challenge Freud. For an instant, Freud attempted to control his growing unrest, but he could not conceal his emotions.

"Dr. Freud, isn't the fact that you were persecuted as a Jew by those you knew as Christians one of the very reasons that you reject religion?"

Freud quickly attempted to regain his composure. He looked like a man at war within himself. He wanted to remain true to his teachings, but he was attempting to overcome his emotional self. He looked at Luckhoo several moments before he ventured an answer.

"NO!" His answer was terse.

"Then why have you taken such a position as a scientist who is supposed to be devoted to exploring all realms of reasoning?"

"Because I am convinced that humankind has reasons for behavior, and reason itself is sufficient for humankind to give place to emotions. Humankind's place in nature is the source of religious philosophy. I find no need to allow for faith conceived as a relation to anything supernatural. If faith lacks an object, as it must have, it is not a relation at all but a condition in the people who say they have faith. Faith in anything unseen or unknown does not allow for an object of faith. In psychology, to understand a religious belief, one must adjust the logical analysis of religious thought."

He took a quick breath and continued without emotion.

"The psychoanalytic condemnation of religious beliefs goes only as far as faith substitutes for psychotherapy. For example, peace of mind as a religious promise, such as the biblical quote about the 'peace of God, which surpasses all understanding,' is really one that can well be understood in psychoanalytic terms. My rejection of religion is purely scientific."

"Dr. Freud, you once wrote a book about the Jewish patriarch, Moses, is that correct?"

"I wrote about a man named Moses, yes!"

"Was it then your belief that Moses was an Egyptian who deserted his own land of Egypt?"

"I believed that was a distinct possibility, yes."

"Did you also believe that Moses was a follower of the

Aten religion, which was founded by Akhenaten of Egypt?"

"Again, yes, I believed that was a probability."

"And did you believe that Moses was the person who led a group of foreign peoples out of Egypt?"

"Yes, I believed that as a possibility, also."

"From your knowledge of the Aten religion, did it compare with the Jewish religion in many respects?"

"Yes, it did."

"Do you believe that a supernatural God called Jehovah . . . called a man of Jewish parentage named Moses . . . to lead a captive Jewish people . . . out of bondage across a desert and through a divinely divided Red Sea . . . and that people is now known as the Jewish nation?"

Freud's answer was short. "No. I do not!"

"Dr. Freud, I have one further question." Luckhoo opened his eyes and fixed them on the psychologist.

"Have you ever submitted Exhibit A, the Bible, to scientific study of any kind?"

"Only the stories about the life of the accused, which I did in college. I believe it to be mostly fable."

"Thank you for your opinions, Dr. Freud."

Luckhoo turned to the lord chief justice.

"My lord, I have no further questions of this witness for the prosecution."

The lord chief justice turned to Darrow and asked, "Mr. Darrow, do you wish to reexamine?"

Darrow shook his head. "No, Your Lordship."

The lord chief justice looked at Freud.

"Then, Dr. Freud, you may leave the witness box and return to your seat."

He turned back to Darrow. "Mr. Darrow, do you have any further witnesses to call for the prosecution?"

Darrow stood and addressed the bench.

"Your Lordship, if you will give me just a moment to confer with my colleague, please."

The lord chief justice nodded his head, and Darrow sat down next to Houston and whispered to her.

"What do you think, Houston? Should we call up Lucifer, or do you feel that is too risky with Luckhoo asking the questions?"

"You said yesterday at lunch that Lucifer would do well on the direct examination but would fall to pieces under cross-exam, isn't that right?" Houston whispered.

"Yes, he'd look like a bouquet of roses in the chief examination and like a bunch of thorns after Luckhoo got through with him in cross. He has a hard time telling any truth, much less backing up what he said in the first place. He's the liar of liars." Darrow's face showed concern.

"My vote is to forget Lucifer and stay with what we've got. You've still got closing arguments and the summation to pick up all the pieces and put them together. You're great at that, Darrow!" She gave Darrow a pat on the arm.

Darrow nodded his head in the affirmative.

"I think you're right, Houston, I think you're right. We still have the cross-exam on anybody that Luckhoo brings in. Let's close it up."

Darrow stood up and looked back at the bench.

"Uh, thank you, Your Lordship. The prosecution will call no further witnesses."

Luckhoo looked at Darrow, then at DiPietro, but said nothing.

The lord chief justice said, "Sir Luckhoo, we will start tomorrow morning with the witnesses for the defense. This trial is recessed and will resume at eight o'clock on the morrow."

The bailiff of the court rose in his place.

"Be upstanding in the court."

All the people stood as the bailiff recited his traditional statement. The lord chief justice stood and exited, and the spectators lost no time in clearing the courtroom.

Darrow and Houston walked toward the barristers' room and were talking quietly. Darrow seemed confident as he left the courtroom.

Luckhoo and DiPietro sat for a few minutes in the courtroom after everyone left. He turned to her and said, "Diane, I believe that tomorrow will hold the key for us in this trial. I believe that the jury will see the truth of this matter with just the witnesses we have. We must be very sensitive to God to see what He would have us do. I believe that there are some legal surprises coming!"

DiPietro agreed by shaking her head affirmatively.

"But God is big enough for any surprises. . . . I promised Lady Jeannie that we would go to Sir Norman's for a fine English dinner this evening. His lovely wife, Kathryn, oversees the kitchen, and she is an excellent cook. Meet us there at McDonough Square at six o'clock to miss the crowd. Then I want to get a good night's sleep. Eight o'clock comes very early in London."

DiPietro led the way out of the courtroom.

"Go ahead and ring for Crawford to bring the car. We'll invite him and his Julie to have dinner with us." He smiled. "Jolly good idea even if I did think of it myself!"

It was evident by his humor that he felt the defense had made a strong case for that day.

Only time would tell.

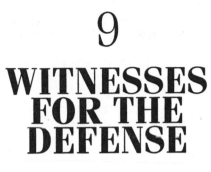

9

WITNESSES
FOR THE
DEFENSE

MORNING, DAY FOUR

Umbrellas were everywhere, looking like differently colored flowers moving in the morning showers. A major portion of them were black, depicting what appeared to be a somber day. Londoners were used to the rain, the pedestrian congestion caused by the umbrellas, and the dangers that cars and buses presented with splashing through large puddles of water.

The thunder seemed louder than ever. It had rumbled about London since about six o'clock that morning when the weather had moved in over the city. Inclement weather always seemed to affect people until they got inside where it was dry.

The bailiff spoke his time-honored lines, and the preliminary legal requirements for the day's trial were completed. The lord chief justice looked at counsel for the defense.

"Sir Luckhoo, you may call your first witness for the defense."

Luckhoo rose and bowed slightly to the bench.

"My lord, the defense wishes to call as its first witness, Mary, wife of Joseph of the house of David, the mother of Jesus."

The bailiff stood, turned toward the witness section, and called out her name in a loud voice.

"Mary, wife of Joseph of the house of David, mother of Jesus. Call for Mary, wife of Joseph."

A dignified woman rose from a seat in the witness section and made her way to the witness box. Her hair, once black, had turned mostly gray in the seventy-seven years she had lived. Her face still held the beauty that had first attracted her husband, Joseph, to her when both were very young.

Small crow's-feet could be seen at the outside corners of her dark eyes, which still sparkled like precious stones touched by sunlight. They contained the same peaceful look that they had received when she became pregnant with her first child. That conception, which she said was fathered by the Holy Spirit of God, had later brought her world acclaim and the religious title of the Virgin Mary.

Mary wore a richly decorated traditional full-length linen dress. A multicolored robe hung loosely from her shoulders. Over that was a colored girdle bearing the stripes denoting that she was of the tribe of Judah. She wore a scarf on her head that hid much of her face. She walked in handmade leather sandals.

When she was directly in front of the jury, she stopped and turned to her right toward the prisoner's dock and smiled at her son. Her teeth were almost perfect. Her smile brought an immediate response from Jesus. He rose from

His chair and bowed to her in respect, giving her a warm, loving smile.

Anyone could tell that there had been very positive communication between mother and son. She took her time, and she walked steadily to the witness box. A woman who knew who she was, she was a vision of gentle strength.

Once there, she pulled her scarf around her shoulders. She stood quietly and waited, looking straight ahead.

The bailiff laid a Bible in front of her, and she placed her hand on it before he could say a word.

"Do you understand the language being spoken here today?" he asked.

She nodded her head. "Yes, I do."

"Then please repeat this after me: I solemnly swear to tell the truth, the whole truth, and nothing but the truth, so help me God."

Her voice came forth soothing, yet strong: "I solemnly swear to tell the truth, the whole truth, and nothing but the truth, so help me Jehovah God."

Luckhoo stood and gazed at this woman. She had lived seven years more than the seventy promised to people by God. She had the appearance of being in her early sixties. Perhaps she was the greatest woman of all time. But if her son was called a fraud, that would mean she was a fraud, also.

Luckhoo knew he must examine this witness in such a way that the jury would know, beyond a shadow of a doubt, that Jesus of Nazareth was her natural-born son, fathered by the Creator of the universe through His supernatural Spirit. Luckhoo would not close his eyes one time during the examination of this witness.

Mary's hands were on the front edge of the witness box.

Her right hand was on top of her left. She wore one ring on her hand bearing the emblem of the Star of David with a fish across it.

Luckhoo picked up his Bible. "I am reading from the Bible, Exhibit A, from the book of Matthew, chapter one, verses fifteen and sixteen: 'Eliud begot Eleazar, Eleazar begot Matthan, and Matthan begot Jacob. And Jacob begot Joseph the husband of Mary, of whom was born Jesus who is called Christ.' Are you the Mary spoken of there, the wife of Joseph and the mother of Jesus of Nazareth?"

"Yes, sir, I am."

"I again read from the Bible, from the book of Mark, chapter six, verse three: '"Is this not the carpenter, the Son of Mary, and brother of James, Joses, Judas, and Simon? And are not His sisters here with us?" So they were offended at Him.' Was your oldest son, Jesus, a carpenter, and did you and Joseph have sons by the names of James, Joses, Judas, and Simon?"

"Yes. That is true."

"Do you believe that there is a supernatural God, one called in Hebrew as Yahweh or Jehovah?"

"Yes, sir. I absolutely do believe that."

"Why do you believe in God?"

"Because, as a child, I heard about the miracles that Jehovah God had done for His people through the stories passed down from one generation to another generation. I heard firsthand of how Jehovah God did great things for people of my father's generation. I have never ever doubted that there is a supernatural God. I have never doubted that a supernatural God can do supernatural things!"

"It is said that you were a virgin, yet you were pregnant with your first child, Jesus. Is that a true statement?"

"Yes, sir, it is truth." Her eyes were fastened on Luckhoo.

"Were you born and raised in Nazareth?"

"Yes, sir, I was."

"If you compared your family of origin to other families in Nazareth, would you say that you were an average family in size, in income, in lifestyle?"

She paused for a moment and turned her eyes upward.

"I would say that we were an average family, yes, sir."

"How old were you when the betrothal took place between your parents and those of Joseph?"

"I was thirteen. Joseph was seventeen."

"Once the betrothal was completed, was it not lawful for you and Joseph to have sexual relations?"

Mary smiled.

"You know some of our traditions, sir, but not all of them. About five hundred years before I was born, that consummation of the marriage had been renounced, and thereafter, the engaged couple were expected to maintain sexual purity until their final marriage vows were taken. Joseph and I were under that tradition of Hebrew law."

"How did you come to know about these things?"

"My father did not believe that there was a difference between people, whether they were Hebrews or Gentiles, whether they were freeborn or slaves, male or female. He taught all of us children the heritage of our past and those things that were normally taught at the synagogue to boys only."

"So you received almost the same education as your brothers did at the synagogue schools, only you received it from your father. Is that correct?"

"Yes, my brothers would talk with my mother and father

every day about what they had learned. Then my father would teach us on the same subject as well."

"I want you to think about your entire life as I ask this question. My question is, Have you ever told a lie to anyone about anything in your entire life?"

Mary's eyes flashed with fire. She spoke pointedly.

"Sir, I have never told a lie to anyone about anything in my entire life. I have so much fear and respect for Jehovah that I felt that if I had ever done such, I would have been stricken dead on the spot for telling a lie."

Darrow leaned over and whispered to Houston. "Give her two credits, Houston. She claims to be the Virgin Mary, and now she claims to be Snow White. That's some combination!" Houston smiled and nodded her head.

Luckhoo continued.

"Were you intimate with your betrothed, Joseph, or anyone else at any time before the birth of your firstborn son, Jesus?"

Mary's face flushed red.

"Sir, I did not and I would not EVER have done such a sin against Jehovah!"

"There are those in the jury who may not have enough facts to believe you. Will you tell them just how you became pregnant with your firstborn, Jesus, since you were not intimate with a man?"

A tear escaped from her eye, and she reached inside her girdle and pulled out a linen handkerchief. She turned her head and stood looking at her son for a moment. Then she looked back over at Luckhoo. Her countenance had changed from anger back to a very peaceful look.

"The day it happened my father was in his shop, and my mother had gone to the market. My brothers were at school, and my sisters were either doing their assigned tasks or playing outside."

Mary tilted her head back and looked at the glass dome in the ceiling of the courtroom. She took a deep breath and a glow came upon her face.

"I was alone in the house preparing food for the evening meal when I sensed something very peaceful and very powerful in the room with me. I looked up and noticed that the room was brighter than I remembered just a few moments before. I turned around, expecting to see the setting sun shining through the window. Instead, the brightness was coming from a large manlike figure standing across the room."

Mary smiled and held her hands to her chest. Her face was radiant as she spoke.

"I trembled with fear when I first saw him. And yet within me I knew that this creature was going to cause me no harm. I somehow knew that this was one of Jehovah's angelic beings! Somehow I knew he was an angel!"

"And what happened next?"

Luckhoo spoke in a quiet voice, not wanting to miss even one word of her testimony as she spoke from the witness box.

"What did this being say to you?"

"He said, 'Rejoice, highly favored one, the Lord is with you; blessed are you among women!' When he stopped speaking, I just stared at him. His eyes were as blue as the sky. I tried not to stare at him, but I couldn't help it."

"Why did you try not to stare at him?"

"We had been taught that it was bad manners to stare at another person. But I just couldn't help myself. I'd never

ever seen anyone that large or that powerful-looking or that beautiful . . . never before in my entire life!"

"Do you remember your thoughts at that very moment?"

"Oh, yes! I was captivated by his appearance. But I was extremely concerned about his words. He said I was favored and blessed among women. I didn't know what his salutation meant. I didn't feel afraid. Yet I looked down at my hands and they were trembling."

"What happened next?"

"I shall never forget his words to me. They seemed to contain the complete essence of what I believed Jehovah God to be. They were almost melodic. My heart was trembling just as much as my hands. The angel said, 'Do not be afraid, Mary, for you have found favor with God. And behold, you will conceive in your womb and bring forth a Son, and shall call His name JESUS. He will be great, and will be called the Son of the Highest; and the Lord God will give Him the throne of His father David. And He will reign over the house of Jacob forever, and of His kingdom there will be no end!'"

Darrow had been listening intently, his reference Bible opened to the first chapter of the book of Luke. His finger pointed to every word she spoke. She had quoted Luke 1:30–33 verbatim. He pointed it out to Houston. She had already compared what Mary said with Exhibit A. Houston had a concerned look on her face.

Luckhoo was nodding his head in the affirmative.

"What was the next thing that you did?"

Mary's voice expressed her excitement.

"My head was reeling with what was going on and what was being said by this majestic angelic being. I knew in my spirit that this angel was talking of the long-awaited Messiah of our people. He was telling me that I was going to be the mother of the Messiah."

"What did you do or say next?"

"I just stood there for a few moments and thought about what he said. I was in awe of the presence of Jehovah God. Tears of joy were coming out of my eyes so hard that he looked just like a huge light standing before me. I remember that after a while, I stopped crying, and then the thought came to my mind that the only way to give birth to a child was to be pregnant. I knew at that moment that I was not pregnant."

Luckhoo, somewhat embarrassed, put his head down as he asked his next question.

"How did you learn about sex and reproduction?"

Her reply was quick and bright.

"Oh, that was basic to our education. We all grew up around farm animals. They were right in our home, in our backyard. At an early age, each of us children was given a male and a female animal and expected to take care of them. I had a pair of sheep. When the ewe came into heat, the sheep bred, and they produced lambs. Every spring I had at least one little lamb that I was responsible to care for."

Houston punched Darrow as he stared at the witness, totally engrossed.

Darrow shrugged his shoulders and turned back to watching the witness. Something about this woman held his rapt attention.

Luckhoo put his hands on the table.

"Back to the angel. Did you make any kind of reply to this being?"

"Oh, yes, sir, I did. I asked him a basic question. I asked

him how this was to happen since I had not married or known a man."

"By the phrase you just spoke, 'known a man,' do you mean to have sexual intercourse with a man?"

Mary's face flushed with embarrassment. "Yes."

"Did the angelic being reply?"

Mary nodded. Her eyes sparkled as she spoke.

"I shall never forget the words he said: 'The Holy Spirit will come upon you, and the power of the Highest will over-shadow you; therefore, also, that Holy One who is to be born will be called the Son of God. Now indeed, Elizabeth your relative has also conceived a son in her old age; and this is now the sixth month for her who was called barren. For with God nothing will be impossible.' Then he stopped talking and just looked at me."

"What happened after this?"

Mary smiled.

"I felt my faith arise in me as if I had never felt it before in my entire life! I closed my eyes and bowed my head to this messenger from God and said words that seemed to bubble up out of my spirit: 'Behold the maidservant of the Lord! Let it be to me according to your word!'"

Mary's gestures became quite animated as she was tell-ing her story.

"I remember raising my hands toward heaven and sing-ing. My whole body felt like it did the hot day when I was a little girl and my sisters and I jumped into a cold mountain stream, only this was even more wonderful than that. I sang and danced around my home. My mother, who was my best friend, came into the house and I hugged her and cried. We both sang and danced. Finally she wore out and sat down. She beckoned me to sit with her and tell her what was happening. It was then that I realized that the angel wasn't there anymore."

Luckhoo was caught up in her enthusiasm. His face was a wide smile, and his eyes were like two shining buckeyes.

"Did you tell your mother what happened at this time?"

"Yes, sir, I did."

"And how did she respond to your sharing this supernatural event with her?"

"She cried and held me and told me that it was every woman's hope to be the mother of the long-promised Messiah. She said that she had prayed and prayed that her firstborn son would be the Messiah, and if he were not, her prayer was that one of her daughters would be the mother of the Messiah."

"Did your mother say anything else?"

"Yes, sir. She reminded me that she and my father had always brought me up to never be fearful of telling the truth, and that she believed that I had never told them or anyone else a lie. She said that she knew . . . that she knew . . . that what I was telling her was truth. My mother never doubted me."

"Did she offer any advice?"

"Yes, sir, she did. She told me not to share this event with anyone else in the family for the moment. She said that since the angel had told me about my cousin, Elizabeth, being with child, I should go and visit her and her husband, Zacharias, who lived in the hill country of Judea. She felt that would strengthen my faith."

"And did you go to visit your cousins?"

"Yes, sir, I did. Before the week was out, one of my brothers took me and left me at their home. I stayed with them about three months."

"What happened upon your arrival at the home of your cousins, Zacharias and Elizabeth?"

Mary smiled, her eyes glistening.

"My brother helped me off the small donkey I had ridden, and I ran to the front door and called out to Elizabeth."

Luckhoo interrupted.

"Did anything unusual happen physically with your cousin?"

"Yes, oh, yes. When Elizabeth heard my voice, the baby in her womb moved. She said it felt as if it just jumped inside her!"

"What was Elizabeth's reply to you?"

"She looked more radiant in that moment than I have ever seen her. I believe that the love of God swept over her, and she closed her eyes and spoke these words to me that I have never forgotten. She said, 'Blessed are you among women, and blessed is the fruit of your womb! But why is this granted to me, that the mother of my Lord should come to me? For indeed, as soon as the voice of your greeting sounded in my ears, the babe leaped in my womb for joy. Blessed is she who believed, for there will be a fulfillment of those things which were told her from the Lord.' Then Elizabeth raised her hands to heaven."

"What did you do?"

"I just felt the love of God flow over me again, as when the angel gave me God's word. I began to speak words of praise to God as if they flowed right out of my inner being."

"Do you recall those words?"

"Oh, yes. Oh, yes," Mary sighed. "My soul magnifies the Lord, and my spirit has rejoiced in God my Savior. For He has regarded the lowly state of His maidservant; for behold, henceforth all generations will call me blessed. For He who is mighty has done great things for me, and holy is His name. And His mercy is on those who fear Him from generation to generation. He has shown strength with His arm; He has scattered the proud in the imagination of their hearts. He has put down the mighty from their thrones, and exalted the lowly. He has filled the hungry with good things, and the rich He has sent away empty. He has helped His servant Israel, in remembrance of His mercy, as He spoke to our fathers, to Abraham and to his seed forever.'"

"Then at the end of three months you returned to your home in Nazareth?"

"Yes, sir, I did."

"By this time you were three months pregnant. Is that correct?"

"Yes, sir, I was."

"When was your betrothed, Joseph, told?"

"Within a day of my return to Nazareth."

"When had you last seen Joseph?"

"I only saw him one time. It was after the betrothal ceremony and just before I went to see Elizabeth. He came with his parents for dinner at the home of my parents. He didn't see me because I stayed behind a shutter in the kitchen."

"Was that traditional?"

"There were several acceptable ways for a bride and a groom to meet. Generally they did not meet until the wedding."

"Were you ever alone with him before the wedding?"

"Yes, sir."

"When was that? Before or after you became pregnant?"

"It was after I became pregnant and I had just returned from Elizabeth's home."

"Will you tell the jury what happened, please?"

"My brother came for me on the donkey. When I returned home, both of my parents were waiting for me. We sat and talked, and I shared the news about Elizabeth's pregnancy. She had not yet delivered when I left her home." Mary paused.

"Then I looked at my mother to see if she had told my father that I was pregnant."

"And what did she do?"

"She nodded her head that he knew and I rushed to his arms. My father held me ever so tightly, and I cried and thanked God for such godly, loving parents."

"What happened next?"

"I told them about the babe jumping in Elizabeth's womb and about what she said, then about what I said. Both were totally understanding. Then my father said that I must tell Joseph myself."

"How did you feel about that?"

"For a moment I felt gripped with fear. Then I laid my hand on my stomach, which was starting to show, and I knew that I was pregnant because of a supernatural miracle of Jehovah God. If He could cause me to get pregnant, He could help me to have the right words to tell Joseph. So I agreed with my father."

"When and how did you tell Joseph?"

"The next day my father sent a message to him to come to our home for dinner, only this time without his parents. He showed up looking quite perplexed, especially when I stepped out of the kitchen and sat down with the family for the meal. We ate dinner, and then my father spoke to Joseph, who was very nervous."

"What did he say?"

"My father said that there was something very important for him to know and he felt that I should tell Joseph privately. My parents excused themselves and went into the next room."

"I told Joseph about my being alone in the house and about the angel who appeared to me. His eyes lit up when he heard this and then he asked me about how big he was. Did he carry a sword? And what color were his hair and his eyes?"

Mary laughed.

"I almost gave up telling him because he was more interested in the angel than he was in me!"

She continued.

"Then I told him what the angel had said to me, and he got this strange look on his face. Even when I told him about being the mother of the Messiah of Jehovah God, he still didn't understand what I was saying. Finally I said to him, 'Joseph, I am pregnant with child.'" Mary put her hand to her mouth and closed her eyes as if she were reliving that painful moment.

"What was his response?"

"I could tell by his face that he was deeply hurt. He sat there shaking his head, as if in disbelief. I told him of my experience with Elizabeth and her miracle of being pregnant, and how the angel had told me about her being pregnant before I went to see her. The only thing he could say was, 'Who knows about your being pregnant?' I told him that just my family and Elizabeth and Zacharias knew."

"Did he reply?"

"He rose from the table and walked toward the door. He turned around and looked back at me. I can remember every word. He said, 'Mary, I have loved you almost all of my life.

When we played together as children, I dreamed that you would be my wife. I never told anyone that secretly I loved you and that one day I hoped we would be joined in marriage. When we were betrothed, my heart sang. Now my heart breaks. It is heavy. I feel that I have more than I can carry. I want to believe you with all that is in me. I can't even think about you being pregnant and unmarried and the consequence of stoning you to death under our religious laws. I must go and pray and think about what I must do.' He started to leave the house."

"Did you say anything to him?"

"Yes. I mustered up everything that was in me and said, 'Joseph, by faith you shall have to trust Jehovah God and me . . . and as Jehovah God Himself provided Abraham with the ram as he was about to sacrifice his own son, Isaac . . . God Himself will provide you with the answer as to what you are to do.'"

"What did Joseph do?"

"He walked out of our home looking dejected. His face was a picture of gloom. It was the first time that I felt pain because of my son, Jesus. I learned that it wouldn't be my last."

Mary looked over to the prisoner's dock at Jesus. He sat there with tears of love flowing down both sides of His face, stopping in His beard and glittering like diamonds. His eyes shone with the love and respect that He had for Mary.

Luckhoo spoke quietly as he continued.

"When did you see him again?"

"The next day he asked permission to see me that evening. He arrived right at supper time, and his face was bright and shining."

"What did Joseph say?"

"Since my brothers and sisters were at the table with us, he asked my parents for permission to share a dream that he believed was from Jehovah God. My mother asked my father if I should first share with my brothers and sisters what had happened to me, and he said yes. I shared my story, and then Joseph told of his dream in which Jehovah God had confirmed that I was pregnant by the Holy Spirit of Jehovah God."

Luckhoo was smiling.

"What happened then?"

"We all had a wonderful time hugging each other and praising God. That was the first time I hugged Joseph. Then my parents said that Joseph must tell his parents every detail and that the wedding date must be set."

"You heard the testimony of your husband, Joseph, in this court. Is that correct?"

"Yes, sir, I did."

"Did he tell it accurately and truthfully?"

"Yes, sir, he did. He even told some details that I had forgotten about."

Mary's eyes showed that she was pleased with the way in which her husband had recounted their lives together.

"Did you ever lie to your husband?"

"Sir, I would have never thought to lie to him or anyone else, for that matter."

"As Jesus was growing up, when did you or your husband tell Him about the miraculous events that took place at His conception and birth?"

Darrow finally came alive and stood very quietly. Every eye in the courtroom turned to him, expecting his usual forceful objection to what was being said. But he said nothing. The lord chief justice turned to him.

"Mr. Darrow, do you have something to say?"

"Yes, Your Lordship. I object to the word *miraculous* that my esteemed colleague just used in his questioning of this witness. The word has not been defined or entered into this trial, and I wish it stricken from the record."

Luckhoo was quick to reply.

"My lord, if you would be pleased to check the record of the court recorder, I believe you will find that in the testimony of Joseph, he quoted verbatim a Scripture from Exhibit A, which I now quote: 'Do not be afraid to take to you Mary your wife, for that which is conceived in her is of the Holy Spirit.' We can recall that Joseph heard these words in a dream from God. One would think that my learned colleague, even in his lack of faith in acknowledging such a supernatural God, would allow that to be called a miraculous conception."

Several of the barristers and solicitors laughed. Luckhoo continued.

"At that time, my lord, the prosecution did not object to the use of such terminology. I would find that conception of a child in a human virgin by a supernatural God as being classified as miraculous by even the most uninformed human being. I would also remind counsel that the entire Bible, Exhibit A, has been introduced as evidence by my esteemed colleague, and the word *miracles* appears in nine of the books!"

"Objection overruled. Proceed, Sir Luckhoo."

Darrow sat down with a loud sigh, indicating his displeasure at the defeat of his objection.

"Do you remember the question?"

"Yes, sir. I told Jesus about His conception and birth when He was about eight years old. He would come home from school and tell me about the things He had learned that day. Then He would always relate to me that somehow He already had learned those teachings from somewhere else. Even the rabbis would chide His father and me because they said we must be teaching Jesus more than they were."

"What did Jesus say when you told Him that you believed that He was the Messiah?"

"By this time He was thirteen years of age. He came home from school on the Sabbath and told me that every lesson He had been taught that week by the rabbis was about the Messiah of Israel. He said that they had studied the Torah about the many prophecies concerning the promised Messiah's birth and life. It was then that I told Him the miracle of His birth was the same as prophesied about the Messiah. When I finished speaking, He looked up at me and said, 'Mother, it is as you say.'"

"What Scriptures did you share with Him? Can you remember any of them from memory?"

Mary reached into her girdle and pulled out a very old piece of parchment. She carefully opened the neatly folded parchment and held it at arm's length from her face. She squinted her eyes as she read.

"Yes, sir, I wrote them down, all of them. I did it when I told Him the first time. I wrote them here on this parchment."

Luckhoo turned to the lord chief justice.

"My lord, I should like to request the court linguist, Mr. Norwood, to verbally identify to the jury from Exhibit A the precise Scripture from the Old Testament that the witness is giving from her parchment."

The lord chief justice nodded his approval.

"Mr. Norwood, if you will take the parchment from the

witness and take it to my chambers. Please make a photo-copy of it for your use and then return the parchment to the witness. Then identify for the jury the Scriptures as she presents them as evidence."

The court linguist rose from the table and walked over to the witness box. Mary looked at him and said, "You will give it back to me, won't you? I kept very few of the things from His childhood."

Norwood nodded his head up and down and left the room. Luckhoo held open his Bible toward the bench.

"My lord, I believe that if the evidence foreman, Mr. Longworth, will open Exhibit A and turn to the back of the Bible, he will find a section marked 'Prophecies of the Messiah Fulfilled in Jesus Christ.' I would ask, my lord, that the Bible be presented to the court linguist upon his return so that he can also give us the subject of any prophetic Old Testament Scripture the witness may provide, as well as the New Testament Scripture that proves the fulfillment of that Scripture."

Darrow rose to his feet and spoke simultaneously.

"Your Lordship, although Exhibit A has been entered into this trial as an exhibit by the prosecution, neither the defense nor the prosecution has proven its creditability as an exhibit from which quotes should be readily accepted per se."

Darrow spoke slowly and distinctly.

"Since Exhibit A contains the most information about the life of the accused and the events surrounding His life, the prosecution has allowed it to be quoted in that sense, without objection. Then, for the most part, we have asked witnesses to verify, by testimony, whether or not that part of the exhibit is correlative. I feel that—"

Before he could continue Luckhoo spoke up.

"My lord, I am not here to defend the Bible, Exhibit A. The Bible certainly needs no one to defend it as it is a collection of books that is historically, scientifically, and spiritually correct. We have already had witnesses for the prosecution and for the defense who have quoted verbatim from the Bible. The words that they spoke were exactly the same words recorded in the Bible."

He continued to speak quickly so as not to be interrupted by Darrow.

"It is also a book of prophecy, and the defense wishes to demonstrate to the jury and to the Crown that this Bible is filled with prophecies concerning the Messiah, which the accused, Jesus of Nazareth, fulfilled in His lifetime on this earth, thus proving His messiahship."

Luckhoo's voice rose to a higher pitch as he continued to speak without interruption.

"It is the intention of the defense to show, beyond a reasonable doubt, that hundreds of prophecies were spoken centuries before fulfillment, and that these exclude the human possibility of fulfillment."

His fist went into the air to make a point.

"The prophecies in this collection of books called the Bible are in such infinite detail as to be well beyond all human power to predict, even with the sophisticated computers of our age."

Luckhoo had a determined look on his face.

"While the defense can adequately reveal over three hundred specific prophecies about the Messiah that Jesus of Nazareth fulfilled in His earthly lifetime," Luckhoo lowered his fist and turned to the lord chief justice, "we ask only that we be allowed to produce a few of them as evidence from the mouths of the witnesses and confirmed by the Bible."

As if it were an afterthought, Luckhoo added a point.

"And I would hasten to state that according to the laws of simple and compound probability, these three hundred plus prophecies concerning the Messiah could have had only one chance in one hundred and ninety-seven ciphers of fulfillment. Yet in Jesus of Nazareth, they all were fulfilled!"

Luckhoo pounded his fist on the desk in front of him with each statement he made.

"The defense will show that only a Creator God could foretell such future events, thereby proving that the Bible is a revelation of God by inspiration. There have been men who have prophesied great events in history, but none of these mere men have been one hundred percent correct . . . as has been the Bible. No one has ever found one failure in the prophecies in the Bible of any single detail of prediction. No one dare refute such a claim. The Bible has stood the test of time, and it has been accepted on every continent and in every nation of the world."

He turned again to the bench.

"The defense is prepared, if necessary, to go through every one of the more than three hundred verses of Bible prophecies. We will prove that they were written prior to Jesus' birth and they came to pass in His lifetime and after His death. This court has the responsibility to allow the accused, Jesus of Nazareth, every rightful piece of evidence to prove He is who He says He is."

Luckhoo held out his open hand toward the bench.

"My lord, we wish to question this witness concerning prophecies from the Bible to ascertain whether or not, from her testimony and that of others, the prophecies were fulfilled in Jesus of Nazareth. My lord, we are dealing with the one witness in all of recorded history who spent the most time with the accused while He was on this earth!"

The lord chief justice stroked his beard for a few seconds and then spoke.

"Inasmuch as the esteemed prosecution did enter the New King James Version of the Bible into evidence at the beginning of these proceedings and specified that the exhibit did contain most of the historical writings concerning the accused, and inasmuch as the esteemed defense did not object to such entering of this exhibit, the Crown finds no offense in Exhibit A being used throughout this trial. The objection is overruled. As soon as the court linguist has returned to the courtroom, you may proceed with the witness, Sir Luckhoo."

Norwood entered the room just as the lord chief justice spoke Luckhoo's name. He walked to the witness and returned her parchment. He went to the evidence table and sat down with his copy and the Bible in front of him.

"Mr. Norwood," said the lord chief justice, "you are to call out the book, chapter, and verse of the Scripture as the witness presents the word of her testimony, using Exhibit A. You also are to call out the subject of the Scripture from the helps section of Exhibit A and read aloud the reference to the New Testament that is given in that section."

He turned to the court recorder.

"Sir Brooks, you will record all that is spoken by the court linguist and show in the record that he is reading from Exhibit A. You may proceed with your examination of your witness, Sir Luckhoo."

"Will you take your parchment and read the holy Scriptures, one at a time, that you wrote when Jesus was a child?"

"Yes, sir. I told Him that Jehovah God had prophesied in the first book of the Torah that there would be a virgin birth of the Messiah from a woman: 'And I will put enmity between you and the woman, and between your seed and her Seed; He shall bruise your head, and you shall bruise His heel.'"

Norwood spoke loudly and clearly. "Genesis 3:15: 'Seed of a woman.' Galatians 4:4: 'But when the fullness of the time had come, God sent forth His Son, born of a woman, born under the law.'"

"Your next Scripture if you please."

"In the book of beginnings, I read to Him where Jehovah spoke to father Abraham: 'I will bless those who bless you, and I will curse him who curses you; and in you all the families of the earth shall be blessed.'"

"Genesis 12:3: 'Descendant of Abraham.' Matthew 1:1: 'The book of the genealogy of Jesus Christ, the Son of David, the Son of Abraham,'" Norwood read.

Luckhoo nodded to Mary.

"I told my son that He was of the prophesied tribe of Judah: 'The scepter shall not depart from Judah, nor a law-giver from between his feet, until Shiloh comes; and to Him shall be the obedience of the people.'"

"Genesis 49:10: 'From the tribe of Judah.' Luke 3:33: 'The son of Amminadab, the son of Ram, the son of Hezron, the son of Perez, the son of Judah.'"

Norwood smiled to himself that he could pronounce the names he was reading.

"I told Jesus that according to God's holy Word, He was an heir of King David as written by the prophet Isaiah, spoken in the year 734 B.C.: 'Of the increase of His government and peace there will be no end, upon the throne of David

and over His kingdom, to order it and establish it with judgment and justice from that time forward, even forever. The
zeal of the LORD of hosts will perform this.'"

"Isaiah 9:7: 'Heir to the throne of David.' Luke 1:32–33,"
Norwood called out, "'He will be great, and will be called
the Son of the Highest; and the Lord God will give Him the
throne of His father David. And He will reign over the house
of Jacob forever, and of His kingdom there will be no end.'"

Mary smiled as she read from her parchment.

"In 700 B.C. it was prophesied by the prophet Micah that
the Messiah would be born in the little town of Bethlehem:
'But you, Bethlehem Ephrathah, though you are little among
the thousands of Judah, yet out of you shall come forth to
Me the One to be Ruler in Israel, whose goings forth are
from of old, from everlasting.'"

"Micah 5:2: 'Born in Bethlehem.' Luke 2:4–5, 7: 'Joseph
also went up from Galilee, out of the city of Nazareth, into
Judea, to the city of David, which is called Bethlehem, because he was of the house and lineage of David, to be registered with Mary, his betrothed wife, who was with child. . . .
And she brought forth her firstborn Son, and wrapped Him
in swaddling cloths, and laid Him in a manger, because there
was no room for them in the inn.'"

Mary stood straight in the witness box as she heard of
the confirmation of what she believed. Her voice seemed to
get stronger with every Scripture she read. A slight smile
was on her face as she looked over to her son from time to
time. His eyes were on her, radiant with respect.

"The prophet Isaiah prophesied around 735 B.C. that the
Messiah would be born of a virgin: 'Therefore the Lord Himself will give you a sign: Behold, the virgin shall conceive
and bear a Son, and shall call His name Immanuel.'"

"Isaiah 7:14: 'To be born of a virgin.' Luke 1:26–27, 30–31: 'Now in the sixth month the angel Gabriel was sent by God to a city of Galilee named Nazareth, to a virgin betrothed to a man whose name was Joseph, of the house of David. The virgin's name was Mary. . . . Then the angel said to her, "Do not be afraid, Mary, for you have found favor with God. And behold, you will conceive in your womb and bring forth a Son, and shall call His name JESUS."'"

"I told my son, Jesus, as best I could, that innocent children had died because of the evil in humankind. I read to Him the prophecy from the prophet Jeremiah written almost six hundred years before it happened: 'Thus says the LORD: "A voice was heard in Ramah, lamentation and bitter weeping, Rachel weeping for her children, refusing to be comforted for her children, because they are no more."'"

Norwood read the reference. "Jeremiah 31:15: 'Slaughter of children.' Matthew 2:16–18: 'Then Herod, when he saw that he was deceived by the wise men, was exceedingly angry; and he sent forth and put to death all the male children who were in Bethlehem and in all its districts, from two years old and under, according to the time which he had determined from the wise men. Then was fulfilled what was spoken by Jeremiah the prophet, saying: "A voice was heard in Ramah, lamentation, weeping, and great mourning, Rachel weeping for her children, refusing to be comforted, because they are no more."'"

Luckhoo nodded again to Mary as she spoke. He was very pleased that she had the parchment with her. He had planned to bring up many of the age-old prophecies in another way, but she had solved his dilemma of how to accomplish his task.

"Jesus was told also that the prophet Hosea had foretold

of our family fleeing to Egypt. The prophecy was written seven hundred twenty-five years prior: 'When Israel was a child, I loved him, and out of Egypt I called My son.'"

"Hosea 11:1: 'Flight to Egypt.' Matthew 2:14–15: 'When he arose, he took the young Child and His mother by night and departed for Egypt, and was there until the death of Herod, that it might be fulfilled which was spoken by the Lord through the prophet, saying, "Out of Egypt I called My Son."'"

Luckhoo interrupted as Mary looked to be near the end of what was written in Aramaic, years before.

"Did you ever give Jesus a prophecy concerning what His cousin John was saying and doing?"

Mary looked at her parchment and nodded her head.

"Yes. I told Him about the prophecy of Malachi, spoken about 430 B.C.: '"Behold, I will send you Elijah the prophet before the coming of the great and dreadful day of the Lord. And he will turn the hearts of the fathers to the children, and the hearts of the children to their fathers, lest I come and strike the earth with a curse."'"

"Malachi 4:5–6: 'Preceded by Elijah.' Matthew 11:13–14: 'For all the prophets and the law prophesied until John. And if you are willing to receive it, he is Elijah who is to come.'"

"Did you ever tell Jesus that He would be betrayed by a friend for exactly thirty pieces of silver?"

Again, Mary nodded her head. "Yes." She looked down and ran her finger down the parchment until she stopped.

"I shared with my son from the writings of King David: 'Even my own familiar friend in whom I trusted, who ate my bread, has lifted up his heel against me.' And from the prophet Zechariah I shared: 'Then I said to them, "If it is agreeable to you, give me my wages; and if not, refrain." So they weighed out for my wages thirty pieces of silver.'"

Norwood ran his finger up and down the page, looking for the reference. Finding it, on the top of the next page, he began his reading.

"Psalm 41:9: 'Betrayed by a close friend.' Luke 22:47–48: 'And while He was still speaking, behold, a multitude; and he who was called Judas, one of the twelve, went before them and drew near to Jesus to kiss Him. But Jesus said to him, "Judas, are you betraying the Son of Man with a kiss?"' And from Zechariah 11:12: 'Betrayed for thirty pieces of silver.' Matthew 26:14–15: 'Then one of the twelve, called Judas Iscariot, went to the chief priests and said, "What are you willing to give me if I deliver Him to you?" And they counted out to him thirty pieces of silver.'"

Luckhoo asked, "Do you have other Scriptures that you shared with your Son, Jesus?"

"Yes, sir, I have many more."

"Rather than cover them all, do you have any that foretold that your son, Jesus, would die on a cross like a criminal?"

Mary stared at Luckhoo for a moment as tears welled up in her eyes. Her once-strong voice could barely be heard as she looked at the lord chief justice and then the jury. One could see the agony in her face as she was asked to remember the cruel death of her son.

"Do you know what it is like to see the fruit of your womb hanging on a barbarous Roman cross of execution between two common criminals? Do you have any idea what it is like as you watch your son slowly and painfully die, innocent of every charge against Him?"

There was no noise in the courtroom except the quiet

voice of Mary speaking. She spoke very softly, yet every person present heard each word. One could imagine hearing the sound of her tears as they rolled down her cheeks and fell to the floor at her feet. Luckhoo stood motionless.

"Do you have any idea of the amount of faith it takes to believe that you carried the promised Messiah of Israel in your own womb . . . so that one day He would eventually be the sacrifice for the sins of even those who sit here today?"

Mary wiped her eyes with a white linen handkerchief. Her tone changed from gentleness to firmness and strength. She stood straight again and looked at Darrow and Luckhoo. Her eyes shone with pride.

"If you desire to know whether or not my son is the promised Messiah of God, you must search the written Word of God. In it you can find the truth and testimony of my son, and in God's Word you can have eternal life."

She looked back at Luckhoo.

"To answer your question, sir, I can quote from my memory what the prophet Isaiah spoke almost seven hundred years before I became pregnant by the Holy Spirit of God. He told of my son's birth by the power of God when he said, 'Who has believed our report? And to whom has the arm of the LORD been revealed? For He shall grow up before Him as a tender plant, and as a root out of dry ground!'"

Norwood kept his finger in the back of Exhibit A and turned to chapter 53 in the Old Testament book of Isaiah. He followed along as Mary quoted word for word with her eyes closed and her face turned upward.

"And after they had beaten my son . . . and after they had pulled out His beard by the roots . . . and after they had placed the crown of thorns on His head and driven in the thorns with the flat sides of their swords . . . and after they had given Him thirty-nine stripes across His naked back with the whip . . . and after He carried his own instrument of death to the hill . . . there He died as a sacrifice for the sins of all people. Isaiah said these words concerning my son: 'He has no form or comeliness; and when we see Him, there is no beauty that we should desire Him. He is despised and rejected by men, a Man of sorrows and acquainted with grief. And we hid, as it were, our faces from Him; He was despised, and we did not esteem Him. Surely He has borne our griefs and carried our sorrows; yet we esteemed Him stricken, smitten by God, and afflicted!'"

Mary lifted both hands upward as if she were in prayer or praise to God.

"'But He was wounded for our transgressions, He was bruised for our iniquities; the chastisement for our peace was upon Him, and by His stripes we are healed!'"

She lowered her head and arms and clasped her hands together.

"'All we like sheep have gone astray; we have turned, every one, to his own way; and the LORD has laid on Him the iniquity of us all. He was oppressed and He was afflicted, yet He opened not His mouth; He was led as a lamb to the slaughter, and as a sheep before its shearers is silent, so He opened not His mouth. He was taken from prison and from judgment, and who will declare His generation? For He was cut off from the land of the living; for the transgressions of My people He was stricken!'"

Hot tears of the deep hurt of memories flowed down Mary's cheeks to form glasslike pools at her feet. One could almost feel the depth of her pain as she spoke words written hundreds of years before she was chosen to bear the Son of Jehovah God and then to watch Him die. Every time she had thought of that horrible day when she watched her innocent son die as a criminal, she would read this chapter from the prophet Isaiah to reassure herself that it was all true.

She continued, "'And they made His grave with the wicked—but with the rich at His death, because He had done no violence, nor was any deceit in His mouth. Yet it pleased the LORD to bruise Him; He has put Him to grief. When You make His soul an offering for sin, He shall see His seed, He shall prolong His days, and the pleasure of the LORD shall prosper in His hand. He shall see the labor of His soul, and be satisfied. By His knowledge My righteous Servant shall justify many, for He shall bear their iniquities. Therefore I will divide Him a portion with the great, and He shall divide the spoil with the strong, because He poured out His soul unto death, and He was numbered with the transgressors, and He bore the sin of many, and made intercession for the transgressors.'"

Mary looked to her son, who had fastened His eyes on her. Their eyes met, and He smiled at her. With tears freely flowing across her cheeks, Mary spoke words of encouragement to her son.

"I never doubted that You, my own son, are the long-promised Messiah of Israel. I watched You grow in wisdom and stature, and gain favor in the sight of Jehovah God Your Father and of man. I am not a learned rabbi, but I know enough of justice to know that the trials of the Sanhedrin and those before the Romans were mere shams . . . and they are a stench in the nostrils of Jehovah God. Every day of Your life, I came to weigh in the scales of life the knowledge that You were my son on the one hand . . . and that one day, You would be my Lord on the other hand. As I watched You die on the Roman cross and even after Your resurrection from the dead, I had to weigh in the balance the things of a mother's heart and the things of a handmaiden of the Lord. I speak to You this day as my Lord. I say that knowing how my heart almost burst with love at Your coming and it almost burst with pain at Your dying . . . I would again welcome the honor to bear the only begotten Son of God in my womb."

The silence was broken by sobs from people in the courtroom. Jesus rose quietly from His seat and extended both hands toward her in a gesture of strength and honor. The holes in His hands were clearly visible where He had been nailed to the cross.

Tears of joy and admiration flowed down His cheeks and into His dark beard. His smile displayed the gratitude that He felt for Mary.

There seemed to be an unexplainable warmth in the room. It was as if someone had opened the door and the fragrance of apple blossoms could be smelled throughout the courtroom.

Jesus bowed slightly to His mother in a gesture of respect and sat down. She turned her head back to Luckhoo, who was wiping his eyes with his handkerchief.

Darrow rose to his feet and looked at the lord chief justice. He knew that it was a poignant moment in the trial, and he dared not desecrate it. Yet he felt an objection was in order. He spoke very quietly.

"Your Lordship, I have been moved greatly by this godly woman's affection for her son, the accused. However, the witness has been allowed, by the esteemed defense counsel, to ramble on without legal direction and to make a very beautiful statement toward her son, which is out of order in this trial because it does not bear on the question posed by counsel. It is an expression of her feelings rather than an answer to the direct question of counsel."

Darrow sat down and awaited his answer.

Luckhoo turned to the lord chief justice.

"My lord, I recognize that my esteemed colleague is correct in his assessment of a very short bit of testimony of the witness. However, my lord, neither the court linguist, Mr. Norwood, nor I have yet verified the prophetic Scripture from which the witness quoted verbatim, nor did counsel have the opportunity to press the issue of the witness's statement to her son, Jesus of Nazareth, which she just uttered."

Luckhoo kept his voice in a quiet and respectful tone.

"If it please, my lord, I should like to ask the witness one question and save the court time and effort. If my action should not please my lord, then I shall yield to my esteemed colleague's objection."

The lord chief justice nodded his head. "Proceed with your one question, Sir Luckhoo."

"Thank you, my lord."

He turned to Mary.

"Do you believe, beyond a reasonable doubt, that given all you know of this man whom you call your son; that given all you know of this man whom you call Lord; and with all the prophecies that have been foretold about His birth and resurrection from the dead . . . without equivocation, do you believe Jesus of Nazareth to be the promised Messiah of Israel?"

Mary looked straight at Luckhoo.

"With Jehovah God as my witness, I believe that man sitting there . . . ," she pointed directly at Jesus, ". . . is without a doubt the Messiah spoken of by the prophets of Jehovah God of Israel. For I know whom I have believed and

I am persuaded that by the prophecies of Jehovah God from hundreds of years before the birth of Jesus, and the miraculous way that each one of them has been fulfilled concerning Jesus of Nazareth, even against this day, I speak to you the truth. I believe, with all my heart, that He is the Messiah, the true Son of the living God."

Luckhoo turned to the court linguist. "Mr. Norwood, please provide the proper quotations as requested."

Norwood turned to Luckhoo.

"The witness quoted verbatim the entire fifty-third chapter of the book of Isaiah from the Old Testament. Do you wish the New Testament Scriptures in response, sir?"

Luckhoo looked first at the lord chief justice. "What say you, my lord, on the objection?"

"I overrule the objection by Mr. Darrow. However, I do wish to encourage the witness to answer only in response to the question asked. Proceed, Mr. Norwood, with the fulfilled Scriptures from the New Testament."

"Isaiah 53:5: 'Vicarious sacrifice.' Romans 5:6, 8: 'For when we were still without strength, in due time Christ died for the ungodly. . . . But God demonstrates His own love toward us, in that while we were still sinners, Christ died for us.' The witness also quoted Isaiah 53:12: 'Crucified with malefactors.' Mark 15:27–28: 'With Him they also crucified two robbers, one on His right and the other on His left. So the Scripture was fulfilled which says, "And He was numbered with the transgressors."' The witness also quoted from Isaiah 53:9: 'Buried with the rich.' Matthew 27:57–60: 'Now when evening had come, there came a rich man from Arimathea, named Joseph, who himself had also become a disciple of Jesus. This man went to Pilate and asked for the body of Jesus. Then Pilate commanded the body to be given to him. When Joseph had taken the body, he wrapped it in a clean linen cloth, and laid it in his new tomb which he had hewn out of the rock; and he rolled a large stone against the door of the tomb, and departed.'"

Norwood nodded to Luckhoo, indicating that he was finished.

"I have a few final questions for you. The first is this: Did your son, Jesus of Nazareth, die a physical death on a Roman cross of crucifixion at a place outside Jerusalem known as Calvary?"

"Yes, sir."

"Did you hold His lifeless body on your lap before He was wrapped for burial?"

"Yes, sir."

"Did you watch them wrap your son's dead body for burial, and did you watch them place that dead body of your son in a tomb?"

"Yes, sir."

"Did you watch them roll the heavy stone over the entrance to the tomb after the dead body of Jesus was placed in that tomb?"

"Yes, sir."

"And did you ever see your son alive again, prior to coming to this court?"

"Yes, sir."

"Will you please tell the jury about that experience?"

"It was just three days later when several of us were gathered in Jerusalem. A report came that our Lord Jesus had appeared to Mary Magdalene. Then another report came from two disciples who were on their way to the village of Emmaus. They saw Jesus and ate with Him. We were all talking excitedly of these things when our Lord Jesus Himself stood in the midst of us. We thought we were seeing a spirit, and we were somewhat afraid."

She smiled and wiped her eyes with her handkerchief.

"However, our Lord Jesus showed us His hands and His feet with the holes in them. He even sat down and ate some fish and honeycomb with us. He talked to us awhile. He blessed us, and we watched Him as He ascended up into the heavens. He just rose in a cloud toward heaven until we could see Him no more."

"And when did you next see the Lord Jesus?"

"In my seventy-seventh year, my spirit became absent from my body and became immediately present with my Lord. I have been with Him in heaven ever since."

"Thank you so very much."

Luckhoo turned to the lord chief justice.

"My lord, I have no further examination of this witness at this time."

The lord chief justice looked at the clock and then at the prosecutor.

"Mr. Darrow, you may cross-examine this witness until we recess."

Darrow rose from his seat, straightened his gown and his wig, and looked at the elegant woman standing before him. He took his time before starting and then looked over at the accused and then back to Mary.

"Do you love your son?"

"Yes, sir, I do."

"Do you love Him more than anything else in this entire world?"

"Yes, sir, I do."

"Do you love Him even more than your own life?"

"Yes, sir, I do."

"Thank you. It is so easy to understand the testimony of a very loving, dedicated, concerned, protective seventy-seven-year-old mother, as we believe you to be. Certainly, no one will dispute that."

Darrow looked at the lord chief justice.

"Your Lordship, the prosecution has no further questions of this witness."

He sat down amid the whispers of the barristers and solicitors sitting behind him.

"Where are you, Darrow?" Houston asked with a scowl on her face. "You had a golden chance to nail the mother of the accused to the cross and you turned that down? What is going on?"

Darrow leaned back against his bench and turned his head to Houston. "Houston, you don't crucify the mother of Jesus, regardless of the opportunity you have. When you get someone who oozes with mother-son love like that, you don't have a chance of making any kind of a rebuttal out of it without seeming like you want to crucify the Virgin Mary. She's a biased, loving mother, and that's the way I want the jury to see her."

Luckhoo leaned over to DiPietro. "Diane, you just saw one of the reasons that Clarence Darrow has been famous in the courts of law. He's a man with a heart, but he knows when to rush in and when to stand. He looks like a softy now, but you watch out, he'll be back like a wise serpent this afternoon."

The lord chief justice banged his gavel on the wooden block before him.

"Do you wish to reexamine, Sir Luckhoo?"

"No, my lord."

"This court will recess for lunch and will be in session

at one o'clock this afternoon. The defense will be prepared to call its next witness at that time."

"Bang! Bang! Bang!" The rapping of the court scepter could be heard all over the courtroom. The bailiff closed the session with the age-old traditional words.

The people stood as the lord chief justice departed through his door. The jurors filed out to their room as the witnesses moved out to their room for lunch. Because there was still an aura of love in the courtroom, people moved out quietly and orderly. The courtroom was empty, yet the sweet aroma of apple blossoms still filled the room.

The first of twelve strokes on the bell at St. Sepulchre's Church began to chime and was joined immediately by Big Ben. Nothing had changed much in the weather. The London sky was still overcast, and a mist was blowing in the wind. The big change was in the people streaming out of the Central Criminal Courts Building. They were different today as they left Number One Court. They seemed to be carrying love out into the streets.

10

WITNESSES
FOR THE
DEFENSE

AFTERNOON, DAY FOUR

The faces of the courtroom participants were bright. They appeared to be jovial as they sat and talked while awaiting the call to order in the courtroom.

The lord chief justice entered the courtroom, and after the traditional opening, the trial resumed.

"Sir Luckhoo, you may call the next defense witness." The lord chief justice spoke in his usual strong tone of voice.

"Thank you, my lord. I wish to call as a witness for the defense John ben Malchus, former servant to the high priest, Joseph Caiaphas."

The bailiff called for the witness.

"John ben Malchus, former servant to the high priest. Call for John ben Malchus."

All eyes turned to the witness section of the courtroom as a man in his early sixties began to make his way to the witness box.

His almost white hair was receding slightly on both

sides of his forehead and was combed neatly back, hanging down to his shoulders. His moustache and beard were white, speckled with black. There was a brown mole just above the left side of his moustache. His classic face was enhanced by dark brown eyes.

He was dressed in an inner garment made of linen that extended to his wrists and hung down to his ankles. He wore simple leather thonged sandals on his feet. A multi-colored outer garment was wrapped around his body. The two corners of the material met in front, with fringes of elegant blue ribbons encircling the hemline.

A wide belt wound around his waist, decorated with delicate embroidery. A gold Star of David and a fish hung around his neck on an elaborate gold chain. As he walked steadily toward the witness box, he displayed a very slight limp. He stopped in front of the jury and made a slight bow to them, then turned and bowed even lower to Jesus. Jesus acknowledged the bow with a smile.

Malchus entered the witness box.

"Do you understand the language being spoken here today?"

He looked the bailiff in the eye and replied, "Yes, sir, I do understand."

The bailiff spoke the oath so that everyone in the courtroom could hear. Malchus repeated it loud and clear. The bailiff took his seat.

The lord chief justice looked at Luckhoo and said, "Sir, Lionel, you may examine your witness."

"Thank you, my lord. Mr. Malchus, would you explain something of your lineage and religious heritage to the jury, please."

"Yes, sir. My mother's family were from Greece, and my

father's family were from the northern part of Europe. She was a devout Jewish believer, and he . . . uh . . . became a believer later in his life. They are both deceased." His voice was very strong and clear.

"I was educated in the synagogue and with private tutoring as a child. When I became older, I departed from religion. I would say that I was forty-two years of age when I came back to practice my religion. Eventually, I ended up as one of the servants of the high priest, Joseph Caiaphas."

"Do you have brothers and sisters, and if so, what are their names?"

"Yes, I have an older brother, Jachin; a younger brother, Patrobas; and three younger sisters, Mary, Rebekah, and Philoga."

"You are married?"

"Yes, sir, my wife's name is Susanna."

"Do you have children?"

Darrow rose from his seat with a look of disgust on his face.

"Your Lordship, why must we go through the complete unrelated genealogy of this mere servant of Reverend Caiaphas and waste the time of the court?"

The lord chief justice glanced at Luckhoo with a questioning look on his face.

Luckhoo answered the challenge immediately.

"My lord, the defense is attempting to show that this so-called mere servant was a respected citizen of Jerusalem at the time the accused, Jesus of Nazareth, was in the city. The defense wishes to know what this witness knows about the accused and to enter his testimony into evidence. The defense wishes for the jury to understand the creditability of the witness."

"Your objection is overruled, Mr. Darrow. Proceed with your examination in chief, Sir Lionel."

"Will you answer the last question, Mr. Malchus, concerning your children?"

"I have three children: Tamara, a married daughter, a son Erech, and a daughter Cristus."

"Are you still a servant of the high priest, Joseph Caiaphas?"

"No, I left the services of Joseph Caiaphas some twenty years before my last birthday."

"Will you tell us how you came to work for Caiaphas, Mr. Malchus?"

"I was raised and educated in Greece, and I married the daughter of a wood merchant from Normandy. He encouraged us to move to Israel to buy exotic woods and send them back to him in Greece. As Greek citizens, we got along well with the Romans and with the Jews. We had met Pontius Pilate in Rome at several gatherings, so when we arrived in Israel, we presented ourselves to him. Because of my knowledge of world affairs, we found ourselves at several parties hosted by the Roman procurator. It was at one of those parties where we met the Jewish high priest, Joseph Caiaphas."

"Were you active in any synagogue or in the temple?"

"I became interested again in my basic religion, Judaism, and began to practice it again. As I did, I saw the high priest on several occasions, and we gave ample tithes into the temple treasuries."

"How did you come to actually work for the high priest, Mr. Malchus?"

"I gave the high priest some beautiful carved wood furniture that my father-in-law had sent to me. I delivered it to his home one day, and he asked me to come to a private meeting with him."

"Will you tell us what happened at that private meeting with the high priest, Joseph Caiaphas."

"A meal was served, with all the blessings, and he asked about our business. I told him that it was doing very well and that I had a very good man, Donylus ben Wirtman, working with me in it, who took care of most of the details. Reverend Caiaphas then asked me if I would consider being on his personal staff."

"Did he know that you were a Greek citizen?"

"Yes, sir, he did. He mentioned that fact, but he said that since I came from a family of Jewish believers, my citizenship didn't make that much difference. He said that my position would be one of administrative duties, not religious ones. He did indicate that I should keep the fact of my citizenship as 'our business only,' as much as possible."

"What did you do for the high priest, Joseph Caiaphas?"

"Anyone who wanted an audience with him had to schedule it through me. I composed letters for him, I wrote some of his sermons, and I represented him at various functions with the Romans and Gentiles."

"Did he ever ask you to go to any function where the accused, Jesus of Nazareth, was speaking?"

"Yes, sir. He sent me to a number of those functions."

"Why did the high priest, Joseph Caiaphas, send you to events where the accused, Jesus of Nazareth, was speaking?"

"Reverend Caiaphas said that he trusted me to bring back an objective report of what Jesus was teaching."

"Can you recall one or two of the most significant functions where Jesus, the accused, was speaking?"

Malchus put his hand to his chin and stroked his beard

as he thought about his answer. His eyes seemed to light up, and a smile broke across his face.

"Oh, I can recall many. One day, I had been sent to find Jesus and listen to Him and then, of course, report back to Reverend Caiaphas. I found Jesus and His followers coming through a gate to the city. There was a man, who had been blind from birth, sitting among the many beggars at the gate daily."

"Can you recall some of what was said as well as what happened on this occasion, Mr. Malchus?"

"Yes, sir. One of Jesus' followers pointed to this particular blind man and said, 'Rabbi, who sinned, this man or his parents, that he was born blind?' And Jesus answered, 'Neither this man nor his parents sinned, but that the works of God should be revealed in him. I must work the works of Him who sent Me while it is day; the night is coming when no one can work. As long as I am in the world, I am the light of the world!' When He had said that, 'He spat on the ground and made clay with the saliva; and He anointed the eyes of the blind man with the clay.' And Jesus said to him, 'Go, wash in the pool of Siloam.'"

"And what did the man do, Mr. Malchus?"

"He did exactly what Jesus had told him to do. He groped his way to the pool of Siloam, washed his face, and came back with his sight."

"What were your thoughts at seeing this, Mr. Malchus?"

"I thought it was absolutely wonderful. In fact, I took the man who had been healed to some of the Pharisees because I thought they would be pleased to see what I believed to be a miracle of God."

"And what did they do, Mr. Malchus?"

"A few of them were sincerely impressed, but most of

them complained because it was done on the Sabbath and it was against one of their petty laws. They even got the young man's very poor parents and questioned them about him, trying to make it seem as if it was all a sham. I had seen the man begging for several years. He had never had any sight before Jesus sent him to the pool. When he came back, the man could see!"

"Did you hear the questioning of the man and his parents by the Pharisees?"

"Yes, sir. I was there as the representative of the high priest."

"And what did you see and hear, Mr. Malchus?"

"The Pharisees asked, 'Is this your son, who you say was born blind? How then does he now see?' His parents appeared to be afraid of the Pharisees. I remember their answer. They said, 'We know that this is our son, and that he was born blind; but by what means he now sees we do not know, or who opened his eyes we do not know. He is of age; ask him. He will speak for himself.' That made the Pharisees mad, and they brought the man who had been blind before them again and questioned him a second time. They told him that the man who had healed him was a sinner because it was done on the Sabbath."

"Mr. Malchus, what did the former blind man say to them?"

"He got into a shouting match with them. The man said to them, 'Whether He is a sinner or not I do not know. One thing I know: that though I was blind, now I see.' Then they asked, 'What did He do to you? How did He open your eyes?' The man yelled his answer back to the Pharisees. You could tell that he was frustrated because it was like they were trying to tell him that he didn't have the right to see! He shouted at them: 'I told you already, and you did not listen. Why do you want to hear it again? Do you want to be His disciples?' That, of course, rankled the Pharisees. They shouted back that they were disciples of Moses."

Malchus seemed to forget where he was in telling his story. He clapped his hands and rubbed them together.

"They shouted that God spoke to Moses, but they didn't know who spoke to the person who had performed the miracle. They also said that they didn't know where He was from! I'll tell you that fellow may have been uneducated compared to that bunch of Pharisees, but he had more common sense than all of them put together! The next thing he said set them off again."

"What did the man say, Mr. Malchus?"

"He mocked them and said, 'Why, this is a marvelous thing, that you do not know were He is from; yet He has opened my eyes! Now we know that God does not hear sinners; but if anyone is a worshiper of God and does His will, He hears him. Since the world began it has been unheard of that anyone opened the eyes of one who was born blind. If this Man were not from God, He could do nothing.' That made them even angrier, and they told him to get out of their midst. I watched him walk out, carefully looking at everything around him as he left the area. He asked the people he met if they had seen the man who gave him his sight. That was the last I heard of that man."

"Did you report all this to Reverend Caiaphas?"

"I did."

"And how did he receive it?"

"I told it just like I told it to you, and it all appeared to bother him. He kept saying, 'That's not good. That's not good.' I had no idea what he was talking about at that time."

"Was there another time you saw this Jesus do something unusual, Mr. Malchus?"

"Yes. It was just after Herod had murdered John the Baptist."

"Why do you say 'murdered,' Mr. Malchus?"

"There was no formal charge against the man. John did nothing but speak against the fact that Herod married Herodias, the wife of Philip, his half brother. By every stretch of Roman law, it was unlawful, but Herod was a powerful tyrant."

"Go ahead and tell of the incident with Jesus, Mr. Malchus."

"Jesus drew multitudes of people wherever He went. The size of the crowds was one thing that concerned both Pilate and Reverend Caiaphas. On this occasion, I and several others were sent to hear Jesus teach. He appeared to be trying to get alone with His closest disciples, but the crowds just wouldn't leave Him alone. They wanted to hear what He had to say."

Darrow jumped to his feet.

"Your Lordship, I object to the hearsay statement of the witness. He obviously had not talked to every member of these alleged crowds of people who followed this Jesus. To make such a statement as 'They wanted to hear what He had to say' is hearsay."

With that he sat down and looked at the lord chief justice.

"The witness will refrain from expressing any views other than his own or other than those that have been told to him by someone else he can clearly identify. Strike that from the record, please. Proceed, Sir Luckhoo."

Malchus frowned at Darrow for being rebuked because

of his enthusiasm. His face reddened, and he pointed a finger at Darrow.

"You weren't there, Mr. Lawyer. But there were five thousand men, plus women and children, WHO DID WANT TO HEAR WHAT JESUS HAD TO SAY!"

Luckhoo moved quickly before any objection could be made by Darrow or by the lord chief justice.

"How many men, plus the women and children, were at this one gathering, Mr. Malchus?"

"We counted five thousand men. The high priest wanted to know how many people were coming to hear Jesus. Each of us was to count the people and report directly to Reverend Caiaphas. When we got back the next day and reported, each had counted the same number, within fifty to one hundred people, in attendance."

"Did anything happen at this event that you would consider unusual, Mr. Malchus?"

"I watched Jesus as He moved among the people. I saw, with my own eyes, older people, younger people, and children being healed of all kinds of ailments when He would touch them and pray for them. I talked to hundreds of them. I had my scribe with me. He took down the reports of these things as we heard them. The people we talked to said that they were genuinely healed. We recorded the reports of their being healed. We even checked some of them out with local physicians to see if the ailments were valid."

"How long did He stay there and heal the people?"

"About two or three hours."

"Why did He take so long?"

"He appeared to be very concerned for each and every person He touched. He spoke to them before healing them, and then He spoke to them after the healing. He took His time with each person."

"Then what happened?"

"Jesus sat down on a mountainside and taught for several hours."

"Where were you as He taught?"

"Because of the way I was dressed and because I was from the temple, people allowed me to sit near the front."

"Were the healings the only unusual happenings you witnessed?"

"No, sir."

"What else happened that appeared unusual?"

"Some of Jesus' disciples sat right in front of me, and I heard them say that they should ask Jesus to send the people away into the villages to get something to eat because the hour was late. They got up and went to Him. I don't know what they said to Him, but I could hear what He said to them."

"And what was that, Mr. Malchus?"

"He said, 'They do not need to go away. You give them something to eat.'"

"What did Jesus do next?"

"Sitting on the front row was a little boy who had some food with him. Jesus pointed to him. One of His disciples ran over to the boy and asked his mother if he could have the little boy's food. I heard him say, 'It is for the Master.' I saw the boy's mother give him five small loaves of barley bread and two small dried fish. I supposed that they were going to give it to Jesus to eat."

"And did He eat the food or give it to His disciples to eat?"

"No. I heard Him tell His disciples to make the people

sit down in groups of fifty. Each group was told to send one basket to the front of the entire congregation of people."

"So there were one hundred baskets up front?"

"There were more than one hundred baskets."

"How long did that take?"

"That took about a half hour."

"Since Jesus didn't eat the food or give it to His disciples, what did He do with it?"

A look of wonderment came over the witness's face as he recalled that miraculous scene from his past.

"I saw Jesus take the five barley loaves and the two dried fish and hold them toward heaven. And I heard Him bless them. I sat a very short distance from Him, and I saw with my very own eyes . . . I saw this man break those loaves and break those fish over and over and over again until every one of the baskets was full. I saw the disciples take a basket to every one of those groups of fifty people, and I saw them eat until they were filled. I and my scribe and others with us . . . all ate till we were filled. I then saw Jesus' twelve disciples take twelve empty baskets and fill them with left-over fragments of bread and fish from the hundred or so baskets. My scribe and the other ten members sent out by Reverend Caiaphas saw it and testified of it, too."

"Did you report this to Reverend Caiaphas?"

"Yes, sir."

"And again, what was the response of the Jewish high priest to this?"

"I told him myself. All he could do was sit and shake his head. Once in a while he would stare into space and say, 'By what power does He do this?' I left him after a while because he seemed to forget that I was there."

"Did you hear of any such acts or miracles that this man Jesus did?"

"I did witness another act or two that I believe to be miracles."

Darrow rose to his feet almost casually.

"Your Lordship, this witness is not a scientist. Nor is he qualified to speak as a parapsychologist. Any opinions he might have certainly would be suspect and therefore would be hearsay evidence. I, for one, certainly do not wish to bore our esteemed jury with such trivia of what this man does or does not believe to be a miracle."

Luckhoo turned to the lord chief justice.

"My lord, we have already determined that this man was a well-respected, Greek-educated citizen who served in a high position in the Jewish religious government. As my esteemed colleague so aptly states, he is not qualified to speak as a parapsychologist. There was no such science of that day. However, Mr. Malchus had completed sufficient education to be considered a doctor of law in his day. His testimony is valid, and his observations are reputable. Certainly Mr. Darrow would consider it a miracle to feed over five thousand people on five loaves of bread and two fish, even during the depression of his day!"

The lord chief justice looked over at Darrow.

"Mr. Darrow, I must agree with Sir Luckhoo. Your objection is overruled. Proceed, Sir Luckhoo."

"Mr. Malchus, you made reference to another act that you said could be considered supernatural. Please describe that for the jury."

"Yes, sir. There was always a crowd following Jesus. On many occasions the high priest commissioned me to be part of the crowd and to factually report what happened on that day. First of all, we had faithful people everywhere."

"What do you mean by 'faithful people'?"

"I suppose they could be called spies because that is what they had been asked to do."

"Were these 'faithful people' or 'spies' paid by someone?"

"No, they were devout Jews who wanted to curry favor with the high priest and the Sanhedrin. They would report anything that was unusual, suspect, extraordinary, or contrary to the Jewish religion."

"Would that include the actions of Jesus?"

"Yes."

"Were you the person in charge of gathering such data for the high priest?"

"Yes, sir. That was one of my responsibilities. I was a liaison between the high priest and these informants."

"Why was Jesus monitored?"

"Because He drew large crowds of people to hear Him speak, and that apparently concerned the high priest."

"Again, what did you see and hear?"

"On one occasion, a crowd followed Jesus almost to Bethany, which was about two miles from Jerusalem. We learned, from our local informants, that a Lazarus had died, and his body had been in a sealed tomb for four days. One of Lazarus's sisters, Martha, came to meet Jesus, and she complained to Him."

"What was her complaint?"

"I heard her say, 'Lord, if You had been here, my brother would not have died. But even now I know that whatever You ask of God, God will give You.'"

"Did Jesus say anything to her?"

"Yes, sir. I heard Him say, 'I am the resurrection and the

life. He who believes in Me, though he may die, he shall live. And whoever lives and believes in Me shall never die.' Then the Nazarene, Jesus, asked her a question: 'Do you believe this?'"

"Did Martha reply to this question?"

"Yes, she did. She said, 'Yes, Lord, I believe that You are the Christ, the Son of God, who is to come into the world.'"

"Then what took place?"

"Jesus and His disciples sat down under a shade tree. Then Martha left and came back with her sister, Mary."

"Tell us what happened next."

"Mary said almost the exact words to Jesus as did her sister, and it really seemed to touch Jesus. He groaned and began to weep."

"Did anyone else say anything?"

"By this time, a small crowd had gathered. I heard several remarks about how much Jesus must have loved Lazarus. One of them said, 'Could not this Man, who opened the eyes of the blind, also have kept this man from dying?' I could not identify any of these people by name. They were identified to me as neighbors and friends of the Lazarus family."

"What did Jesus then do?"

"He apparently asked them to take Him to the place where Lazarus had been buried. My party and I followed very closely, and we all came to a cave in the hillside. A great rock had been rolled in front of the cave entrance. Jesus told them to roll the stone away. I walked quickly to assist those who were moving the great rock, so I could see and hear what might happen."

"Did either sister say anything when Jesus asked to have the stone removed?"

"Martha, the sister of the dead man, spoke out. She told Jesus that he had been dead four days and there would be a stench if the grave were opened."

"And, Mr. Malchus, what happened next?"

"Several men and I used a large tree limb to pry the bottom of the stone to get it moved. The flies and gnats were all around the tomb, and believe me, the dead man's sister was right. I've smelled dead human flesh before . . . and I was smelling that again as that tomb was being opened."

"Did Jesus help to open the tomb?"

"No. He just stood looking up toward heaven."

"Could you see anything in that tomb?"

"Yes, sir. When the stone was rolled back and blocked so it wouldn't roll closed again, I looked into the tomb and saw a body lying on a stone bench. It was wrapped in the traditional burial wrappings. The body had swelled and I could see the swelling against the wrappings, like it was bloated. There were flies and gnats on it, and the smell coming out of the tomb was almost overwhelming."

"What did Jesus do, Mr. Malchus?"

"He was standing just a few feet from me. He looked toward the heavens, and He prayed loud enough for all of us to hear."

"Can you repeat any of that prayer, Mr. Malchus?"

"I don't think that I will ever forget it. Jesus said these words: 'Father, I thank You that You have heard Me. And I know that You always hear Me, but because of the people who are standing by I said this, that they may believe that You sent Me.' And then Jesus shouted into the cave: 'Lazarus, come forth!'"

Luckhoo was quick to ask, "Mr. Malchus, what did you see happen?"

"Well, suddenly there was a very bright light in the cave. I don't know what it was, but it was so bright that I had to shield my eyes. Then I heard this thumping sound, like a person hopping on two feet. I heard it several times. A few seconds later, my eyes adjusted, and I could see the same body that had just been lying in that tomb . . . only this time it was upright and moving in jumps and it wasn't bloated."

"How do you know it was the same body?"

"Because the bright light had disappeared from the tomb, and I could see the spot where that body had lain. The flies and gnats were still around the body as it hopped out of the tomb."

"What then did Jesus do?"

"He commanded that the graveclothes be removed from him, and we did."

"And who was under those graveclothes, Mr. Malchus?"

"The man known as Lazarus."

"Was he known as the brother of Martha and Mary?"

"Yes, sir."

"Was this the man your informants said had died just over four days previously?"

"Yes, that is what they had reported."

"And you, Mr. Malchus, were seeing him alive before your very eyes?"

"Yes, sir. I saw him alive."

"And as an educated man, what is your opinion of how this happened?"

"Sir, I have thought again and again about what I experienced. There is no logical explanation for a man being raised from the dead after being confirmed as dead four days. I can only attribute it to being a miracle performed by God and—"

Speaking before he was on his feet, Darrow interrupted the witness.

"Your Lordship, the witness has already testified that he was not attached to the office of the high priest in any religious sense. It has already been brought to testimony that magic and illusion were parts of their culture. On that basis I object to his statement that it was a 'miracle performed by God.'"

The lord chief justice looked at Luckhoo, who was waiting for a statement, and rendered a decision.

"The objection is overruled. Counsel asked for an opinion, and that is what the witness provided. Proceed, Sir Luckhoo."

"What did Jesus and the people do after that?"

"Many of the people who came and saw that miracle believed that Jesus was the Christ, the Messiah. Still others, who stood on the fringes of the crowd, said that it was magic, and that Jesus was a charlatan. Jesus ministered to the people and then was invited into the home of Lazarus. I left and returned to Jerusalem. There I reported what I had seen to Reverend Caiaphas."

"And what did the Reverend Caiaphas do, Mr. Malchus?"

"He immediately called a council of the Pharisees and elders and instructed me to tell my story to them."

"What did they say or do then, sir?"

"They were very apprehensive. One elder stated, 'What shall we do? For this Man works many signs. If we let Him alone like this, everyone will believe in Him, and the Romans will come and take away both our place and nation.' They all started talking among themselves about Jesus until the high priest called them to order."

"What did the highest priest of the Jewish people say next to the Sanhedrin, Mr. Malchus?"

"There was some discussion, then he said, 'It is expedient for us that one man should die for the people, and not that the whole nation should perish.' The Sanhedrin started shouting in agreement. I saw a couple of them leave in disagreement, so I left, too. That meeting gave me the same feeling of being in an angry mob with blood in their eyes."

Luckhoo's face showed great anger.

"John ben Malchus, you are stating under oath that the president of the Sanhedrin, High Priest Joseph Caiaphas, made a public statement in front of the Sanhedrin calling for the death of a man who had not yet been charged, arrested, or tried in the legal system. Is that a correct statement?"

"Yes, sir."

"Mr. Malchus, who was the man that the high priest referred to in that instance?"

"It was Jesus of Nazareth, sir."

"Did it appear that he was setting Jesus up for an illegal trial?"

"Yes, sir."

Darrow stood, with a pencil in his hand.

"Your Lordship, counsel is leading the witness to make an inference as to whether or not the trial of the accused by the Jewish Sanhedrin was fair. The witness is not qualified to sit in a judicial capacity and make such a decision." Darrow didn't bother to stand fully erect but made his objection with knees bent. He then sat down again.

"Objection sustained."

"Mr. Malchus, will you tell the jury about your experience the night that Jesus was arrested in the garden, please."

"I was sent to the Garden of Gethsemane as the high priest's personal representative, along with others from the temple. I was not in charge. The captain of the temple guard was in charge. Our entourage carried lanterns, torches, and weapons. A former follower of Jesus, a man by the name of Judas Iscariot, guided us to Him in the garden."

"What do you mean, 'guided us to Him'? Didn't you know where Jesus would be and who He was?"

"Oh, yes, we knew His general whereabouts but not His specific whereabouts on that night. In the darkness it is sometimes difficult to tell one man from another, so the plan was that Judas would lead us to Jesus and kiss Him on the cheek in the customary fashion of greeting. Then there would be no doubt as to who the guard should arrest."

"Did Judas do his dastardly deed?"

"Yes, sir. He walked up to Jesus, greeted Him by calling Him 'Rabbi,' and kissed Him on the cheek. Jesus said something to him, which I could not hear. Jesus then looked at the temple guard and asked them whom they were seeking. They told Him, 'Jesus of Nazareth.' Now I can't tell you why this next event happened . . . all I know is that I was part of it."

"What was that, Mr. Malchus?"

"Jesus simply said, 'I am He,' and everyone in our entourage fell backward to the ground! It was as if someone unseen had pushed us down. Only Jesus and His disciples were not affected by whatever it was!"

"What did you see happen next, Mr. Malchus?"

"Since I was near the front, I saw Judas slip out of the light and off into the darkness. Then I heard a shout, and the next thing I saw was a sword coming straight down toward my head. I ducked to one side and felt it hit me. I immediately grabbed the right side of my head. It felt as though I had been hit with a firebrand."

Malchus impulsively put his hand up to the right side of his head. He held it there for a moment, then realizing what he was doing, he put his hand down again.

"In the torchlight I could see my blood running down my arm and onto my clothing. I pulled down my hand from my ear and my ear was lying in my hand, covered with my blood. I closed my eyes and screamed in pain. When I opened them seconds later, I saw Jesus coming toward me. My thoughts raced to the many times He had healed people with all kinds of ailments. I couldn't comprehend that He would heal me at the very time when He was being arrested. Yet I felt His hand go under my right hand and He forced my hand, with my ear in it, to the right side of my head."

"What happened, Mr. Malchus?"

"The pain stopped instantly. My ear was again attached to my head . . . I don't know how. All I know is that I was struck with a sword . . . my right ear was cut off and it was lying there in a pool of blood, right there in my hand . . . Jesus laid His hands on me and my ear was miraculously attached to my head. Praise be to Jehovah God!"

"You said you had blood on your hands and arms?"

"Yes, oh, yes. It was on my clothing and on that of several of the temple guard who stood around me."

"Was there any other bloodshed that night?"

"No, sir. Jesus told His disciple, whose name was Peter, to put away his sword."

"Why do you believe there was not more bloodshed?"

"They had their prisoner, Jesus. He told them to let His disciples leave. They did that very quickly."

"What did they do to Jesus, Mr. Malchus?"

"They bound Him with ropes and led him away to the home of Annas, the father-in-law of Reverend Caiaphas."

"Were any Romans there that night?"

"Yes, I saw a party of twelve or so men waiting in the background. They didn't do anything except watch."

"Did you attend any of the trials at the home of Annas or with the Sanhedrin or with Pontius Pilate?"

"No, sir, I did not."

"When next did you see Jesus?"

"I was ordered by the high priest to observe His crucifixion, to see who would come."

"And did you?"

"I did."

"Was this the first Roman crucifixion you had ever attended."

"No, sir, I am sorry to say, it was not."

"Was there anything different about this crucifixion from others you attended?"

"Several things were different. One was the manner in which Jesus died, which was rather quickly. Then somewhere around the sixth hour it became unusually dark and stayed that way until about the ninth hour. At that time, Jesus, who was hanging on the cross, cried out, 'Eli, Eli, lama sabachthani?' In your language, that means 'My God, My God, why have You forsaken Me?' Jesus cried out a second time and died. Precisely at that moment there was an earthquake. I learned later that the veil at the temple had split from top to bottom. People reported seeing loved ones, who had died, walking about Jerusalem, talking to people about God and His salvation."

"Didn't you think those things were strange, Mr. Malchus?"

"In my lifetime, I had never seen anything like that."

"Did Jesus of Nazareth die a physical death on that Roman cross of crucifixion that day, Mr. Malchus?"

"Jesus died that day on that cross, sir. I have no doubt of that. The Romans were very efficient in that area."

"Did you ever see Jesus after that, Mr. Malchus?"

"Yes, sir, I did. I was directed by the high priest to watch a gathering of Jesus' former disciples, about five hundred of them. They had gathered on the side of a mountain in Galilee. I arrived at the gathering somewhat late, and one of their leaders was already teaching. All of a sudden I realized who was doing the teaching. It was Jesus! For the most part He kept His hands in His lap. But one time He made a gesture, and I saw the large hole in His hand where the nail had been driven in to affix Him to the cross. I then made a special effort to look at His feet. There were holes in the tops of both feet! It was Jesus! He was alive! The religious officials had heard reports that He was alive. I saw Him for the first time myself! Even my personal scribe verified it to be Jesus!"

"Did that have an impact on you?"

"Only a callous fool would be unmoved by what I saw and heard. With all that I had witnessed before the Crucifixion and now to see Jesus alive . . . believe me, it made an impact. It was then that I became a believer that Jesus of Nazareth was the Messiah."

"What did you do about your position with the high priest once you became a believer in Jesus?"

"Well, the first thing I did was to go home and tell my family. They were full of joy! My wife revealed to me that she and the children had been believers in Jesus for months, but in secret! I told them that I must resign my position with the high priest, but not reveal why I was resigning. I knew that the Sanhedrin would question and harass any and all believers in Jesus that they could find. I knew of their political power as well. So I went to Caiaphas and resigned from his service. I told him that we were returning to Greece to be with our families. Within the year we moved back to our homeland, and we found other Christians already there."

Luckhoo paused, looked at Malchus, and quietly spoke.

"John ben Malchus, you are a living page in the history of Jesus of Nazareth. From your experience and based on your education and training, do you believe that Jesus of Nazareth, the person you saw in human body form, is the Son of the living God, the Promised One of Israel, the Messiah?"

Malchus pointed to Jesus, sitting in the prisoner's dock. He stood straight at attention as he spoke.

"Sir, that person, Jesus of Nazareth, as I knew Him, is, as far as I'm concerned, the true Messiah, the Son of God. Yes, He is that and much more!"

"Thank you, Mr. Malchus, for your unquestionable testimony."

Luckhoo smiled at his witness and turned to face the lord chief justice.

"My lord, the defense has no further questions of this witness at this time."

"Thank you, Sir Luckhoo. Mr. Darrow, the prosecution may cross-examine the witness at this time."

Darrow rose from his seat, laid some notes on the desk in front of him, and straightened his court gown. He pulled his cuffs out of his sleeves, making special effort to gain the jury's full attention.

"Mr. Malchus, you told our esteemed jury in your sworn

testimony that you received private religious teachings as a child, as well as being taught by a rabbi in a synagogue. Is that what you said?"

"Basically, yes, sir," Malchus answered cautiously.

"You also said that you departed from your religious teachings. Is that what you said?"

"Yes."

"You also said that you did not practice your religious beliefs until you were in your early forties and then you ended up on the staff of the Jewish high priest, Joseph Caiaphas. Is that what you said, Mr. Malchus?"

"Yes."

"How old were you when you departed from your religious beliefs, Mr. Malchus?"

"I would say when I was sixteen or so."

"Mr. Malchus, you stated that you were a spy of sorts and that you spent so much time with this charismatic Jesus that you became an adherent of the religion He preached. Is that a true statement?"

"Yes, sir. That's what happened."

"And eventually, you rejected your religious upbringing, you rejected the leadership of your high priest, and you rejected the wisdom of the entire Sanhedrin. You rejected a several-thousand-year-old set of beliefs in order to follow this itinerant Jesus with His three-year-old beliefs. Is that true, Mr. John ben Malchus?"

"Yes, sir."

"Now one thing further, Mr. Malchus. You told us that in the garden on the night that they arrested Jesus, you suffered a hard blow to the side of your head by a sword and the sword cut your ear off. Is that also true?" Darrow was very deliberate.

"Yes, sir."

"And you said that after you had been hit on the head, you put your hand to your head, and the next thing you saw was your ear lying in your hand in a pool of your blood. Was that your statement?"

"It was."

"You then screamed from the pain of this blow to your head, and Jesus came over to you and put your ear back on your head. Is that what you want the jury to believe?"

"That is a true statement of fact, sir. I have a scar completely around my right ear if you would like to look at it, sir!"

"I certainly believe that you have a scar around your ear, Mr. Malchus. Now, am I correct in saying that you did not become a believer and follower of Jesus until after you suffered this blow to your head? Is that true . . . sir?"

"Well, uh, yes, but—"

Darrow quickly interrupted.

"That's very interesting, Mr. Malchus, that's very interesting. Thank you." Darrow paused. "Your Lordship, I have no further questions for this witness for the defense."

Darrow slapped the file closed in front of him and sat down with a look of satisfaction on his face. It was like he had just beaten an opponent in a fencing match.

Luckhoo jumped quickly to his feet.

"My lord, the defense requests reexamination of the witness."

The lord chief justice turned to Luckhoo.

"The defense may reexamine."

Houston bumped Darrow in the ribs. "I thought these Christians always turned the other cheek. He sure sounds like a regular lawyer!" Darrow nodded his head affirmatively and watched Luckhoo intently.

"Mr. Malchus, after you became a Christian, did you write letters to your friends and acquaintances, telling them of your past and of how your belief in Jesus of Nazareth, as the Messiah, released you from the guilt of your past and changed your life?"

"Why . . . yes, I did, sir. I shared my testimony of what God had done for me . . . how He had changed my life and the joy that I had, which I had never had before . . . and the fact that I had a personal relationship with my Lord and Savior, Jesus Christ."

"And in your testimony of these letters, did you hide the fact that you had been a religious person but that your Jewish religion had little or no meaning as a boy; however, you found new meaning in your Jewish religion as you became more knowledgeable in it?"

"Yes, I shared that."

"And in your letters, Mr. Malchus, did you share the facts of your newfound religion in Jesus of Nazareth, of the fulfillment of the prophecies of the Torah and the Talmud, and of the miracles you saw performed before your eyes, time after time?"

"Oh, yes, sir, I did."

"And what did you write in your letters as to who Jesus was?"

"I wrote that Jesus was the Christ, the Messiah, the Promised One of Israel and of the world."

"Thank you, Mr. Malchus."

Luckhoo turned to the lord chief justice.

"My lord, I have no further questions for this gentleman."

The lord chief justice looked at Darrow.

"Mr. Darrow, do you wish to reexamine?"

"No, Your Lordship."

The lord chief justice banged his gavel on the pad.

"The witness is excused. Sir Luckhoo, are you prepared to call the next witness for the defense?"

"My lord chief justice, the defense rests. We have no further witnesses in this trial of the Messiah."

There was a stir in the courtroom as people whispered concerning this unexpected change. Most of the barristers and solicitors believed that Luckhoo would have several more witnesses. Luckhoo, now sitting in his seat, waited to see what would happen next.

The lord chief justice banged his gavel, then looked from the jury to where Darrow and Luckhoo were sitting. He called their names and they stood.

"Does either of you wish to recall any of the witnesses to this trial?"

Both Darrow and Luckhoo stated that they did not.

"Then, gentlemen, it is the decision of the Crown that there will be a change in the procedure of this trial. There shall be no closing arguments or rebuttals. There shall be only closing summations. Whatever your final arguments are to be, they must be contained in your summation."

Both Darrow and Luckhoo responded with looks of concern. Usual criminal trial procedure allowed for closing arguments, rebuttal of the closing arguments, and summations of a trial, but the lord chief justice had exercised his rights to set trial limits. This restriction placed added pressure on both barristers to be specific and complete in the closing summation because there would be no second chance. There was no higher appeal above the lord chief justice.

The lord chief justice continued.

"Mr. Darrow, Sir Luckhoo, this court takes privilege to instruct the prosecution and the defense on the presentation of the closing summations."

He used two fingers together as his pointer in his instructions to the two barristers standing before him.

"This is the last opportunity either of you will have to communicate directly with the jury. It is imperative that your summations logically and forcefully present your position on the contested issues and the reasons you are entitled to prevail."

Darrow and Luckhoo kept their eyes on the lord chief justice as he spoke to them.

"The Crown expects your closing summations to contain two characteristics: they must be simple, yet they must respect the jury's intelligence. Your closing summations should present your theory of your case explicitly to this jury and demonstrate why your theory most logically incorporates and explains both the contested and the undisputed facts admitted at this trial. I remind both of you experienced barristers that we are not in an age when spectacular oratory impresses the jury. It will certainly not impress the Crown. The members of the jury are well informed and perceptive. They have been specially picked to decide this matter, and they will be persuaded only by facts of your case. Their final decision will be to find the defendant guilty or not guilty as charged. Are there any questions from the prosecution or from the defense?"

Both men shook their heads and stated, "No, sir."

"Then since the prosecution began arguments in this

trial, Mr. Darrow, you shall be prepared to begin your closing summation at eight o'clock in the morning. Court is adjourned for this day. Mr. Bailiff!"

The court scepter was banged three times on the floor, and the people automatically stood as they had for the past four days in court.

"Be upstanding in the court."

The people stood as he recited his closing call and banged his scepter on the floor.

Everyone was already moving toward the exits. In the mild rush to leave, no one talked.

The last one out of the courtroom was Luckhoo. DiPietro had gone to call for the limousine. His lips were quietly moving as he walked toward the door.

The sun had come out of hiding and was shining through the translucent glass-domed skylight, held up by wrought iron work. It cast a shadow on the courtroom floor before Luckhoo, looking like a net into which he was about to step. He stopped suddenly as if it were real.

Something on the inside rang out: *Caution! Caution!* He heard a hiss, like that of a snake. He saw nothing as he looked around and left the courtroom to go for a meal. But food was not foremost on the mind of Lionel Luckhoo. Spiritual things were.

11

CLOSING SUMMATIONS

MORNING, DAY FIVE

Dark clouds loomed over London in the early morning light. On the horizon, lightning was darting out of the distant clouds and smashing its fury somewhere into the English countryside below. Ominous thunder could be heard as people scurried to their shops and offices. Rain was one thing in London; thunderstorms with fierce lightning were quite another. As the storm was moving toward London, the church bell and Big Ben chimed eight times in unison.

Inside Number One Court the officials, the jury, the witnesses, the accused, and the spectators were all in place. The lord chief justice's door opened, and he moved quickly to his place.

Bailiff Griggs completed the formal preliminaries.

The lord chief justice looked at the jury and spoke to them as a body.

"Ladies and gentlemen of the jury, the past four days,

you have heard evidence from witnesses and the exhibits concerning the charge against the accused, Jesus of Nazareth, who is charged here with capital fraud."

His voice was steady and pleasant as he continued his instructions to the jury of how they were to receive the closing summations of the barristers.

"You, the jury, will now be presented with closing summations from the prosecution and from the defense. Closing summations, simply put, are the chronological culmination of evidence presented in this jury trial. You are to follow the Crown's instructions and decide this case on the basis of the evidence presented. You will be given further instructions as the trial proceeds. You've been a wonderful jury, thank you."

He paused and pointed to Darrow.

"Mr. Darrow, you may proceed with your closing summation for the prosecution."

The famous Clarence Seward Darrow stood to his full height. Although he was an American, Darrow had been specially chosen to be the prosecutor for this trial held in Old Bailey because all of his life he had been known to take the unpopular side of a subject, even when he knew that almost everyone disagreed with him. He was exhilarated by standing by himself in a case, appearing defeated before he started, fighting the impossible foe.

His temperament was strengthened by the system of logic found in both Roman and English law. As a promising young lawyer, he had found mental stimulation in trying imaginary cases in his mind where he would stand for justice against the forces of evil.

But this day would be different from ones in his professional past. He had defended Eugene Debs against the transportation giants; he had defended Richard Loeb and Nathan

Leopold, Jr., the two thrill-killers of Bobby Franks; he had accepted the offer of the American Civil Liberties Union and defended John Thomas Scopes in the famous Scopes Monkey Trial, where evolution was on trial; and he even had to defend himself against a charge of bribery in a trial in California.

This day Clarence Seward Darrow was taking the unpopular position of prosecuting the founder of Christianity, Jesus of Nazareth, naming Him and His religion as a fraud. Darrow had a reputation as being antireligion. This would be his last chance to expose what he believed to be a cruel hoax on the world. Darrow began the prosecution's summation.

"Ladies and gentlemen of the jury, I am a stranger here, a foreigner. It is only by the grace of the Crown that I can stand before you as the prosecutor in this case of capital fraud. I stand here in this silly wig and this court gown feeling ridiculous, even though these other barristers and solicitors are wearing them, too. If I were back home wearing this getup, they'd laugh me out of town. But I'm not. I'm right here behind this bench talking to you. I'm here as the prosecutor, not particularly because I was the most appropriate person to prosecute the accused. There are many, many others who would relish an opportunity to prosecute Jesus of Nazareth. No, I'm here because I am one of many who fought against injustice, against villainy, against oppression and, most of all, against tradition."

Darrow's comments obviously unsettled a number of the barristers and solicitors in the courtroom. Their faces displayed the disdain they felt for the statement because most of them thrived on tradition. But Darrow knew they were not part of the jury.

Darrow closed his eyes for a moment, a sign he was in deep thought. His voice remained unchanged.

"You see, part of what is on trial here is tradition. In this particular case, it happens to be . . . Jewish tradition." He opened his eyes. "The specific tradition we are dealing with in this trial is the tradition concerning that elusive person called . . . the Messiah."

Darrow turned to look at Jesus sitting quietly in the prisoner's dock, just as He had done during the complete trial. Darrow's hands were thrust deep in his pockets. His voice was questioning, somewhat accusing.

"Who is the Messiah? Or specifically, what is the Messiah? Is the accused the Messiah? He says He is! Exhibit A says He is. The tradition of the Christian religion says He is. The defense has ably produced witnesses who say He is. But what say you?"

Darrow had placed a number of books on the bench in front of him, with their spines turned toward the jurors. Most of them could read the large titles: *Psychology, Evolution Science, Physics, Anthropology, Astrology,* and *Religions of the World*. He pointed to them as he made his next statement.

"These books came from a local library, right here in London. Most of you, in your lifetime, have studied one or all of these kinds of sciences." He picked up the top book, *The Changing World*, and pointed to it. "Perhaps you studied a book like this about the evolution of scientific evidence from early civilizations to today. You probably remember reading that the traditional view once was that the earth was the physical center of the universe, around which the sun, moon, stars, and planets moved in a complex rotation. It was thought to be flat. Today, science has shown us that the earth is a small, round satellite of an average star, which is only one of a large galaxy in a vast and unfathomed universe."

He put the book down and looked back to the jury.

"Traditions once limited people's vision to only what they could see. They could travel only a few miles in one day because the usual method of transportation was walking or riding an animal. In those days sailing ships took months to cross the Atlantic. But now, they say, you can travel to the moon and back in only a few hours!"

Darrow slid the first stack of books to his left, and Houston placed them on the seat beside her. She placed another stack of books in their place with their spines facing Darrow.

"Archaic concepts and antique transportation are remnants of the past. Today, we find such in museums. But unfortunately, ignorance and prescientific superstitions still prevail in the area of religious traditions." He pointed at the new stack of books.

"Here I have some religious books from the local library. They have all been published within the last fifty years."

Darrow purposely did not read more than just titles because they could not be placed in the trial as exhibits. He turned the titles so that jury members could read them.

"Here are modern books on Buddhism, Islam, Jehovah's Witnesses, Mormonism, Karma Yoga, New Age religions, Scientology, Unitarianism, religions of the world, Judaism, and Christianity."

Darrow contrived to appear as cool and as unemotional as ever, but on the inside he was running full steam. He enjoyed the oratory of painting word pictures for his many audiences, and the picture he was painting now was one with many embellishments around the edges.

"Let me refresh you on some of what that wonderful book of great stories, Exhibit A, the Bible, says."

He picked up his well-worn copy and thumbed through it as if he were going to read to the jury.

"You remember that I mentioned in the opening statement to the esteemed jury that the Jewish Torah was adapted as part of the Christian Bible, called the Old Testament. The Old Testament is filled with the history and traditions of the Hebrew people. I'm also certain that you recall hearing stories about Moses and the Ten Commandments. Even before Moses got his Ten Commandments, after being up on a mountain for forty days, the Hebrews had long been looking for their traditional hope . . . their Messiah."

Darrow held the Bible in his hand as he talked.

"You folks remember that I told you about the great Gautama Buddha and his unusual conception after his mother had a dream about a white elephant entering her womb. In this Bible, the mother of the accused said that she became pregnant after a visitation from an angel. Mohammed apparently believed he was the prophet of God after his visitation from an angel."

Darrow pulled his finger back, tapped his chin, and smiled at the jury.

"You also remember that I gave you the historical fact that five of the world's great religions were founded between 600 B.C. and A.D. 600, including Buddhism, Christianity, and Islam."

Darrow paused with one of his effective pauses, pointed toward the south, and resumed his statement.

"These three religions were founded in the area of the

Arabian Peninsula of Mesopotamia, Palestine, Lebanon, and Syria. These three were religions of primitive Semite tribes. These three religions were propagated by people who were called prophets of their gods. These three claimed to be human beings at one time or another. These three ran into severe problems from groups and local governments who opposed their beliefs and the methods by which they propagated their beliefs."

He paused and stared at the jury for a moment.

"And, oh, yes . . . all three . . . DIED!"

Every eye in the jury was upon Darrow as the jurors weighed every word he spoke. His voice rang in the courtroom.

"You folks remember how we proved to you that the accused did not meet the qualifications of a historical character. We found it difficult to come up with any reliable historic sources concerning the validity of a historical religious leader in Israel named Jesus of Nazareth. The information that we were able to ascertain from historic sources, going back to His birth, simply attested to the fact that Jesus of Nazareth certainly did exist. Now, folks, we believe that the man did indeed exist . . . but not as a historical religious leader of His own day. His religious leadership came after His death. It was pursued by His disciples."

Darrow was walking a very fine line in bringing to remembrance all the details of the prosecution's case to the jury. His responsibility was to accentuate his case, eliminate as much of Luckhoo's case as possible, and persuade the jury to vote against the accused. His voice was strong and sure. He pointed to Jesus.

"There sits the leader of a worldwide religion with hundreds of thousands of followers gathered over two thousand years. True! But, my friends, true history records only a few words about the man! You can see why it would be easy to understand why a charge of capital fraud was filed against the accused!"

Darrow pointed to the exhibit table.

"You remember that in Exhibit B, Celsus wrote a book, which was against those who called themselves Christians, about A.D. 180. But his historic book had no direct reference as to whether or not the accused even existed."

Darrow paused and slowly turned a page in his notes. Suddenly, he found what he was looking for and spoke excitedly.

"Ah, yes, here it is in Exhibit B. There was supposed to have been some sort of an official document between Pontius Pilate and Emperor Tiberius that mentions the accused. The historians Justin and Tertullian believed there was such a document. But when Governor Pilate was on the witness stand, he did not mention such a document. Historians argue even today over the validity of such a document. But one fact is evident . . . the defense did not produce such a document!"

Darrow tapped the desk in front of him with his finger. He looked at the jury and then to the lord chief justice, then back at the jury.

"His Lordship told my esteemed colleague and me that you, the jury, wanted nothing but facts. Well, I am giving you facts . . . and here are more facts."

Darrow became very logical and less emotional.

"Another historian of the time when Jesus was on this earth was Philo of Alexandria. In Exhibit B, he did not make even the smallest reference to the accused or His followers."

Darrow's voice became condescending as he attempted to persuade the jury of his case.

"But, ladies and gentlemen of the jury, one man did . . . a Jewish historian by the name of Josephus. He actually called Jesus the Messiah. I find it very interesting that for a man who was part of a nation that longed to see the coming of their Messiah, Josephus wrote just over one hundred words about Jesus."

Clarence Darrow appeared to be just warming up his oratorical skills. His voice was pleading.

"Isn't a Messiah supposed to be someone who saves His people from the sins of the world? If that is so, then why . . . tell me why we human beings have not been saved from the suffering? Why have we not been saved from wars and rumors of wars since this man was on the earth? Why have we not been saved from pestilence and famine that span the globe? Why have millions upon millions upon millions of God's chosen people, the Jewish people, died needless, horrible, barbaric deaths around the world? Are not these unanswered questions?"

Darrow clasped both hands together and looked expectantly at the jury.

"Now, folks, let's remember what the witnesses said about the accused. The first witness was Joseph, who said he was and wasn't the father of the accused, whose ancestors included women of ill repute. Joseph was that young boy of seventeen when his fiancée became pregnant. Joseph suddenly had a dream and then he married the girl. Joseph came from a superstitious Semitic tribe. Joseph had a minimal education and was a carpenter. Joseph had some more unusual dreams and some unusual experiences with some shepherds and with three foreign astrologers. Joseph and his wife and baby ended up in a land where magic and illusion were common practice. Joseph said that he taught his son about how wonderful it would be for the long-awaited Jewish Messiah to come on the earth and save His people. Joseph said that he was a good father to the accused. Joseph said he was honest. I believe Joseph was a very honest man. I believe that Joseph was A VERY . . . HONESTLY . . . DECEIVED MAN!"

Darrow dropped his hands to his sides and looked down. He then reached up on the desk before him and turned over one of his notes, scratched out on a yellow legal tablet. He looked back to the jury, who sat waiting for his next statement.

"You long-suffering people also remember the Jewish high priest, Reverend Joseph Caiaphas. He was a very important man in his day. He was the chief justice of the Jewish Supreme Court, the Sanhedrin. The Sanhedrin was made up of the leaders of the Jews. Joseph Caiaphas had been appointed high priest by the Roman curator, Valerius Gratus. He was the high priest in office when Gratus was succeeded by Pontius Pilate in A.D. 26, and he held that religious position through Pilate's term of office. You heard with your very own ears about the cat and mouse game played between the ruling Roman procurator and this oppressed Jewish leader. You witnessed this gentleman break down under the pressure of the badgering of the defense counsel and the pressure of remembering the pain of the occupation of his beloved homeland by a foreign army. You also heard this chief justice of the Jewish Supreme Court of his people in his day say that the accused was a charlatan and a fraud as a Messiah. I hope you will remember that statement from a legalistic Jewish Sadducee who knew beyond a shadow of a doubt what to look for in the Jewish Messiah."

Darrow's eyes went back to his papers as he reminded the jury of statements that had been given in evidence in this trial.

"In fact, the statement from the chief justice was this: 'I must say, Mr. Prosecutor, that during the time I first knew of this Jesus and went to see Him, I did indeed have hope that He was the promised Messiah. I have dreamed of Him in my sleep, and I have tried to be as fair and as impartial as I can be to examine His claim to messiahship. But I cannot find sufficient evidence that would lead me to believe that Jesus of Nazareth, the man we found guilty of blasphemy and subsequently executed, was the Messiah of Israel. Many things that happened were very coincidental, making Him look like He could be the Messiah, but I do not believe that He was or is the Messiah-King!'"

Darrow looked back to the jury. He was almost fatherly in his tone of voice as he gently rebuked the jury.

"Now, ladies and gentlemen of the jury, we heard the testimony of the highest religious and legal figure of the Jews at the time the accused lived. You and I weren't there when this chief justice ruled in all religious matters, along with the Sanhedrin. You and I weren't there watching all the events happen in his oppressed country. You and I weren't there when these Jewish leaders had to make pressured decisions that affected all of their beloved people. You and I weren't there when they took the accused to judgment with their own esteemed leader, Annas; then to their own courtroom; then to the Roman leader, Pilate; then to Herod; and finally back to Pilate, the man with the absolute authority to pronounce the death sentence on the accused. No . . .

you and I weren't there. That is why we must accept the testimony of a qualified man who was there, and Chief Justice Joseph Caiaphas WAS THERE ALL THE TIME!"

Clarence Darrow was perfectly calm and composed. He looked at the accused, and their eyes met. That seemed to unsettle Darrow for the moment. But he cleared his throat and went on with his argument.

"Now I am certain that you fine folks of the jury remember the witness of the governor of Judea, the distinguished equestrian, from the noble Pontii family of Italy, Pontius Pilate. He was appointed to his high office by the great Tiberius Caesar himself. You remember that Governor Pilate had no religious or ethnic ties to the accused. History records that when it came to ruling and maintaining law and order, Pontius Pilate apparently was a fair and impartial prefect."

Darrow smiled at the jury.

"Now you surely remember that Governor Pilate, a witness who lived at the time of Jesus, made a number of statements concerning the accused."

As Darrow talked, he made a number of hand gestures, including holding up his fingers as he made each point.

"One, he had spies gathering information everywhere. Two, he informed us of the cousin of the accused, a strange man named John the Baptist, who supported the religious beliefs of the accused. Three, he told us that the accused was charismatic, that He attracted great crowds of people, and that large crowds of people were always potentially dangerous to Roman rule. Four, he told us that both he and the high priest were in agreement about law and order in the land. Five, the Roman governor told us that he alone had the authority to put the accused to death . . . and on that authority . . . as the highest tribunal in Israel . . . he ordered the death of the accused for a crime against the Roman Empire."

Darrow simply held out his hands, palms up, toward the jury. His voice was quiet but firm. His eyes were on the jury.

"Now, folks, Governor Pilate acted in a fair and an impartial way in his rule of the Jews, the accused being a Jew. He made a decision based on the law of his nation. He carried out that law. The accused was executed. Governor Pilate stayed in his position of authority in Israel until A.D. 36, when he returned to Rome. Do not all of these facts speak to you, as members of the jury, that this honorable historic character was just one more authority who verified that the accused was a Jewish troublemaker and not the Messiah? The answer of intelligent and informed jurors is YES!"

Darrow clapped his hands as he made his point. He could see that some of the jurors were yawning once in a while. He woke them up with the sound.

Darrow now had to move to the next witness and to another controversial subject: Darwin and evolution. He reached down, took a drink of water, then looked at the jury, holding the glass up for them to see.

"It's interesting, folks . . . to note how almost two thousand years ago this was just plain water. Now today, because of the scientific knowledge that we have, this is known not only as water but as H_2O as well. I want you to remember that fact for a moment as I remind you of the testimony of the world-famous scientist and naturalist, Mr. Charles Robert Darwin. Now, folks, what kind of testimony did Mr. Darwin bring into this court of law? He showed us that there are two conflicting theories about the beginnings of humankind. One they call creationism, done by a higher power they call their supernatural God. And remember, the God in this case is supposedly the supernatural father of the accused. The second theory is the theory of evolution, which has been accepted for years by the scientific community."

Darrow picked up one of the testimony sheets, looked at it for a moment, and then looked back at the jury. Again, he acted as if he had a delightful tidbit of information for them.

"I would like to read from the official testimony of Mr. Charles Robert Darwin: 'I feel that my life's work has been the demonstration that the evolving of plants and animals, and the adaptations that they demonstrate, provides no substantial evidence of a divine or providential guidance or purpose in design as the Christian Bible purports. Natural selection of fortuitous variations provides a scientifically plausible foundation for evolution and does not necessitate miraculous interposition or any supernatural interference with the laws of nature as we know them.' That was from the testimony of a world-renowned scientist, Mr. Charles Robert Darwin. What more could this scientist say to convince you?"

Clarence Seward Darrow was masterful in legal oratory and in convincing juries of the innocence of his clients as the attorney for the defense.

This time he was the prosecutor. Yet the eighty-one-year-old lawyer's skill at law was still evident. He looked at the jury with anticipation.

"Our next witness who presented scientific testimony was a man of world-famous reputation, Dr. Sigmund Freud. Dr. Freud is recognized as the father of psychoanalysis. He is one of the outstanding pioneer scientists who probed the intricate human mind. Now, my dear jury, I invite you to again remember the testimony of Dr. Freud."

Darrow again picked up the batch of testimony papers that were provided for use by the prosecution and by the defense. He read from one page, then turned the page as if he were speed-reading the transcript. He spoke softly.

"Now, folks, this psychiatrist stated, in his testimony, a couple of important things. He first stated, 'I once did a sample case with this Jesus as a patient, such as we would do in a textbook case provided by our tutors. My diagnosis was of a man who became so engrossed in His idea of being a holy Messiah that He became a classic case of grandiose paranoia.'"

Darrow paused, put the paper down, and looked over the entire jury. He picked the paper up again and went on reading from the testimony. His voice increased in volume.

"Dr. Sigmund Freud also said, 'I do not believe He is the Messiah of the Jewish people, if they have one. I believe the man is a fraud. I believe that anyone who shares the man's delusion shares in perpetuating that fraud.'"

The leonine counsel had accomplished his purpose. He had captured the attention of not only the jury but all who were in the courtroom. Only the ticking of the clock could be heard throughout the courtroom as they waited for his next words.

He laid the testimony sheets down in front of him. He looked at them for a moment, then he looked back at the jury. His voice was reassuring as he spoke.

"That . . . was a direct quote from a man who is known as a world-recognized authority on psychology and psychiatry. I remind you that psychology is the science of human behavior. Dr. Freud is a medical doctor who has received additional specific training in the areas of mental health and disease. He is a pioneer in the area of human thought, feeling, and behavior in normal development and aberrations. His theories are accepted by adherents of psychology worldwide. Can we accept this man's testimony as true? Absolutely! This man's testimony cannot be challenged."

Picking up his yellow legal tablet, Darrow flipped a page, looked at it, and then turned to the next page and stopped. He smiled, nodded his head to himself, and then looked up at the jury. His voice was soft and gentle.

"Now, folks, let's remember what the esteemed defense counsel has attempted to provide as evidence. The very first witness that my esteemed and titled colleague brought before you kind folks was that wonderful and kind woman, the mother of the accused. She is known around the world as the Virgin Mary or Mother Mary.

"She very definitely corroborated the testimony of her husband, Joseph. Mary even gave us the details of her very supernatural experience as a teenage girl, when she said that she became pregnant by the Holy Spirit. She is the only person in the world to have had this experience. I am certain that for this young girl who was facing death by stoning, to be able to live, marry, and have a baby was indeed supernatural!"

Darrow shrugged his shoulders quickly a couple of times and looked inquisitively at the jury as he made his point.

"Now, folks, Mary told us about her visions and dreams and also about having to tell her seventeen-year-old husband-to-be that she was pregnant. That was an impressive story. Then we learned that this young boy had a dream, and he changed his mind and decided to marry the very pretty thirteen-year-old who claimed that she was a virgin."

Knowing he was possibly playing with fire, the able criminal lawyer moved circumspectly. He chose his statements with precision.

"Mary testified that every woman in Israel dreamed of having a baby boy who would become the traditional Messiah to deliver God's people from bondage. Well, they had a baby boy. And they had some real unusual events happen to them, folks."

Darrow wanted the jury to believe that the testimonies of Joseph and Mary were fabrications.

"You see, a lot of unusual things happened to them . . . or at least they said happened to them. Her pregnancy . . . they had to go to the little town of Bethlehem in her ninth month, and upon arriving there, they found there was no room at the inn. So she had to deliver her child in a stable with no midwife. Next they told us about the sheepherders. Then they told us about three very unusual men who came and gave them gifts and about how the men had talked to King Herod. Remember that this well-known despot was reputed to have said to these three men that he wanted to find this newborn king they were talking about and to worship Him. With this information and with the gifts the men had given them, and . . . oh, yes, they had another dream . . . they left Bethlehem to go to Egypt . . . the land of ancient sorcery, magic, and illusion. They lived in Egypt for a short time, and they even managed to come out of Egypt at the time of their traditional Passover, just as their ancestors did. It seems that the wicked King Herod had died just prior to Passover."

Placing both hands on the desk in front of him, Darrow smiled and leaned toward the jury. He looked at the faces with his boyish grin. He knew how to play to a jury and use every tool of oratorical skills to make what he was saying the absolute truth.

"And then, my friends, this devoted mother and father raised their child in the nurture and admonition of their Jehovah God. They fed into this young mind the wonders of their religion. Both admitted in sworn testimony that they taught this child to believe in their traditional, promised Messiah of Israel. That, my friends, is the way this young man grew up. Oh, yes, please remember that He was in almost constant contact with His parents until He was thirty years of age because He lived with them and worked daily in His father's carpenter shop."

Darrow looked at his papers, then back to the jury.

"I am certain that your parents had a great influence on you, one way or another, good or bad, didn't they?"

Darrow stood up straight behind the barristers' bench and thought briefly of his parents, Amirus and Emily Eddy Darrow. He remembered how they had encouraged him to study Greek and Latin and to read every book he could. His father was strongly antireligious. He remembered how much of an influence they had on his life.

Darrow felt a tug on his court gown.

"Darrow, you can't hold this trial out there in your never-never land or wherever you are. You're in the closing summation . . . so close," whispered Houston.

"Oh, yes . . . and you remember that the mother of Jesus and the esteemed defense counsel went through a number of very impressive Scriptures from Exhibit A. It was their conclusion that the accused met every one of their statements, based on prophecies from this Bible of theirs."

Picking up his own Bible, Darrow held it up for the jury to see. He took his thumb across the pages and stopped where he had a cigar wrapper as a marker. He looked up at the jury.

"Now this part of the Bible, Exhibit A, has four books in it called the four Gospels—Matthew, Mark, Luke, and John. Folks, these religious books contain almost all the known historical information on the accused that exists."

He took his right hand and scratched his chin as if he were in deep thought.

"These four books probably reached their final form somewhere between thirty-five and sixty-five years after the trials and death of the accused. They present us a problem of determining which portions of these four books refer authentically to the teachings and career of the accused and which, on the other hand, are really additions or inventions by followers of the accused. That is a distinct possibility, you know."

With a look of dismay on his face, he picked up the testimony sheets again and turned the pages until he located another cigar band page marker.

"My friends, remember the very similar witness who was brought forth by the defense, the former servant of the high priest, a Greek citizen by the name of John ben Malchus. This man, at first, seemed to be a very creditable witness. He told of things that he saw and things that he learned on a firsthand basis in his official capacity. He saw some very great and wonderful things, folks. Let me ask you . . . were they supernatural or were they illusions, practiced by magicians?"

He placed his finger on his mouth.

"I remember seeing the great Ehrich Weiss who attained an international reputation for his theatrical tricks and daring feats of extrication from shackles, straitjackets, ropes, and handcuffs and from various locked containers. I'm sure that most of you have heard of him by his stage name. He was known as the Great Harry Houdini. Weiss was a magician. Weiss was an illusionist. We don't know what this witness, Malchus, saw. We don't know if he knew what he saw. He did testify as to what he thought he saw. Did he see the supernatural? Or did he, like thousands of others, see another Great Houdini, an illusionist at work in His craft? Oh, but what about Malchus's ear getting cut off in the garden by one of the followers of the accused? What about its being put back on his head? What about his so-called healing?"

Darrow put his hand over his own ear to illustrate.

"Is it possible for a man, who has been hit on the side of the head by a blow from a sword and made to bleed profusely, to make a rational statement as it appears here in Mr. Malchus's testimony? For a proper answer, we would have to recall Dr. Sigmund Freud. Now, Dr. Freud probably could verify for us that if, in such an extreme case, a man could make a rational judgment of whether he actually held his ear in his hand or whether he held something else. Or perhaps it was nothing more than a great deal of his own blood, and the man was in a state of shock. Or perhaps it was some psychological twist of the man's mind for a moment . . . or perhaps it, too . . . was an illusion!"

Luckhoo sat motionless. He had wanted to jump to his feet and refute each one of his opponent's statements from the beginning of the summation. But he knew that the rule of law set by the lord chief justice would not allow him to do so, and if he did, it would register against his client. He sat with his eyes closed, waiting.

Darrow shook his head doubtfully. He picked up one of

the library books from the barristers' bench in front of him. The title on the book spine was *Psychology*. He held it with the front toward the jury, so they could see the title; then he laid it down. Holding his forefinger in the air, he used it as a pointer and a point of focus for the eyes of the jury.

"Is it possible that the healings and the miracles attributed to the accused were perhaps illusions? We would have to call on the Great Houdini for that explanation. But since he is not here, you of our jury will have to answer that. It is interesting to note that the Great Houdini campaigned against mind readers, mediums, and others who claimed supernatural powers. His argument was that they were charlatans."

Darrow pointed down to some papers on the barristers' bench before him. He nodded to the jury, and a great expression of satisfaction settled over his face.

"Now, do you know something, folks, when time moves quietly through our lives, it takes us away from significant events that happened in our lives. We tend to remember what we like to remember . . . especially when we look back at that event after a number of years have passed by. We tend to remember the good old days and forget the bad old days. We asked Mr. Malchus to remember, and that's what he did. But one thing we must all remember, and that is that now, Mr. Malchus sees these events of his past through his eyes as a Christian. Now, Mr. Malchus is a believer and a follower of the accused. Now, Mr. Malchus is another person who has become a Christian. Now, my question to you is this: Can you trust the testimony of Mr. Malchus as being unbiased?"

Darrow let his suspenders go with a snap, put his hands out with the palms up, and once again shrugged his shoulders, accentuating his words. He shook his head, indicating a negative answer to his own question. Darrow took a deep breath and plunged in again.

"So much for the testimony of the Christian, Mr. Malchus. Let's all remember that the accused's family came from a Semitic tribe, a superstitious tribe. Let's remember that they spent some time in Egypt where religion was focused upon a quest for the immortal, the permanent, the eternal. Let's all remember that Egypt is a land where ancient religions, much older than Judaism, held that there was a deity that was supposed to be human as well as divine. Their deity was supposed to be resurrected from the dead. Their deity's resurrection was supposed to signify that all righteous people could likewise rise from the dead and have eternal life if they did right in the natural life span. Does that sound very familiar to you? It should. It's the same concept as Christianity."

Darrow caught himself going off his plan for his close. He regretted that he did not have some professor of comparative religions to testify, but he really had longed to do that himself. That was hindsight, he concluded. But he had to continue.

"History has been greatly influenced by religion. It has proven to be the strongest human motive operating on this earth. Its influence has sometimes been good, as the lives of countless thousands of godly men and women reveal; and sometimes it is inherently evil, as the squalor in the Near East and India and as the religious wars around the world portray. Although these are not done in the name of the accused, the warring factions have used His name for their purposes."

Darrow began to pace back and forth.

"When we look at the accused through the eye of a historian, treating Him in exactly the same way as we would any other figure in history, we must search ancient literature, which is capable of yielding historical information. We have done that, and we find precious little information. What we do find is somewhat contrary to that portrayed in Exhibit A. We find no meek and gentle Lamb of God, as the defense would have us believe. The officials of His day were concerned with His religious activity that had the potential of becoming political activity, and that presented a severe problem for them. On the one hand, His teachings were great messages of 'turn the other cheek, love thy neighbor, welcome sinners, and render unto Caesar.' On the other hand, His acts were systematically dedicated to the success of His great mission, that of being accepted as the Messiah of Israel and of the world."

Once again Darrow felt as if he were walking through a mine field. He knew that each juror had some kind of feeling toward religion, but that the jurors had been picked because they indicated they were without bias. He balanced his closing summation between a capsule of the evidence, a concern for the feelings of the jury, and an all-out attack on the traditions of religion, especially where it concerned Jesus of Nazareth.

"What kind of a picture of the accused do we have, my friends? Certainly we would be foolish to think that He has had no effect on humanity. He is perhaps the most significant figure not only in the history of religion but in world history as well. So why is there very little available history of the accused, except in the Gospels from the Bible? They appear to give precious little information about the accused except what had to do with their own doctrines, their own rituals, or their own apologetics. Biblical scholars have studied the sacred texts of Christianity and historical documents for hundreds of years, attempting to understand the historical Jesus of Nazareth. Most people understand that there have been many inexplicable and conflicting traditions, plus the accretions of later generations, which were added when Christianity became a religion following the death of the accused. We cannot lay those to His blame. We can only bring before you the evidence that Jesus of Nazareth is not the promised Messiah of Israel and the world."

For just a moment Darrow's eyes met those of Jesus, sitting in the dock. His expression held something curious for Darrow. He found it hard to look away, but he forced himself back to his task. He stood straight as he could, looking from one side of the jury to the other.

"My friends, as sacred as Exhibit A, the Bible, is to people around the world, much of it has never been historically proven! If you're going to believe it, it's one of those things you have to accept by faith. Members of the jury, what then IS historically proven?"

He opened a file folder, glanced at it, then looked back at the jury.

"You folks remember the documents I presented to you in Exhibit B. The lack of any creditable Jewish or historical testimony concerning the life and person of a Jesus, son of Joseph and Mary of Nazareth, Palestine, seems improbable, almost inconceivable to us. How in the world could the accused, who certainly has a place in history, be so incredibly lacking in history? Exhibit B, the statements of accepted historians, has meager information, and most of it is about the followers of the accused and not about Him."

Once again his hands were on the bench in front of him

in an attempt to get as close to the jury as possible. His voice was almost pleading in tone.

"My friends, it is obvious that the Jewish chroniclers and the world historians did not find that this religious movement in Jerusalem, led by the accused and His small band of disciples, was worthy to occupy any place in the authentic Jewish history of their day. I submit to you this fact: the silence of these historians . . . concerning the accused . . . speaks so loudly . . . that you, the jury, must consider that fact in your deliberation as you judge the defendant is GUILTY as charged."

Clarence Seward Darrow looked once again at Jesus of Nazareth sitting quietly in the prisoner's dock. He avoided looking into Jesus' eyes. Jesus had not shown any emotion in the entire trial, except to those who were close to Him. Darrow just shook his head back and forth as he looked at Jesus. Then Darrow looked back at the jury.

"The fact is that the dreams of this itinerant Jewish preacher, which He announced to all who would listen, did not happen. His kingdom of peace and love and joy . . . which He said would be coming . . . still has not arrived here on earth. Instead, the accused violated the civil authority of His nation and was tried by an authority of the Roman Empire. He was found guilty by that authority, and He was executed. By one method or another, the tomb, where His followers placed His dead body, was found empty. Then several hundred of His devout believers claim to have seen this man alive after His death."

Darrow paused to let this information sink in.

"Now here is the one big difference between Christianity and other religions that, you remember, I mentioned to you at the beginning of this trial. The Christians say that their

Messiah was raised from the dead by their Jehovah God. Yet we see that very little of the dream of their Messiah, for poor and downtrodden people, exists today in a religion named after Him . . . Christianity. Many theologians have said that Christianity today is very unlike its founder. He neither foresaw what it was after His death nor did He desire it to be what it is today. You see, not only was the accused a fraud, but His own followers have defrauded Him of His futile dream. What was His futile dream? Let me read it to you and let us see if He . . . or they . . . have made it come to pass."

Darrow reached for the black Bible in front of him. He took out a cigar wrapper he had placed in the book of Luke. He ran his finger down the page until he came to the verse he had marked.

"I want to read this man's purpose statement as He gave it from the Jewish book of the prophet Isaiah. He was in His hometown of Nazareth in front of His neighbors and friends with whom He had grown up."

Picking up the book and holding it in the palm of his hand, Darrow read the passage with eloquence.

"I'm reading from the book of Luke, chapter four, verses eighteen and nineteen, the New King James Version, Exhibit A: 'The Spirit of the LORD is upon Me, because He has anointed Me to preach the gospel to the poor; He has sent Me to heal the brokenhearted, to proclaim liberty to the captives and recovery of sight to the blind, to set at liberty those who are oppressed; to proclaim the acceptable year of the LORD!'"

Looking up from the Bible, he spoke with conviction to the jury, who sat with rapt attention.

"That is a beautiful purpose for humanity, and the

prophet Isaiah, who wrote those words in the year 690 B.C., had a wonderful thought."

Darrow turned sideways and looked at Jesus. He felt compassion for Jesus because, in life, both had tried to help the underdog. Both had fought for similar causes. Jesus was destined for religion; Darrow was destined for law.

"But when the accused read Isaiah's words to His devout Jewish friends and neighbors on that Sabbath day . . . in His local synagogue in Nazareth . . . something very predictable happened. Let me read it to you from some succeeding verses of their Bible."

Again he held the Bible in the palm of his left hand, out where he could read the small print. With his right hand he pointed to each verse as he read it.

"I am now reading the verses immediately below the verse from the Jewish prophet Isaiah, beginning with verse twenty: 'Then He closed the book, and gave it back to the attendant and sat down. And the eyes of all who were in the synagogue were fixed on Him. And He began to say to them, "Today this Scripture is fulfilled in your hearing." So all bore witness to Him, and marveled at the gracious words which proceeded out of His mouth. And they said, "Is this not Joseph's son?" He said to them, "You will surely say this proverb to Me, 'Physician heal yourself! Whatever we have heard done in Capernaum, do also here in Your country.'" Then He said, "Assuredly, I say to you, no prophet is accepted in his own country. But I tell you truly, many widows were in Israel in the days of Elijah, when the heaven was shut up three years and six months, and there was a great famine throughout all the land; but to none of them was Elijah sent except to Zarephath, in the region of Sidon, to a woman who was a widow. And many lepers were in Israel in the time of Elisha the prophet, and none of them was cleansed except Naaman the Syrian.'"

Darrow kept his finger in place as he looked up from reading. He squinted his eyes as he looked at the jury, then at Jesus, then back down to his Bible.

"Now I want you to hear what these devout Jewish friends and neighbors tried to do to 'Joseph's son' when He finished reading and speaking. The next verses . . . verses twenty-eight and twenty-nine: 'So all those in the synagogue, when they heard these things, were filled with wrath, and rose up and thrust Him out of the city; and they led Him to the brow of the hill on which their city was built, that they might throw Him down over the cliff.'"

Laying his Bible down in front of him with the page still open, Darrow locked his fingers together in front of him. He looked quizzically at the jury.

"I've been to some very hot-tempered union meetings, some very hot-tempered debates, and some very hot-tempered court proceedings in my lifetime, folks. But the accused sat among His elders in His hometown synagogue and told them, in essence, that He was their Messiah, and," Darrow raised his voice, "their own words tell you that they believed He was a liar and a blasphemer. Their law said that such a person should be thrown down a cliff and stoned . . . and they started to do that to the accused, but He got away."

Unlocking his fingers, Darrow made his final thrust in his summation in a very steady voice.

"Ladies and gentlemen of the jury, the elders of Nazareth, Palestine . . . the hometown of the accused . . . who saw the accused grow up as the son of the carpenter, Joseph . . . did not believe that the accused was their promised Messiah. The elders of the hometown of the accused . . .

judged their own adult citizen . . . and they found Him guilty of blasphemy against their God, Jehovah. My dear friends . . . they were devout Jews who knew their religion. My dear friends . . . they were a very clannish group of people who knew well their neighbors. And my dear jury, the elders of Nazareth found the accused, Jesus of Nazareth . . . GUILTY OF FRAUD ON THE VERY FIRST DAY OF HIS QUEST TO BECOME A RELIGIOUS LEADER."

Darrow reached over and closed the files on the barristers' bench in front of him. He straightened up the books that had been sitting there and once again picked up the Bible in front of him. Standing to his full six-foot height, he held the Bible out to the jury as if he wanted them to read it from his hand.

"This Bible is what the believers in Jesus of Nazareth call the truth. What I just read to you about the accused is from their book. The statement from their book of truth is that His own peers found Jesus of Nazareth guilty. During this trial, the prosecution has provided you with historical proof . . . with scientific proof . . . with witnessed proof . . . and now using their truth . . . with traditional and religious proof. You now have the proof of the guilt of Jesus of Nazareth as a fraud, and you must return a verdict of GUILTY."

Darrow quietly closed the Bible that he held and laid it on top of all the books before him. He turned to the lord chief justice and, as a show of courtesy, bowed very stiffly from the waist.

"Your Lordship, that concludes the case for the prosecution."

A hush fell over the courtroom as Clarence Seward Darrow sat down. He believed that he had done his very best, as was his custom. For the first time in many years, he felt comfortable again. Houston patted him on the back.

At that instant the bells from Westminster and St. Sepulchre began to chime eleven o'clock. During the morning, no one had noticed the bells ringing up until that moment.

The lord chief justice looked down at some papers in front of him and made some notes. Finally he looked up and spoke to those in the courtroom.

"The court will recess for lunch and return to session at one o'clock this afternoon. At that time the defense will begin the closing summation. We will not recess for tea at four this afternoon but will recess at five o'clock, for one hour. At six o'clock, this court will reconvene for the general instruction from the bench. The court is now recessed."

The lord chief justice rose from his seat as the bailiff quickly stood and carried out the formal adjournment of the court.

Luckhoo looked at DiPietro. "Diane, I will not be eating. I will be next door at the church in prayer. I have a very important task this afternoon. Mr. Darrow alluded to the truth when he used the Bible. What he read was simply 'a truth' from the Bible. I must convince the jury that they must be seekers of all of the truth, not just 'a truth,' and that it is dangerous to make 'a truth' into 'the truth.' I'll meet you back here after lunch. Check to see that the intercessors are still hard at work. The proof of their pudding will be shown today."

He took his well-worn Bible and walked out the door. DiPietro picked up her briefcase and headed out to get lunch. She noticed that everyone else, including Darrow and Houston, had already left the courtroom. As a very qualified solicitor, DiPietro had not participated much in the trial, except to follow Luckhoo's instructions and take voluminous notes.

After Darrow's summation, DiPietro felt insecure in their defense of Jesus. She looked up through the skylight and said, "Oh, God, help us." These words began to form in her mind: *Yea, though I walk through the valley of the shadow of death, I will fear no evil; for You are with me; Your rod and Your staff, they comfort me. You prepare a table before me in the presence of my enemies; You anoint my head with oil; my cup runs over. Surely goodness and mercy shall follow me all the days of my life; and I will dwell in the house of the LORD forever.*

She left the room with joy rising in her heart as she thought: *Amen . . . so be it, God!*

12
CLOSING SUMMATION

AFTERNOON, DAY FIVE

The London skies had brought heavy rain and light-ning for most of the morning, but by noon there was only a light steady rain descending on the city. A thick mist had enveloped the Central Criminal Courts Building, and the afternoon forecast was for more thunderstorms and lightning.

People were returning to the courtroom with wet shoes and umbrellas. They hurried to their places, folding their raincoats and umbrellas so that they could fit them under their seats.

Darrow and Houston were in their seats and smiling. They had presented as much evidence as they could, and both felt as if they had done their best. Besides that, both had enjoyed a good meal at lunch. They were content for the moment.

DiPietro's face showed the strain of the trial and the coming closing summation. She glanced at the prisoner's dock and saw that Jesus was looking at her. He smiled a reassuring smile, and she felt comfortable once again.

Luckhoo sat beside her with his eyes closed and his lips moving in prayer. On the desk in front of him lay one red file folder. He sat clutching his well-worn Bible, waiting for the trial to begin again.

The dome in the courtroom suddenly lit up as lightning once again struck somewhere in the distance, and the lights flickered in the courtroom.

A moment later, the lord chief justice's door opened and he entered. The bailiff got the proceedings legally under way.

The lord chief justice looked over at Luckhoo and spoke.

"Sir Luckhoo, you may present your closing summation to the jury."

"Thank you, my lord."

Luckhoo bowed from the waist, then turned and did the same toward the prisoner's dock. Jesus looked at him and smiled, then gave him a single reassuring nod. Looking up and down then into the faces of the jurors, Luckhoo began what he felt to be the most important closing summation in his career at law.

"Ladies and gentlemen of the jury, each of you, as a hand-picked member of this jury, does not sit in judgment here of a mere human being. No, you sit here in judgment of Deity. You sit here in judgment not only for yourself but also for humanity itself. You sit here in judgment of the accused, Jesus of Nazareth, the founder of Christianity. Your judgment in this matter brings eternal reward or eternal damnation."

Luckhoo's impeccable use of the English language, with his British accent, was part of his legal trademark. He was known throughout the former British Empire as a brilliant barrister.

"This trial began with what we know as a man. But this man was different from most men. He was a religious man. But this man was unlike other religious men. He was the founder of a world religion, Christianity. But this man was different from any other founder of a world religion."

He took his Bible in both hands and held it up to them. His voice was strong and assuring.

"This man is the only founder of a world religion who has ever claimed to be wholly man and wholly God. He is the only religious leader who was resurrected from the dead. And He is the only God who led a great portion of the world to believe that He is who He says He is, even centuries after His death and resurrection. He is Jesus of Nazareth, the Messiah of the Jewish people. He is the only One who fulfilled all of the prophecies of the historic Old Testament. That fulfillment was recorded in the historic New Testament of the Christian Bible. That, ladies and gentlemen, is WHY He is on trial before you here."

Luckhoo ended his statement by pointing to Jesus. He dropped his hand and looked back at the jury. They were anticipating his next words.

"I am well aware that such beliefs will bring forth both honest critics and sincere fools. But regardless of either, there is a God, and He has made ample provision for the honor and support of His Word to His people, the gospel, the good news of the Messiah, which we find throughout Exhibit A. The evidence that we proposed and have presented with our reliable witnesses, people who were with Jesus of Nazareth, shows an orderly design of events that have withstood the test of an eternity of time. Any great design of doctrines and precepts, which Christianity is, must therefore come from Jehovah God's divine promise of the Messiah. That promise reveals that Jesus of Nazareth is the Messiah. Christianity itself is a divine fulfillment from the great Creator, and it is the religion of the Father, the Son, and the Holy Spirit."

Luckhoo laid his Bible down carefully before him and continued his summation. He had never summed up a trial as he was now doing.

"My esteemed colleague based the prosecution's entire case on the evidence that there were no written significant historical documents concerning Jesus of Nazareth, and yet he placed before you sixty-six of the most significant historical documents ever produced! There, in Exhibit A, are sixty-six books of historic proof of the facts that we seek in this trial! Historic facts? Yes! My friends, the Bible has been with us for centuries, accepted by kings and peasants, poets and lawyers, fishermen and farmers, singers and soldiers, priests and physicians, statesmen and tentmakers, preachers and publicans, and on and on. Forty authors, from those professions and occupations, wrote those sixty-six books of Exhibit A. And they did it over a period of one thousand five hundred years . . . and they did it on three continents . . . most of them never seeing one another or communicating with one another or knowing what the others were writing! Yet, my friends, when these sixty-six books came together into one book, known as the Bible, there is not one contradiction between the forty writers! Amazing, isn't it?"

Luckhoo picked up his Bible again, holding it out to the jury. His face was a picture of love and respect for what he held in his hand.

"What do you think would happen if we chose forty

psychiatrists, such as the esteemed Dr. Sigmund Freud, and asked each of them to write a book about either the causes or the cures of mental illness? What kind of unity in the creation of an answer do you think we would get?"

Luckhoo pointed in the direction where Freud and Darwin were sitting in the witness section, holding his arm out as he talked.

"My friends, we already have that answer in literally hundreds of concepts and theories in psychiatry and psychology."

Luckhoo dropped his arm and pointed around the courtroom.

"Cannot we use judges and juries, theologians and thespians, authors and artists, and all manner of people who, if we picked forty of them to write on one subject, would not also produce works that were filled with severe contradictions?"

Luckhoo turned and pointed to the two stacks of books that Darrow had used in his summation.

"And once more, my friends, we have the evidence in our public libraries, volume after volume, that severe contradictions exist in all subjects! Why then does Exhibit A, the Bible, become the most remarkable book ever made? How can the Bible be a divine gathering of sixty-six books, some of considerable size, some of just a few pages, containing literature, drama, history, prophecy, biography, allegories, poetry, riddles, proverbs, parables, hymns, laws, letters, and elaborate directions for ritualistic worship? How can the Bible contain all manner of literary styles and not be excelled by all comparison?"

Luckhoo opened his red file folder very slowly.

"The defense now presents you with the theory or presupposition of the proof of the messiahship of Jesus of Nazareth. It simply starts with this acknowledgment: GOD IS! We have provided you with witnesses who saw and heard, firsthand, the things that Jesus did and said! We can spend hours in this summation with apologetics from theologians, with cosmological, teleological, and ontological arguments for the existence of God. No amount of apologetics or no amount of arguments can prove God, but GOD IS!"

With no particular expression on his face, Luckhoo turned and looked directly at the witness section.

"'The fool has said in his heart, "There is no God."' My friends, God is a person who is Spirit, immortal, infinite, impartial, eternal, perfect, immutable, invisible, self-existent, omnipotent, omnipresent, omniscient, holy and just, full of knowledge and wisdom, and who is the beginning and the end of all things . . . and much . . . much . . . more! God is the reason why, across fifteen hundred years of time, that forty authors could write sixty-six books with one central theme of the creation and redemption of the entire human race by Jehovah God through His divine Son, Jesus the Christ, and through the power of the Holy Spirit. There before you in Exhibit A is the Holy Bible . . . without contradictions!"

Lightning flashed nearby as several people held their ears so as not to hear the crash of the thunder. Luckhoo was unmoved by the noise.

"Is Exhibit A accurate? For years, historians called the Genesis story of Joseph and the seven years of famine in Egypt a myth. Archaeologists have proven their myth is a myth. Historians said the story in the biblical book of Daniel concerning Belshazzar being king at the time of the destruction of Babylon was false. They said that Nabonidus was the only king. But, my friends, archaeologists discovered a cylinder, inscribed with curious records, taken from the mounds that marked the almost forgotten site of that once great city. The records indicated that Belshazzar was the son of Nabonidus and was regent under him, sharing the throne of his father. Once again the very stones cry out in confirmation of the historicity of Exhibit A, the Bible. Five thousand places mentioned in Exhibit A have been located and verified by geographers and explorers. Add to that the Codex Vaticanus, Codex Sinaiticus, Codex Alexandrinus, and the Dead Sea Scrolls. These important discoveries confirm the accuracy of the Hebrew and Greek translations of Exhibit A, the Bible. What say you to these things?"

Luckhoo pointed to the witness section, then dropped his hand to his side.

"Does the defense need to provide you with an endless parade of scientific witnesses against evolution and for God? If so, then, for a start, be referred to one location, the Bodleian Library at Oxford, where eight hundred scientists of Great Britain, students of the natural sciences, signed a statement expressing their regret that fellow researchers had perverted scientific truth concerning evolution and denied the teachings of the Bible, Exhibit A! What say you to the testimony of mere people who have attested to the validity of the Bible? George Washington, Queen Victoria, Thomas Jefferson, W. E. Gladstone, Napoleon Bonaparte, Andrew Jackson, Theodore Roosevelt, John Quincy Adams, Alfred, Lord Tennyson, Benjamin Franklin, Zachary Taylor, William Cullen Bryant, and on and on."

Luckhoo picked up the paper that he had in his red file folder. He looked at the paper for a moment and then looked up at the jury.

"Let me close my summation with this."

A rustling went about the room. The barristers and solicitors in the spectator section were whispering to each other
about the brevity of Luckhoo's summation. Some couldn't
believe that he would not go on for his full allotted four
hours. Instead Luckhoo concluded.

"Exhibit A, the Bible, is an inspired supernatural revelation from God! *Revelation* means 'to unveil, to uncover, to
reveal, or to lift up a curtain to see what was previously
veiled.' The method of disclosure and the truth disclosed
are alike called revelation."

Luckhoo laid his paper down and picked up his Bible
and opened it.

"The Bible was a revelation given to people by divine
inspiration. For 'all Scripture is given by inspiration of God,
and is profitable for doctrine, for reproof, for correction, for
instruction in righteousness, that the man of God may be
complete, thoroughly equipped for every good work.'"

Laying his Bible down, Luckhoo picked up his paper.

"Revelation discovers new truth, and inspiration guides
the communicating and recording of that truth. Exhibit A
is a book of truth. Some words recorded therein are the
exact words of God. Some were words revealed through the
mouths of speakers who spoke as the Holy Spirit of God
inspired them. Some words were written as people were
moved by the Holy Spirit to write them. Other words in
Exhibit A were given to speakers and writers, and they were
inspired to write as the Holy Spirit directed them. But the
Holy Spirit guided all the words to be written! That is why
there are unity and order, and there is not one contradiction
in the writings of forty authors!"

Luckhoo picked his paper up again and read from it.

"Let me share a few important facts about Exhibit A. Fact: it has a unique unity of authors. Fact: it has been the best-selling book of all times. Fact: famous and not-so-famous people around the world attest to it. Fact: my life and the lives of countless millions of people have been changed by its contents and its power. Fact: no editor has ever improved it. Fact: no critic has ever stifled it. Fact: it has been preserved for thousands of years, and it is as relevant today as the first time it was read. Fact: it responds to the deepest human soul. Fact: its height and depth of ideals attest to a divine author. Fact: there are over three hundred verses of prophecy . . . predictions of the future . . . and over half of them have already been fulfilled and proven as truth. Fact: verified miracles prove its divine revelation. Fact: the Old and New Testaments verify each other. Fact: it is scientifically correct and so proven. Fact: it is historically correct. Fact: it has universal adaptability for all ages and peoples. Fact: it has spiritual power. Fact: its doctrines are contrary to human teachings. Fact: almost twenty-one centuries of time have not improved it."

Sir Lionel Alfred Luckhoo put his paper into the red file folder and closed it. He picked up a second Bible and turned to the eleventh chapter of the book of Hebrews in the New Testament.

"'Now faith is the substance of things hoped for, the evidence of things not seen. For by it the elders obtained a good testimony. By faith we understand that the worlds were framed by the word of God, so that the things which are seen were not made of things which are visible.' These are verses one through three."

He put his finger on the opposite page.

"Let me read to you from this Bible study edition. I think

you'll find it helpful. It talks about faith: '*Faith (pistis)* is defined in a practical way in Hebrews 11:1: "Now faith is the substance (or substantiation) of things hoped for, the evidence of things not seen." The writer of Hebrews goes on for thirty-nine additional verses to illustrate these who took God at His word and had faith in what He said. They were not all outstanding believers. Jacob, Gideon, and Samson were all too human in their failure, and even father Abraham slipped up a few times. But they were believers. What is faith? It is confidence that someone or something is reliable. Our whole life is based on faith. Without it, banks and post offices would not be possible. Paper money and credit cards (the very word *credit* is from the Latin verb "to believe") would never be accepted.'"

Luckhoo placed his Bible on top of the folder. He looked up at the jury.

"Ladies and gentlemen of the jury, I conclude the defense of Jesus of Nazareth with this statement. Exhibit A, the Holy Bible, is the revealed inspired word of a holy, supernatural God. Exhibit A says that Jesus of Nazareth is the Son of God, the Promised One of Israel, the Messiah Savior of the world, sent to the world because of the great love that a Father God has for the world . . . and you. That should be more than enough evidence for you to make your decision . . . to render your verdict . . . FOR . . . JESUS OF NAZARETH!"

Luckhoo turned to his right and faced the lord chief justice.

"My Lord Chief Justice, this completes the summation of the defense of Jesus of Nazareth. The defense rests!"

With that, Sir Lionel Alfred Luckhoo sat down, picked

up his Bible, and began to pray silently. No one moved in the courtroom.

Thunder could be heard in the distance again, and flashes of lightning were evident in the courtroom. Even with the raging storm outside, there was a peaceful feeling in the courtroom that was beyond description.

The bells at St. Sepulchre and at Westminster began to chime. The wind and rain howled across the glass dome.

The lord chief justice banged his gavel. He spoke to the jury in a strong, but very pleasant voice.

"Ladies and gentlemen of the jury, it is your solemn responsibility to determine if the Crown has proven its accusation of fraud against Jesus of Nazareth beyond a reasonable doubt. Your verdict must be based solely on the evidence, or the lack of evidence, and the law as presented to you here in this court. The charging document against the defendant is not evidence, and it is not to be considered by you as any proof of guilt."

The lord chief justice gestured from time to time to illustrate his point. He was very methodical in his instructions to the jury.

"In every criminal proceeding, a defendant has the absolute right to remain silent. At no time is it the duty of the defendant to prove his innocence. From the exercise of a defendant's right to remain silent, the jury is not permitted to draw any inference of guilt, and the fact that the defendant did not take the witness stand must not influence your verdict in any manner whatsoever." He paused, took a breath, and continued.

"It is up to you to decide what evidence is reliable. You should use your common sense in deciding which is the best evidence and which evidence should not be relied upon in considering your verdict. You may find some of the evidence presented by the witnesses as not reliable or less reliable than other evidence. Here are several points that you should consider as you remember the witnesses. First, did the witness seem to have an opportunity to see and know the things about which he or she testified? Second, did the witness seem to have an accurate memory? Third, was the witness honest and straightforward in answering the barristers' questions? Fourth, did the witness have some interest in how the case should be decided? Fifth, does the witness's testimony agree with the other testimony and other evidence in this trial? Sixth, did the witness appear to be honest and of a good reputation?"

The lord chief justice reached over and took a drink of water from the golden goblet on his bench.

"Here are some general rules that apply to your deliberation of this trial. First, this case must be decided only upon the evidence that you have heard from the answers of the witnesses or what has been presented in the form of exhibits and evidence and these instructions. Second, this case must not be decided for or against anyone because you feel sorry for anyone or angry at anyone. Third, remember that the barristers are not on trial. Your feelings about them should not influence your decision in this case. Fourth, feelings of prejudice, bias, or sympathy are not legally reasonable doubts, and they should not be considered by you in any way. Your verdict must be based on your views of the evidence presented to you and the law contained in these instructions. Fifth, you must decide a verdict of for or against, which is not guilty or guilty. Deciding a verdict is exclusively your responsibility. It is a heavy responsibility. It is the most important decision you can make in your life at this time. You will retire to the jury room to make your decision. God bless you in your decision."

The lord chief justice nodded to the bailiff. The bailiff stood and rapped the court scepter on the floor three times.

"Silence. Be upstanding in the court."

Everyone stood. Outside, the sky was almost black. The wind was now raging and accompanied by heavy thunder and lightning.

The lord chief justice stood and faced the jury. A clap of thunder resounded immediately throughout the courtroom as a bolt of lightning hit a power pole somewhere next to Old Bailey. People gasped with fear.

In that instant, the lights went out and the room was in total darkness. Within seconds of the thunder, another bright flash of lightning lit up the courtroom with an eerie glow.

In that flash, the lightning revealed the face of the lord chief justice. His head and His hair were now like wool, as white as snow, the prisoner's dock was empty, and JESUS OF NAZARETH WAS THE LORD CHIEF JUSTICE!

About the Authors

Sir Lionel A. Luckhoo, a citizen of Guyana, South America, is the ambassador extraordinary and plenipotentiary of Guyana. He is listed in the *Guinness Book of World Records* as the "most successful criminal lawyer," having 245 successive murder trial acquittals. Luckhoo, knighted twice by the Queen of England, is the only man in the history of the diplomatic corps to represent two sovereign nations at the same time. He has been a trade union leader, a Guyanese Supreme Court Justice, and mayor of Georgetown, Guyana, four times. Luckhoo has authored a number of publications and presently resides in Fort Worth, Texas.

John R. Thompson, Ph.D. is a licensed clinical pastoral counselor and director of The Pastoral Counseling Center in Temple Terrace, Florida. He is an associate pastor of Calvary Temple Church of Temple Terrace and chaplain of a psychiatric and addictions hospital. Thompson, a former congressional staff member, attended Indiana University and is a graduate of International Seminary with a doctorate in pastoral psychology.